The Devil's Blade, Mark Alder

'Alder's glorious romp draws inspiration from the already incredible life of 17th-century noblewoman and duellist Julie D'Aubigny, spinning a fast-paced tale of pacts with the Devil, love and revenge'   *The i*

'From backstage at the Paris Opera to the court of the Sun King himself, this bloody, funny and very literal bodice-ripper shows that the devil may have the best tunes, but Mark Alder runs him a close second.'   *Daily Mail*

'If you're looking for swashbuckling, diabolical intrigue, class hatred and a rather touching lesbian romance, this is going to fill in your empty hours rather neatly.'
Roz Kaveney

'It is dark, very violent, very sweary but at the same time quite good fun.'   *Mark Yon, SFFworld*

D0524344

By Mark Alder from Gollancz:

THE BANNERS OF BLOOD SERIES

Son of the Morning
Son of the Night

The
DEVIL'S
BLADE

MARK ALDER

Dedicated to the memory of Aslan King,
a bright star gone too soon.

Paris 1687

Prelude: Nocturne

They say the Devil made her, but I know better. She told me all her stories – and I witnessed a few – yes, I remember the night it began. I remember the night it ended, too, but I'll tell that tale another time.

I had become interested in a certain group of gentlemen of great quality and had heard they were planning to meet by midnight on All Hallows' Eve in the Bois de Boulogne, that deep, dark wood that leaks from the western edge of Paris like a pool of blood from a vanquished duellist's side.

Now, this was the time of King Louis XIV – the Sun King who very rightly spent his reign ignoring the poor and raising monuments to his own splendour. Neither he, nor his police force under the baleful rule of Mssr de la Reynie, were interested at all in what happened beneath those trees, so long as it did not involve fomenting insurrection. It would have taken a brave revolutionary or a lusty one to visit the Bois at night, thronging, as it was, with whores and thieves and any other whose business proceeds better unseen. A man took his life in his hands to go there, and no woman of virtue would set foot beneath the trees. Which was the point of these gentlemen choosing it for their little rendezvous, I think.

These great men, you see, were lovers of 'frisson', of the charge that ignites the senses when mild danger is near, of pushing the edges of experience, of daring to do what others would not.

Their idea of what that might entail might not be yours (it is probably a little extreme for your modern tastes) but let me just say that, on a foggy autumn evening when the moon hid her face – I can't really be bothered to paint the picture more clearly, you carry my drift – they had assembled with the noble intention of summoning the Devil.

As if you can summon the Devil! That is an illusion fools have indulged in for centuries. You don't click your fingers and have Hell come running. No, you make yourself interesting to Hell and then Hell comes to look at you, quite freely and of its own accord.

First, of course, they did summon someone, the young woman, by sending a letter to her lodgings and asking her to sing for them. She was unique, you see, even then, her voice so pure a soprano that such had not been heard on the Paris stage in living memory. Beauty like that from a girl of no professional training, delivered with the sort of innocence that so stiffens the dicks of men of dark tastes, could only be the work of God, they surmised. And what better way to delight the Devil than to destroy one of God's rarer creations? They had brought her there to kill her, for sure, and in no pleasant way either, as we shall see. A virgin, an artist, a flower of God. Yes, how could Beelzebub refuse such a sacrifice?

But let me present her not in a dry tale told in this tawdry way. While I may not have the enthusiasm to describe the clinging fog, the torches in their veils of light, the deep smell of the horses, the wet autumn mud that encroached on the fine footwear of those gentlemen and threatened their pale stockings, I have nothing but enthusiasm for describing her.

I will show you her, here nervous and flushed as she steps from the coach that has delivered her to the woods. She rearranges her skirts as she steps down, feels the cloth of the skirt to try to adjust a stray garter. She has to fight her instinct to simply lift up the dress and secure the garter herself. High men might be close, she needs to watch her manners.

2

Of course, she would not have gone willingly into the woods, but she has not been looking out of the windows, for reasons that will later emerge. She has no sense of what she might become, this girl of sixteen. She has not yet taken the grand name they will howl through their tears as they lower her coffin down into the dead earth. Two or three times, as it happens. She was never very good at staying dead. For now, she is plain old Julie d'Aubigny, who has been panting by the door of the Grand Opera in Paris for a month in hope of an audition. Her voice may be wonderful but that is not enough. She needs introduction, presentation, the right people to speak for her. You might think, given her upbringing in Alsace as the daughter of the secretary to the Comte d'Armagnac, that she would find such contacts easy to come by. But a secretary is a functionary, a tradesman really, and though the Comte might entrust the education of his sons and other pages to such a man, he would not speak to him beyond business. The Comte found Julie amusing when she was a younger girl and laughed to see how her father had raised her as a boy among boys, teaching her to sing exquisitely, to dance very well, to fence well enough to beat the boys and to draw with a steady hand and a curious eye. But, one drunken attempt to fuck her when she was fourteen aside, he has shown her little attention or interest since. She could not ask for his patronage without risking the sternest rebuke.

So Julie has paid her way in the world by singing in the street, where she came to the notice of the Band of Thirteen, the Black Tredecim as they call themselves – in order, one presumes, to show they know Latin and are gentlemen. She was flattered when they invited her to sing for them. Such rich men, so much poise, so much refinement.

Julie thinks these are men of influence. She is right. She thinks they might do her some good, get her the audition she seeks. She is dead wrong.

But let me get on and tell this tale in the way she would have liked, as a drama, as an opera. Here, by torchlight, Act One. Enter Julie and Paval, her lover, in a carriage.

Act One

Scene One

The Chorus of the Diaboliques

The torchlight is yet distant as she steps from the coach. The carriage they sent to fetch her has creaked and jumped its way over the potholes of the cinder road from the east gate to the woods and then rattled along a little track to stop here.

She kisses her companion Paval to mark an end to their fun. He is a nice boy who she met in her fruitless quest for an audition at the Grand Opera. He is the attendant on the stage door, running errands for Arcand, the stage manager. If she is to sleep her way to the top, she has joked, she has left herself a long haul from these beginnings. Still, sometimes the long road is the most enjoyable and Paval is a dear.

Paval buttons his breeches as she exits the coach into the cold of the foggy night. She lifts her doe mask on its stick to her face, shifting her weight on her feet to stop her shoes sinking into the mud. These are her only pair and she is mortally afraid of marking them.

'Over there,' says the coachman. 'A footman will fetch you.'

Paval is next to her now, searching for her hand, but she dismisses it. 'Wait here,' she says. 'This is high company.'

He nods, smiles his big grin.

'So many mistakes to make with these aristos!' he says. 'Best have only one of us making them.'

She kisses him once more, deeply, and he takes her head in his hands.

'I love you,' he says.

'Don't do that,' she says.

'Why not?'

'I am not made for it,' she says. She almost believes it. Her plans don't involve love for a long time yet. And yet, and yet, Paval is so kind and so warm. Could she love him? Perhaps, in a way she never thought she could love a mere man, but she must try not to. Men, to her, have always seemed too uncomplicated, too simple to love. You get things from men – money, position, names, and the centre of their souls that lies in their breeches. You share things with women, who are far more complex and interesting. Yet these simple qualities are what she has come to admire in Paval.

There is something else, though, that makes her warn Paval away. She has always felt somewhat, she cannot quite put her finger on it, somewhat, well, dangerous, for want of a better word. Her life is to be an opera, a grand work, and lovers never fare well in those.

'You want the audience to love you.'

'That is a different kind of love,' she says. 'You are a love, Paval.'

'I know you only hold back from me to lead me on.'

'Was I holding back in the carriage?'

He blushes, sweet boy. 'Not like that.'

'Then like what?' She comes close to him, still careful of her shoes in the mud, gives his dick a squeeze as she lowers her mask.

'I've forgotten,' he says, close by her mouth.

'Well, tug on that until you remember,' she says.

A light cough from behind her like one of a lady's more demure spaniels suggesting it might like another biscuit.

She turns. A tripping servant, wigged, powdered, heavy with satin bows, comes towards her and takes her hand to lead her. She doesn't really like that. She knows she is only the same station as he and that it is no affront to be led this way, but she does not want to appear as his equal among the great men she is to meet. One day, after her singing career is done, perhaps before, she will be a duchess. Julie may have been born poor but she will die rich, whatever it takes.

She rejects the man's hand, gives him a look. 'Suit yourself, dear,' he says and heads off up the track into the deeper woods. She collects herself, stands straight to her considerable height and strides following him along the track, humming a few scales under her breath. That is all she has ever needed for a warm-up. She was born to sing, born singing if you listen to her father, and she has been singing all her life. Warm up? Her lovers say she sings in her sleep and she has had enough of them to make a reliable jury.

The wet smell of autumn chills her, the track is slippy and she does her best to retain a good bearing as she walks along it. Head up, shoulders back, as if she is about to burst into song. She commands the stage of her imagination as she is sure she will one day command the stage at the grand opera. These gentlemen she is to meet – the Tredecim as the group of patrons style themselves – are the gatekeepers of her future.

She is met in a clearing by a group of four men who bear lanterns that make soft webs of light in the foggy air. They are masked, as is the fashion at soirées and balls. The theme they have chosen is unusual – the masks are all in the style of devils. She does not find it disconcerting. This is the high society to which she aspires. Masks, feathers, stomachers trimmed with gold and silver braid, emeralds, diamonds, rubies, things she has glimpsed as they flit between carriages and the gilded interiors she peeked into as a child.

Instinctively, she knows what she must give these men. The Comte's sons, before they went up to court, were as dirty, flea ridden and naive as she was but she has learned enough from the men those boys became when they returned from court, and later from war, to understand them, at least a little. They do not have the sentimental tastes of the bourgeoisie – they favour the disturbing, the elegant, the challenging. It is here she will learn to belong.

The gentleman devil who takes her arm to lead her further through the trees is perfumed with a rare violet scent and wears a coat of the silvered cloth they call Gros de Naples – a lustrous silk inlaid with crimson half-moons. She has seen this cloth before only outside dressmakers as it is delivered and, yes, she makes it her business to haunt such places to know better how to furnish her dreams. Here, conjured from its long slumber on the roll, bid to rise and take life as a coat, the cloth transforms its wearer into a fabulous animal, a shimmering leopard who leads her to the magnificent Court of the Beasts.

And what a court. Twelve more men, all masked as devils, stand in a circle, each one a statue raised in tribute to excess, self-love, love of life. The torchlight makes deep pools in brilliant silk coats, glints from buckles and rings, turns the milled brass of a cane tip – shaped as a toad – to fire. It glitters from the jewels of the masks, sparkles from the gilded hilts and scabbards of their fine slim court swords. These are gentlemen and they wear the latest weapons – short and slender blades, no lumbering long rapiers here, like the ones her father taught her to fence with. She tries to distinguish the men in some way for, if she meets them again, she could use this connection to her advantage. One has roses on his shoes, another an emerald ring that glints green even in the red light, one more has an uneven stance, one leg shorter than the other, another has the monograph of a hart upon his coat, still one more pats his friend's back and says, 'Courage, Diablo!' Is that a name or a nickname?

One of the men in the circle speaks. 'This is the virgin?' A voice, old and dry with vowels so strange and clipped that Julie has to suppress a giggle. He sounds like a comic actor aping a nobleman, rather than a nobleman true.

The speaker is tall and stands with one foot forward, a hand on his hip as if posing for a portrait. He wears a coat of blue silk inlaid with gold. The hand that supports his cane, Julie notices, has two fingers missing. So a duellist, or a warrior. No wars for a couple of years now. He must be bored, poor lamb, she thinks. A man like that needs action. She wonders what it would be like to lie with him. Would he just strike poses while she did all the work? She smiles to herself. She knows a few tricks to rattle an icy composure but she would get nothing back from him, she is sure. And so what? In lifting her skirts for a man like that she'd be after so much more than a tremble and an 'oh!'. She'd be seeking a destiny.

'This is the street singer,' says another man, his voice equally mannered. It is as if he has made scissors of his lips and is trying to clip and trim the words as they emerge. Not that she can see his lips. His face is only that of a leering devil, horns and long nose, a painted mouth of teeth.

The first man lifts his hand to his mask.

'Let her sing,' he says. 'And let us see if she is, as you claim, Abaddon, God's creation.'

The man raises his hand. A splendidly dressed servant in a powdered wig turns to a servant who is merely impressively dressed and raises a finger. That servant turns to a servant who is well dressed and he to another who is certainly no scruff and raises a finger. This servant turns to her and raises a finger of his own.

'Now?' says Julie.

The unscruffy servant nods.

'Well, by God's bollocks,' says Julie. 'You might have just said so yourself!' Oh no. Nerves, the masks, the night, the fog have conspired to make her forget herself.

'God's bollocks?' says one of the devils. He carries a stick of silver and prods it forwards as if the words are on the ground before him and he is jabbing them to inspect them.

'Begging your pardon, it is an expression we use when we are . . .'

The three-fingered gentleman inclines his head.

'Who are "we"?'

'The people.'

'The word "we" should be outlawed,' he says. 'There is no "we" wide enough to pair me with the likes of you and the mob.'

'Oh do fuck off,' says Julie. Oh no! The nerves again. They have betrayed her. She wants to smile and nod and be pretty but from somewhere this defiance has emerged. She curtsies. 'Begging your pardon, sir. I am inclined to such outbursts when nervous. Think naught of them.' Do they say 'naught' for 'nothing'? She hopes so and hopes it might make her seem more refined.

He inclines his head, studies her as a cat might a spider.

'She's a mite coarser than one might have assumed, Diablo.'

'Her singing bears no mark of it,' says one of the masked devils.

Three Fingers raises his hand again and the chain of command ensures a much lower status hand is raised in front of her to tell her to sing. Well, she'll take the evening so far as a success. She has never spoken directly to such a great man before, even if she did tell him to fuck himself.

She imagines herself his wife, he away hunting or at war, or poking about in the woods dressed as a devil, she at the opera, singing in his jewels, in the dresses he might buy, riding home in his gilded carriage, riding the grooms, riding the maids, giving the tall, thin duke some bonny fat children he would have to call his own or face dishonour. She sees herself in black, at Versailles, looking out at the fabled lawns, loudly cursing the Spanish or English or whoever's ball of lead so conveniently killed him and left her a rich widow. She would be comforted by some gorgeous duchess, yes, a widow too and she would fall in love and be loved. She could fuck a man, she could laugh and play and be ever so fond of a man, but she could only ever really love a woman – this fantasy duchess with her hair in a tower of stolen curls, a shepherd's crook of gold in her hand, little tame lambs in diamond collars to wander behind. Yes, she could love a woman like that madly. Perhaps Paval might be there too, as her secret, or not her secret. He could fuck one woman well enough, why not two?

She would commission arias just for herself and sing to the golden angels on the ceiling of the Opéra so well those angels would think she was one of them. She has not seen Three Fingers' face, but already she has married him, killed him and is spending his money becoming – what? Great. Yes, great, grand and beautiful. She is already pretty but she wants something more, to have an awing beauty that makes the world her slave. All love, to give and receive love magnificently. Yes, she will become the world's lover and be loved by it in a mad amour that will lift her to the heavens. Well, a girl can dream, can't she?

She clears her throat and begins. These great men will not be charmed by sweetness or by coyness the way a street crowd would. For them, something more sharp, piquant, more challenging. She must sing of love, though, and everything that goes with it. She must stir their blood, stiffen their pricks and then they are hers and she can get what she wants from them. She dismisses the song she was going to sing. Instead she will sing one she heard not weeks ago after Paval smuggled her in to the Opéra. She only needs to hear such things once and then they are lodged in her mind. She will sing 'The blood that unites me with you', from Lully's great work *Armide*. And she will sing both the part of Armide the enchantress and her lover Hidarot, her range great enough to accommodate both.

She doesn't need the note, doesn't need the harpsichord to bounce her in. She begins and the wood holds it breath. No bird has ever sung like this, no footpad trilled or whore hummed in such a tone. It is as if something new and strange is being made, coming to birth in the world. A night flower unfurls and offers its inky petals to the moon. Probably, anyway. Somewhere that must be happening, she thinks. She sings of it, which is how the song begins. The gentlemen are statues. Only one paws at the air with his hand as if it is floating on the melody.

She allows a brief silence when the low part is finished, to create a tension, spark desire through denial. And then, and then, Armide herself. She begins. Unaccompanied, there is no wavering, no guess for the note. Can any of the gentlemen believe she has never been trained beyond what a country estate had to offer her? They cannot.

The notes tumble from her, so pure, so clear and delicious in the still air of the foggy wood. The conclusion, when it comes, seems torn from her soul.

'Against my enemies at will I unleash
The dark empire of Hell;
Love puts kings under my spell,
I am the sovereign mistress of a thousand lovers.
But my greatest happiness
Is to be mistress of my own heart.'

They are enraptured. They are entranced. There is a long silence. No one speaks, as if the merest chance that this flat fog, these damp trees, might offer an echo of the song's magnificence.

'Truly a creation of God,' says Three Fingers. 'A rare talent indeed.'

'Mwah!' One man makes a kissing gesture to his fingers before snapping them out before him in approval.

Another devil just nods furiously before taking out an over-large snuff box decorated with a dragon, pinching out a mighty nip, shoving it beneath his mask and inhaling it with a snort of delight. She sees a gobful of dark teeth as he casts back his head and the snuff goes in, a sure sign of wealth. They say it's sugar that makes the teeth go rotten and who but the very well off can afford that?

Julie's heart skips. With patrons such as these, what things might she aspire to? There would be no limit to her ambition. She sees herself on stage at the Opéra, bathed in candlelight, filling that great space with the music that flows through her.

'A virginal flower,' says another, a fat man who carries a gilded, finely wrought pistol in his belt.

'Let us do what we came for,' says a tall, thin man who waves a pristine white handkerchief. 'Let us sacrifice her and call forward the Devil. It is your turn to lead, Bissy,' he says to the little fat man.

'Sirs?' says Julie. She doesn't understand, not at all. Sacrifice? What does that mean? If you wrote those words down, passed them to her and asked her to read, she would know what was meant. But there in the wood, they come as such a shock that she cannot make sense of them.

Swords are drawn, the blades shining tongues of fire. Now the words make sense, terrible sense. Julie feels her stomach fall to her feet as she knows she is the victim of an awful trick. She pulls out her hairpin – useless of course against these blades – but she will not go down without some sort of fight.

A snort of laughter from behind the masks.

'Beelzebub, we have paved the way,' says Three Fingers. 'We have spoken your names, we walked the circle widdershins, we have cursed God and his angels!'

'We spit on the name of Jesus!' shout the men.

'We praise the names of Judas and of Satan and of the great Whore of Babylon!' shouts Three Fingers.

'We praise the Whore!' the men chorus.

They close in on her like wolves upon a stricken deer, pacing forward slowly, confident their prey cannot escape, their dead-eyed masks fixing her with lethal stares.

'Take the virgin!' says Three Fingers.

'I am no fucking virgin!' screams Julie. The men pause, as if partway through a dance whose music has frozen.

'What?' says the man with the scissored vowels.

'I am no virgin!'

The masks turn to each other.

'You are a country girl of sixteen,' says a man who twirls his sword as if he is an idle lover twiddling a stalk of grass at a girl's gate.

'And I have not been a virgin these two years!' says Julie. 'Sirs, if you seek to kill a pure woman, you will not find one here. There is little to do in the countryside but horizontal pursuits and, once the love of that pastime is secured, there is very little that can shake its habit. Why, the Comte d'Armagnac fucked me himself on my fourteenth birthday and I was glad to have him!' This is not quite true. The Comte had dragged her to his bed, but he had been so drunk he fell unconscious when he got her there.

'You are merely trying to save your skin. You are an untouched girl. You country women save yourselves all for one sweating oaf, I know,' Three Fingers says.

'I don't know,' says one devil. 'They are at it like dogs from as soon as they are able in my estates in Évreux. With me quite often.'

'I had a man not half an hour ago,' says Julie. 'In the carriage that brought me here.'

'In the carriage here?'

'I was nervous. You know what they say, sirs, "a fuck for luck".'

'They?'

'The people. Or rather I do. The act is very calming, sirs, and I do believe it enhances the female voice! I sing so well for a reason, sirs, think of that. The contact with men enables my low notes, I am sure of it!' Her heart is racing. She is speaking the words, but it is as if she is outside her body, looking in. She did not come here to die. She has so much, so much, to do.

'Is the carriage still here?' says Three Fingers.

'It is,' says a man in a coat adorned with butterflies. 'At a distance, with the servants.'

'Go and see if the groom is there.'

'Why don't we kill her anyway?' says another devil.

'It's a matter of how, not when. I've another two hundred lines of summoning to get through before we're meant to kill her,' says Three Fingers. 'I can save a lot of effort if I know it will come to no good.'

A devil lifts his mask, takes a nip from a bottle of brandy. She sees his face briefly, an eyepatch on his right eye, a mess of scars beneath.

'Are we required to fuck her for this ceremony?' asks another devil.

'Yes.'

'But not if she's a strumpet, right? My syphilis has gone away, and I don't want it back. I will only fuck virgins and my wife, you know that, dear boy.'

'No need to fuck her, we just kill her.'

'Excellent. I've just had these breeches made by Daquin. I don't want them stained with mud,' says another voice.

She hears a cry from the trees: 'get off me!' and realises, with alarm, that it's Paval. What will these men do to him? If she is to die, must he? She has placed him in great danger and must protect him. He is prodded in at the point of a sword.

'Paval, I lied and said we had fucked in the carriage. Deny it. Sirs, I am a virgin, I admit.'

'Too late,' says the devil with Paval. 'He has confessed it already. Twice in the carriage and many times before, it seems.'

'Oh, in the name of Satan, Villepin, do you not check these things before dragging us to the woods for nothing?' She cannot tell who is speaking beneath the masks.

'Bring wine,' says Three Fingers, loudly to the darkness.

Swords are sheathed and the servants bring wine. One of the devils leers at Paval, says 'boo!' and the boy shrinks away, terrified. She must do something.

'Would you like another song, sirs?' she says. All her life she has been able to charm with song.

'A swansong, why not?' says a devil and she does not know what he means.

Paval is glancing from mask to mask but the devil who grips him still has his sword drawn.

'And if I sing well enough, will you let us go?'

'I might keep you as a servant,' says Three Fingers. 'Who knows?'

'And my friend.'

No one says anything. There is no sound in the woods. The fog muffles everything to silence.

Begging will not help her. She knows these to be proud men who expect and respect pride, courage and arrogance. And so she sings, one of Lully's death songs.

'Shades, ghosts, companions of death,
I do not ask of you, I do not want mercy.

I do not complain of this my lot,
This exchange I do not call cruel.
Shades, ghosts, companions of death,
Let not such just piety offend you.
An unknown force that I feel in my breast
Gives me courage, spurs me on to the test,
Makes me greater than myself.'

She lets the words babble from her, sweet as a brook, and then burst out, cold and pure as a spring torrent. The men stand rapt, masks tipped back just enough to allow them to drink the offerings their servants bring, sipping brandy from crystal glasses. All the time they never take their eyes from her. She sings, sings for her life, for Paval's life. She goes on from the song to the whole opera, every part, effortlessly transposing the key of the lower parts as the men drink. While she is singing, she is not dying. She does not stumble on the words, nor the tune. Such things imprint upon her and need no memorising, no work to hold them. She lets the music flow through her as the night grows colder and the men drink, do nothing but drink, their masks tipped back, easy in their command, their control of Paval and of her. Paval is terrified, shaking. She cannot run, in her silly shoes and skirts, but Paval can and she wants him to, but he is there for her and will not leave her.

'I warned you not to love me,' she thinks. 'And now see the good it has done you. Paval, don't share this fate.'

She does not drink – of course, she is not offered a drink – not beer, not water, not brandy and after two hours, maybe more, it happens. She has sung almost every part, transposed and moved up a register here, down here, but every part. Her voice cracks and the spell is broken.

The chief devil, Three Fingers, shakes himself.

'Enchanting,' he says. 'Quite enchanting.'

He walks up to her, his eyes black pits in his leering mask, and inspects her as one might a work of art. The blow sparks white light in her head, sends her to the earth as if all the bones were knocked out of her. She hits the ground like a fish smacked onto a slab. He has punched her, she realises, hard in the face.

'Fuck her!' shouts someone. Paval screams. She looks up. A devil grips him from behind and draws a knife across his throat. Paval falls, a wound like another great mouth at his throat. 'Paval, Paval!' she cries out.

She is kicked, punched, two devils have her, but she bites, kicks and is free. Her head is spinning with the force of the blows, but she fights to regain her senses, blinking, gulping in air.

'Bitch!'

Another – this one in a much plainer mask than the rest - lunges for her but the music is in her; she is a dancer turning aside and letting him stumble over a root, so he lands heavily on his knees.

'My silks! My silks!' he cries out, but she steps in behind him and draws his sword from his scabbard.

'You will leave me, sirs!' Her heart is pounding. Paval! Is he dead?

'Montfaucon, you fool,' says a voice, 'you let a girl take your weapon. We should never have had you along as a prospect!'

Three Fingers approaches. She looks up at him. Her senses are scrambled, and he is like a creature from a dream, blurred, an assembly of colours, a wavering flame himself among wavering flames. She is going to black out, wants to black out.

'My father taught me the art of defence, sir,' she says. 'You'll not find me easy with a sword.' She thinks of her father now. He blessed her as she left to go into the world, thought it a wonderful thing she sought to carry her gifts to the highest stage in Paris. He had always known she would go, he said, right from the time she was small. But he had put a sword in her hand early, taught her the arts of defence because he knew that a lone woman in the world of Paris would need such a thing.

Three Fingers laughs a little laugh, puts his fingers to the lips of his mask like a maiden aunt hearing a saucy story. 'This is the best swordsman in France!' says a mocking voice from behind him.

Three Fingers flashes his sword like a whip, through the torchlight.

'If in France, then in the world!' says Three Fingers. 'Put up. Fellows, stand back.'

She points the sword at him, in line, as her father had told her, arm straight, the point as far from her body as it can be held. Whoever wants to kill her will have to deal with that first.

'Oh dear,' says Three Fingers. 'Oh dearie dear.'

He steps in and, with a squeeze of his fingers, he has beaten the blade aside, extending his arm to offer the merest snick on the fabric of her sleeve with the tip of his blade.

'I can take your weapon and make it mine!' he says, encircling her blade with his so it feels it will spin from her fingers.

She regains her grip, straight arm quivering.

'I can oppose you, steel to steel!'

He shoves his sword forward, angling the hilt wider to deflect her blade, using it to guide his point to its target. Another snick on the sleeve. Her arm is cut, and she cries out in pain.

'I can ensnare the blade!' he says. 'Bind and cross, transport and deflect, make your arm my arm and move it where I like!'

In a whirl he has caught her sword with his and moves it at will.

'A straight arm is a fine defence against a village thug!' he says. 'For me, it is a gift! And I give you my best gift in return.

Without crosspiece or blade breaker, with no dagger, buckler or cloak but with only fingers and wrist, I give you the disarm!'

In a flick her sword is out of her hand and flashing through the torchlight.

She steps away but he has trodden on her foot and, unbalanced, she falls to the ground.

He has the tip of his sword at her breast and she cannot move at all.

'Had I the surgeon's art,' he said, 'I would cut your throat so nicely that you would not die but never sing again.'

'I would rather die!' she says.

'Well, that's rather the point,' he says.

He moves the sword up to her neck.

'But what's to lose?' he says. 'If I kill you, I kill you. A risk I shall take. Perhaps a pressure here.' He pushes the sword in under her chin and she cries out in pain.

'Yes! The base of the tongue. That should do it! Indeed, yes!' She screams as the needle blade pierces her flesh, screams up at the blank-eyed mask above her. Warm blood covers her chest, the tip of the sword feels so unnatural, so unwelcome in her throat.

A plunk on the back of the white silk glove. A raindrop.

The rain comes in across the torchlight, great golden berries from the dark sky pattering the leaves and the mould. A consternation among the gentlemen – silk may be ruined, lace muddied and, worse, those who had stinted on expense in ribbons, pleats and hats might see colours run, exposing them as cheapskates.

'My God,' says Three Fingers. 'This coat is by Boileau of St-Germain!'

The rain in an instant is a wash, a descending veil.

He draws back his sword hand but then puts his free hand up before his eyes. The white glove is stained with the purple dye of his head ribbon.

'I'll kill that haberdasher,' he says. 'A cape, gods, a cape!'

He turns away and rushes for his coach.

She spits at him, spits blood.

'You will go to Hell for this!' she says, the words agony, bubbling with blood. 'This is not my final scene!'

She is right. It is, however, the end of her first scene as a kick from God knows where sends her reeling into darkness as the curtain of the rain falls.

Scene Two

Entrance of the Fury

'So soon departed.'

She awakes. It is still night, though the rain has gone and somewhere behind the horizon a milky morning is trying to be born. The taste of blood is in her mouth. She tries to breathe through her nose, but it is blocked, maybe broken. Her arms feel wrenched and pulled, her legs numb where she has been kicked and stamped on.

She puts her hand to her throat. It's agony. Her voice! She tries a note, a simple 'ah!', but there is too much pain and she coughs herself raw. Blood is streaming over her fingers and she tears a piece of her ripped sleeve to stem the flow.

'He has ruined me,' she croaks. 'Ruined me!' Paval! She must find him, see if he has survived.

'This is irregular. This is insulting. This will not do.' Someone else is there. The voice is musical, the vowels like an oboe, the consonants crashing like timpani. Her head is disordered. Is she dead? She does not know.

She coughs again, spits out blood, crawls forward or tries to while holding the cloth to her neck, tries to look for Paval. It is cold and the ground is filthy. Her hand slips on the mud.

'Paval,' she says.

'Dead,' says the voice. 'Murdered.'

A great wail rises inside her, but it does not find expression in voice. Instead she grunts, low like an animal, like a mastiff thrown down by the bull but preparing for another attack.

'The Devil take them,' she says but her voice is guttural, shredded. It's as if the sword is still stuck in her throat. She wants to die. If her throat is ruined for good, then her life is over. She is near to crying, though she has never cried. She was not made for it.

The voice continues.

'Well, the problem is they'll all be shriven before morning – roll into church, confess their sins, a couple of Hail Marys and they're white as snow, ready to do it all again, safe from Hell. It does not seem right. They are too rude – to call a ruler, a potentate, a grand and royal personage of a most noble domain from princely works and then to depart before they arrive. An egregious lapse of manners, don't you agree?'

Only now does she see the man in front of her and at first she mistakes him for one of her tormentors, he is so finely dressed, the slim sword he twiddles in his fingers so well wrought, so light and quick. But, is it even a man? If it is a man, it is a young one, so dainty and pretty that he might be a girl. Only his voice, low like hers, says he might be male. The hands, on which rubies flame, are pale and long like a woman's. The figure wears a coat of shining gold, laced and decorated in blue sapphires and adorned with a brooch of golden angel's wings. The breeches are palest primrose, the shoes . . . There are no shoes. Instead, where the shoes should be, are a pair of shining black hooves.

'I know you, sir, madam,' she says. She tries to get up, levers herself onto her hands and knees.

'All men know me. All women too.'

'You are Lucifer?' Her throat makes speaking agony, though she feels she must talk.

'Yes. Lately. Though I have many names. Ishtar and Astarte, Goddess of the dawn. Venus and Aphrodite, lady of pleasures, whose number is 666. And yes, Satan. Of course, now they call me the Devil. King of Hell. And queen.'

'You are a woman?'

'We're all a woman sometimes,' says the Devil. 'If we've got anything about us. Man, woman, other things too. I am legion. Sometimes I wonder if I am even one person, or one thing.

The Devil takes her hand. Her arm cannot be broken, as she thought, for there is no pain. Instead a strange tingle spreads throughout her body. His, her, their hand is hot, very hot, but not unbearable. She stands, she doesn't know how.

'If you are the Devil, then I am dead,' she says. She shivers. 'I thought Hell would be warmer.'

'No,' says Lucifer. 'You are not dead, though you are grievously injured. I think you will recover. But you risk rudeness yourself to concentrate on your own minor problems, when mine are so much greater.'

She retches blood. The world wobbles on its axis. It never felt more like a globe. She feels she could slide off.

'I am waiting,' says Lucifer, 'for you to express some concern about me.'

Julie wipes the blood from her mouth, dizzy. All of her life she has dreamed of having access to powerful men, to bend them to her will. Now, though she may be delirious, may be reeling from her beating, she is before the second most powerful being in creation. She had thought a great deal on how to approach this sort of wealthy and important person. Flattery. No one is immune.

'You are certainly the injured party here,' she says, coughing.

'I am indeed. I am not used to being called like a dog and then left out in the cold. Not used at all. They called me, imagined that they "summoned" me, as if I could be compelled by such as they in any way. They simply descended to a level of depravity that sparked my interest and I chose to come. Then they abandoned me. Rude, rude, grievous rude!'

'Will you let me help you?' she says. There is a whistle in her voice.

'How?'

She doesn't know, so she just says, 'I could sing for you.' She retches. Blood, blood, blood.

She cannot sing now, she is sure. Her throat is raw, her head spinning. But it is all she knows. What else can she offer the Devil but the gift God gave her?

'Not necessary,' says the Devil. 'Your voice is beautiful but reminds me too much of those of the angels. I miss Heaven and would not wish to be melancholy.'

'Then what can I do?'

'Well, you're not going to be of much use down there feeling sorry for yourself. You have much to work with. You have many of the Seven Diabolic Virtues but not all. You are lustful, you are proud. You do not envy – though you do want, greatly – but you are greedy for all life has to offer, all the riches, all the gain, all the experience. You are not slothful, no one could call you lazy and contented, and you are not a glutton but . . .'

Now, Julie sees. There on the wet ground, in the pale light of the predawn, lies the body of Paval.

'Wrath,' she says. 'I have wrath.' The word is like a heat coming from her.

'Yes,' says the Devil. 'Yes you do! It is . . .' the Devil sniffs, scent the air. 'It is delicious. Palpable.' Lucifer explodes the consonants of the final word like fireworks popping at a fete.

'Then, sir, let me help you take your revenge on them?'

'Madam, I am a lady tonight.'

'Then, madam, let me help you!'

27

'I don't need your help, you mad bitch!' The Devil is suddenly angry, and that anger seems to shake the ground beneath Julie's feet.

'Well, you just said you fucking did!' Speaking is agony. Julie holds the cloth of her sleeve to her throat, the previous rag being quite soaked.

The Devil takes a pace back, raises a delicate brow.

'Sorry, sir madam, Mister Lady,' says Julie. 'I am prone to such unfortunate outbursts.'

Lucifer says nothing but studies her.

Julie bows her head. 'So you will kill them?'

The Devil mulls. 'That is problematical.'

'Why?' she croaks. 'You are the dark one, prince of the darkened air, you have stood before Christ unblinking, fought angels. Why can't you kill ordinary men?'

The Devil preens, twirls their flashing sword.

'Well, if they are killed by me, God's enemy, that makes them God's friend. So they go to Heaven when they die. Lamentable but, as I think will be clear to most, I don't set the rules.'

Julie looks at Paval's body.

'Then let me send them to you. Let me be your instrument,' she says, her voice like a barrel scraping on flagstones.

Lucifer shrugs, paces, the black hooves digging up the soft earth.

'What do you want to do?'

'Humiliate them . . .'

The Devil smiles. 'Yes!'

'Corrupt everything that is dear to them.'

'Yes!'

'And kill them!'

'Naturally! Naturally. But how? Some of these great men have enemies by the score and still live confident of seeing the next dawn. How? They have great protectors. Fierce bodyguards, men who kill for a living. That one who wounded you is a rare swordsman, though not as rare as he believes and his skill is that of the practice salle, not the duelling ground. How would you get close enough to kill them? Do you even know who they are?'

'No. Don't you?'

'Well, they do wear masks!' The Devil gives an extravagant shrug.

'But . . .' She does not want to question them, him undermine their authority but she is beginning to think this fiend is half mad.

The Devil laughs. 'Of course I know who they are! Of course. But if I send you then you are my servant, and again we risk them ending up in Heaven. You need to find them. You need to work independently! You need to find a way to be the agent of their perdition.' The word 'perdition' sizzles like bacon in a pan.

The light is coming from behind the eastern clouds now and the woods awake in birdsong. Her pain seems sharper, more unbearable in the light, as if the dark hid it. Never mind. She will go on.

'I remember,' she says. 'One wears a coat with a hart upon it, another is called Diablo, at least one has seen me perform in the street. I heard them called by three names, Bissy, Montfaucon and Villepin.'

The Devil holds up a hand to stop her and passes her a black card. 'Use your hairpin. Scratch the details there!' She does, though her mind is hazy, her vision blurred. Bissy, who she thinks carries a dragon snuff box, Villepin. Montfaucon, one eye, three fingers, scissor mouth, silver cane, emerald ring, one with a hart upon his coat, another with the waddle step, another short and stout, one called Diablo, one more with roses on his shoes. These are small things and little to go on, but she writes them down anyway, thirteen little seeds she hopes to water with blood.

'This is splendid,' says Lucifer. 'This is a traditional arrange-ment, the like of which has been all too rare recently. Of course there has to be a price. I mean, you don't get to join in my revenge for nothing.'

'Nor you mine! Where I come from, prices are paid in the expectation of return,' says Julie. 'In goods or boons! You will not give me their names, so what have you to offer me, Mister Madam, matey boy?' She coughs. Oh dear. She has let her tongue run away with her again.

The air seems to chill. The Devil snarls and Julie is suddenly very aware of the pointed white teeth beneath those ruby lips. She's spoken without thinking, forgotten her place. Her father always said her temper would get her into trouble.

The Devil's face relaxes into a smile.

'I'm afraid that if you ask for the usual, you'll just end up losing all motivation.'

'What usual?'

'Riches, mainly. Immortality.' The fiend yawns the last word out.

'There are immortals?'

'Some such miserable souls exist, yes. You don't want that, do you? It's really just turning your world here into Hell.'

'No, I don't.'

'So what do you want?'

'Give me back my voice first.'

The Devil rolls their eyes. 'I don't do healing. That's God's province. Ask Him. Ask me for something else.'

She thinks of how Three Fingers took the sword from her. She does not intend to give her enemies the chance to fight back but, if they do, she needs to be prepared. She knows now what she will ask.

'I heard a tale that you taught someone to play the violin once.'

'I did. I will. Music is in my gift. Is that what you'd like? I don't see how it would hasten your revenge.'

'I have music. I don't need yours if you cannot heal me. No, I want you to teach me to fence. I have a little skill already, but I want to learn properly. Can you do that?'

Lucifer bows and slashes at the air with their fine sword.

'There is no student of the sword like me, no one who can know better the use of finger and foot, the subtle disengage, the secret thrusts, the dropping soft step, the long overhand thrust or the pass in four. No one can fence like me!' The Devil illustrates the words by stepping daintily, by thrusting and cutting, turning and dropping, all the time the movements as fine and measured as a court dancer.

'But can you teach?'

'Of course. I am a rare instructor, a professor nonpareil, all the books agree on that.'

'So teach me.'

'Why not just learn to kill? I could show you poisons. I could show you traps. I could show you how to lead a man to damnation with powders sweet, tinctures bitter, leaves to chew and smoke and spit. Go to Pomet's the apothecary. He does my work, though he knows it not.'

'Death is not enough. I will find these men and I will, by guile and wile, send their souls to Hell.'

'No,' says the Devil, twirling the fine sword, this time so quick the blade leaves flashes in the dawn air.

'No?'

'Think. Why not?'

'Because I am a woman?'

'Because you haven't got a sword!'

'I will—'

'What? Buy one. With what? Fairy gold? A song? That's a lot of singing to buy a good duelling blade, even if you can sing. That's a nasty wound, by the way, I would get it seen to.'

Julie growls again, her mastiff growl.

'I'll find the first. I'll kill him myself and send him to you. And I will take his sword. After that, you will teach me.'

The Devil smiles. She can see this idea pleases them, him, her, whatever.

'A murder binds you to me and shows good faith. After that I will teach you. One lesson for each death. You will need to be a rare fencer to best some of these fellows.'

'One for each.'

'Yes. But let us set a limit. I like you and it would be sweet to show you the agonies of Hell. I will teach you. But you have a year to kill all thirteen. If, by midnight a All Hallows' Eve, the last one does not lie cold and unshriven in his grave, I will take you, lady, alive to Hell.'

Julie bows her head, glances at Paval's cold body. He died after fucking out of wedlock. He will go to Hell.

'Do you have his soul?' she says.

'I do.'

'Then release him until our bargain is done and we have a deal.'

The Devil considers, seems uncertain.

'All of them,' says Julie. 'In a year. That is no easy task.'

'And you will not confess the murders before a priest before all are gone?'

'I will not.'

'Then let us make it traditional. Midnight on October 31, a year from now.'

'Midnight,' she says. 'Let me see Paval is free.'

'Oh, very well. I grant you ghost sight.'

The Devil waves a hand and Julie sees Paval's ghost, pale and insubstantial, wandering dazed about the forest.

'Paval!' she says.

'He has just been released from Hell,' says Lucifer. 'It will take a while for him to come to his senses. Do we have a deal?'

'We do.'

The Devil smiles and bites their own pretty lips until blood shows. Julie knows what to do, coming forward to kiss the fiend with her own bloody mouth, pressing her bruised lips to Lucifer's, mingling blood. A sensation of crackling fire goes through her, the smell of cinders, cinnamon, everything burned and beautiful.

And then she is alone, in the lightening wood, cold and shivering, only a black card in her hand.

She goes to Paval's body, casts her arms around him, holds him cold to her breast.

A bird sings and the sound of its voice is unbearable to her, too sweet, too much a reminder of what she has lost. She lowers Pavel to the earth and runs for the town, for the Opéra, to tell Arcand to bring a hearse for her dead lover and, as she clasps her ruined throat, she vows she will make a hearse of the bones of the Tredecim for the corpse of her voice, and she will drive it to Hell.

Scene Three
Butterfly Shed Thy Wings!

She runs towards the sound of the tolling bells that welcome in the new day, unimpeded through the gate of the Bois. The gateman mistakes her for a whore and, having paid a bribe to get in, she is not required to pay one on the way out.

She has no money on her and the few fiacres – the cabs for hire – that are by the Bois at this hour would not take her anyway for fear she would bleed on their seats. She pauses, tries to find her way, shivers. The sun of autumn has a cold stare, looking on creation with contempt from its own pale splendour. She hates the sun now, for it exposes her fall. She is changing, she feels from a creature of the light to one of the dark. She longs for the darkness, not so she can hide and be safe but to hide and be dangerous.

Then she is running again, still holding the rag to her throat. What damage has he done? She should stop at the Université for help, but she has heard the doctors there do as much harm as good. She runs through the patchy fields between the Bois and the town, through the smell of morning fires, of burning rubbish, of the shit of pigs and of pig herds, of the wet and warming land. As she nears the buildings at the edge of Paris, she winds through kitchen gardens, the stink of the city already sweeping over her – rot and decay so unlike the autumn of the woods. In the woods and fields things decay because they are meant to – leaves, flowers, the bodies and leavings of animals – and so the decay promises renewal. In Paris, things rot that should not decay – people, hopes, love, kindness, souls – an endless autumn heading towards winter with no prospect of renewal. The smoke of a fire drifts past, acrid and bitter. What are they burning? Perhaps better not to ask.

She hurries on. A ragged woman carrying two pails of water on a pole across her shoulders looks at her and shakes her head in pity or disgust, Julie cannot tell and does not care. Houses spring up and the streets wind through them, like mould through a stinking cheese. And then Julie sees her, coming the other way. Another woman of about her age. She is poor, no one rich is that thin, but she has on a good blue dress and in her hand, she clutches a bonnet set with flowers. For an instant she almost thinks it is herself she sees, a spectre of herself conjured by tiredness, by her rattling headache, by anguish, but it is not. The girl's nose is broken and blood streams down her chin onto the front of the white trim, where the cloth has been pricked in imitation of lace. She is crying.

The girl stops as she sees Julie, her eyes widen. Julie walks up to her. Julie wants to ask what happened to her, to find out if she has suffered at the hands of these horrible men too, but she is exhausted from running and her throat is agony. She cannot summon the strength to speak. The woman's face hardens, her eyes narrow.

'Bitch!' she says, the word like a whip crack. 'This is my patch. My patch!' And then she slaps Julie hard across the face.

'I see you here again, I'll kill you!' she says and moves on, crying again.

Julie looks up to the heavens, though she expects no help from that direction. She is ragged, she is filthy, and she is bleeding, though none of those conditions mark her as unusual in this teeming city of half a million souls, where it is said one in every ten is a beggar. For every beaten girl with a bloody rag at her throat there are a hundred, more, men, women and children, feigning distress, injury, illness and disease to pluck the heartstrings of the rich, or not so rich, and to be given alms.

She stands shocked by the slap for an instant, but nothing can hurt her more. A dizzy, disordered feeling comes up inside her. She senses what it might be like to cry, though she has not cried since she was a small child. The girl was not a cheat, she thinks. She was not feigning distress. She is distressed. Anyone who finds themselves weeping for alms in the street is not going back to a golden apartment on the Île de la Cité in the afternoon.

She goes on down the Grand Cours, a wide avenue. At least she will not have to risk the back streets as she runs, still runs, under the pale gold of the parade of autumn elms. She is not tired, she is possessed. She sweeps past the poor in their doorways, some sleeping, some begging, some just staring into the weak sun; she sweeps past cabs and soldiers, some going about their early morning duties, some ragtagging home from the affairs of the night. A man wanders past with a great metal tube on his shoulder, shouting 'Get your morning clyster! Purify the bowels with a long draught from my health-giving piston! Cleanse the complexion, do not leave to nature what man has perfected! I guarantee my aim is true and I will carry all shit away! Come now, the king bends for three of these a day!'

The blood has stopped by the time she reaches the Opéra. The company is based in the theatre of old Cardinal Richelieu's Palais Royal, in the eastern wing. She does not have to search for the stage door, she has stood at it for long enough begging auditions to know where it is.

She hammers at it. Arcand will be in – has to be in. He sleeps there, has his own bed. It a long time before he answers

– no Paval in the cot by the door this morning. Only now does she know how tired she is, gasping for air after such an effort.

The door swings back and the old man is in front of her, his hair disordered.

'Who the fuck are you and who dug you up?' he says. His voice is reedy, his manner exaggerated.

'Paval,' she says. Her voice is a scrape, no more.

'You're not Paval.' He clearly thinks this is funny.

She coughs, retches, holds her throat.

'He's not here. He's off with some baggage. Are you all right, dear?'

'I'm the baggage,' she says. 'And he's dead.'

Arcand puts his hand to his chest.

'Oh my life! How?'

'We were set on in the Bois de Boulogne. Set on by great men. Deceived and tricked.'

'My Jesus!' says Arcand. 'What were you doing in the wood? After dark? Don't tell me it was after dark!'

'I . . .' And now her voice fails her. She can't speak, though she tries.

Arcand peers at her.

'Oh my good lord. You're that one who keeps coming trying for auditions, aren't you? Hang on. Is this a ruse? Get an old man's sympathy and then be put in front of Master Lully. You can sing well enough, I'll grant you, but you are nothing without introductions. Where is Paval, in truth, where is he?'

She removes the rag from her throat and shows him the wound.

He is quiet for an instant.

'Come in,' he says. 'Come in.' He wipes a tear from his eye.

Stage hands are sent to fetch Paval's body. The doctor is called from the other side of the Palais. Monsieur – the king's brother Philippe – is up at St-Cloud at the moment and that chateau has its own staff, so his doctor in town, an Englishman called Mowbray, is at a loose end. Arcand is a useful man to know for someone of culture like Mowbray, and so the doctor is glad to help. He is a round little man who smells of drink, but he has a soft face and smiles easily.

'Quite a wound,' he says. '*Quite a blessure* . . .' On his lips the French word sounds like a kettle coming to the boil.

She tries to speak, cannot, and Mowbray puts up his hand to quiet her.

'You will have to avoid speaking for quite a while,' he says. 'Well, he was either lucky not to kill you or a fine swordsman with some knowledge of the human form. He missed the major blood canals and I think the larynx. I *think*. Galen, one of the fathers of my art, describes this structure as the foundation of the voice. He has missed it, I am sure.'

'Then she will sing again?' says Arcand. 'She has a wonderful voice, if only she could find the right patron.'

'She will never sing again,' he says. Julie feels her mind boiling with anger at Mowbray, at Three Fingers, and at God for the fate He has visited upon her. 'That is my opinion. Now, I will stitch, I think. Some colleagues prefer to let such things scab, but I stitch. Do you have brandy, Arcand?'

'Will that numb the pain?'

'Not for her, for me. I take brandy and egg for breakfast as the surest guarantee of a long life. Unfortunately I need the egg for the dressing, but I will not forgo my brandy.'

He is sewing her up and the pain is terrible. Arcand holds her hand, calls her little bird and sweet thing but in truth she welcomes the agony. While the needle pierces and the thread pulls, she does not think of what is to become of her. Her whole life has been taken from her, her singing, the thing that thrilled her more than anything. No longer will she open herself up to the air and feel the notes God struck at creation sounding in her. So she will strike some different notes herself.

When he is done, the doctor takes an egg from his bag and mixes it with rose water and turpentine. He soaks a pad and bandages it to her neck. She has been thinking. All her life she has dreamed of being allowed through the doors of the Opéra. Now she is here, she will not leave. If she cannot make the music, she will be near to it. And besides, aristocrats come to the Opéra, don't they? Like so many bright butterflies fluttering to the flowers of the shining riverbank while she, a squat toad, waits for them in the underdark.

Julie turns to Arcand and signals for a paper and pen and they are brought.

'What do you want me to do?' she writes upon it.

'In what way?'

'You need a new dogsbody.'

He looks at what she has written, gives an exaggerated shrug. 'A woman cannot do this job.'

She raises an eyebrow.

'Well, perhaps one could do the work, but the cast would never accept it. Carrying and fetching is a man's job and . . . it is not done, it is not done for a woman to be employed so. You are too pretty. You'll be goosed from dawn till dusk back here in the dark.'

She takes up the surgeon's scissors and Arcand puts his hand to his chest. For an instant, it seems he thinks she will stab him. Instead she cuts off a hunk of her hair. And then another and another.

All the time she watches Arcand. He shoots the doctor a look as if to say, 'well, this is a rum do'.

When she is done, her hair is a hacked mess, not unlike Paval's.

'I am Gilles,' she writes.

Arcand gives a little moue but his eyes are full of pity.

'All right, Gilles,' he says. 'We will get you some man's clothes.'

Scene Four

Oh See the Huntress
'Neath the Silver Moon

She sleeps by night in the cot by the door, still deep with the smell of Paval. She has buried him in the stench of the Cimetière des Innocents near the market of Les Halles. There was no money for a plot for Paval, so he was shovelled into one of the open pits.

She forced herself to watch his dear shape tumbling down into the jumble of limbs and faces, the rotten bodies and the freshly dead, the penny incense she bought from the street seller unable to keep the stink from her nose. That smell, it still hangs on her clothes, she can taste it in her mouth as she falls asleep at night, in the food and drink she forces down her raw throat.

When she sleeps, she thinks she is standing in the cemetery, the dilapidated charnel houses around her, their broken roofs showing skulls and bones. The land is not land, neither is it water, but it rolls and pitches like water and when the skin of green grass parts, corpses and skeletons rise up, arms imploring, before the earth closes over them again and they are swallowed. She sees the broken-in church, the walls of the mausoleum, the ground swollen and bursting with dead. She wakes and holds her ankle. She turned it on the iron cattle grid at the entrance to the cemetery. The ground there is so thin, the soil so sparse, that horses would quickly split it open and reveal the dead within. Coffins have to be carried in on shoulders or, if no coffin can be afforded, the corpse dragged in by its sheet. Few want to shoulder something as leaky as a dead body.

It seemed like a dream there. The Devil had allowed her to see ghosts and she was sure there were a few in the cemetery, wandering like blown clouds among the graves, looking lost and alone.

She tumbles back into a half sleep once more and a presence is at her side, one of perfume and light. 'All Hallows' Eve,' says a musical voice and she is swallowed by the welling land, sucked down to be spat out into wakefulness and morning in the opera house.

She is not even sure now, a week after the attack, if she ever met the Devil. Only the black card, with its pin scratches revealing the red beneath, reminds her. There are the clues, the names, the details of the men – three fingers, emerald ring, rose shoe, all of them. It does not matter if she saw the Devil for true or if he or she or it came to her in a delirium. She will act as if she saw them. She has taken the Devil into her heart, she will become the Devil if she has to. She touches her throat. Still so painful.

A year, no time to lose. Though she must lose some time. She works, she must work, but her mind must turn off for a while, her body heal. Can she speak? Yes, her voice returns, but not the same voice. This one is low and grating, like a man's. She does not like it, though it completes her disguise.

Many voices are in this building, from the careful, worried old woman tones of Arcand to the carpenter with a voice like a flute and the flautist with a voice like a saw. The musicians bustle in for the performances, the singers too – burly baritones, spare countertenors, a fat bass. The women she cannot look at, not directly, for fear that her want of being them will kill her or them. She looks at the floor as they pass and sees only the hems of their drab street clothes and then the shine of their faux silks and ribbons as they await the stage.

She hears their conversations, though, as they ask her to 'be a darling and run for my wig' or, in other cases, simply extend a hand and click their fingers, expecting her to know what it is they want fetched or carried. Everyone clucks for her to serve them, or shouts or commands. She feels as if she is running most of the day, but she is glad of it. It helps her forget. Not forget. Put on hold. Suspend. Wait. Her desire for revenge is a physical thing, lodged inside her like a hook in the gullet, like the pain she feels when she swallows or speaks. She needs to become strong before she can act. The Opéra rests, it repaints, recuperates, practices and renews each day before the performance of the night. She will do the same. She is like a piece of stage design herself, a painted tree or a mountain, convincing from afar. Up close, the illusion does not hold for the tree is no more than daubed paint, the mountain can be moved with one hand, the person is not a person, just a seething spirit of vengeance clothed in flesh.

From four in the afternoon the Opéra is the busiest place she has ever been in her life – busier than any market. People rush everywhere, shoulder and shove, great sound fills the building as the orchestra prepares, tight-waisted dancers squeeze past barrel-chested singers in passageways so narrow a rat would need to breathe in to pass.

The smells of the backstage are wonderful, paint and turpentine, grease and candlewax, make-up and perfume. Paris is not Paris here. Paris rots. The Opéra blooms, like a great garden of wondrous flowers sunk in the stinking soil of the city.

At the centre of it all, the god of this Eden, is Lully. Lully is the master, Lully is the great composer, Lully is the conductor, the impresario, the man who pays the rent, the wages, the upkeep and the man who takes the money. Yes, Lully is like God, or maybe not like God because sinners cannot rely on God's wrath – his mercy is mysterious and unpredictable. Lully's anger with those who annoy him is a certainty and terrible in its execution. Lully, though, Lully is all. His are the only works ever performed at the Palais as none can compare to his genius. Although it also helps that Lully is in charge of commissioning operas and so is in a position to recognise and foster his own talent.

But there is talk of another opera – one from another composer, not Lully.

'This,' says Arcand, 'will set a cat up Lully's arse.'

'Don't you mean "set the cat among the pigeons"?' says the boy Diandré, a waif of ten years old who has inveigled himself into the Opéra by the twin strategies of making himself useful and just refusing to leave. He plays with a button as he speaks, one of a number he has collected by hook or by crook from the costume department. His invention with them is legendary at the Opéra – he can juggle, flip, palm and flick them high to catch them in his teeth.

'It'll be far worse than that,' says Arcand. 'Have you never had a cat up your arse?'

'No,' says Diandré.

'It's awful,' says Arcand. 'Watch out when you change your trousers. First a mouse runs up there, then the cat chases it and all Hell breaks loose. You're lucky if you can walk for a week. That's if you pull them up quick enough to stop a dog following the cat in! Next thing you know a man's got his hand up there, trying to get his dog out.'

'This has happened to you?' says Diandré.

'Countless times,' says Arcand with a wink at Julie.

Diandré takes Julie's hand. 'I'll look out for mice,' he says.

43

Julie smiles. The first time since that night in the Bois, the first time since the cauldron of steaming, grasping dead at Les Innocents. She touches her throat. It is no longer sore, though she will not risk speaking if she can help it. She takes her hand out of the little boy's. Why? It's just a feeling, not anything she can put into words really. She has the sense of being poisonous, dangerous. Yes, Three Fingers shot poison into her like a great wasp with his sharp sting. Or was the poison always there? Was that what killed Paval?

'Why will Lully care?' says Diandré and Arcand explains.

Everything comes from the king. The king is the sun, shining his light on the land, choosing who is nurtured and who is left in darkness. Lully has stood in the full glare of the monarch's admiration for decades now and all his power comes from that fact. Lully does not want one ray of that sunshine falling on anyone else.

The problem is that Louis would like to see something new or different. Impossible at the Palais Royal, of course, even for Le Roi Soleil; the season is booked years in advance and everything, *everything* would be thrown into disorder and chaos were anything at all to be changed, says Lully.

Louis is a man who gets what he wants, however. France is his opera house. Here *he* pays the rent, the wages, the upkeep and here *he* takes the money. So much that it cannot be counted – from the taxes he levies to the interest he charges the nobles he is bankrupting by his insistence they dress like gods in silks, brocade, gold and jewels. Of course, a god never wears the same thing twice.

Yet nothing can be done at the Opéra, even by the king. But with such a large cast, so many singers, so many players and dancers, so many understudies waiting to be given their chance, cannot the Opéra come to Louis at Versailles? It can, of course, and the king commands it. There will be a performance of Angelica by young Plamondon at Versailles, to break the dourness of Christmas, with all its masses.

The king's man Bontemps has put in an appearance at the Palais to make sure things are going well, that the right singers are being made available. No talk of understudies now. Fanchon Moreau is to sing, come in from Vienna at the request of the king. Lully is fuming, the walls of the Palais seem to tremble. A first violin is beheaded by Lully on the spot after a squeaky note and his innards spilled across the orchestra pit, so say the gossips. Lully took out an axe, yes, an axe, and chopped him up right there and then. Julie sees the first violin later and he appears remarkably well, considering his ordeal, if a little cowed. Lully will not go to see this minor work at the court. It is an insult, a monstrosity. He will not go! He will not go! He will go. He must. Moreau. She must sing for him. Plamondon cannot properly serve a talent like that.

Julie doesn't see Bontemps of course, all persons of dubious appearance are swept aside for his arrival, but the Opéra clucks with talk of his visit. A month later, songs of Jesus's birth are on the breath of the opera singers as they practise and trill. It is time to have her stitches removed. They itch so, and the scar at her throat is nearly healed. However, Monsieur is back at the Palais, so it is inconceivable that Mowbray will see her. She is not paid at the Opéra, simply allowed to sleep and eat there, so she cannot pay a doctor to do the work. She takes a small sharp knife from one of the tailors and pulls out the stitches herself. It does not hurt, as she expected it would, there is just the sensation of tugging and then the stitches are gone. She sits at one of the backstage mirrors, studies herself in the candlelight. She could be a boy, tall, pale, dark. She takes one of the great wigs from its stand and puts it on. She could be a woman, tall, pale, dark. She tries a note, but the voice is low and growling like a dog. She does not cry, she is not made for it. There are nobles at Versailles, great men. She studies her black card. 'Three fingers, waddle step, Montfaucon, rose shoes.' As she says the words, she notices her voice sounds better. Yes, her speaking voice is healing. She tries to sing again. No. Quite ruined, her talent gone and the men who did it walking free. She puts the small knife into her sleeve. One day it may be useful.

The Tredecim could be there, at this performance at Versailles, and the Opéra will need someone to fetch and carry. As it is, she doesn't even need to ask to go. She is told she will attend – though she must wait with the wagons at the edge of the park once they are unloaded and in no way make herself visible to noble personages, who might be offended by the sight of her.

So the costumes are loaded, and the carriages drawn up for the orchestra and singers. The king – even for the rehearsals – has deemed that standard city fiacres will not do to move the company. Accordingly, grand carriages have been requisitioned, borrowed, or even bought to take the Opéra to Versailles.

Julie finds herself, nevertheless, on a drab dray pulling the scenery through the frosty streets. It is to be driven within a mile of Versailles and then the scene panels carried the rest of the distance to the grand house, lest sensitive eyes be shocked by the sight of such base transport. She is glad of the frost. The shit and slurry of the streets has frozen solid and the horses make good progress.

The rehearsals are Sunday and Monday – Lully would not spare his company for later in the week – and the performance on the Tuesday. The scenery drays pull up in a wood and a nobleman is waiting to direct the stagehands down to the palace, his retinue around him. No, it isn't a nobleman. It's a servant but with his own servants. A tripping, powdered, wigged and bowed servant. Is it him? Is it the one who greeted her at the Bois de Boulogne?

If it is, his master can't be far away. She scrabbles for her little card even though she knows she has written nothing about a servant there. She touches it for reassurance.

She hops down from the dray and tries to speak to him. Her throat is tight from so long without words and she rasps at him.

'Where do you want the horses?' Her breath steams in the cold air.

'I'm sorry, I don't speak peasant, dear,' says the servant. 'You'll need a translator if you want to address me.'

'Dear.' The word is like a gong struck inside her. Julie has an ear for timbre, for voice, for stress and emphasis, accent and breath. This man, she is sure, is not the servant who greeted her in the woods.

She is to wait with the horses, along with Diandré, but she is determined to get into the grounds of the great house. The boy has constructed a draughts board from a piece of wood, stolen buttons for pieces. She plays for a while but cannot concentrate, thinking only of how she can get to the house. When the scenery panels are unloaded, she takes a corner of a forest scene, but Arcand waves her away.

'You've not been with the Opéra long enough for perks,' he says. 'You stay with the horses. Maybe next year you'll get to see the palace. Light a fire or you'll freeze!'

She knows it's useless to protest, once Arcand makes up his mind he makes up his mind. Lully, bossy, firm, never accepting dissent or challenge, sets the tone for the whole Opéra. Everyone in the backstage crew is a little Lully, bossing whatever he can of his own domain – right down, she guesses, to the Opéra cats bossing the mice. No wonder the mice run up people's bums.

She lets go of the panel and returns to the horses. The retinue of servants from Versailles make no effort at all to help with the scenery as the stagehands manoeuvre the images of trees through the real trees and down the road to the palace. Behind them stream the other stagehands from the Opéra, carrying all the trunks, costumes, and wig boxes the performance needs. Well, not quite all.

Tied beneath the cart Julie came on is the box containing soprano Langlois's best wig. It is the one she always wears when the top aristocrats are in and she is sure to wear it at Versailles.

The evening of the rehearsal passes serenely, the breathing of the horses and the sounds of the winter wood lulling her into sleep before the fire. The next day is bright, clear and bitter, a breeze from the east. She eats some bread, sees to the horses, fetches wood for the fire and that is the extent of her activities until a party of servants come up from the great house to tell her to move the wagons deeper into the wood. Friends of the king are coming to the performance and there must be no risk of offence to their vision. They must put out their fires and not relight them. These are the king's woods.

'We will freeze!' says Diandré.

'Invisibly, so it won't matter,' says a servant.

She does as she is bid, setting up camp at a greater distance from the house. But as dusk falls she makes her way, shivering, to the edge of the wood in order to overlook the road, unseen. She touches the black card inside her tunic, feeling the scratchings of the pin.

The king's servants line the road here every fifty paces or so, each carrying a flaming torch though it is not yet full dark. She is cold, wrapped in an old horse blanket she has got from the bottom of the dray.

The first carriage rattles up the road, a splendid painted blue affair pulled by four white horses whipped on by a coachman in a livery of scarlet and led by four pied carriage dogs who lift their paws high as they run as if disdaining to soil them on the dirty ground. She tries to remember if such a thing was present at the wood on All Hallows' Eve, but she cannot. Neither can she see inside the carriage, for the curtains are drawn. Others follow it, one or two at first but then a great train. Within them, she sees flashes of feathers, of jewels, a sleeve of blue or scarlet but nothing she can attach with certainty to that terrible night in the Bois de Boulogne.

She winds herself on to a torch-bearer's arm.

'Hello, handsome,' she says.

'I don't do boys,' he says. 'Fuck off before one of the great men sees you and has us both flogged.'

'Well, that's a bit of luck, because I'm not a boy.'

He squints at her.

'Aren't you?'

'No.'

She takes his hand, presses it to her breast.

'If you're a woman, you're a rough one with a voice like that,' he says. 'But it doesn't matter because I've no money for whores.'

'Well, that's the sort of thing a girl could find offensive,' says Julie. 'I want no money. I just want you to tell me who all these pretty people are who are trotting down the lane.'

'And what do I get for that?'

'What do you want?' she says.

He smiles at her unevenly.

'Who do you want to know about?' he says.

She thinks of her card.

'Just tell me who is who and all about them as they come in. It's so romantic.'

So he does and she gets little profit from it. The names of the nobles come and go but there is nothing she recognises but she jollies the torch-bearer along, expressing interest and cooing at the bits of gossip he tells her.

'Some of these great people are fine enough to rival the angels,' she says. 'Or the Devil.'

But he just shrugs.

'The last of them should be in soon enough,' he says. 'Then you can suck me off before I go back.'

'I'm looking forward to it,' she says. 'But tell me, do you know a Montfaucon?' She won't ask for the other two yet – that may raise suspicion if, by chance, this man knows of what binds them.

He snorts. 'The cheapskate? He's trying to gain influence, aren't they all, but he lacks the bollocks for it so only comes up here for things like this. That'll never do, the king will just look at him and say, "we hardly see him". But he won't come any more than he already does. He doesn't have the nuts for it.'

'Nuts?'

'Financial nuts. You have to spend to be seen here and the cost of it bankrupts everyone. Everyone. They have to borrow from the king. It's a fact of life, you can't get round it if you're ambitious. But Montfaucon won't lay out. I bet he fucks off back to town tonight, even. That'll mean he saves on having to have clothes for breakfast. He holds on to his money, but others are bolder, cough up and have a say in shaping the world.'

'What does he look like?'

'Why do you want to know?'

'He made my sister pregnant. I'd just like to look at him.'

'He looks like a noble. They all look the same, don't they? Wig, flashy coat, rotten teeth.'

The last of the carriages rattles through the gates.

'Now,' says the torch-bearer.

She leads him into the trees. He hugs her, tries to kiss her but she won't have any of that. She pulls out his dick and gives it a few strokes. It is long but thin, strangely tapering and she tries not to laugh. It reminds her of an under-watered carrot. He puts his hands on her shoulders, trying to push her down but she just keeps stroking, dragging her nails, or what is left of them, across the underside of his dick.

'You said the mouth,' says the torch-bearer. 'Come on, I'm ready to go. In the mouth. In the mouth.'

She gives his dick one last squeeze. He sighs, his breath sharp with cloves.

'Not until you show me Montfaucon,' she says.

He shoves her.

'You don't bargain with me, whore. You made a deal.'

She smiles, lifts her tunic to show him her tits.

'When you show me Montfaucon,' she says. 'Then you'll get to blow all over my face and over these. Until then—'

'I don't do deals with the likes of you,' he says. 'You'll fuck me, whether you like it or not!'

She takes her little knife from her sleeve, holds up her finger in a 'No, no, no' gesture.

He looks at the knife.

'Oh God,' he says. 'Come on then!'

'Wait,' she says.

She fetches the box from under the axle of the carriage.

'Now,' she says. 'Let's go.'

Scene Five

Hark the Angel Sings!

When they finally break from the trees, she draws in her breath. The palace is not a building but a floating island of light. Versailles has lit its candles and its windows shine across the dark gardens as if suspended on an invisible sea. It's huge, far bigger than any building she has ever seen. It's as if the old Greeks were right, that the sun does plot his course across the sky in a chariot of fire and comes to rest in his palace by night. She imagines the king inside, all burning bright, his skin a flaming gold, his courtiers dancing in his shining light. Once she would have seen herself in that vision, a jewel to catch the king's light, reflect it back in colours rich and deep. Now she imagines herself as a little blob of darkness moving inexorably towards the palace, a piece of the night come to the court of the sun.

Through the trees she sees lines of torches parading up a grand promenade, their light doubled in the water of a canal.

'I will show you his carriage, that will be enough,' says the torch-bearer.

'You will show me him.'

'We can't go inside, you stupid strumpet,' he says.

'I can,' says Julie.

'You'll be locked up, if you're lucky,' says the torch-bearer. 'I'll show you the carriage and no more. They wait by the stables.'

Julie can see she's going to get nothing more from this man, so she follows him out of the trees and skirts around the back of the building.

They arrive at the stables, where coachmen play dice or stand and drink from bottles. A few have made a little fire in the courtyard and a man stands playing a scratchy fiddle.

'Which one?' she says.

'That one,' he says, pointing to a low two-horse gig.

'How do I know?'

'You are a presumptuous slut,' he says. 'Because I say so.'

'Whose carriage is this, sir?' says Julie to the driver.

'The Marquis de Suaval,' he says. 'What's it to you?'

'Which is Montfaucon's?'

'Over there, the one with the silver tree.'

There it is, a canopied carriage bearing the image of a spreading tree on the door.

'You got it wrong,' says Julie.

'You still owe me,' says the torch-bearer but he says it to empty space.

She has gone, run away from him past the stables and out towards the big house, bearing the box under her arm.

She has no idea where she is going, nor what she might blunder into. She streaks down the length of the building, past an interminable row of windows where visions of firelit gold blur against the night's dark.

There are doorways, plenty of doorways but she dare not go in. Which door is suitable for the likes of her? Which door will not see her imprisoned or beaten for the temerity of trying to enter? No, she must try. There, there is a door with two footmen in scarlet livery outside it, both of them stamping in the cold. She calms herself, walks and approaches them, holds out the box.

'Sirs, I have a delivery for . . .'

'Opéra three doors down,' says a footman.

She walks on to find a door with carved comedy and tragedy masks above it. She knocks but there is no reply. She pushes open the door and enters. The corridor is quite the most splendid place she has ever seen. Grand portraits line the wall – the king in costumes of emperors, divinities, portrayed as a man in a toga declaiming before rapt audiences. She knows Louis liked to act in his youth. There is a rail of fine dark wood, the ceiling is in gold leaf. She gulps. This is the backstage area? This is the staff entrance?

The door to her right opens as a young boy steps through and the corridor floods with noise. A huge room lit by golden candelabras is packed with the cast of the Opéra. Ladies adjust wigs in front of mirrors, apply make-up and earrings, boys fetch and carry. David Boucher, the great bass, takes a swig on a bottle and gargles; a violinist comes in, screams and shouts until someone can finally understand that he can't find his case. It's discovered under a soprano, or rather under the chair she is sitting on. A young apprentice singer heaves at the laces of a mezzo-soprano's dress. Everyone else is warming up, 'a be be be,' 'ah, ah, ah,' 'oh, oh oh', like so many splendid birds chirping in a forest of costumes. A violin runs scales to help.

Julie finds Langlois, who is sitting for make-up so heavy that it is as if another face entirely is being painted upon her own.

'You forgot your wig, ma'am,' she says.

A brow is arched, a lip curled.

'I forgot nothing,' she says. 'I am here to sing, not to remember. It is the costumier who forgot.'

'Sorry, yes,' but Langlois is already ignoring her, turning her attention back to the mirror.

No one even seems to see Julie, other than to tell her to get out of the way. Everyone is so busy, so distracted. She would like to see the opera room, for sure, so she takes a door out of the room. She's surprised that she doesn't come into a grand opera space but into another corridor, lit by candles in glass lamps.

It is even more richly adorned than the corridor she entered through – wood panelled, hung again with paintings in golden frames, fine carpets on the flags of the floor.

She steps in and closes the door behind her. All along the corridor are doors, each with a symbol on them picked out in gold. Here is a lion, here a griffon, here an eagle.

She walks on. A door opens and a waft of deep perfume comes through. It is followed by a young woman in a shimmering dress of pale blue velvet, her hair a mass of dark curls. In her hand she holds a silver mask, sparkling with jewels in the candlelight.

'Shit!' she says. 'Shit, shit!'

She sees Julie.

'Shit!' she says again, almost into Julie's face. She gives a big smile.

She turns back into the room and emerges clutching a fan and disappears down the corridor away from the Opera's backstage. An instant later, a maid sticks her head out of the door. She sees Julie but completely ignores her.

'She's gone,' she says. 'Over to the pavilion and get ready for them to come back from the opera.'

'We won't get to bed before midnight tonight,' says another.

'Unless old Dacre gets his paws on you,' says a maid.

'Don't,' says the other and shivers. Then they are gone, tripping down the corridor. As another servant, and a lowly looking one, Julie is invisible.

She is alone in the corridor. Out of curiosity, she tries the door. It is unlocked.

She pushes inside. She cannot see, it's so dark, so she takes a candle from the wall of the corridor and gives life to a fabulous line of shining dresses in colours of greens, reds, blues and yellows that nature could only envy.

She steps inside, in wonder. This is a room as she should have had, if her rightful destiny had been granted her, a trove of silks and taffeta, brocade and even lace. There are masks here, there are extravagant fans and tall shoes and pale stockings. There is one huge chest, big enough to swallow her, full of scarves. If she had found a genie lamp, and been granted wishes, a room like this would have been one of them – after the restoration of her voice and the death of her enemies. She strokes a hand down the long rail of dresses, holds one against herself in the looking glass. A noise at the door. She drops the dress and folds herself back into the clothes rail.

It's a maid, carrying a candle. She enters the room, picks up a roll of ribbon that must be worth a year's bread to an ordinary person, and leaves quickly. Thank God she ignores the candle already burning by the mirror. Perhaps she wants the palace to burn down or perhaps she is one of the wiser servants who concerns herself solely with things she has been told to concern herself with – in this case ribbons, not candles.

Julie steps out. She does not think. Julie can think, and often does, but now she proceeds as if driven by some external force.

She takes off her workday rags and stands naked before the mirror. The bruises on her arms have healed, but one on her leg remains, a devil's kiss of yellow and black. She will not bother with the undershirt, she wants to feel the material against her skin.

She puts on a pale gold underskirt, its silk cold against her legs, its brocade scratchy on her chest and back. Then the overskirt, a sweep of deep green. Now a high wig. In an instant, she is transformed from a pretty boy in a skirt to a woman, a lady of the court.

She has played this game as a child, being a great lady preparing for the ball, tried on thousands of imaginary skirts, balanced thousands of non-existent wigs on her head. She takes a ribbon choker from its case and clasps it about her neck. It covers her scar perfectly. As she clicks the clasp shut, she swallows. She could be hanged for what she is doing here but she doesn't care. One night of this seems worth it. She holds out a sleeve, feels its velvet weight dropping away from her, breathes in its smell of musk and roses.

She cannot bring herself to rush. This dressing is as sensuous, as transforming as any undressing by a lover's hand. A bracelet now adorns her wrist and she holds it up to the mirror in the candlelight, transfixed by its gold. It must only be costume jewellery, no one would leave a real gold bracelet lying around but that doesn't matter to her. She feels like a goddess, dropping fire from her hands.

The dressing takes her ten minutes, though she struggles with the lacing at the back. She gazes at herself for ten more, an image of what she might have been, an image of what she is. Imposter, thief.

She goes back out of the door and walks down the corridor, the way she saw the young woman go.

She opens another door to find herself outside, where footmen carry sedan chairs creaking through the dusk, where gentlemen escort ladies on their arms as if showing them like horses at a fair. Streams of fine people are passing through an archway of flowers guarded by scarlet footmen. The candlelit gold of the windows shines like the light of another world.

She goes through the archway. The footmen don't give her a second glance as she passes within.

She is in a tunnel of paper flowers that extends a couple of minutes' walk before opening on to a large courtyard in front of a grand building that curves in front of her in a crescent of arches.

She has heard in her village of doors to the otherworld – to the land of the odd folk and strange people where it is never night unless they wish it to be night and there are mice as big as horses, horses as tiny as mice.

It seems it is such a door she faces now. She steels herself, stands tall and approaches the footmen standing guard. She doesn't address them or even acknowledge them, just stands staring ahead. They open the door and she steps into a grand salon, a dazzle of glass and silver, a confusion of conversation and colours, a clinking of bottles as gilded servants move among fabulous aristocrats.

A maître d' bows before her, then rises to look uncomfortably at her. He doesn't recognise her, she sees, and she has no servant to pass him a card. She stares at him, feigning arrogance.

He lowers his head and then announces.

'The lady . . .' He has a fit of coughs, bows extravagantly and she passes him by without a second glance.

The candlelight dances on glasses, on jewels, on the gold of rings and buckles, belts and brooches. This is the kingdom of light, she thinks. Heaven could not sparkle so. She looks around. There is a man in exactly the coat that Three Fingers wore! But this man is short and stout, Three Fingers was tall and bony. There is a man with the design of a hart on his coat. But it is not quite the same hart as the one she remembers. A lady puts her hand on Julie's arm, says 'Darling!' and passes on.

Another floats past. 'Your dress, dear, has a loose lace at the back. People will think you're plying for trade. Ask me about replacing your maids.'

She puts a hand up to the lace on instinct but cannot reach it.

A servant passes her a glass of wine and she takes it, stands against a wall.

'Be a dear and point out my lord Montfaucon to me,' she says in her best – not very good – posh voice to a splendidly dressed fellow in scarlet but he just says, 'We never see him, we never see him' and she gets the same answer from two others.

Finally she asks a servant. 'My lord Montfaucon?'

'The gentleman over there in the white coat,' he says. 'That is Montfaucon, though his star is waning. We never see him. He has been here no more than twice a week for that last year!'

There he is. She had imagined him old, but he is not really old. He is perhaps forty-five, handsome in his way, with long dark hair and a fine, strong chin. His eyes, though, are lined, pained almost, and he dabs at his nose with a handkerchief. He looks about him as he talks to a gentleman in a coat of pale green, his eyes searching the room. He passes limpingly from that gentleman without excusing himself to another who wears an extravagant black wig but only talks a few moments there, his eyes still darting, before passing on again abruptly to stand as if marooned in the centre of the room, stiff on his toes as if unsure which way to go. Julie touches the black card in her sleeve, touches the knife in the other. She feels she could stab him here.

She sidles towards him and smiles. He smiles back, dabs at his nose, which is red and sore-looking. She guesses he must have a cold and she hopes it is a bad one.

'Some cloth,' he says, and she realises he is talking about her dress. 'I don't know you, lady. Is your father a rich man?' Yes, it is the voice she recognises, the clipped tones, the way of speaking that is as near to nature as are the pale gold roses on his coat.

Julie swallows. She can't talk to this man. Her common way of speaking will give her away even if the gravel of her voice does not. She nods.

'Very rich?'

She nods again.

'Silent, demure. I like that in a woman. I will make enquiries of you, lady. You . . .' He extends a finger as if it is a sword and he intends to knight her. 'You have caught my eye! What is your name? Your family name?'

Before she can reply, a bell is sounded, and the performance announced.

'Princes, lords, ladies, we commence very shortly, very shortly indeed!' says the maître d'.

She smiles at Montfaucon, lowers her eyes. She is afraid her voice will give her away, so 'sit with me,' she mouths. He smiles back with his mouth of rot and takes her arm as they go through to the next room.

The auditorium is bigger even than that at the Palais. There must be space for a thousand here, all stood or seated on whatever chair, stool or chaise longue their rank and state of favour allows.

'If I am with you, cannot I take a seat nearer the front?' says Montfaucon. 'Does your father sit there? Perhaps you should introduce me. Is your father a duke? I think he is a duke to have sired such a handsome woman as you. And yet I do not know you, I do not know you. You are a puzzle, lady.'

She smiles and lowers her eyes and he laughs.

'I like puzzles,' he says. 'As long as I quickly find out the answer. I am not a patient man.'

It seems to be his wish to sit further up and it is hers too. This will be the first time she has seen an opera from the auditorium, not the wings. So she walks down the aisle to where she sees the young woman from the changing room. She is a vision in pale blue, her hair, no wig, piled up in lavish dark curls, a diamond choker at her throat. She looks enchanting and, Julie guesses, will not recognise one of her own dresses if she sees it. She has so many. At least Julie is sure she is wearing something that will announce her as this woman's social equal.

She sits down next to her and smiles, Montfaucon sliding in at her side.

The young woman smiles. 'A nice dress,' she says. 'You must give me the address of your designer. I can tell you and I shall be friends, so much do I like your style.'

Julie returns the smile, but the young woman leans across her.

'You're with him?' she says, almost prodding Montfaucon as she points at him.

Montfaucon has the air of a mouse who is frozen for a moment, not quite sure if he is in the eye of a hawk. He says nothing but smiles weakly.

'Don't be his step, darling,' says the young woman. 'That's all you'll be to him. He'll tell you what you want to hear until you marry him then he'll spend all your money and leave you marooned on some country estate dropping children every five minutes until one of them kills you on its way out and he uses your fortune to marry a duchess. To whom he will do the same.'

'Really!' says Montfaucon.

'Don't "really" me,' says the young woman. 'I know you, Montfaucon, we hear all about you at court. You'll do to her what my father did to my mother – lock her up, force her to pray for half the day and search her rooms for lovers every midnight. No wonder she ran off with a woman!'

'I will not!'

'Yes you will!' She turns to Julie 'Do you know, my father had all the girl servants' front teeth knocked out to make them less attractive to men and he wouldn't let the milkmaids touch the cows' udders because it reminded him of spunking a cock? That's what you're in for with the likes of him.'

'Madam. You are too much.'

'You see, a tight little bourgeois through and through. Spunk a cock! Spunk a cock! Does that offend you, sir?'

'Young women should not talk that way.'

'You'd be happy enough to hear one of your maids say that to you by candlelight. You are a pane of glass to me, sir,' says the young woman. 'I see through you, though it would please me greatly if I did not see you at all.'

'I have friends in high places!' says Montfaucon.

'I am the high places,' says the young woman, 'and the likes of you are no friends of mine.'

'I am a prospect for a society of most distinguished gentlemen.'

'Not that distinguished if they'll consider you for membership,' she says. The woman extends her hand towards Julie. 'Charlotte-Marie de La Porte Mazarin de La Meilleraye,' she says. 'I know what you're thinking. "One of the infamous Mazarinettes". But don't worry, we don't bite unless you ask us to.'

Julie takes her hand and wants to speak, wants to laugh along with this bright, witty, fierce woman. But her voice! Not just its gravelly ruin but the mark of its class it bears. She sounds like a farmer's wife unless she sings.

A hubbub, a clattering, a door opens, and the musicians enter the room to stand before the stage, each bowing to the nobles. No one acknowledges them, of course, but voices become more muted. The opera will begin. Even now, with the card up one sleeve and the knife up the other, hell-bent on revenge and sick with nerves for the murder to come, she is desperate to see the great Moreau.

Montfaucon whispers to her, his breath hot against her ear.

'Beware of her. The Mazarinettes are a coven of witches. They are unnatural. Her mother left her father for a woman. And as for social climbing, she was cut off without a penny by her husband and whored herself out to the king of England. Got a pension of four thousand pounds a year, I heard.'

Julie can't but wonder what this woman was like – if the English king wanted a whore, he had his pick and at a lot cheaper than four thousand a year.

A note on the violin.

'So marks the beginning!' says Montfaucon, still close, still in a low voice. 'Let's hope the king has not prepared another of his twelve-hour delights. Professional dancers, they say tonight. And women too! Imagine it. Still, no courtiers. I am glad of it. My ascent would have been faster had I been able to dance. Or ride. Or fence. But do not think me without prospects, madam. I am in society with some of the highest in the land and have proved myself a capable man to them. At some cost, I tell you. Those who would be truly great must often do things that lesser men would shirk away from.' He blows heavily into his handkerchief.

She smiles at him, inclines her head.

'Do you ever speak?' he says. 'I hope not. A woman, a woman of status, who does not speak is a rare gift, one La Mazarin here could do with learning. Oh God, there's the king!'

Now the room does fall silent. Five, six, seven, eight, more courtiers sweep into the room, bowing to all as they do, forming two lines. First a man bearing a mace steps tall into the room. He is wearing a coat of shimmering silver cut in with little moons, his wig silver too. She cannot count his fingers from where she is sitting.

Then two more come in, one a tall fellow wearing a long black velvet mantle decorated with red flames and secured by a huge badge – an eight-pointed cross, each point ending in a golden ball. Beside him walks a hard-faced man in a long black coat, spare and lean, she thinks, like a butcher too mean to eat his own meat. He wears no adornment, no badge or ribbon and he surveys the room as if he suspects a rat on the premises.

'All kneel. The sun rises and the land bows before his glorious rays.'

Everyone in the room kneels, those that are sitting sliding forward off their chairs, those that are standing sinking to one knee.

Like a dancer himself, the king emerges, treading carefully and delicately into the room, as if he suspects the ground in front of him and is testing each step for support. As he walks in, he turns out his feet, exposing the high heels of his red soled shoes. She has never seen anyone dressed so finely, guesses no one else has ever seen anyone dressed so finely. Above his red heels, he is entirely in gold, from his stockings to his wig, and his tunic bears the image of the sun spreading its rays. In his hand he carries a gold wand and his wig is full of gold stars. The king does not move as a normal man moves but rather like a marionette, slowly, carefully, one leg extending, testing the ground daintily, before descending to take his weight, the other leg gliding to join it.

He is shown to his place by a man who rises from kneeling, almost dancing himself. He is upright, tall, and glides across the floor to lead the king to his seat. He wears white gloves, each finger carrying a glittering ring of ruby or emerald. Not each finger. Not each. Two of the gloved fingers on his left hand are bare. Something about the way he moves. Could it be? Could those fingers bear no ring because the glove is empty there? In the candlelight, she can't quite see if they look empty. She has strange thoughts – the fingers could be stuffed to give the appearance of a full hand. The king sits and the room relaxes, gets off its knees to resume its former position. Oh my fucking God, if it is him. To kill a man who sits at the right hand of the Sun King. If it's him. If it is him.

Montfaucon snuffles, sniffs, dabs at his face with his wet handkerchief, assumes an air of affected awe as he gazes on the king, mouth open, eyes wide. She thinks he almost appears as a child sarcastically aping great interest in something.

The music begins, uplifting major chords undercut with sad minors, and she imagines instantly a great court like this one full of pomp and elegance but where sad stories play out under the protective eye of a monarch. Others do not imagine things like that, music does not affect others so, but that is how it moves Julie – each note a syllable in a grand story. The dancers take the stage, four men in stockings and wide wired skirts high stepping, precise and elegant. She gasps. They wear the leather masks of devils – not the same as the ones that the men wore in the wood but like enough to send a shiver through her. They carry candelabras and the light of the flames cuts trails in the dark air. Her throat feels tight and her fingers bite her palms as she recalls that terrible night.

The men twirl and bow, cross and recross. The pattern is lively, their strong limbs whisking them across the stage in turns and leaps. Then the lady comes in, her long white skirt seeming to float above the ground. Her hair is dark, her skin olive and her eyes deep, her natural colours wonderfully offset by the rubies at her neck.

Julie has never seen such a vision as this. This must be Moreau and when she sings, it is instantly confirmed.

'Damned by the deeds of another
Hell bound for the sins of my brother.'

Her voice is pure like the mountain air, though it summons spectres whose shadowy fingers reach out to stroke chills down Julie's bones.

Julie sees immediately how this woman has been put into a terrible position by her brother – her virtue gambled away at dice. She sees the tiny room she has been forced to live in, the grand palais in which she was raised. She . . . Montfaucon sniffles and clears his throat and the vision is lost.

'I am thrice undone,
Betrayed by this wayword son.'

The singer is more than a human. She is a creature of rainbows, of light and air, a thing that weaves sounds that could be colours and colours that float to become music. The music lifts Julie and the words touch her soul. Is she not damned anyway, if she kills? That was the Devil's bargain, truly. If she kills the men she saves herself from immediate damnation but will be damned when she does die. She has no gold to pay for prayers for her soul, nor to build churches or houses of the poor to offset a murder. Her mind feels wide, expansive, as it ascends on the melody. What will more killing do? Is she afraid? Yes, she is. Murder is a mortal sin and if she is caught, she will die in torment. She will not do it. She must go to the church and have the bargain undone, it must be possible.

Montfaucon snorts. There is no more colour. Mundanity is restored. People are still taking their seats. Someone calls for a drink and someone rich and powerful enough to do so farts heavily.

Montfaucon sniffles again.

'In the darkness I long for the sun
In the darkness I long for the sun.'

She sees a brilliant dawn over a dark plain, sun firing the surfaces of lakes, metalling the mountainsides, where rivers of quicksilver flow through the land. She feels as though she is a cello string vibrating at the pitch of this voice. Montfaucon hawks up a good quantity of snot.

She cannot sit here in the presence of divinity and have it soiled by such baseness. Better to have not heard this at all than to hear it through this snuffling, hacking and wheezing.

Montfaucon stares miserably into his handkerchief.

She forces a smile.

'Not like?' she mouths at him.

'Music is no pleasure to me,' he says and seals his fate. He doesn't like music. No point being alive, then.

She takes his hand, puts it to her leg.

'Fuck me,' she whispers. He sees only the movement of her lips, but his eyes widen.

'Er, when?'

'Now.'

'I . . . The performance. What if we're seen leaving?'

She shrugs and points to herself, silently shaping the words.

'Forty thousand livres a year.'

He wets his lips with his tongue.

'Forty?'

She nods. 'If you please me.' Her voice is low, almost sung to disguise her country vowels.

Worry clouds his face.

'Yes, right. Yes. I suppose it's dark enough we won't be recognised. Oh God, I should be seen here! What best, what best? Forty thousand you say. Will it be quick?'

'*Prestissimo!*' she says, in her best Italian accent.

'Yes, then where?'

She stands up, trails her fingers across his shoulder and he stands to follow.

'Oh, don't go,' says Charlotte-Marie.

Julie smiles at her. She sees something in her eyes. Attraction? Longing? Something more. A will for adventure, for this, their meeting, to be an adventure. It cannot be. She has adventures of her own to attend to.

Scene Six

Oh Praise the Blood Joyous!

'In here?'

'Yes.'

She will use the changing room in which she found her dress. Her stage boy's clothes are there, and she can put them on and disappear.

She takes a candle from the corridor wall in one hand and his hand in the other. It's cold and clammy. Perhaps he has a fever. Perhaps he will die anyway. That won't do. She needs to kill him to cement her bargain and fulfil her need for revenge.

She opens the door and pushes inside. There are three maids inside, who come smartly to attention when she enters.

'Yes, ma'am?' says one and they all bow.

'Get out,' says Montfaucon.

'This is Lady Mazarin's chamber. I—'

'She'll have it back soon enough, get out!' He flicks a coin towards them. The skinny one picks it up and the maids are gone.

'I have little experience of this,' he says. 'Beyond whores, of course. You don't mind whores, do you? I mean, I have no disease, but a man has needs and whores are—'

'Uncomplicated,' she sing-says.

'Quite!' He dabs at his nose. 'Women have always fled me before. They are too demanding, expect too much. What is the fault in them that they will not have me? I have thought long and hard on it, lady. I have even produced a pamphlet. *The Faults and Duties of Women*. Many seemingly unattractive men such as I have great qualities that might be passed on to their sons. Women who will not look at us go against nature.'

'What qualities?' says Julie. She still tries to act, to make her voice sound refined. It does not work very well.

'What do you mean?'

'What qualities do you have that you might pass on?'

Montfaucon looks stunned. His mouth gapes and he looks lost in contemplation, like a man pausing as he prepares to leave his house, wondering if he needs to shit.

'Qualities that might become visible only in a son. You have a rough voice for the daughter of a duke. What was his name again? There are so many of them pouring in nowadays, one can hardly keep track.'

She does not answer him, only says in a low voice:

'It is the fancy in my province for great ladies to pretend to be the daughters of the land. Sheep in little bows and all that. Will you play shepherd while I play the shepherdess?'

'Yes, I suppose. I shall be glad to marry you. Will the forty thousand livres be in addition to a dowry? There must be a dowry, I have debts. I love you, er, what is your name?'

He pauses, looks at her expectantly.

'Marie,' she says. It is the first thing that comes into her head.

'Marie. I have had to do some bad things in hope of advancement. I have asked for forgiveness for them, but I fear that to continue is to stain my soul. Great men can be evil men, I tell you that. The things I have had to do. The things I will have to do to gain full membership of their society. But with you, of course, I can tell them go hang. I will not do what they bid any more.'

'What have you done?' She speaks low. Has this wretch the spleen to feel sorry for his sins? He thinks he is sorry now. In a moment she will carve regret into his skin. Her little knife is ready, small and very sharp. He coughs. She will cut that cough out of him, the cough that ruined Moreau.

'You would not believe.' He snuffles, wipes his eyes on his sleeve.

She sits next to him on the couch.

'Tell me.'

'I cannot. For shame I cannot. I go to mass twice daily. I am of God, but I have been forced. I should not tell you this, you my prospective future.'

'You can tell me what you will. How forced?'

'By ambition, do you not see? Anyone would have done what I have.'

'What have you done?'

'You will not marry me if I tell you,' he says.

'I swear I will. I knew from the second I saw you, you were my heart's desire. Nothing could shock me. Nothing. It might even excite me. I have the blood of greatness in me.'

'Really? Your voice is exceeding rough.'

'I have a cold. A little rheum,' she says and coughs.

He looks at her softly. She almost feels sorry for him. He blows his nose again. She feels sorry no more. He holds her hand and she sees what he is. A greedy man but a soft one. He has not had the spine to resist the opportunities that the Black Tredecim have afforded him. She should feel sympathy for him. And yet, the snuffling and hacking when Moreau sang seems too great a crime, even if he was not the instigator of Paval's death and her ruin. He was there at the Bois and he snuffles in the presence of beauty. It is enough for him to die. And worse.

She says the words.

'The Black Tredecim?'

He crosses himself, looks surprised. 'Yes. How do you know?'

'My father is a great man. How do you think he came to greatness? Tell me, sir, let me know you are connected. What are the names of the other twelve gentlemen in that distinguished group?'

'Lady,' says Montfaucon. 'That is one test I shall pass. Of course, we are sworn to secrecy. I would not give their names on pain of death. You see, your father's secret is safe with me. Tell me, is he the duke?'

Julie makes a sign of horns at her head.

'Oh my word, Diablo!' says Montfaucon, waving his hand at his face like a maiden aunt overcome by the sight of a carthorse's cock.

'I would know their names,' she says.

Montfaucon shakes his head.

'My lips are sealed,' he says. 'I would face any torture before I divulged such a secret.'

'I will not marry you unless you tell me.'

'Who do you know them to be? You cannot ask me to break a secret you would not break yourself, dearest.'

There is noise outside. The handle of the door is turned, then it closes again. She has little time.

Julie swallows. 'Indulge me,' she says. 'Are you shriven? Are you confessed?'

'Before I came here. I do the rosary whenever I can, even here when no one sees. I fear so for my soul, you see, but I must be progressed. Above all I must be progressed.'

'But I would not lie with a shriven man. Great people are strange. We are not the bourgeois and I can teach you how to leave that ugly world behind, your tender conscience. I have known the Black Tredecim, believe me. I too have felt the benefit of their works.'

'You, a girl? How so?'

'They love to corrupt the young, do they not?'

'I have not seen you.'

'The inner circle of the Tredecim do not admit women. But they can use us.'

'There's an inner circle?'

'I have felt their influence.'

'Can I be so wed to corruption? To flirt with it is one thing, to do and then be sorry, but to commit? What of my soul if I marry you?'

'What of your debts if you don't? I'm sure you will find a way. Come, say you love the Devil, say so nicely and then fuck me until I come, my ecstasy showering silver and gold upon you.'

He wets his lips, clears a little phlegm.

'How do I know you do not toy with me? How do I not know you won't mock me when I have said these things, that this isn't a cruel game? I've been the victim of them before.'

'Undo my laces.'

She turns her back to him and he pulls open her dress.

She turns again to face him, pulling down her underskirt, her breasts naked, her arms still in her sleeves.

'Say you love the Devil.' He looks at her in a way that reminds her of how her father looked at the drystone wall the day after the storm had knocked it down, as if to say, 'No use complaining, best get started'.

'It might provoke me, I suppose,' he says.

He pulls at his crotch. The handle on the door clicks again.

'Someone is coming,' he says.

'Then we will prevent them.'

She takes a chair, places it against the door handle so it can't open.

'I ask you, sir,' she says. 'For forty thousand a year, are you man enough to fuck me?'

'Just needs a little encouragement,' he says, unbuttoning his breeches to tug at his limp flap of a cock. 'Forty thousand. Yes?'

'Yes.'

'I love the Devil. Say the number again, it stiffens it.'

'Forty thousand a year and my father's patronage. Say you hate Christ and spit on his works.' She approaches to run her fingers across the tip of his floppy member.

'Come on,' he says to his nethers. 'Yes. I hate Christ and spit on his works. Forty thousand and never no more to have to meet with the Tredecim!'

'Forty thousand! You recant every confession you have ever made and are proud of your misdeeds?'

'Yes. I recant them. I have been a bold sinner and so I remain. Ah, there, relative turgidity,' he says, damply.

There is a huge heave at the door, the chair flies away and tumbling into the room comes Charlotte-Marie.

'Crikey, blimey, blinking flip!' she says, as she sees Montfaucon's cock, sagging already like a small, wet loaf.

'Oh my word!' says Montfaucon.

'Well, don't let me stop you,' says Charlotte-Marie. She brusquely closes the door.

Montfaucon stands ridiculous with his breeches at his knees, as if struck in bronze.

'I've only come back for a bit of my tincture,' says Charlotte-Marie. 'The divine Moreau isn't on again for another two hours apparently. Isn't she divine, don't you think? Don't you think?'

She begins to rifle through a dresser. 'The whole thing's going to be twelve hours and I need a little something to get me through.'

'Lady, I am sorry,' says Montfaucon.

'Don't apologise like a country butcher,' says Charlotte-Marie. 'Do what you want and do it proudly. That is the way of a man of breeding. Go on, fuck her if you want. If you can. It'll be entertaining. Will it be entertaining? I don't know.'

She glances him up and down, a side-eyed look of the sort that either crushes or inflames a man. Montfaucon seems to fall into the former camp. He slaps at the slack dangling thing between his legs, trying to get it to come to attention.

Charlotte-Marie takes a little jewelled box off the table and removes a stoppered bottle. She sits on the couch and pours a little liquid onto her finger. She pops the finger into her mouth and sucks at it, winks at Montfaucon and then sticks her front teeth out bunny like, crossing her eyes, mocking him.

Montfaucon gives a reluctant cry, like a heifer refusing to go back in its stall.

'Here's for forty thousand!' he says and grasps his cock. 'Curse Jesus and let Satan reign! For that much a year I'll laugh at the fires of Hell!'

Julie feels her heart thumping. She has what she wants but she can't kill him in front of this woman.

'Damn Jesus and stiffen my resolve!' says Montfaucon.

'Crikey!' says Charlotte-Marie as her eyes close. It's as if a sudden and magical sleep has come over her as she falls back on the sedan. Julie swallows, her throat tight. Now. It must be now!

'Is she all right?' says Montfaucon.

'She's fine,' says Julie. 'Tell me, sir, can you sing?' She has her knife hidden behind her back, grasping it in a fist. Her hand is trembling. She has never done this before, never.

'Not a note,' he says.

'Neither can I,' she says and drives the blade into Montfaucon's neck.

The look on his face does not satisfy her. He first grasps at her arm and then he shrugs as he dies, as if to say 'much as I expected. Just my luck.'

His blood, though, is like a benediction, a warm fountain in which she can bathe. It spurts pleasingly to the ceiling, covers her face, her arms, her wig. She is enchanted by the blood.

She touches her throat, feels the scar, tries a note. Still ruined, a frog's call. She tastes his blood. A deep tingle goes through her. Another note. 'La'. She does it on instinct. Still awful, still cracked but not as awful. Is there a way back here? Is this her cure?

A scent of primroses, a tinkle of bells.

'Hello,' she says, without turning around.

'Hello,' says Lucifer.

'You have come to honour your bargain?'

'I have.'

The fiend walks to the body, takes Montfaucon's head in their hands, which seem transformed, long, very cruelly taloned.

'In Hell,' says Lucifer, 'we will heat forty thousand silver livres every day until they are red as burning coals. Then we will apply them, one by one, to his tender flesh!'

The candle has gone out and dark is tight around the bud of light that surrounds the Devil. The room is cold.

Lucifer is so beautiful, all moon glow and glitter – this devil is so pretty and so dainty they must be a woman, not a sun king but a lunar princess, shimmering silver like the moon itself caught in the waters of a midnight lake.

'You have killed me,' says Montfaucon, holding his neck.

'He lives!' says Julie and raises the knife again.

'No,' says Lucifer. 'I have let you see with other eyes. It is his soul who stands here now.'

'I was forced into this!' says Montfaucon. 'I meant none of it!'

'Do you know what we call that defence in Hell?' says Lucifer.

'No!'

'Correct,' says Lucifer. 'It is no defence.'

'Before you go to Hell, tell me the names of the Tredecim!' says Julie. 'You can lose nothing now.'

But Lucifer twiddles their fingers and a fine silver needle appears. The Devil makes a sewing gesture with the needle and instantly Montfaucon's lips are sealed with silver thread.

'Why do that?' says Julie.

'Because I want you to accompany me to the pit. I have not sworn to help you. I have not even sworn to refrain from hindering you. What will we do to you, Julie d'Aubigny? As yet I am undecided. Perhaps we will just make you sing, with your croaking frog's call, put you in a swamp full of flies with the only company that creaking throat of yours. Or worse? Perhaps we will keep you singing forever until your throat swells, your ears burn, and your mind goes numb with its need for silence. Time is ebbing away. It will soon be the New Year. Do you even know who your enemies are, Julie? Who are those gentlemen who call me by moonlight?'

Lucifer extends a finger to point at Montfaucon. A ring of primroses springs up on the floor of the room and then the floor within the ring vanishes to reveal a raging fire beneath. The clothes of the wardrobe spring to dancing, vaunting life, circling Montfaucon's ghost in a mad whirl of flapping arms, flying skirts. Then they descend upon him like crows upon a dead rabbit and he is pulled down to Hell.

'Blinking flip, this is better than the opera!' says Charlotte-Marie, who is waking groggily on the couch.

'You saw Montfaucon's fate?' says Lucifer.

'Yes,' she says. 'Yes, I did.'

'I have not granted you the power to see souls. Ah, but wait. Dr Pomet's excellent remedy. You have taken the poppy milk?'

'Yes.'

'My favourite flower,' says Lucifer. 'When God made it, I put a little of my own soul in it too, I believe. It grants true visions of Heaven and Hell.'

'You worked with God?'

'We were once great friends,' says Lucifer. 'But he is not, I regret . . .' They search for the words. 'A democrat.'

Julie wipes the blood from herself with the coat she took off for Montfaucon, casts aside her wig and pulls back on her rough shirt, her skirt still around her waist.

She looks at Montfaucon's sword.

'I don't want to have to kill this one,' she says, nodding to Charlotte-Marie.

'No need,' says Lucifer. 'She will think it all a dream. Perhaps she will take the blame, though I doubt it. She can pass it off as just defence for an assault on her virtue. Your father is a friend of the king, no, lady?'

'They are as one,' she says.

'Then there is no need to worry on her account. You will never see her again.'

Julie glances at Charlotte-Marie. Such a strange mix, so sophisticated, beautiful and yet something unformed about her, as if she was younger than her years. She would like to see her again.

'Then you owe me a lesson,' she says to the Devil.

'I think so,' says the Devil and a sword appears in their hand. 'You know the step dainty, you can pass and duck and weave, I take it?'

'I can.'

'So let us begin with the Devil's Forms, that you will find in no gentle book of fencing skill. Do not look for this in your Saviolo, your Marozzo, your Sainct-Didier or even your George Silver, though the Englishman fights like a dog in the street. You know the Italian, who fights with a cloak on his arm?'

'Yes.'

'He uses it to block, to ward and above all to obscure.'

Lucifer clicks their fingers and Montfaucon's corpse, which has remained, floats to its feet, draws its sword.

Another click and the corpse lunges at Lucifer but the Devil has taken a fur stole from a chest and uses it on their free hand to deflect the weapon, to catch it and to return thrusts into Montfaucon's side. The corpse moans as they do so.

'I can learn such tricks from any boy in the street,' says Julie.

'Yes, yes, you can,' says Lucifer, as they throw the stole into Montfaucon's face. The fox wraps around his head and eyes as if it has set upon him and then Lucifer finishes with a thrust to his chest.

'First, take this stole. This will be your protector. A fox, which is your sign, so cunning are you.'

'Any man of skill will see that coming,' she says. 'I need more.'

The Devil takes the stole from Montfaucon's re-fallen corpse. She is surprised to see the fox wink at her.

The Devil clicks their fingers and the fox runs up Julie's leg to curl around her neck, as warm and supple as if living.

'This is a fine gift, but you promised me a lesson.'

'Fencing is life in miniature. You learn to fence, you learn to live. And what is the first lesson of life?'

'Get the servants to do the dull stuff,' says Charlotte-Marie.

'Exactly!' says Lucifer. 'Exactly! Let us distil and condense this estimable lady's message. Let us boil it down. What is she really saying?'

'I don't know,' says Julie.

'Do you get your servants to do the dull stuff, Julie?'

'I have no servants.'

'Then . . .'

'I must make do myself.'

'Genius!' says Lucifer. 'Genius! You are correct. The first lesson of fencing, the first lesson of life, is that you work with what you have! No point in dreaming about tomorrow, you use what you have today. Do you have a great skill with a blade?'

'I have some.'

'More than a gentleman raised to the *esquive*, the bind and the *pasata soto* and trained by the greatest masters of France?'

'No.'

'So you must win your fights by more than skill! I could teach you to take the dirt from the street, carry sharp coins or ground glass and throw it into your opponent's eyes. Or I could teach you what the masters never will!'

Suddenly the sword is in her hand and the Devil is in front of her, their sword at her throat. She parries and returns a thrust. 'Lean back on the parry, so teach all the masters!' says Lucifer. 'Not I!' They step under the thrust and leans in to her body, shouldering her back onto the couch to sit next to Charlotte-Marie.

'Hello,' says Charlotte-Marie.

The Devil leans in, stoops to where Julie has plonked.

'But no need for that just now. The stole will suffice until you please me with more deaths. I'll leave you two together, you make a nice pair.'

With that, Lucifer makes a circle in the floor with Montfaucon's blood. Little flowers burst forth around its rim and, within, a shining light burns. Lucifer steps in and is gone, the circle vanishing behind.

Charlotte-Marie clasps her hands together.

'Cripes! I have to say, when I saw you in my dress, I immediately thought you would be by far the most entertaining person I have encountered in years and now I see my first impression was entirely correct. Entirely. I am never wrong in such matters, never!'

Julie gets up.

'I am glad I am an entertainment to you,' she says.

She starts to change quickly, casting off her dress and pulling on the rough breeches.

'My gosh,' says Charlotte-Marie, 'you are a creature of surprises.'

'I have to be,' says Julie. The fox curls around her. One instant it appeared as a lady's stole. Now it is more like a trapper's pelt, mangy looking, worn from shoulder to waist like a musketeer's bandolier, its tail in its mouth.

'Don't worry about the dress,' says Charlotte-Marie, in her arch way, seeing it trampled into the floor.

'You knew I had stolen it.'

'Of course.'

'How?'

'Though you are beautiful you don't quite have the bones of a lady. And your hands, dear. Wear gloves in any future deception, you look like you've been peeling potatoes.'

'I have.'

'How extraordinary,' says Charlotte-Marie.

'So you saw me for a servant?'

'Yes, and a bold one. I had no idea how bold. I wish I could cut throats. Is it very like peeling potatoes? Could you teach me?'

'To cut a throat?'

'No. Anyone can cut a throat, that's practically my birthright. To peel a potato. I should think it such a hoot. Think, to take one ripe from the tree and skin it there and then.'

Julie's face darkens.

'I am not here to provide diversion to great ladies.' She hears herself as she speaks. Wasn't that once her life's ambition? Didn't she long to take the stage and bask in the admiration of women like this? Wouldn't she wish so now?

'It's not all been hoots,' says Charlotte-Marie. 'I mean, this is quite a mess.' She gestures to the body.

'I doubt it's you who will have to clear it up,' says Julie. She bends to Montfaucon, puts her finger to his wound, licks at his blood. It tastes good to her.

'What a funny thing to say. Of course not! Were you paid to kill him? I can't think Montfaucon has enemies who would pay to see him killed. Why, if I were his enemy, I would think the nastiest thing I could do to him was to allow him to continue being Montfaucon for a long and miserable life. If I hated him, I'd pay his doctors' bills. So why kill him?'

'My own reasons.'

'He has made you pregnant? A sister? Repossessed a house? I know all about the lower orders and how annoying they find these things, I asked my aunt Minette about them.'

'You know nothing of my life,' says Julie.

'I know you are a remarkable person. Was that actually the Devil?'

'I believe it to be, yes.'

'Fascinating. Quite beautiful, wasn't she? I didn't think he'd be a she, if you see what I mean. Are you embarked upon some great and diabolic work together?'

'Yes.'

'I knew it. Do let me join in for a while. I can't tell you how dull this place gets. A pact with the Devil is just the thing to liven things up, now I've bored of cards.'

Is it right to involve this pretty, funny, fascinating, silly young woman in her schemes? *Well, she did ask, didn't she?*

'You can help me if you so wish, and in so doing help the Devil too.'

'Now that does sound fun.'

'I need to identify certain gentlemen of this court.'

'To kill them?'

'Yes.'

'Oh, whizzo! Blood, danger, I love it!'

'This is not an opera,' says Julie.

'Life is an opera!' says Charlotte-Marie, singing out the words. 'Now, take those clothes back off and put on a dress. We will go to see Moreau. But before that, there will be an intermission and I want you to meet *everyone*!'

'What of Montfaucon? Won't the corpse be found?'

'We'll take a sedan,' says Charlotte-Marie. 'Pretend he's drunk and dump him in the woods.' She takes a little locket, shaped like a bottle, and puts it around her neck.

'Will no one miss him?'

'Quite the reverse,' she says.

'Will not the palace guards investigate?'

'Maybe, but I'm not going to tell them anything, are you?'

'What if they ask the sedan carriers?'

'My Lord, what an idea! Why would they talk to servants? And no servant is going to admit anything or say anything for fear of being caught up in it. Even if they were to find his body, they'd run off for fear of taking the blame. The facts are simple. You have killed someone of little importance to the court. Kill the more important people and that's when the trouble starts. The only embarrassment might be being caught red-handed, so to speak. What romps this is! I'll call a sedan.'

'The blood?'

'The servants will clean it.'

'Won't they ask where it came from?'

Charlotte-Marie laughs. 'Oh, you dear thing. They don't speak until they are spoken to. Do they have curiosity like us? I don't know but if they do, they never show it. Now, let's get that sedan!'

'Yes,' says Julie, and scratches the name 'Montfaucon' off the Devil's card.

Scene Seven

Not Cupid's Arrow but Jove's Thunderbolts Strike Love Into Thine Heart!

Both women, now splendidly dressed, lurch from the shadow of the palace into the blue night, Montfaucon carried between them as if drunk and needing support. There are two sedans, one for the ladies, one for Montfaucon. Their chair is carried by four stout men, Montfaucon's by two and each of the chairs is extravagantly decorated in patterns of flowers against a pale background. In the darkness Julie can't tell its true colour.

'Convey us to the northern woods!' says Charlotte-Marie.

'My lord is drunk, and we wish to play a trick on him,' says Julie.

'Very good, ma'am,' says a footman, though Charlotte-Marie raises her eyebrows. Julie realises the mistake she has made. She has offered an explanation to a servant. The nobility does not do that, it wouldn't even occur to them to do so. She looks at the corpse. They have tied a scarf around the wound in Montfaucon's neck and, if any of the servants have noticed, they make no comment on it. There she goes again. She must not consider what servants think if she wants to blend into this company. But wouldn't that entail not caring what she herself thinks?

The ladies decant Montfaucon into his sedan and get into the other. Charlotte-Marie is so pretty in the moonlight, but

Julie wants to shake her, tell her this isn't a game. Or perhaps it is; perhaps if you are born well enough then everything is a game. She's playing at being a killer in the same way that the ladies of the court play at being shepherdesses or milkmaids, white lambs on silk ribbons.

They squeeze in, Charlotte-Marie commands the chairs 'forward!' and off they go, bobbing along under the big moon. Charlotte-Marie sprawls out, as much as she can sprawl, on her seat while Julie sits tightly, nervous.

'You may kiss me if you wish,' says Charlotte-Marie.

Julie feels the stir of desire within her. She would like to kiss this fascinating, silly, spoiled, funny, captivating young woman but she is too nervous, and she suspects Charlotte-Marie's intentions. If the pail falls from the wagon, so to speak, and they are discovered, it will be she – not Charlotte-Marie – who takes the blame.

'You may have a kiss when you have earned it, lady,' says Julie.

'And how might I do that?'

'You can deliver me my enemies.'

'Being?'

Julie takes out her list and reads.

'These are their descriptions. They are all men of the court, I believe. Roses on the shoes.'

'A mania for it at the moment.'

'A very fine pistol.'

'All pistols here are fine.'

'One eye.'

'The wars claim many eyes.'

'An affected way of speaking, like his lips are scissors.'

'I'm afraid there are rather a lot of those,' says Charlotte-Marie, mimicking an affected posh voice.

'A silver cane.'

'Here we do gold.'

'A dragon snuff box, a big thing.'

'It doesn't ring a bell.'

'A white hart upon the coat.'

Charlotte-Marie shrugs.

'Villepin.'

'Oh, Villepin, I know him, I'll gladly help you kill him. Do I get a kiss now?'

Julie smiles. Charlotte-Marie makes her laugh, gives her a glimpse of the person she was before Paval, before her voice was taken from her. It is a wild night, a night of devils and murder and music. Why not a kiss?

Charlotte-Marie leans forward. Ridiculously, Julie has to twist sideways to allow her to kiss her, their high hairstyles butting in the confines of the sedan. Charlotte-Marie tastes of strange spices Julie has never known before, of the fat of her make-up, of something else quite dizzying – a flowery, pungent smell that you could plunge into, lose yourself forever. She is intoxicating and, when Julie's tongue enters her mouth, Charlotte-Marie sucks at it in a way that makes her feel as if she could disappear into her, fall away from herself, become a strange hybrid creature lost in its own ecstasy.

'Stop that chair, fellow.' A voice from behind them.

Julie breaks from the kiss and manoeuvres her head out of the window.

The moonlight is strong enough for her to see they are followed by three other sedans, each carried by two. Torches, mounted on the front of one sedan, illuminate the face of a man who leans out of it.

'Who says we should stop?' says Charlotte-Marie, twisting around to poke her head out of the other side.

'Chevalier De Bissy of Évreux. Madam, you have been abducted by a murderer and we are here for your rescue!'

Bissy! That was one of the men at the wood! The one with the pistol!

'Bollocks,' says Julie, ducking back inside. 'If that were the case there'd be a party of guards. These are killers. They're the ones who killed Paval and ruined my throat.'

'Who, what?' Charlotte-Marie manoeuvres her wig back inside the sedan.

'Never mind.'

'How have they found us to chase us?' says Charlotte-Marie. 'How do they know you're a murderer?' Julie sees it in an instant – Lucifer has told them. The Devil wants her soul. He, she, it has set her a task and is trying to make sure she fails it.

'The Devil!' she says.

'That one in my changing room!'

'The same.'

'What a fucker!'

She leans back out of the sedan.

'Go away!' shouts Charlotte-Marie. 'There is no murderer here!'

Julie cranes out of the sedan to get a better look behind.

'Lady, for your protection I must disobey. You have a dangerous woman with you who may have seduced you with lies! Her name is not what she says it is. This is Malory Malherbe of Malmaison! She has killed, oof.' A trailing branch strikes him and his head pops within.

Another head emerges from another sedan.

'We must detain her, madam!'

'You'll have to catch us first!' shouts Charlotte-Marie. 'Footmen – away, as quick as you can.'

The sedan lurches forward at a jangling clop. Julie looks out to see the chairs behind follow, their footmen running too.

'Is that really your name?' says Charlotte-Marie.

'I think they've been sold a pup,' says Julie.

'What?'

'Misled, steered wrong. Someone has taken the piss.'

'What a pity. I like you as Malory Malherbe. Malory Malherbe of Malmaison. How bad can she be? Very bad, if you're lucky.'

Bang! A shot from behind.

'Have you gone fucking mad?' shouts Charlotte-Marie, leaning out of the window.

'We know what we're doing, ma'am!' shouts a voice.

'Acting like twats!' shouts Charlotte-Marie. 'If that hits me, they'll hang you and hang you again to make sure! It'll be the breaking wheel for you!'

'I am a crack shot, ma'am!'

'Crack twat!' shouts Charlotte-Marie. 'My father won't miss your arsehole when he sticks that pistol up it and pulls the trigger!'

'Why don't they get out and chase us on foot? They'd easily catch us,' asks Julie.

'They don't want to damage their shoes,' says Charlotte-Marie, putting her thumb to her chin and flicking it away in a gesture of contempt. 'Stocking doublers! I bet you wear them two days in a row!' shouts Charlotte-Marie through the window. 'I bet some of you would wear the same ones for a season if you could. Cheapskates! Faster, footmen!'

'Yes, lady!' A panting voice from the front.

'To the woods! We'll lose them there!'

The chair thunders on, the crunch of footsteps on the gravel path behind, the groans of the footmen raising up a dissonant counterpoint. Julie can see the pursuing chairs are neither gaining nor losing but keeping their distance, their footmen cursing and uttering oaths as they totter and lurch after her under the moon. A gaggle of servants out in the moonlight leap from the path as they come thundering down. A set of boxes, stored out of sight at the entrance to the woods – stage equipment or something – blocks the path and the first sedan with its dead passenger flopping from the window crashes through them, knocking them aside. Thank God they were empty!

'What are we going to do if they catch us?'

'You'll die and I'll be sent to my room for a week!' says Charlotte-Marie. 'Isn't this exciting? Gosh, I'm glad I met you. Nothing ever happened before you appeared and now, this! Isn't it wonderful?'

'You'll hang, Malherbe!' shouts a voice from behind them.

'If you're killed, I'll never forget you!' says Charlotte-Marie.

'That will be a magnificent consolation,' says Julie. It is said entirely without sarcasm. To be remembered with affection by someone as beautiful as this. To be treasured by the glittering world. It would be the grandest consolation, if she did not have another twelve men to kill.

'What is your name, by the way? Something exotic, I bet.'

'Julie. I hope you didn't bet much.'

'Such a lovely name,' says Charlotte-Marie. 'Like a wild flower!'

Now they're leaping, the sedan almost flying before dropping heavily back into the footmen's arms.

'What was that?' says Julie.

'Lovers' Leap!' says Charlotte-Marie. 'A couple on the bonk! I think we'll have surprised them!'

To anyone else, it would seem foolish, arrogant, missing the point to a ludicrous degree, that Charlotte-Marie could find this exciting.

Julie, though, feels a thrill inside her. She draws Charlotte-Marie close and kisses her again, breathing in her odour of wine and burned flowers. 'I have only ever sought to be remembered,' she says, 'or to live the sort of life that is worthy of remembrance.' A jolt as a footman stumbles and she falls back from Charlotte-Marie.

They are galumphing along a track in a wood. Julie cranes out of the window. Montfaucon's chair is the row behind, three others pursuing, just visible careening through the dappled moonlight.

'They're closing on us!' says Charlotte-Marie.

'Faster!' says Julie.

'As fast we can, miss!' heaves a footman.

'Come back!' shouts Bissy from behind.

'I'm dying!' shouts a footman.

'Fuck this. We should get out and run,' says Julie.

'In these skirts?' says Charlotte-Marie.

'Ma'am, there is a stream ahead!'

'Jump it!' shouts Charlotte-Marie.

The footmen leap and the sedan bucks as they land. Julie sees the sedan directly behind has cleared the jump but one of the footmen of a pursuing chair cries out and it goes tipping into the brook.

'Hide, hide!' says Julie. 'Go into the woods! Now's our chance.'

Their chair reels to one side, tipping like a boat broadsided by a wave.

After ten or twenty more paces the chair is dropped and a chorus of panting and curses rises up from the footmen.

'Fools, be quiet!' says Charlotte-Marie.

'The sedan is wrecked!' says a voice from the direction of the stream. 'God, this is turning out to be an expensive evening.'

God. There's an oath that could damn a man.

'Get in mine!' says another voice.

'Sir, there are only two of us!' says a commoner's voice.

'Put your backs into it, you lazy dogs. Can you expect your betters to walk?'

There's the sound of enormous straining, like a giant on the toilet, and the footsteps begin again, which the footmen on Montfaucon's chair take as their signal to drop it and leg it.

'Lie low!' Julie hisses to the remaining servants. The footmen by her chair are panting, retching, their breath sawing into the night. The only thing that masks the noise is the groans and complaints of the pursuers' footmen. Julie peers from the chair. The top of a pursuing sedan is visible, moving slowly and stealthily above a bush against the moon. In a second, they'll be on them.

'Move,' she whispers to the footmen.

The footmen pick up the chair, tiptoe ten paces and set it down.

She sees the top of the pursuers' sedan pause. Then it moves slowly on again, coming towards them.

'Circle behind them,' says Julie.

Her chair lifts again, but a footman loses his grip on his pole and their chair crashes heavily and noisily to earth.

'We know you're in there!' says Bissy. 'Men, patrol the area and allow me to search for them.'

'They're over there, sir,' says a footman. 'I can hear them.'

'I found them, not you,' says Bissy. 'Head towards where I have directed you.'

'Where's that, sir?'

'Where you can hear them.'

The sedan comes creaking and rustling towards them. Julie sees it loom across a patch of moonlight, like an upright coffin.

'Run for it!' shouts Charlotte-Marie.

'We can't, lady, we're done for!' replies one of the footmen.

'Run!'

The chair is lifted, and the men burst forward with a roar, but they only get a few steps before their strength gives out. The sedan cants sideways and is tipped over. Julie's wig is knocked askew and she lands on top of Charlotte-Marie.

Julie plants a kiss on her cheek and stands up in the chair, emerging like a rabbit from its hole, scanning for hawks.

Her footmen have gone, run for it, and Bissy steps down from his sedan, a blanket placed on the ground to save his shoes and stockings. From the other chairs, gentlemen squeeze out, two standing awkwardly on a single blanket, one on a blanket of his own. They are in a rough clearing and the moon is a lantern above them.

'Where is Montfaucon?' says Bissy.

Julie levers herself out of the overturned chair and drops onto the wet ground.

'In there,' she says, gesturing to the abandoned sedan.

'Montfaucon! Come out!' shouts Bissy. 'Our infernal friend said you are dead but that is too awful! I say you live! Footmen, get him out, get our friend out!'

The footmen wheeze to the sedan, open the door and Montfaucon flops out onto the ground.

'He's dead!' says Bissy. 'No gentleman would allow his clothes to soil like that if he lived, not one of Montfaucon's tight purse anyway. It's just as the Devil said! She has killed Montfaucon and now she is coming for us!'

'I should say he's dead,' says Julie. 'That tends to be the effect of a cut throat.' The fox stirs at her neck. She has the idea it is chuckling.

'For that you will die!' says Bissy.

He draws his pistol in an extravagant gesture, levels it at her and pulls the trigger. Nothing happens.

'Flint's fucked!' he says. He cocks the pistol again and squeezes the trigger experimentally. There's an explosion, a groan and one of his footmen collapses to the ground.

'That was not my fault,' says Bissy. The moon at his back, smoke wreathing the cold air, Bissy seems a devil himself.

The other footmen bend over their fallen colleague. 'There's another pistol in the sedan, get it for me,' says Bissy.

'I'd say you've had enough of pistols, sir,' says a footman.

'Damned cheek! Take hold of her, fellows,' says Bissy to the footmen, but Julie has drawn Montfaucon's sword.

'So it's as the Devil told us,' says a stout little man. 'The slut from the Bois de Boulogne!' He takes out a large snuff box with a dragon carved on top of it, takes a pinch and sneezes.

'A slut who has come for your life,' says Julie.

'You didn't fare very well the last time you fought with a sword! Women should stick to needles! Footman, take her, I say.'

'Will his family be recompensed for this, sir?' says one of the footmen, pointing to the corpse of his colleague.

'For what?' says Bissy. 'It's not my fault the pistol went off at the wrong time. Get hold of that woman!'

'I would prefer to discuss the matter of compensation first, sir,' says the footman. He hovers uncertainly and Julie sees her chance.

'I challenge you to a duel on this matter of honour,' she says. 'You have refused to pay what you owe. You are a cheapskate, sir, and should answer for that at the point of a blade.'

'What?'

'A duel! You are challenged. Now, footmen, know this. Duelling is banned and seconds, which you undoubtedly now are, are banned from attending on pain of death from the king.'

'No one has ever been executed,' says Bissy.

'No high man. Would these fellows be sure of the king's indulgence?' The fox stirs at Julie's neck again.

'No one will witness it,' says Bissy.

'I will,' says Charlotte-Marie, who has finally extracted herself from the overturned sedan.

'You, woman, can't challenge me to a duel,' says Bissy. 'We are not social equals.'

'I challenge you then,' says Charlotte-Marie.

'You can't fight me! It would be unfair, you are not schooled in the art of the sword! And what if we killed you? We'd be signing our own death warrants.'

'Julie is a fencer. She's my second. The second steps in when the duellist cannot fight. Servants, various, you are now seconds in a duel and will hang for it. If I were you, I'd hop it before anyone finds you or any of us take a note of your description, though the lower orders all look the same to me.'

The footmen glance at each other and then run for it, pounding heavily away through the woods.

'Are we going to have to do this ourselves?' says Bissy. 'Look, you couldn't just come here, could you? These shoes cost me a fortune. Tourdonnet, you go, you're already filthy from falling out of the sedan.'

'Well, I can't fight, I don't do that sort of thing,' says a tall man. He is weedy looking, in that he is thin, but also in that he is covered in weeds.

'It's a woman, for God's sake. Think of your ancestors, Tourdonnet, who fought under the sign of the white hart . . . Where did they fight?' The white hart! Another of her degenerate prey!

'Everywhere, all the time,' say Tourdonnet.

'Exactly, live up to that!'

'In the name of the Devil, I am not my ancestors! Half of them married their sisters. Am I to do that too?' says Tourdonnet. 'Can't Dreux do this?'

'I'm not getting dirty,' says the short, stout man with the snuff box.

Julie feels her heart skip. Tourdonnet has called the name of the Devil. He can die now, safely assured of Hell. The other? She will see.

'Know that I am Lucifer's friend!' she says. 'He protects me.'

'It was Lucifer who led us to you, whore,' says Bissy. 'He is our friend. Our ally. We have called him, bound him with strong magics and made him our servant. He's told us what you will do

93

to us if we let you and he was right by the start you've made on Montfaucon. It's your soul he wants, and we will give it to him.'

That will do. Of course, she should have seen it immediately! They are at this moment on the Devil's business. No confession or absolution will save them. Well, not in time anyway.

'I came only to support you,' says Dreux. 'I cannot fight, not since the wound I took at the siege of Dendermonde!'

'What, when a lowlands whore bit your cock?'

'Cannon!' says Dreux. 'Cannon! I stared into the mouth of the cannon! Kill her, Tourdonnet. You're covered in the filth of the field anyway.'

'I threw the shoes out before I got into the stream. They're silk faced, you know!' says Tourdonnet.

'Kill her!'

'I'm no fighter, Bissy.'

'Kill her. She's a woman. How many fencing lessons have you taken?'

'Well, it's different when they're trying to hurt you. If my fencing master cuts me I can have him flogged. I mean, she might scratch me!' says Tourdonnet.

'Do it or our high friend will know.'

Tourdonnet sighs. He takes out his sword, looks at it as if he doesn't quite know what it's for. He steps forward.

'Don't run off,' he says. 'This ground is marshy. Just stay where you are and make this easy on me. You owe me that as your social superior.'

He speaks as if to a nervous puppy as he treads gingerly, placing each step as if he fears the ground will swallow him. 'There'll be no saving these shoes after this, Bissy,' he says. 'Oh, my silk! This is insupportable. Have you any idea how much I paid for this pair?'

He steps forward, looking at the ground for mud or puddles. This is ill advised. Julie's father always told her that the best place for a swordsman to look is at the opponent. The ground, the puddle, is not going to run you through. 'Finest silk, finest silk,' says Tourdonnet.

As soon as he is within distance, Julie juts out her arm, kicks forward on the front foot to lunge and runs him through. The sword slides in so easily, until there's a jolt as it strikes his spine.

'Your shoe worries are over, sir,' says Julie as she withdraws her blade.

'Oh, God almighty!' says Tourdonnet. 'I told you no good would come of this, Bissy. She's fucking killed me. That's really, really the absolute limit. Really, no gentleman should . . .' They never discover what a gentleman should not do as Tourdonnet collapses and dies.

'Zookers!' says Charlotte-Marie.

Bissy throws up his arms. 'That's ridiculous,' he says. 'Ridiculous.'

Bissy draws his sword. From the instant he walks towards her, Julie can see he is a different proposition to Tourdonnet. He steps lightly and confidently, his legs well bent, his arm in front, point first.

Julie crouches, as her father taught her to do. As they close, Bissy stands, ready for the play of blades but she withdraws. Bissy looks puzzled and steps forward again. She searches for his blade, looking to catch it with hers, sweep it aside and make space for a thrust but he is clever. He allows her to take the blade, to think she's caught it, but at the last instant a flick of the fingers sends the point of his sword whizzing beneath hers to push it aside. He slides his blade down hers and nicks her hand. It's all she can do to hold on to the sword.

They close again, a shooting pain in her arm. This time he pushes on her blade and she, like a fool, pushes back. Again he whips the point under her blade, allowing her blade to move aside, and stabs forward. The point finds its mark again, just a touch, but it is enough to lacerate the palm of her hand and she drops the sword.

He bows a little bow, puts the blade aside in a curtsey, and Julie lifts her skirts.

'If you think you can bargain your way out of this by offering your twat . . .' he says. She kicks him so hard in between the legs that it's amazing his bollocks don't pop out of his eyes.

Bissy staggers backwards but Julie follows him, picking up the blade in her left hand and stabbing at him. Unluckily for her she only snags his arm. Still he reels away, clutching the wound, sword still in his hand.

'Now you die!' gasps Bissy. 'I swear by the Devil who led me to you!'

'Allow me!' says Dreux. He has the pistol from the sedan. He points it directly at Julie, at a distance of no more than twenty yards, fires and blows Bissy's brains all over her dress.

'Fucking cheap shit pistol!" says Dreux.

The moon darkens, a chill wind blows. Then the Devil is there, in lustre, in shining coat and sparkling wig.

'This gentleman has died calling on my name,' they say. 'Unshriven and out of favour with God. He is mine forever.'

'Shit!' says Dreux and runs for it. Julie tries to give chase, but her dress is like a rope around her legs.

'What do we do?' says Julie. 'Dreux will tell the Tredecim I am here! They'll come for me.'

'They don't know you in your servant guise,' says Charlotte-Marie. 'Return to that! They won't imagine a servant could be their undoing!'

'There is a greater problem here,' says the Devil. 'You were to kill all the men, were you not?'

'I was.'

'And yet Dreux killed Bissy. Your bargain is unfulfilled, Julie. You must come with me to Hell!'

Julie smiles, bows. 'And were I not here, would Dreux have fired his pistol?'

The Devil gives a little purse of the lips to acknowledge the cleverness of the argument.

'Who can tell?' they say.

'You, surely.'

The Devil puts a hand to their breast. 'Me! I have no special insight to such things, lady.'

'I think you do,' says Julie. 'But if you would prefer to win by cheating . . .'

'Yes,' says the Devil.

'Yes what?'

'I would prefer to win by cheating. Clearly. I'm the Devil. That's the sort of thing that really appeals to me.'

'I ducked the shot,' says Julie. 'That is why Bissy died. If I had stood and taken it, it would be me dead on the floor.'

'That's not true,' says the Devil. 'Bissy spent more on his gun's decoration than he did on its barrel, that's why.'

'It's a kind of true,' says Charlotte-Marie. 'We don't have to limit our understanding of what happened here to the immediate facts. There is a setting to these events. The diamond of Bissy's death is set in the foil of Julie's involvement, thereby appearing all the more lustrous.'

'Not convinced,' says the Devil.

Julie speaks. 'Then let me promise you more souls. Are you so sure you will gain every last one of the Black Tredecim without me? If they live to be old men, might not one of them die on his way out of the confession box? Will the heated irons, the whips and the other torments you have prepared for them be put to no use?'

The Devil casts back their head in thought. They um, ah, stamp and scratch.

'Very well,' they say. 'This one, I concede, died because of you. But let us be clear. These gentlemen must all die by your hand in the future. You must personally dispatch them to me. Will you swear it?'

'I swear it,' says Julie.

'Good.'

'But while we're at it, this thing you gave me proved a fat lot of good,' says Julie. She gestures to the fox at her neck.

The Devil just shrugs and prods Tourdonnet with a hoof. 'For this one,' they say, 'we will invent a torment involving shoes. Perhaps we will make them of gold, he loved riches so, but burning gold and a poor fit at that. The other here, well, he called me his servant. So let me serve him. I will serve him dishes of briars and glass, cups of gall and bile. Let me dress him in shirts of thorns, let me wash him in lime, scrub him with burning coals.'

'You betrayed me,' says Julie.

The Devil gives a little moue. 'I was afraid you were finding it too easy,' they say. 'I do so long for your company in Hell, Julie.'

'Are all my enemies to know I am coming for them?'

'No.'

'Good.'

The Devil laughs. 'They are not to know. They already know! Or they will by the time Dreux gets changed and presents himself to the rest again.'

'He needs to get changed?'

'He has stained his socks,' says the Devil. 'He will not appear before great men in a state of dishevelment. But they will know who you are.'

Julie puts her hand to her dress, wipes a little of Bissy's blood. Then she puts her fingers to her mouth and licks, tasting the iron and salt. She feels a thrill go through her, an erotic shiver.

Bissy's ghost stands up now, Tourdonnet's too, staring down in disbelief at their own corpses.

'Who shot me?' says Bissy. 'You, woman?'

'Your own accomplice,' says the Devil. 'Dreux killed you with your own flintlock.'

'Oh God, he was always a lousy shot.'

'Not his fault,' says the Devil. 'You chose the decorated gun from Piaget of the Marais. Should have gone to the Belgian De Bruyne and spent the money on the barrel. Those balls come out like a rat from a hole – they could go anywhere.'

'I couldn't be expected to walk around with a plain pistol!' says Bissy. 'I have my reputation to think of!'

'So pride is truly a deadly sin,' says Lucifer.

'And are you an angel, come to take me to Heaven?' says Bissy.

'Guess again,' says the Devil.

Bissy crosses himself but his fingers make a cross of fire at his chest and he leaps back, howling.

'You led me into this!' says Tourdonnet, jabbing a finger at Bissy. 'You said we could be shriven, sup with the Devil but return to God!'

The Devil smiles.

'I would point out,' they say, 'that Theology is not an exact science. Like most things, there is the theory on the page and then there is the practice, which so often falls down in the timing.'

'Look what you have done!' says Tourdonnet. 'Look what you have done!'

He jumps at Bissy, pushes him and Bissy pushes back. The two ghosts fall brawling to the ground. The Devil makes a shape with their hand and the ground opens in an explosion of primroses, swallowing them both.

Julie takes out her card and crosses the White Hart and Bissy, the snuff box, off her list.

Scene Eight

The Wolves' Song of Themselves

'Two lessons,' says Julie.

'Of course,' says the Devil with a deep bow. 'Use Montfaucon's blade. A revenger fights better with a dead man's sword. The bitter comes out better with a stolen rapier.'

'It's not a rapier,' says Julie. The sword she has in her hand is a good small sword, much shorter, lighter and quicker than a rapier.

'As you please,' says the Devil.

'My hand is in agony,' says Julie.

'Do you want the lesson or don't you?'

'I do.'

They come en garde, Julie quite high, inviting the low attack as her father taught her.

'You know,' says the Devil, 'that the best way to block a thrust is with the back hand – the glove or the cloak or the dagger used to deflect?'

'I do.'

'It is not! Use the blade to block the advancing thrust, come at me!'

Julie lunges at the Devil, who knocks aside the tip of Julie's sword with only a kiss of their blade before returning the thrust to go straight through her wig.

'That way the defence and the attack are one! Practise!'

The Devil throws a series of thrusts towards her and she blocks and returns.

'You are too straight, Julie. Are you a Protestant in your angles and your austerity? Twirl and circle the blade. Let it make curlicues! The answer to the raw brutality of nature – the direct and threatening attack – is art! The movement of the sword must be like the age! Baroque!'

The Devil's blade dances and hers follows their lead. Lucifer's blade circles, spins, pirouettes and twists, finally coiling and ensnaring Julie's sword. They do not move or step much, but sway and duck to avoid each other. This ground is far too uneven, and the big moon throws shadows that make deep holes seem shallow; shallow holes seem like wells. The play of the blades is like music and Julie's body sways and turns to the rhythm the Devil sets, her feet fixed, her body playing like a flame.

'Yes!' says the Devil. 'The blades dance, as the stars in their glasses dance in the sky, as the planets whirl! Do not block the enemy's way! Lead him prancing into strange lands, dizzy his head and befuddle his wits with corkscrews and arabesques! Turn and dodge, be there and not with Lucifers's dance, the Devil's Esquire!'

It seems as though they have been training for hours. Her wounds ache dreadfully, and the blade is heavy in her fingers, but it is in her fingers that she must carry it. If ever she employs the wrist to send the point zinging or, God forbid, the arm, the Devil raps her on the back of the hand with the flat of the blade. Finally, it seems her legs can bend no more, the skin on her hand is chafing beneath the glove, her shoulder is tight.

'Enough!' says the Devil.

Julie falls to her haunches, pants, steams in the cold air. Charlotte-Marie is quite still, watching, enchanted and enchanting, a beauty in aspic, it seems.

'You promised me two lessons!' says Julie.

'So I did. If you want the fox to help you, why don't you ask it to?'

'I should speak to a fox?'

'Oh yes. Creatures of great intelligence and insight. That's it. I am gone, for I have souls to roast.'

'Wait! You will promise not to interfere in my quest!' says Julie. 'You must play fair.'

The Devil turns, and anger transforms their face. Where there was once a beautiful boy, girl, man, woman, there is a leering, full-fanged man with hairy chops and twisted horns.

'I must? Must? Another once said "must" to me and I led a cohort of angels against him!'

'How did that go?' says Julie.

For an instant, she thinks the Devil will strike her, but the hairy face relaxes, melts away and the beautiful features are restored.

'Oh Julie, pretty, witty Julie,' they say. 'What a game you have begun!'

The sound of a bell, a pressure in the ears and she and Charlotte-Marie are alone under the moonlight, the upturned sedans around them, the bodies lying on their backs, eyes staring vacant at the moon. Such a pretty sight, her enemies, blank eyed as hares on a butcher's table, their skins waxen under the moon. Three dead. Ten to go.

'How long did that take?' says Julie to Charlotte-Marie.

'Well, don't ask me!' says Charlotte-Marie. 'I took a nip of my tincture. You should try it, you need never be bored!' She rechecks the little bottle locket she wears around her neck.

'I haven't felt at huge risk of boredom this evening,' says Julie.

'Nor I, though the tincture enhances even the sweetest moments.' She squeezes Julie's hands and gazes at the bodies.

'This is a rare sight,' she says. 'To think of all the times I have been goosed, or laughed at or even bargained for by these

idiots and many like them. Well, who's the idiot now, corpsey?'
She pokes Bissy in the gut with her foot.

'Dreux will undo us,' says Julie. 'I need to find him while
he dresses and kill him.'

'Well, I'm all for that,' says Charlotte-Marie. 'But there's a
problem.'

'Yes.'

'Won't we miss Moreau?'

Julie's stomach leaps. She cannot miss the angelic Moreau.
A flush of anger comes over her when she thinks of Dreux.
He and his kind ruin everything. First Paval, then her voice,
then Moreau.

'We can't do that.'

'The safest thing to do is kill Dreux now,' says Charlotte-Marie.

Julie speaks, and it is as if some outside force has gripped
her, as if in meeting Charlotte-Marie she has encountered
Destiny made flesh and, for the first time in her life, she sees
things clearly. Her one glimpse of Moreau has convinced her
that salvation, a cure for her voice, some nameless, obscure
good, will come of contact with her. Moreau is an angel on
earth, and Julie needs to stand in her light.

'Charlotte-Marie, we are not creatures of safety, with our
little murders. We are not sheep who huddle in the pen, we
are wolves, who howl at the moon for joy, no matter that we
bring the hunter on.' Where did she learn to talk like this?
These words seem to spring from her in Charlotte-Marie's
presence.

'Exactly that, that's exactly who I am!' says Charlotte-Marie.
'Oooooooh!' She puts back her head and howls into the frosty
night. Julie howls with her and they hug and laugh. Something
has happened to Julie since she has been with Charlotte-Marie.
The brave, bold person she has always been has transformed
into something entirely wilder. With Charlotte-Marie in her

arms, Julie feels reckless, mad. La folie d'amour. Whatever, it is dizzying.

'We have to try to see her even if it kills us. She is the marvel of the age.'

'We'll risk death for beauty! Well, you will,' says Charlotte-Marie. 'How romantic!'

Julie bends to the gentlemen's bodies and relieves them of their purses.

'Why are you doing that?' says Charlotte-Marie.

'So I might have food to live,' says Julie. 'And for Paval's mother.'

'Gosh,' says Charlotte-Marie. 'You have to worry about food. The romance redoubles. How wonderful. How picaresque. Perhaps I will pretend to be poor for a while.'

Julie laughs. 'Until you die? You're not pretending properly if you don't die.'

'Isn't that how all romantic stories end?' She takes Julie by the hands, looks into her eyes. 'You and I are wolves, Julie, we are!' she says. 'It is not enough for us to eat the meat of the table. We need to kill. I am so glad I found you!'

'Moreau first, and then Dreux,' says Julie. 'Let's go to it!'

'But Julie, you are covered in blood! And your hand!'

Julie looks down at herself beneath the moon. The dress is darkly stained, her hand is slashed along the back.

'Then we will make two strikes with one stone,' she says, and begins to strip.

'What are you doing?'

'Bissy is my size. I'll take his clothes and be a man for the evening. They are looking for your female companion. The fucker's got gloves too!'

'His collar's covered in blood!'

'Then I'll take Tourdonnet's collar.'

'It'll be too big for you!'

'Then "too big" will be the fashion I set,' says Julie.

'Spiffing!' says Charlotte-Marie. Julie has never heard the word before, but she takes it for approval.

Scene Nine

Alas! Alas! My Enemies Surround Me!

A couple of clips is all it takes to attach Tourdonnet's wig to her head. She pulls its lovely curls around her shoulders and the little fox stirs and moves to accommodate her. She needs his coat too – she put a hole in Bissy's sleeve. The coat is long, but the blood will not show if she keeps it buttoned. She takes a pair of fine dark gloves from Tourdonnet. They are loose on her hand but not so anyone else would notice.

She does one other thing before she goes. She takes the discarded dress and puts it on Bissy, clips the woman's wig in place on his head.

'Why do that?' asks Charlotte-Marie.

'No one can have sympathy for the ridiculous,' says Julie.

'No one thinks it is ridiculous to dress as a woman,' says Charlotte-Marie. 'The king's own brother, that lion of the battlefield, does so.'

'Yes,' says Julie. 'But the dress is too small, the wig askew. No one thinks it ridiculous to dress as a woman, but plenty think it ridiculous to dress badly. And look.' She pulls up the skirt. 'No drawers. See his little shrivelled cock like a mouse poking from a bush.'

Charlotte-Marie smiles. 'A man with a cock like that cannot

be mourned.' She kisses Julie. 'You look quite handsome,' she says, straightening Julie's collar.

'Why only quite?'

'In the English sense of "very",' says Charlotte-Marie. 'I think I love you, Julie.'

Julie grasps her hands. 'Do not,' she says. 'Delight in me, kiss me, send me letters and gifts, lie with me, wake with me but never love me.'

'Why not?'

'I am not made for it. I can give love, I am full of it, I will gladly love you, Charlotte-Marie, if that blossoms in my heart but, my dear Charlotte, do not love me. I have work to do on this earth now and, if I do not complete it, then I am bound for Hell.'

'Then you must complete it. Let me help you.'

'It is too dangerous for you.'

'Nothing is dangerous for me,' says Charlotte-Marie. 'My father is the Marshal de La Meilleraye, a childhood friend of the king. I am danger to all who oppose me, for my father stands in the light of the Sun King and tells him where to direct his withering rays.'

'These men will not respect place or position. They will not hesitate to hurt you, should you stand in their way. They will pursue you.'

'Then they should look out,' says Charlotte-Marie. 'For, if they pursue me and their luck fails them, they will catch me. And then they will know what it is to be sorry, believe me. Now, let's watch Moreau!'

They head back to the tunnel of flowers, arm in arm beneath the paper blooms. They emerge to make their way through the thicket of sedans that crowd the entrance to the huge crescent building.

'This is the stables,' says Charlotte-Marie. 'I wonder where they've put all the horses while the Opéra is here.'

They duck inside. Charlotte-Marie knows everyone, everyone wants her attention.

'Darling!'

'My dear!'

'Who is this young man?'

Charlotte-Marie says nothing to them. 'Nothing is without significance here,' she says. 'There are fifty, perhaps a hundred families here who would like to see me married to them. Gossip of a new suitor will travel fast.'

They find their places near the front – a couple giving up their seats for them in deference to Charlotte-Marie's status.

The performance restarts and Moreau takes the stage again. She is a little thing, a slender woman who is taking the role of the Princess of Colchis here. However, when she turns, her arm a little stiff, her pose a little mannered, it is as if a sorcery is cast over the room and the audience holds its breath.

She sings and it seems to Julie that she flies. The background fades away, the set, the sweating, stinking aristocrats around her, the gold of the auditorium, everything, and Moreau is suspended as if on a cloud.

She sings of being a spurned lover, of her hatred for the woman who has replaced her. She sings of how hate can become an animal, a thing that has a life of its own, a beast that calls you to follow down dark paths. Julie has never heard such a pure soprano, like sunshine on snow, like the earth bountiful in spring, like all that was ever good and right in the world given a physical expression. She sees more – Moreau has wings but not those of a bird or an insect, wings of rainbows, of light split through the spray of a weir, of beauty that can normally only be glimpsed but here is everlasting.

There are noises behind her, but she can pay them no attention.

Charlotte-Marie is speaking, saying something about how she has been seen. Is Dreux there?

On stage Moreau is an angel, an actual angel, this is no flattering comparison. She floats on light, moves on light, is light.

To sing so, to sing so! And then it is as if Moreau faces her directly, like there is no one else in the room. She sings, high and clear.

'Damnation's roads you have walked,
Hand in hand with the Devil,
Your voice will never soar to holy Heaven,
Until your soul is purified.'

'Can you cure me?' says Julie. 'Can you cure me?'

Moreau smiles and it is as if waves of love are sweeping towards her. She feels lifted up, ennobled and yet, and yet, she is aware that within her, as if lodged in her throat like a plum stone, there is a core that the light does not touch, dare not touch.

And then she sees it, as clear as a country dawn. The Devil said fiends cannot heal and yet angels can. Moreau is an angel, a real angel sent from Heaven. If the Devil can walk the earth, why not angels too? She will know what to do, she will know how to get out of this terrible deal, restore Julie's voice and let her resume her life as it was.

'Try,' says Julie. 'Try to save me, Angel Moreau.'

The singer extends her arm and a beam of light and love, a beam of lovelight, stretches towards Julie but as it touches her, it recoils.

Moreau puts her hand to her forehead, finishes the part and all but staggers from the stage.

It's as if Julie is spent. All the strength goes from her. She looks around. Charlotte-Marie is talking to a tall burly man in a scarlet coat. He carries a wooden staff. Dreux is at his sleeve, gesturing wildly. He has changed, she notes – his wig is blond where it was dark before. The man with the staff raises his arm to calm him. She must get to Moreau, she must get to her!

'Are you all right?' someone is saying to her. 'Are you all right?'

There is a hubbub around her. 'I thought the fashion for swooning had died out,' says a voice.

'Hold her up!'

Someone has an arm around her. Has she fainted? Has someone caught her? She appears to be on her feet.

'I'm fine. I'm fine,' says Julie. She must make it to Moreau, must tell her of her admiration, she must be healed. Another man is at Charlotte-Marie's side. He is lean, spare-looking and severe, dressed in a coat of black silk. His face bears a scar from his eye to his lip.

She walks to Charlotte-Marie. It's as if she is enchanted.

'The music,' she says. 'The music.'

'That's Bissy's coat!' says Dreux. 'This must be one of this lady's abductors! There were ten of them! I killed five! Take this man, de la Reynie.'

'This is my good friend,' says Charlotte-Marie. 'How dare you implicate him.'

'Monsieur,' says the burly man, touching the lapel of Julie's coat. 'I am de la Reynie, chief of police here. If you would . . .' He withdraws his hand, looks at his fingers. 'Your coat, Monsieur. It is wet with blood. Monsieur, you will come with me.'

Julie snaps from her reverie. All eyes are on her.

'This is my special friend,' says Charlotte-Marie.

'This villain has enchanted you, madam,' says Dreux. 'The only other explanation is that you are in league with him and, as you are a lady and the daughter of a powerful man, that cannot be. Now reveal what happened to the woman, the woman you were with, the one the Devil sent.'

'The Devil sent?' The lean man speaks now, his voice dry and slow.

'A manner of speaking,' says Dreux, 'but there was a woman there, a woman involved in this lady's abduction.'

'All will become clear under my questioning,' says de la Reynie. He addresses Julie. 'Now, sir, if you will come with me.'

Julie turns to run, but three other men appear from nowhere to bar her way.

Scene Ten

Dance of the Beasts

If this is a cell, then it is an opulent one. The walls are crimson, the floor a polished dark wood. She is seated at a grey marble desk facing de la Reynie. Two guards are at the door, dressed like de la Reynie in scarlet.

'Well,' says de la Reynie. 'We have been to the woods as Monsieur Dreux instructed. A fine pickle there, don't you think?'

Julie says nothing. Her sword has been taken from her and leans against the wall behind the policeman. She is left to wonder if she could overcome De la Reynie in a fist fight. Though she was raised with boys and fought every day of her childhood life, she concludes she could not. De la Reynie is a bulky man who carries himself with the confidence of someone who has seen many confrontations and come out best from all of them.

'Two gentlemen dead, one lying half naked in ladies' clothes. It's easy to see what happened there.'

Julie raises an eyebrow.

'Yes, very easy. You are clearly not a manly man. So my bet is that you are a boy whore, brought to those woods for some sort of entertainment by those gentlemen, perhaps it pleases them to play the lady with you and be called pretty. Then you kill and rob them, plain and simple. You will hang for this.'

Julie feels her anger rising.

'Load of shite,' she says. No point in pretending to be high-born in front of this man so she'll be rougher than she is, more convincing as a man, she hopes. Then she just has to wait until Charlotte-Marie uses her connections to free her.

'That is not gentlemanly speech,' he says.

'I beg your fucking pardon,' says Julie, 'but it's not gentlemanly speech to go flinging accusations at people with nothing to back them up.'

De la Reynie smiles. 'Of course it is not. But I am glad the slur on your virtue has led you to the truth. What was it then? I have files on everyone at this court, everyone, some as thick as my arm. On your friend Charlotte-Marie Mazarin, I have enough for a library. Does her father disapprove of your relations with her? Are you not rich? Has her corruption descended from women of her own rank to street meat? She has the German Vice, does she not, but does she dally with men too?'

'The German Vice? That's a new one on me.'

Julie is aware of her little knife tucked in her sleeve. Could she free it and do for him? She doesn't quite trust her hand, numb beneath her glove from practice and from the wounds upon it.

'She likes other women. And she is wild, though that is not a sin limited to Germans. Her father despairs of ever finding a match for her. How does a guttersnipe like you, for that is what you are by your rough speech, how does such a person end up in the company of Charlotte-Marie Mazarin, grand-daughter of the Great Cardinal?'

Julie smiles.

'I'll just wait here, squire,' she says. 'I think it won't be too long before Charlotte-Marie gets me out .'

De la Reynie cracks his knuckles.

'Look at the walls,' he says.

She does. They are an opulent crimson, as she has noted before.

'Now look at the floor.'

She does. It shines like the top of a piano.

'And this desk. What do you think of the decoration?'

'Very liveable.'

'Yes. Red walls, a floor that is easily mopped, a desk that cannot be stained. Why do you think I use this room to ask my questions? What is your name?'

He asks the final question quickly, fairly barks it out.

She says the first thing she thinks of.

'Jean Lully.'

'Like the composer?'

'Yes.'

'Are you related? I can't imagine that you are.'

'No, I . . .'

A noise at the door and a footman comes in to pass de la Reynie a note. He reads it and sniffs.

'Very well, very well,' he says. 'I have business to attend to. When I return you will answer my questions. Do you understand?'

Before she can reply he has leaned forward across the desk and caught her a hefty slap across the face. She slumps back in the chair.

'Too slow, sir, too slow,' he says. 'When I return you will answer more quickly if you want to avoid further such treatment.'

He steps outside and the guards withdraw. Julie feels the blow ringing through her. She is alone in the room. And de la Reynie has left her sword. Very odd. She shivers, looks at the big window, the dark outside.

At the desk, she takes a heavy chair, takes it to the window and hurls it through the glass. An enormous crash, but the hole is not big enough. She takes a second chair, hurls that too. For an instant, almost on instinct, she pauses. She had expected footsteps, running, to be chased. But no. She takes up her sword and slips through the hole in the glass into the night. From two wings of the building, like rats after a stricken duckling, men appear, moving purposefully across the grass.

She runs, though she doesn't know to where, just into the darkness. There is no hue and cry from the men; none of them carry lamps but they are quick, closing the distance between them with every step.

She runs hard, but soon can go no further. Water blocks her way: a long canal. She turns right, goes as quickly as she can but the night's exertions are catching up with her. Her limbs are heavy, her breath short.

A shape looms against the moon: a wall, a gate within it. She opens it, slips within. There is nothing to bar the gate behind her, so she heads on. A path cuts through two neat lawns to another gate, this time of steel bars in a fence of wood. It's barred on the inside but not locked, so she reaches through to slide back the hasp. She goes through that and closes the gate behind her. Birds, everywhere, such strange pale birds too, squat big things with pouches beneath their mouths waddling on the grass. Above looms a tall building, angular at the bottom, domed on the top like a grand hatbox, dark against the moon. A shape separates from the bulk of the building, an extraordinary shape. At first she mistakes it for a giant man, bent over, a long arm stretched out to scrape the ground, or searching the way in front of him with a walking stick but when it moves she sees it is on all fours – a massive thing, far taller than she is and bulky too, with a great nose before it, huge protuberances either side curving skywards like great knives. This, she realises, is an elephant – something she had only ever seen in pictures before. It looks at her, munching. Is there no one here to control it, to care for it? No – with the Opéra at the court, every lazy servant has taken advantage of his master's absence to do what he will.

The gate opens. Eight men enter the garden. The creature moves away and the birds flap uncertainly.

'Stay right where you fucking are.'

These are not aristocrats, evidently – their voices are too rough, their coats too plain, they carry cudgels and staffs, not swords.

'I have done nothing wrong,' says Julie. 'You have no right to detain me.'

'We're going to detain you six feet down, matey boy,' says one of the guards.

So why did Dreux get the police to arrest her if men have been sent to kill her here? Because he is unstrategic. Because he doesn't think. Someone above him does think and has decided that whatever has been going on is best solved without the involvement of de la Reynie and, through him, the king. She almost laughs. She bets there is another gang of men searching for the mysterious woman who was with Charlotte-Marie.

The gate opens again and the men look around. It's the lean man in the black, slim-fitting justaucorps coat, the one who accompanied the man with the eight-pointed cross to the Opéra. His sword is low on his hip.

'This gentleman will come with me,' he says. 'You have no business with him.'

'Fuck off, skinny,' says one of the men. 'We're on orders from better than you.'

A man runs towards Julie and swipes at her with his club. She jumps backwards and he comes again but there is a stir at her neck. She remembers, at last!

'Fox, get him!' she shouts.

The stole slips from around her shoulders, darts across the grass and shoots up the man's body to curl around his eyes. He can see nothing. Her sword is free, and she does for him. She feels the contact, the sudden stop of his breastbone against the hilt and her fist, hears his shout, sees his stuttering fall, like a foal first standing but in reverse, stumbling out of life, not into it. She feels sick. This is no enemy, no hated torturer or killer. This is just a guard doing his job and she has killed him without thinking.

A thump and a rush and she is down, she doesn't know how. She rolls away, half gets up, but a man is on her, his arms about her, pulling her down again. Then another piles in. She sees the shadow of something against the moon, then a flash of white light as if the moon itself has struck her; she realises she has been hit. A man draws back his foot to kick again, but the fox is on his eyes in a streak and he shouts and blunders. The birds rise up in a great squawk, some strange creature roars in the darkness. She bites the man on top of her, tears off his ear but he hits her hard, smashing her in the eye.

'You have failed to notice!' shouts a voice but the beating continues, blows smashing into her arms, which she curls around her head. She takes a blow to her guts that makes her retch.

A thump next to her and the blows stop in an instant.

'You have failed to notice,' says the man in the black coat, 'that I have killed one of you already and one of your compatriots lies dead at this gentleman's hand. Know that I am Sérannes, fencing master, adviser and protector to the Marshal de La Meilleraye. On his authority, know that if you continue, you will die.'

Five men turn towards him; the one on the ground tries to stand and tear the clinging fox from his face, but loses his footing and falls, rolling and cursing, to the floor. Two corpses on the ground, dark shapes of birds in the air. Beasts roar, deep sounds of anger and warning.

'You're going to fucking die!' says a man.

'Inevitably, but not this evening, I would wager,' says Sérannes.

They leap at him, but he dances backwards through the gate, trapping a hand between the gate and the post as it grasps for him. A man cries out in pain and then another. A body falls. One, two, three are at the gate and one, two, three are dead, a sword like a shard of moonlight dancing through the bars . . . but then he is forced to take a step back when the butt of a quarterstaff is driven at his face.

The men wrench the gate open and Sérannes backs off, turning aside from the blows, and kicks like a drunk man playing crazy at a country dance. Julie looks around her. The great elephant is blowing and stamping in panic, roaring and squealing like it was being fried alive. Still one man rolls on the floor, the fox clinging about his face like an expansive and very noisy beard.

The two remaining men retreat inside the garden, locking the gate as they do. Sérannes is now on the outside; she locked within. Any attempt he makes to put his hand through and open the bolt will be met with a blow from a cudgel or a staff, for sure.

'Get him!' says one of the men. She realises he is talking about her. 'If he dies then there's no one to rescue. I'll watch the fencer.'

A man is in front of her with his quarterstaff. She puts forward her – Montfaucon's – sword.

The man laughs but he has panic in his eyes. 'You're a boy,' he says. 'And my staff outreaches you by two arms' length!'

He attacks, jabbing the butt of the staff towards her. She ducks, but he has led her into a trap, knocking the staff down on her head. She sees it coming in time and twists aside, but his attack is relentless – he comes on swiping the air in great arcs, the iron shoe of the staff fairly singing in the night air.

She backs off; he runs, trips on the uneven ground, goes sprawling, but she has retreated too far to finish him, doesn't want to finish him anyway. She can kill for hate, easily, but not gladly kill these who have been sent to kill her only for pay, or for duty. She glances behind her. The elephant is bellowing near the fence, fretting behind a pile of earth and a jumble of stonework.

She sees her chance – she runs hard for the mound of earth, leaps from the top of it onto the elephant's back, up and over the fence to land heavily on the other side. She hits the ground winded, the sword knocked from her hand. She scrambles to pick it up, panting for breath.

Beasts roar from within the angled building and the birds wheel against the moon. The fox runs through the fence to take its place as a limp skin around her neck.

Sérannes stands at the gate, his sword warding the final three men away.

'You'll hang for this, Sérannes!' shouts the quarterstaff man.

If Sérannes does hang, the quarterstaff man will never get to see it, nor his two fellows who stand on each shoulder. A noise like an infernal trumpet sounds, and the elephant flattens all three.

Scene Eleven

A Conversation of Blades

They run for the woods. Sérannes is tall but rangy and runs with an easy step, almost as if he floats upon the ground. She runs by his side, matching him for pace. Her eye is swollen, her lip is split, and she coughs blood as she runs. From the pain, she thinks she may have broken a rib.

'Why are we running?' she says. 'Our enemies are gone.'

'I was running because you were,' says Sérannes. 'I assumed you knew something I did not.'

'I don't,' says Julie.

'Then I suggest we walk,' says Sérannes. 'Let us take the air. I shall be Jove and you Ganymede, what do you say?'

He offers her his arm and she links it with hers. This is a wise course of action, she thinks. If they are seen, no one will think it remarkable that two gentleman friends are out strolling together.

'I'm sweating like a blacksmith's bum,' says Julie. She is too, still boiling hot, though she can feel the sweat beginning to chill on her clothes. She bends to catch her breath, panting out plumes into the freezing moonlight.

'I'm no authority on blacksmiths' bums,' says Sérannes, 'though I would conjecture they do produce their fair share of perspiration.'

'Honest toil has that effect,' says Julie.

'I won't pretend I'm so high that I don't know,' says Sérannes. 'I could do with a nip of cologne after that exertion myself. I'm glad I forswear to powder my face or rouge my lips. What a fright I should appear.'

Sérannes looks enough of a fright to Julie anyway. His cheeks are sunken, he is so spare and lean, no palace gorger he, no pastry hound or sweetmeat-sucker like so many of the aristocracy.

'Thank you,' says Julie. 'For your help.'

Finally they sit, she doesn't know exactly where, just under some trees with the moon filigreed by the branches and the leaves.

'You interest me,' says Sérannes. 'I have you down as one of Pomet's men. I am correct, no?'

'What's it to you and who the fuck are you to ask? Begging your pardon for the profanity, it is my habit, sir,' says Julie.

'Decide. If you are going to curse, do so freely and don't apologise. Or don't curse and you won't have to apologise. "Sorry" is a serf's word. Never utter it. I am the protector and fencing master to the Marshal de La Meilleraye.'

'I've never heard of him.' Charlotte-Marie's father. Can this be a coincidence?

'Then you must be a person of very great importance indeed. He's a Marshal of France and one of the richest men in it. Head of the Artillery and much else. He's also your friend Charlotte-Marie's father. Which brings us to the question of what it is to me. I look out for her. He is very concerned about her – particularly when it comes to keeping company with young men. She is beautiful, is she not?'

'She is.'

'And you have designs upon her?'

'None that need worry you.'

'Monsieur,' says Sérannes. 'It would do you benefit to answer my questions graciously. And besides, it is good manners. A gentleman repays his debts and I have rescued you tonight.'

'You and an elephant. Should I answer its questions? What debt do I owe that tusky fellow?'

Sérannes jabs a finger at her.

'I am your social better, I am appointed by . . .' For a moment he seems lost in thought. 'None of this matters. What matters is, I have a sword, you have a sword. That is where our equivalence in the fight ends. I could kill you any time I choose and call you another cutpurse I have found in the woods. Now answer me or I will run you through.'

The fox on Julie's neck flicks open an eye.

'And do not imagine,' he says, 'that I am so slow that I will not kill that thing, whatever it is, before it moves.'

The fox looks quizzically at Julie as she faces Sérannes in the moonlight and then Sérannes smiles.

'Come,' he says. 'No need for this. Let us talk as gentlemen. And let me be frank. I did not rescue you—'

'You are correct, you did not.'

He inclines his head, smiles. He is old, maybe thirty-five or forty, but he has a confident air about him and, strangely for such a killer, a gentleness that she finds disarming.

'Let us stick to facts. I killed only a portion of the eight men assailing you. In the chaos of the fight I have quite forgotten how many. Four, I think. I give due credit to you and to our long-nosed friend. I killed those men out of concern for Charlotte-Marie. I rescued you because Dreux talks too freely and imagines that because I am a servant, yes that is what I am, that I am deaf and incapable of having concerns or opinions. But the Marshal has always employed me as much for my mind as for my hand. I think and act independently, forestalling problems before he even knows they exist. Dreux received a message after de la Reynie took you away that left him white. He then scribbled a note to give to de la Reynie's man. I was intrigued to see you released and more intrigued to see how quickly those men were assembled to attack you.'

'They were guards. They're always there.'

'You are right, the guards are always there. But those men were not guards and the guards were – contrary to the iron law we have just stated – not there. That can only happen for one reason. They were withdrawn. That tells me something very plain. You have enemies in high places and those enemies do not wish you to speak to the chief policeman of the king. Well, while it might be desirable to watch you die and have the matter returned to silence, I wonder which others are with you, what else I need to know to protect Charlotte-Marie. Who are your accomplices?'

'I have no accomplices.'

'Excellent. Then you can die, and we tidy all loose ends. I track and kill the murderer who has been stalking these grounds, making such work for the gardeners.'

'The gardeners?'

'All those bodies will need to be removed before morning. We cannot have news of this chaos reaching the ears of the court.'

He draws his sword.

'As a man of honour I will give you the chance to defend yourself.'

The fox stirs at her neck and in an instant has run up Sérannes's leg, but his free hand is like lightning and catches the creature by the scruff where it mewls, kicks and goes limp, just a skin once more.

'As a man of honour, could you kill a lady?'

'Of course not!'

'Well, then you can't kill me. I am a woman, not a man and I have been grievously wronged by high men.'

'You don't look like a woman.'

She removes her wig, throws off her coat.

'I suppose,' says Sérannes. 'I suppose, yes. I can see that now. That makes more sense, given Charlotte-Marie's inclinations and, well, your hips. No disrespect to your breasts, either. So why are you here?'

'For revenge,' she says.

And then she tells him, though missing Lucifer's appearance, about what happened to her in the Bois de Boulogne.

Sérannes thinks for a long time.

'And you think you can identify these men?'

'Yes. Dreux is certainly one of them.'

'And you will kill them?'

'Yes.'

'How?'

'By whatever means I can. I wish to humiliate them so I was thinking of calling them out in a duel if I can find them.'

Sérannes laughs.

'You cannot do that. They will kill you.'

'I can use a sword as well as any man. And I have my fox fur.'

'Yes, what is this?' He waves the fur in front of her.

'A gift of my father's. He won it in a game of cards with an Arab years ago.'

'Do they have foxes in Araby?'

'They had this one.'

'Extraordinary. But you cannot humiliate a man if you beat him by deceit. And you cannot fight, as I say.'

'I can fight.'

'Really? Then put up and let us see.'

He puts up his sword in en garde, still dangling the fur from his back hand.

'And what do I get if I win?'

'My help, such as it is. I don't like those men either. They are a cancer in the court, and it would be good to remove them. They are too close to the king, which means too close to my Marshal, too close to me. And these activities make them weak, open to blackmail, to coercion. De la Reynie would certainly like to know of them.'

'No one cares if aristocrats are murdering street girls.'

'The king cares. He has already suffered one grievous riot in Paris that nearly cost him his crown. He doesn't want another.'

'And if I lose?'

Sérannes smiles.

'Death, in all likelihood,' he says.

'I have a rare master,' she says.

'Let's see,' he says.

They cross blades and stand in the formal way as if it were a lesson – no tricks of pacing back and forth here on the dark and rooty ground, no cowardly retreats or showy advances, just fencing as it was meant to be – the swords tip-tapping against each other, ready to begin the conversation of blades.

Sérannes does not move but waits for her.

He will not expect her to take him on with strength. He will expect her to duck the tip of her own sword under his to expose his inner arm to attack, then a feint to the arm, another quick dip of the point and a snick to the outer arm with the angled hand or a hit to the foot. Guile in some form.

She extends her arm, scraping her blade down his, trying to shove it aside to expose his outer arm, but it is as if he can see the future. He simply extends his arm and lifts it and now it is her arm and chest that are exposed. She performs the disengage, the dip of the point led only by a twiddle of the fingers to put his blade on the outside of hers and strike at his arm but again, the tip of his blade is a blur and he has anticipated, brought the sword down on hers, blocking it out.

He gives a little slap on her side with his blade, to show he could have run her through if he wished.

'You were expecting that,' she says.

He looks affronted.

'Never,' he says. 'To expect is to open the possibility of deceit. I cannot be deceived because I have no preconceptions. I react to what I . . .' She *expects* he was going to finish that sentence with 'see' but she has noticed that it is a weakness of men that, once they have begun declaiming on a topic, they are possessed of a great hunger to finish that declamation. Therefore his guard is down while he is holding forth.

She snorts, gulps, makes a lunge for his chest. He laughs and blocks, riposting like lightning to her hand but she has not withdrawn her blade to block and parry as fencers are taught to do. She has left it forward and now leaps at Sérannes, blocking his sword's progress with a thrust that snicks his leg.

He does not cry out, merely gives her a little laugh.

'Quite the devil,' he says. 'One more pass, madam!'

Now his blade is a pen writing a calligraphy of threat in the night air in front of her. It dances, bobs, thrusts, withdraws, menaces, demurs, boasts, offers, denies, and her own blade is bewildered. She tries a desperate parry to block him, a desperate riposte that strikes back for his chest – not direct of course, no such blundering reply could catch a man like this, but with two little curls, promising first an attack one way, then another. He deflects the point at the last instant with a graceful nod of appreciation and now they are dancing carefully sideways, mindful of tripping, turning a minuet of steel under the bloated moon.

They close and part, circle and turn but she knows now that her one devil's trick is done and that her homely skills, learned with her brothers and father on the cobbles, are no match for this man's blade work, with the fingers and wrist that are iron one instant, water the next.

Snap, and his wrist is a trap, prying the blade from her fingers and sending it spinning to the ground.

'I'm sorry,' he says. 'That was unforgivably ostentatious.' He drops his sword to his side, bows extravagantly.

She punches him hard in the face, sitting him back on his arse.

'How's that for ostentatious?' she says.

He laughs, holds his nose. 'I think you've broken my nose,' he says. 'Where did you learn to punch like that?'

'You're not the first idiot I've encountered, nor will you be the last.'

He stands, smiles. There is an instinctive understanding between them: the fight is over. She looks towards the house, towards where Moreau is waiting, the angel who can restore her. A ripple across the line of light. Men are massing there, lanterns, dogs too.

'It seems they've found you have not been killed,' says Sérannes. 'I knew we were running for a reason.'

'We will have no time to run now,' she says.

'Oh, I don't know. Dreux or someone won't like being told what to do by the likes of de la Reynie, even if he is chief of police with a hundred times more brains than Dreux and his mob put together. There'll be a dispute about order of precedence in leading the search. On top of that, de la Reynie has quite clearly been asked to let you go, so his interest in capturing you might be slight. That's not to say he won't, and deliver you to whoever tried to kill you in the menagerie, so we can take nothing for granted. One thing is certain, you can't go back to the house. Where do you want to go?'

'To the Opéra camp, to the wagons,' she says.

'I have no idea where that is.'

'Just off the main road as it comes to the gates. Can you show me the direction?'

127

'I regard it as my duty to show you there,' says Sérannes. 'No one has broken my nose before so I must repay you for that lesson. Follow me.'

The hounds at the house let up a great cry and she and Sérannes run into the dark.

Scene Twelve

Run to Earth

'What, what? Who's there?'

A childish voice from the wagons.

It's Diandré, the little Opéra boy, his face pale and dirty under the moon.

'Diandré, it's me, Julie!'

'Thank God, I thought it was bandits! Who is this?'

'Never you mind,' says Sérannes.

'Beg pardon, sir,' says Diandré with a bow.

'Get out of your clothes,' says Sérannes to Julie. 'The hounds will track blood and you can guarantee they'll run them past the corpses to get just the right scent.'

'I have nothing else to wear.'

'A blanket?'

'I have one!' says Diandré. 'There's all your sleeping stuff at the back.'

'That will do! You, child, take these clothes and run a good mile from here. Drop them in a brook and come back, you shall have a sou,' says Sérannes.

'That's too dangerous,' says Julie.

'We have no choice.'

'I'd like a sou!' says Diandré, with great enthusiasm.

She goes behind a wagon to change, throwing down the

bloody coat, the dirty breeches, the gloves. It pains her to discard the shoes and stockings, they are so lovely, but they will betray her now. Diandré stuffs them into a sack as she covers herself with the blanket.

'Don't get caught by the hounds,' says Sérannes. 'You hear them anywhere near, drop the sack and keep running.'

Diandré bows and totters quickly into the night.

'You should leave now,' says Julie. She feels vulnerable.

'I will not go,' says Sérannes.

'Why not?'

'You will see,' he says. 'The blood is still on you. The hounds will find you here. I must wait a while to defend you.'

'You can't fight so many.'

'No, but I can offer a deflection. In the art of fencing is everything in life. Fencing is life, life in steel. Here we shall offer a deflection, not a block or an opposition. Another disguise for you, I think.'

'I have no clothes!'

'We can work with that,' he says.

She watches him strip, wondering what he plans. He removes his dark coat, his shirt, the brooch that holds the scarf at his neck and springs up to sit beside her in the covered wagon. He is built very lean, like a hunting dog himself and his skin is white beneath the moon. She has heard that it does well to be fat at Versailles – the king is fat, and one would not want to make him self-conscious. Sérannes clearly has no hope of preferment.

She pulls the blanket around her tight. The fox curls around her neck. She pats it and says a name. 'Furie.' Not inventive but it seems right for the fox – a useful devil, a gentle tempest, sleeping at her neck.

Sérannes sits beside her and she prepares herself for what comes next. She knows what men are and that such a night of murder and violence is more likely to provoke a man's appetite than dim it. For herself, she has no sentimental thoughts left about sex, with men at least. She uses it to get what she wants. What she wants might be pleasure or affection, it might be joy. Sérannes might do for those things, but not here and now on this night of murder. Perhaps later, if he can show himself valuable, she might let him do what he wants. Now, she will turn him away.

But he does nothing, just sits in the darkness.

'Sing us a tune to while away the hour,' he says.

The words are like a knife in her, a sharp feeling from the base of her tongue to her guts.

'This night isn't yet done,' she says.

He shrugs at her, not understanding. Then he launches into a song about a woman. His voice is worse than hers, even now. It makes her laugh.

'You sing badly,' she says.

'It's a battle song,' he says. 'You don't have to sing it well.'

'About a girl?'

'About anything. You just need a tune everyone knows and for it to be in French your enemy can't easily pick up. It stops you getting shot in the fog of battle.'

'You have been in many battles?'

'A few. There is very little to recommend them.'

A great cry, dogs baying and headlong into the wagon come three or four hunting dogs, claws scratching, tongues licking. Furie shoots from her neck and under a flap at the back of the wagon and two of the dogs fly after then; the other two press noses into Julie, snorting and sniffing at her.

'Out, out, the lot of you!' shouts a voice from outside. 'Out!'

It's then she realises – she has left the sword inside the wagon. If they find that, they are done for.

Sérannes is transformed.

'This is insupportable!' he bellows. He jumps into the back of the wagon, takes the two dogs by the scruff and hurls them out, then he picks up his sword and leaps down.

'Who the fuck are you?' says a voice. Julie pushes away the dogs, peers from the wagon. A magnificent young man on a stamping horse looks down at Sérannes. He wears an epauletted uniform and carries a heavy military sabre at his side.

'I am Sérannes, fencing master and bodyguard to the Marshal de La Meilleraye, and if you address me in that tone again people will be asking who you were, not who you are!'

'I am on orders to search this camp,' he says. 'Which includes that wagon.'

'I am in that wagon at the moment,' says Sérannes. 'Search it and you may regard it a matter of honour.'

Julie hardly understands how some of these gentlemen speak but she thinks Sérannes has just threatened the young man with a duel.

'What are you doing in there?'

'Really,' says Sérannes. Julie takes this as her cue. She sees Sérannes' plan. The blanket wrapped around her like a shawl, she comes to sit at the edge of the wagon, a dog licking her ear.

'I see,' says the young man.

'Yes, you see, now . . .'

A clamour, the sound of hooves and more men pour into the camp.

Dreux is on one horse, puffing and blowing, de la Reynie on another. Julie slides back into the darkness as the two dogs at her side drop to the ground.

'We must search everywhere!' shouts Dreux. 'What's here, Captain?'

'Nothing, sir, but the master of defence with er, a, er, an actress.'

'You have searched the wagons?'

'The dogs seem interested in that one,' says the horseman.

'Really,' says Dreux. 'Let me see.'

'What is in that wagon is my business,' says Sérannes.

'You think yourself a high man, Sérannes,' says Dreux, 'but you are but a high man's shadow.'

'Enough to cast shade on you,' says Sérannes. He steps in front of Dreux.

Dreux bridles. He wants to call Sérannes out in a duel, should call him out in a duel, but that would be a policy of limited return. Out in the woods, two dogs give a cry.

'They've lost the scent,' says a man in the drab coat of a hound master.

'Well, they found something in here,' says Dreux.

He hops from his horse on the side away from Sérannes and, with a suprising agility, runs around the horse and jumps into the wagon. Julie cowers in the dark, completely covered by her blanket.

'What's in here, then?' he says. There's a scrabbling, a sound like a demented baby crying from near Dreux's feet.

'Come down, sir, or—' Sérannes never gets to finish his sentence. Dreux lets out a great cry and tumbles out on to the ground with a thump.

'A fox!' he shouts. 'A bloody fox!' as Furie leaps after him and speeds into the night, the hounds in full cry after them, the riders – who have not quite understood what has gone on – tearing after them.

'We'll have further business for your insolence!' shouts Dreux. 'Ah! My clothes!' He remounts the horse.

'I will be happy to kill you if you think that necessary to satisfy your honour,' says Sérannes.

Dreux curses and spurs his horse off after the hunt.

'You are safe now,' says Sérannes, stepping up into the wagon.

He takes her hands. Does he think to kiss her? Does he think two rescues gives him the right to her? Well they do, don't they? In his world, the world of aristocrats and of men generally, she is now in his debt. In one way perhaps she is. She owes him her gratitude, not her body.

'Thank you,' she says. 'But I do not choose to be safe. How long until dawn?'

'I don't know. An hour, two?'

'Then I must return to the château. Moreau is here for one night only and I need to see her.'

'There will be no more singing tonight!'

'For me she will sing,' says Julie. 'I know what she is.'

'What?'

'An angel,' she says.

'Who told you that?'

She smiles. 'I saw her, and she spoke to me. You need to find me some clothes.'

'Of course,' says Sérannes. He shrugs greatly. 'You are mad, you know, don't you?'

'I only suspect it,' she says. 'Get me to the house!'

She steels herself. Moreau will cure her. Furie will escape the hounds. It will all be all right.

They walk back towards the house, to the buzz of grooms and sedans preparing to take the guests back to lodges and apartments, to the guards who patrol in numbers.

They do not see one horseman turn away from the hunt to follow them.

Scene Thirteen

Let Your Hearts Lament
This is the End of All Mercy

No one looks at Julie strangely, wrapped as she is in a blanket. At this hour most are drunk, and the normal rules of behaviour break down. There has been a killing in the grounds of the menagerie, it has been discovered, and before the guards will be allowed to inspect them, all the people of rank will insist on viewing the corpses, speculating on what happened. It is certain, it appears, that one of the elephants who roams the inner field at night has been spooked and provoked. The animal's keeper is called, and it is placed in a stall so the aristocrats can marvel at what damage it has done to the bodies of the men it has trampled.

Julie sees none of this, but she feels the chateau's life as something out of nature, moving to an energy granted by the strange artificial sun known as King Louis; people moving through the darkness with their lantern bearers before them, the house ablaze in candlelight.

All the gaudy colours of the aristocrats' dresses and coats are here transformed by torchlight into night shades she has never seen. They are strange moths flitting in the dark and she a caterpillar cocooned in her blanket. Does she still long to become one of them? She does not know. Those ambitions seem distant now. Is she a caterpillar? Or is she a worm, a canker eating at the night's bright heart?

Sérannes leads her. What do they think of her? Whore? Beaten servant? Captive? She realises the truth is more mundane. They do not think of her at all. This would be no agony to most but Julie feels the ghost of a sharp distress rattling its chains inside her. This was to have been her audience, the people whose souls she would lift to ecstasy through her singing. She sees them now, staggering drunk, leering, shouting, no more than brightly clad beasts. She could have transformed them, she believes it. As they would lift her with their adulation, she would lift them in song, coax the spirit from the flesh, make them angels. She could have done God's work. She touches her throat. Now she must do the Devil's.

As if sensing her thoughts, Furie runs across the lawn, up her back and takes its place at her neck. She touches the fur for comfort.

Sérannes pushes her on through Versailles, through back corridors of plain white walls and stone floors, through grand, empty state rooms of polished wood and gold, big windows lit up by the moon. In other places nobles stroll or guards wait. The nobles do not acknowledge them, the guards give Sérannes a nod.

'Is she here?'

'She will stay near the king. If she stays,' says Sérannes.

Finally they arrive at a fine corridor on the second floor of the palace.

'I think this is it.'

Julie knocks and, after a moment of kerfuffle from within, the door is answered by a maid.

'We would like to pay our respects to the great Moreau,' says Sérannes.

'And you are?'

'Admirers,' says Sérannes.

'Pretty rag-arse admirers if you ask me,' says the maid.

'Let them in. I know this one, I saw her from the stage.' A voice like a bell chimes from behind the maid.

The maid shrugs, turns and Julie follows her nervously inside.

The room is opulently furnished – it must have taken a whole goldmine to provide the leaf for the furniture alone. A grand mirror flickers above a huge fire and, on a divan, Moreau reclines, a gaggle of ladies around her seeing to her nails, arranging her hair. Racks of dresses stand before another mirror and a table is nearby, laden with make-up, the pots in neat rows. A harpsichord sits in the corner, sheets of music strewn around it, the only note of disorder in the room. Furie slips from Julie's neck to lie before the fire. No one is gauche enough to even comment on the woman in the blanket's pet fox slinking across the carpet.

'The second hour of dressing,' she says. 'Another two and I'll be ready to meet the king.'

Julie rushes up to her, kneels at her feet.

'Great Moreau,' she says. 'I know who you are and from where you come!'

'Lyon?' says Moreau.

'Heaven,' says Julie.

Moreau looks at her quizzically. 'I saw you,' she says, 'from the stage. When I am here before you now, I see you plainly, without insight or knowledge. But when I sing, I understand things. I understand people. You have been hurt. You are looking for healing.'

'Yes.'

'And you are a singer yourself. Music wants to speak through you, I think.'

'I was a singer before I was cruelly cut.' She shows Moreau her neck.

Moreau extends an arm towards her, runs her fingers over the scar. Julie feels a tingle spreading through her body.

'Sing with me,' she says.

'I cannot, my throat is ruined.'

'If you sing, I might be able to help you.'

'Then I will sing.'

Moreau goes over to the harpsichord and plays a scale of E, ascending in a hum. It's only a warm up exercise but the air seems to brighten around her, the heavy scent of candles lifts and a freshness like a spring morning comes into the room.

Julie hums too. It had not occurred to her, she who had never really needed to warm up, that music was still there for her in this way. Humming is not singing but it is music. Her notes come out pure and sweet.

'With me,' says Moreau, changing to arpeggios, still humming. The women hum together and Sérannes cocks his head as the music fills the room. Everyone is silent, everyone enraptured. Julie herself is transported. She is a girl in Alsace, taking her first lessons along with the noble boys in her father's charge. She sees sunlight, the movement of water. And then something darker, visions of that night in the Bois. She is seeing the beginning of her true love for music, seeing its end too and, in duetting with Moreau, she shares something with her, knows she sees it too.

Now Moreau goes to 'ah'. Her voice is like a peal of bells. Julie follows her and for an instant thinks she has it. Then the dog is back in her voice. She coughs, splutters and the spell is broken.

No one comments, no one breathes. Moreau gets up from the harps chord.

'I know your cure,' she says. She goes to the rack of dresses. 'Take one,' she says.

Julie sees these dresses are in fact costumes, some those of queens, some of shepherdesses, others of servants. She chooses the servant. For now, she wants to be invisible.

She dresses in front of the room, unselfconscious beneath the gaze of the women. Sérannes steals a glance at her but suddenly becomes rather interested in the opposite wall when she meets his eye. When she is dressed Moreau comes to her, takes a ribbon from the rack and ties it around Julie's neck.

'This,' she says, 'is a token. I see your path to healing. What is it that healed the world?'

'I don't know.'

'Think, girl.'

Moreau touches her and she has a vision. Christ on the cross, the hill black against a sky streaked with red.

'Blood,' she says.

'Blood will heal you. God will not let his enemies triumph.'

She touches Julie gently on the neck and a deep pleasure shoots through her, a pleasure of the body and the soul, a feeling of homecoming, of deep friendship, of love.

A knock at the door. The spell is broken. Moreau nods to her maid and the girl goes to open the door.

De la Reynie stands in his horse coat, the whip still in his hand.

'I need to talk to you, Sérannes,' he says. 'And your companion.'

There is nowhere to run and no point running anyway. Sérannes is well known to de la Reynie.

The chief of police beckons them from the room, and they follow, the maid closing the door behind them. Julie gives one last glance to Moreau but she is gone.

Julie is surprised to see no guards with de la Reynie, nor any weapon in his hand. Instead he bears a large card.

'You gave the hunt the slip,' he says.

Julie does not reply but shrugs.

'I am not asking a question, I am telling you. I have eyes everywhere and I know what goes on in this palace and a day's march all around it.'

'Then there's little point in interviewing us,' says Sérannes.

'This is not an interview,' he says.

'Then what is it?'

'I am a policeman. I guard property. You dropped this, madam,' says de la Reynie.

'I dropped nothing,' she says.

De la Reynie simply extends his hand with the card in it.

'My reading is not so good,' says Julie. She fears to take the card in case it is something incriminating.

'Sérannes?' says de la Reynie.

Sérannes takes the card and reads it. Then he nods. De la Reynie bids them goodnight and walks along the corridor.

'What is it?'

'It's Dreux's Versailles calling card,' he says. 'It has his address at the palace. He's staying near the Orangerie.'

'So Dreux has enemies other than me. I will visit him.'

Sérannes nods. 'I want to say something to you.'

She looks him in the eye. He seems mildly nervous, not a quality she has come to associate with him in their brief association.

'Yes.'

He coughs, shuffles. 'You hum enchantingly,' he says.

She laughs. Is he going sweet on her? She wouldn't have thought Sérannes capable of tender thoughts.

'Thank you,' she says. 'Do you have a knife? I have mislaid mine.'

It takes her a while to find the Orangerie. She cannot ask nobles and the servants think it a great jape to send her the wrong way. She takes a little knife from a fruit bowl, silver, curved, made for peeling. It will do.

It must be an hour, maybe more, before she finds the room and by that time the hounds are returning outside, baying up a storm.

She finds herself in a long corridor of doors, each with a card upon it. She looks out of the windows. Horses circle, men shout. A horn sounds and the men are silent, shushing the dogs.

A voice cries out. 'His Majesty has taken to his chambers. Silence will prevail in the court.'

'We need to see him, we have great news!' shouts a voice.

'Silence will prevail in the court!'

She cannot see Dreux. She takes the card from her sleeve and examines it. She does not read too well in the half light of the candles, but by comparing it to the cards on the doors she finds his name. She pushes back the door and goes within. Even for a woman who has been in Paris for months, this place stinks. Sweat, masked by the odour of rose-water. The room has huge windows full of moonlight. It is opulent but messy, clothes strewn around, a great bed unmade, shoes all across the floor. Dreux must have instructed the maids to stay away. Too mean to pay for them, more like.

She chooses to hide behind the bed. It is a long time before she hears the door handle turn.

'The king will see you tomorrow. You can present it to him then.'

'Good, Godefroy, good,' says Dreux. 'This will be greatly to our advantage.'

'Indeed.'

In comes Dreux. He is humming tunelessly to himself, some tavern air. He does not bother to change, does not bother even to take off his coat but just gets straight into bed, thumping a bag over onto her side.

Shortly he is snoring, blowing and turning like a pig in a byre.

Curious, she pulls the bag towards her. It's a drawstring affair, and she unties a bow to open it, peeking in by the light of the moon.

She screams and the next thing she knows she is in the corridor, running, having dropped the bag with Diandré's head inside it.

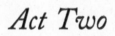

Act Two

Scene One

Blades in the Darkness

Diandré's death is like a noxious fog all around her for weeks. She fled. She fled without killing Dreux and she cannot get that fact from her mind. He was already too deep in sleep and, thank God, she was out of sight before she heard him bellowing 'What the deuce?' behind her.

At the Opéra, Arcand goes about his business with his head downcast. The death of a child is not an unusual thing, but everyone knows what happened to the boy. He had disposed of the sack, the gossips say, but he was found with a button from Bissy's coat – he never could resist a button. Dreux beheaded him on the spot with a woodsman's axe.

Julie shakes and frets when she tries to sleep. She put him in that position, she exposed him to danger. He should not have kept the button, but she didn't warn him of that. Of course he would be drawn to it.

By day, life goes on and eventually normality begins to reassert itself – the jokes, the camaraderie of the backstage crew. Julie joins in but she feels hollowed out, tired. The weather chills and the Seine freezes, and snow cuts Paris off from Versailles. She does not see Charlotte-Marie for a month, though she thinks of her often. Her hand heals, with binding and rest, though as soon as she can she practises with any of the company who will face her, stage swords standing in for the real thing. She cannot be beaten and that feels good. *Do not kid yourself, Julie*, she tells herself. *The challenges you face will be greater than those offered by a candle-boy who fancies himself a swordsman.*

The end of January comes, and it is Arcand's birthday. She eats a piece of sugar from a box he has been given, enchanted by the thrill it sends through her. The cook in Alsace had always kept that well locked away.

Then, with the first let-up in the weather, a letter and a package from Charlotte-Marie is delivered by hand at the theatre door. It arrives in a waft of perfume and the messenger asks that it be given to Miss Julie d'Aubigny. Arcand, however, intercepts it and is waving it and sniffing it when he calls her over to tell her it is for her.

'This is a good cologne,' says Arcand, sniffing the letter. 'A gentleman admirer?'

'Look at me,' says Julie, gesturing to her street boy's clothes.

'Don't run yourself down, darling,' says Arcand. 'Only the other day, I was thinking to myself "now there is a very rentable arse".'

'If I sell it, it will be for a palace,' says Julie.

'Well, yes, dear. Don't hold out too much hope is my advice.' He smiles at her but there is a glumness to him. Diandré's death has hit him hard.

'Do you want to give me my letter?'

'No.'

He reads.

'"My darling, so exciting." Ooh!' says Arcand. 'This is news.'

'Get on with it,' says Julie.

He reads: '"Everyone here is in a grand flap about the killings. Well, what do you think has happened? There is talk of a demon, sent from Hell itself to avenge the excesses of the rich. I don't know what that means, as I survive on the bare minimum a lady of my breeding could be expected to endure and am a stranger to excess in any form. They say it is a female fiend, a harpy with bare breasts, breath of fire and who carries a whip and a spear. What fun that would be, were it true!"

'"The excitement you have brought to the court is wonderful. The morning after you went, two gentlemen squabbled in the courtyard – one accusing the other of leading him into sin and bringing the Devil down upon them. Mention was made of the Bois de Boulogne, I understand – so it could be your devils, though enough ordinary fuckery goes on in those woods to send half of Paris to Hell. I could not find both their names, but one is Villepin."'

Julie swallows, crosses herself.

'Is he one of them that did for Paval?' says Arcand.

'Give me the letter or cut the comments and get on with it!'

He does. '"Anyway, you know how such squabbles finish and these gentlemen are to meet at the Tuileries Gardens by lamplight tonight to settle their score now that the roads are passable again. Duelling at the palace would be insupportable under the present circumstances. I hear it said that the offence is so severe that only death can avenge it. Well, my carriage is booked and waiting for that one, I can tell you. We'll be at the gardens for sunset at five because I want to be sure to get a good view.

'"Won't you be happy, my dear Julie, now your enemies are killing themselves?

'"Your admirer and lover Charlotte-Marie de Mazarin etc."'

Arcand lowers the letter with an expression on his face as if he doesn't know where to begin, but begin he does.

'Enemies?' he says. 'What enemies can someone like you have? Annoyances, rivals and pains in the arse, yes, but I didn't think one got enemies for less than 100 a year.'

'It's some of the people responsible for little Diandré,' says Julie.

'And what are you going to do about that?'

'Kill them, tear them apart as the hound tears the fox.' She feels Furie stir at her neck.

'Good luck trying,' says Arcand. 'And what's this "admirer and lover"? Has some great lady taken a fancy to you? Are we going to lose you to the service of a great house?'

'No,' says Julie. 'I am flirting with her, that's all.'

'You're flirting with Charlotte-Marie de Mazarin? My God, that family always had odd tastes, but I didn't think they'd extend to you. You might as well flirt with the cobra of Inde!'

He passes her the letter.

'Aren't you going to open the box? It's heavy,' he says.

She hesitates. Should she, with him there? Why not? There is a lump in her throat at the thought of what might be inside. She knows it will be nothing horrible, but the image of Diandré's head is still there in her mind.

She unties the ribbons, breaks the wax of the seal. Within are two duelling pistols, a quantity of shot and some powder, along with enough small coins to feed her for a year. 'A blade is sometimes not enough' reads a note in Charlotte-Marie's handwriting.

Arcand lets out a low whistle.

'Those things are dangerous,' he says.

'That's rather the point,' says Julie. 'Do you need me tonight?'

'I don't need anyone shot,' he says.

'Yes you do. You just don't know it.'

'We've had all sorts of stagehands and dogsbodies here,' says Arcand. 'Lazy, industrious, angry, sleepy. I've never had one who scares the shit out of me before.'

'Can I go then?'

'In my life, I've found it generally best to allow people who are armed to the fucking teeth to do as they please. Go. And do something for Diandré, if you can.'

He kisses her on the cheek, squeezes her arm. She kisses him back and then is gone.

Julie's heart is thumping like a rabbit in a bag. Her pact with the Devil is to kill all of these men. At the start of a mortal duel they are bound to have confessed. They will go to Heaven. She needs to fix that somehow.

She has hardly any time. The messenger arrived at three, the fight will begin at nightfall. She clothes herself from the theatre's supplies, becoming a young man with long black wig, moustache and beard. The sword, she unwraps from its place beneath a floorboard and heads out into the night, the pistols in her belt, charged and ready.

She aims to stop them on their way to the gardens, force some blasphemy from them and do for them there in their carriages. She knows it's a desperate plan but what other choice does she have? Quickly she goes out into the sleet-blown day to the Rue de Faubourg St-Laurent. They will have to come past there to get to the gardens; they won't risk skirting the city on the poorer roads. Already the city-sponsored lamps of the main road are lighting, the lampmen lowering them from the chains that suspend them above the street.

The duellists are unlikely to take too many people with them – duelling is illegal and, though their meeting is known in the court, they can't make too much of a display of it.

She has no idea what they will look like, but instead she calls out at every gentleman who passes, whether by sedan, carriage or horse. 'Monsieur Villepin! Monsieur Villepin!' The sky is dark, a cold wind blowing in from the east full of stinging sleet. 'Monsieur Villepin! Monsieur Villepin!'

No one replies, though some pour insults down on her, tell her to stop accosting her betters in the street. The sleet raises dead smells from the street – piss, shit, human and animal. Is the sky darkening because of the cloud or is night approaching?

She can't wait too long here. If the men kill each other it will be a disaster.

She is about to give up, when she sees three merchants. At least she thought they were merchants but then a drab cloak lifts for a second and she sees a flash of bright blue beneath. And look! One of them is carrying a bundle of torches. Such will be needed for a night-time duel!

Julie is ready. She crosses herself, wonders if that is quite the thing to do, given the spirit she serves.

The men are fifty paces away from her when she steps out.

'Gentlemen!' she cries. 'A moment of your time please!'

The horses come on at a light trot. She produces the pistol from her coat and levels it.

'Stand, sirs! I have business with you that will not wait!'

Forty paces. Thirty paces. Twenty. They are moving at a fast clip. Will she have to shoot? She needs to be sure their souls are in a state of sin before she does.

She feels her finger squeezing on the trigger. Should she shoot? Should she shoot? The men turn abruptly left down a side street and, by the time she runs to see where they have gone, it is too late, they are not there. She goes a little way down the street to see if she can see them. She cannot. She turns to see three other gentlemen followed by a doctor, his bag bouncing on the back of his fat horse, and a priest, hoity-toity and nose high on a white palfrey, sail by on the main route. They have to be the duellists.

She cracks off a shot at the priest, but the men just spur their horses forward. She never could hit anything with a pistol.

'What are you doing?' says a passing man, a burly fellow in a tanner's apron.

She produces her second pistol and shows him its muzzle. He backs away and she runs off to the gardens.

Paris is a warren and it's only now that she realises how little she knows of the city. She knows the Opéra, she knows the main routes, she has been to the Tuileries but to find them from here is another matter entirely. The wet sleet slicks the mud of the streets and her cheap shoes slip as she runs on. Every fiacre is taken, the rain forcing pedestrians off the streets and into the hired carriages.

The gardens must be east of her. She tries to run but already the streets are churning up and she has to skip around puddles and ruts. The sun breaks behind a black cloud, crusting it with light, like a glowing coal in the furnace of creation. Soon it will be dusk. Very soon.

A fiacre slows beside her to walking pace as it negotiates a particularly treacherous piece of road. There is nothing for it. She catches hold of the rail, puts a foot on the mounting step and swings herself up besides the coachman.

'Tuileries Gardens, please,' she says.

'Fuck off, I'm going to the Louvre.'

She pulls out her pistol.

'Tuileries please,' she says.

'Robbers!' shouts the coachman, and dives from his seat into the mud and shit of the street.

Julie puts the pistol under her thigh and sits on it to hold it in place, then seizes the reins and whips and cracks the horses forward. A cry from behind her and two brightly clad gentry put all thought of station and separation from the lower orders aside to leap head first from the fiacre to join the coachman in the chill shit mulch of the street.

She careers on, the horses terrified by the noise and the shouting. She still doesn't know which way she is going but she is at least going there quickly.

Flat out over the Pont Royal, the stones providing better grip than the mud, then down by the river. The horses, their panic subsiding, have remembered they have been pulling the cart for ten hours straight now and slow to a weary plod.

She stops, looks around. The river is dark and quiet. She could ask someone the way but, in a place like this, would they know? And a fiacre driver would be bound to know the direction. She would raise suspicion from anyone she asked. But she has no choice, she must ask.

'I say,' she says, imitating the poshest accent she can. No one would believe a well-bred gentleman has stolen a fiacre and, even if they did, no one would risk incurring the wrath of his friends to report him. 'You, fellow with the crutch. Which way to the Tuileries Gardens?'

He smiles up, a toothless grin.

'For half a sou I'll show you! Let me have a lift.'

'Very well,' she says.

The man hops up beside her. He stinks, that is to say, he stands out as particularly malodorous, which is quite an achievement in this city of miasmas, pongs and reeks.

'Straight ahead, sir,' he says.

She flicks the reins and the horses plod on.

The man sits beside her, simply fixing her with a grin.

'Down here,' he says. She turns. 'And down here.' She turns again.

'And down here.' She is about to turn into a dingy alley barely wide enough for the carriage when she sees the knife's dull blade in his hand.

'Give me all your money, all your clothes, that nice sword and all the money you have taken in fares,' he says. 'Didier Pelletier, thief and general bane to the gentry, pleased to make your acquaintance.' He raises his hat with his free hand.

'Take me where I want to go or I'll kill you here,' she says.

'It seems to me you're in no position to be giving orders,' he says.

She takes the pistol from under her thigh and shoves it into his face.

'Take me to the Tuileries now,' she says.

'I see you are in a position to be giving orders,' says Pelletier. 'Just the way I was going. Down here and left.'

'Drop the knife.'

'Could I keep it, if I place it at your feet?' he says. 'It's the only thing I own in the world and, on these streets, I am dead without it.'

Julie holds out her hand and he puts the knife in it.

'You can have it back when we part,' she says.

It is very dark in the back lanes. She thinks of it as a maze, but a maze is not the right description. In a maze you are sure of a way out. Here it is as if she has entered some sealed labyrinth, some contrivance of Hell with no exit, no solution to the puzzle it sets. The sun dips further and Pelletier is only a pair of eyes shining beside her in the blackness. A thought strikes her.

'I haven't died and gone to Hell, have I?' she says.

'Not as I know,' says Pelletier. 'Sometimes that thought occurs to me. Do you think that in Hell, the devils know they are devils? Perhaps they think only of the torments they suffer, never those they inflict. Are you a devil?'

'I'm fairly sure that I'm not.'

'Me too. But sometimes it's hard to be certain, isn't it?'

'Yes, it is.'

This is not Hell, because soon the road widens, and they are on the main drag along the river by the Île de la Cité.

'Down here, sir,' says Pelletier.

The horses clop on and presently they come to the walls of the garden. Here it is, then; all the carriages of the court lined up in the road against the elaborate ironwork, their footmen waiting under the flickering, swaying lights of the street and by the light of their own lanterns. Some forward-thinking souls have brought braziers and they warm their hands and stamp their feet, blowing out steam into the cold air. The footmen have adopted – or been told to adopt – the court's idea of a disguise. That is, they are wearing their own coats, not their liveries. However, they are standing next to carriages that bear the large crests of great families.

'Take the fiacre,' she says.

'No thanks,' says Pelletier. 'I know you are no driver. So news of this theft will be across the town now. This carriage is fast becoming a hearse.'

'Then attend me,' says Julie.

'For what?'

'I don't yet know. But I could do with a man who I can trust.'

'You can't trust me, sir. I am a thief and robber born.'

'Which is why I can trust you. I know what you want in life. If you know that about someone then they are your puppet. Here. Follow me for a silver ecu!'

'I would follow Satan into Hell for such a sum,' says Pelletier.

'You may yet get the chance. I am trying to prevent two gentlemen from killing each other.'

'A noble cause. Are they relatives?'

'They are my enemies.'

'So why do you want to prevent them killing each other?'

'So I can kill them myself.'

Pelletier purses his lips. 'I must improve my victim selection skills in future,' he says.

The gardens are dark, very dark. The street lights are dimmed by the trees and away in the distance, some house lanterns burn in accordance with de la Reynie's ordinance, but no one lives in the Tuileries to light a lamp. Tonight the clouds have smothered the moon, and a light rain begins to falls there. This is why the duellists choose the Tuileries. It offers great safety. Should de la Reynie's men find you there, all it would take to turn invisible would be to throw a torch to the ground. That gives her an idea, at least. She does not know how she will stop this, but she has at least something to work with.

She peers out into the darkness. A flash of light like the first spark our Lord commanded, and a torch is lit, answered by another a distance from it, as if replying to a signal. Then other torches are lit, others still as if the fire is a contagion. Faces appear in the gloom – many masked in the ballroom designs of birds, of gargoyles, or long-nosed devils, of rabbits or foxes. Her own fox nuzzles her neck. 'We may yet need you, Furie,' she says. 'We may yet need you.'

Pelletier crosses himself.

'How much would you pay if I could ensure the gentlemen would not hurt themselves?' he says, close by her ear.

'A lot.'

'Then make a distraction,' he says. 'A good one. I will work upon their blades.'

'How work?'

'Blunt them.'

'A blunt blade can still kill.'

'Not as easily, and if these gentlemen are like other, lower men, they will quickly grasp an excuse to end this exercise. Providence, something like that.'

He produces a roll from his shabby coat. In it are a variety of dull tools.

'I thought all you had in the world was a knife.'

'That and my lies,' says Pelletier. 'No matter what indignity I suffer, what trial the Lord visits upon me, they will never ever take my lies from me. Sir, work now; the gentlemen are assembling.'

'Indeed they are.'

In the torchlight she can see the men are stripping to the waist to show no foul play of padding or mail. One works quickly, nearly tearing off his clothes. The gentlemen have not yet been offered a choice of swords. But already one makes swipes with an imaginary blade. He thrusts and lunges at the air, turning circles with his fingers. He will be the one to die. His arm is stiff, she notes. The other undresses slowly, a lazy grace to his movements.

Oh no, the priest approaches. Both men kneel before him and he blesses them, making the sign of the cross above them.

Julie walks through the throng. There must be thirty or forty people there. Charlotte-Marie is behind her lady's maid, who holds a torch. She bounces on her toes, straining to see. As she passes her, Julie brushes her arm. Charlotte turns, indignant. And then, 'It's you. Oh my, it's you! This is about to become the best night of my life ever! Do something dramatic!'

'I will!' They kiss for a second and, as they break, Julie takes out her pistol and fires it into the air. The report, then the flash, draws a gasp from the crowd.

'In the name of the king and of de la Reynie his chief of police, I decree that everyone here is arrested! Seconds and surgeons, stay where you are, you are culpable in this and will hang! Spectators too will be punished.'

A wave of panic seizes the group; torches are thrown down, women gasp, and men curse.

'Damn impudence!'

Torches bob across the darkness as people run, some lights are quickly extinguished. She sees Pelletier bend to the box that contains the swords but then he vanishes.

'Who do you say you are?' says the man with the lazy movements.

'De la Reynie's man.'

'Your name, sir!'

'It is for me to ask for names!'

'I am Le Comte Villepin, this fellow I am about to kill is

Wimpffen, two generations out of the Westphalian slums, though he carries a stick of silver and tries to talk like a gentleman.'

There is a second, carrying the said stick, just like the one that fellow of the Tredecim held in the Bois de Boulogne. Wimpffen has to be one of the devils! Villepin goes on: 'Now, if I am to hang, I have a right to know the name of the man who accuses me. And where are your men? De la Reynie has sent a single slight fellow to arrest us? I think not. Normally, when he wishes to make a show, he comes with thirty or forty burly gentlemen of the Musketeers or Guards.'

'If this is the king's representative,' says Wimpffen, 'we should at least go with him. We won't hang, Villepin, you know that, the good king pardons everyone.'

'Everyone of your rank,' says the surgeon.

'We'll put in a word for you,' says Wimpffen.

'No need,' says Villepin. 'I would take a better look at this fellow.'

He strides forward but Julie is gone, away into the dark.

'Ha!' shouts Villepin. 'I knew it. He's a do-gooder! Some families lose one son to a duel and then take it as their God-given right to spoil the fun for the rest of us. He's no more from the king than the Devil himself. He's one of these pasty-faced loons who can't bear to see blood spilled. Now let's get on with it, Wimpffen. I intend to kill you and be back at dice by eleven!'

The torches are picked up, the diminished crowd slowly returns, and the men are armed.

Both test the swords.

'This is blunt!' says Villepin. 'Is yours the same, Wimpers?'

'Mine's quite sharp,' says Wimpffen.

'Sharp, my eye! That's as blunt as your dick! Jesus Christ, I don't want to die of gangrene, if I'm to die I will be run through. What's going on here. Challont-Aymavilles,

Challont-Aymavilles! You were charged with providing quality weapons.'

'I swear to you, my friend, these were sharp when I put them in the case.' The second looks mystified, tries his thumb against the tip as if he doesn't believe the swords can possibly be blunt.

'Well, have the elves got them then? Someone, lend us your swords. My God, I hope they're of a length.'

'I will, not fight with an unequal measure of blade,' says Wimpffen. 'That would not be honourable.'

'Stop looking for excuses,' says Villepin. 'I'll take the shorter one if need be.'

'Then people will say I cheated when I kill you.'

'I wouldn't worry about that,' says Villepin. 'Who in the name of the Devil blunted these?'

A cold thrill goes through Julie. 'In the name of the Devil.' That's all she needs to hear from him. Such little sins, little oaths, carry such weighty and eternal sentences.

She steps out of the darkness again.

'I blunted them,' she says. Again, a gasp. Charlotte-Marie makes a noise like a piglet escaping from the grip of a farmer.

'Marvellous! Marvellous!' she shouts.

'You?' says Villepin. 'The one who claimed to be de la Reynie's man. My God, I should report you to the chief of police for using his name in vain. Do-gooder. Men will duel. It's what they do. Where will civilisation end up if a gentleman can be insulted to his face with no redress?'

Julie watches him carefully. He is a big man, wide at the shoulder, barrel-chested. Rolling gait. A hussar or some other sort of horseman. He will be strong, no doubt, and hard to fight. He will also pride himself – as they all do – on his uncommon bravery.

'I thought you would be pleased,' says Julie, 'for I hear you are enormous cowards.'

There are fifteen people in the circle who have remained. Two duellists, four seconds to assist them, two to a man, the surgeon, the priest, Charlotte-Marie and her maid, and five onlookers who were too well connected or too drunk to worry about being caught at a duel. They all hold their breath.

'Well,' says Villepin, 'there's a thing. Sir, I am no coward. I call you out now. You have a weapon, I see. Bring my day sword, Challont-Aymavilles, we'll fix this now.'

'And you?' says Julie to Wimpffen.

'Well, we can't fight you two at a time.'

'No? I don't see why not. Unless you are too scared even to do that.' She is insouciant, contemptuous, but her heart is banging like a grenadier's knees on a bordello bed.

'You'll get in my way, Wimpffen,' says Villepin. 'Stay out of this.'

'I'd get in his way,' says Wimpffen.

'Then fight me first, alone,' says Julie.

Villepin shakes his head. 'No, no, people will say I'm a coward in not going first.'

'They'll say I'm a coward if I don't,' says Wimpffen.

'They already say you're a coward,' says Villepin.

'That's the talk that brought you here in the first place,' says Wimpffen.

'Gentlemen,' says Julie. 'Draw lots, that is the easiest way.'

'Lots! Lots! Lots!' chants Charlotte-Marie, who is clearly enjoying this immensely.

Two twigs are brought, and it is Villepin who picks first. As he picks the longer and gets the choice, Wimpffen breathes out deeply.

'After I kill this fellow, our quarrel still stands,' says Villepin.

'Absolutely,' says Wimpffen, 'Don't exercise him too much, fellow, I want him fresh for our set to.' Julie understands this is pretty much the reverse of what he actually means.

'You need a second,' says Villepin. 'Will someone stand for him?'

'I will!' says Charlotte-Marie.

'Lady . . .'

'It's a ceremonial position, isn't it? I don't have to do anything.'

'You have to fight in his place if he doesn't turn up.'

'Well he's turned up!'

'Very well, let's get on with it,' says Villepin. 'I have a fortune to win this evening, by God.'

By God. Another oath. This man has said enough to damn him.

The ground is even, though wet. Good duelling turf.

She faces Villepin and they salute, each tapping the blade to their nose, extending the arm to their opponents, the onlookers and the priest.

'You are going to die,' says Villepin. 'No man has ever bested me, nor scarcely touched me in practice. I have killed ten men here alone.'

'En garde!' says the surgeon.

Julie's mouth is dry, her grip too tight on the sword. She wills her fingers to relax.

Villepin roars at her and she steps backwards. 'What shall it be? How shall I take you? Italian-style, all back hand and sticky blade? French with a swift parry, a lightning riposte, perhaps the subtle disengage to catch out your clumsy evasion? Or shall I do it the English way and beat you to death with the pommel?'

'A higher power is on my side,' says Julie.

'God cannot help you here!'

'God is all-powerful!'

'God hasn't seen my swordplay! He wouldn't have the guts to face me!'

So God is not all-powerful. God is a coward. What torments await this braggart?

'Ready!'

'Ready!' they both say.

'Set to!'

Julie snaps forward her arm, but Villepin deflects it with a classic parry across his body, holds it in the recommended way for a fraction of a heartbeat to ensure he has caught her blade and ripostes. She parries early, deliberately early to draw the 'disengage', the flick of the fingers that cuts the tip of the blade under the opponent's parry and sends it speeding towards their heart, but Julie has set a trap for him and catches his blade on the opposite side, shoves down on it, and strikes. Villepin takes a step back, twisting away to avoid the singing point.

'Very good,' he says, 've—' He hopes, by striking half-way through a word, to surprise her but – disconcerted by her cunning – he has launched directly from too far away. In a normal duel, this would not be too much of a problem. The opponent would secure a block first, a parry to be safe, before launching their reply. Duelling is not furious, on the whole; it is careful and considered and no one wants to skewer their opponent only to find they have been skewered in return, in an undertakers' jackpot.

But Julie has been taught by the Devil, who scorns such strategies of safety. Instead of catching the incoming blade at its furthest extension, she blocks it out as Villepin's arm begins to straighten, a parry more like a punch in the face than the usual soft-handed deflection. Villepin's sword is pushed aside, its tip pointing to the heavens while hers finds its mark.

The blade enters under Villepin's right arm and, knocked aside by some bone or internal structure, exits through his left shoulder. He grabs at Julie, tries to headbutt her, but she has left her weapon in him and has her hands on his face, her thumbs in his eyes.

'What style was that?' he says as he grasps at her. 'What country fights like that?'

'The country of Hell,' she says.

She drives a knee into his guts, and he sits down heavily on the wet grass, letting out a long, exasperated sigh like a man finding out the tavern had just sold out of his favourite wine. He dies.

'Bravo! Bravo!' shouts Charlotte-Marie.

'Well,' says Wimpffen. 'I don't actually feel all that insulted, really. On reflection.'

'You have been called out,' says Julie. 'Answer to honour's call or live forever in shame.'

'Dead and honourable, living in shame,' says Wimpffen. 'A tough call.'

'You must fight,' says a man at Wimpffen's side, one of his seconds. 'Perhaps he will accept first blood.'

'Will you accept first blood?' says Wimpffen.

'It depends,' says Julie.

'On what?'

'On whether the blood is mine or yours.'

'Very droll.'

'I will make you a promise. Cut me and I will spare you.' She suspects this poltroon will run if he thinks the odds are against him. This way, he believes he has a chance. Will she spare him? Of course not. These men deal in lies, and so will have lies dealt to them.

From somewhere in the darkness there is the sound of little bells, a waft of some perfume, rare and strange, something burned and beautiful.

Julie withdraws her sword from Villepin. Wimpffen is shaking, terrified. She knows such opponents can be dangerous, her father told her so. Fear does not always paralyse. Sometimes it incenses and timid men become tigers, rushing in regardless of their own safety. It's easy to spear such clumsy fools, but easy to get speared by them too. Her father always told her 'fear the fearful!' and she is cautious here. The two salute and 'fight' is called.

Wimpffen does not rush in, though, he immediately backs away, offering the point to her, his body as far away from the tip of his sword as the length of his arm will allow, as she had done to Three Fingers in the Bois. His feet tap out an urgent beat on the slick ground and he looks like a child summoning the courage to make a big jump across a puddle. Julie knows she could just wait for him to fall over but she presses, stepping forward with her dancer's glide. He cannot back away forever. Another twenty steps and he will be through the gates of the park. Another two after that and men will damn him eternally as a coward.

He stands, tall, ill-balanced. If these gentlemen pay for fencing lessons, this one should sack his master. She advances and then she is down. The ground is slippy, the night dark and her foot has caught some divot or hole and sent her stumbling. Immediately he advances and lunges, but she turns aside, the blade snagging on her arm.

'First blood!' shouts Wimpffen. 'First blood!' He waves his sword aloft, dancing with a dexterity entirely absent when he was fighting.

'First blood,' says a second.

'Hold on a bally moment!' says Charlotte-Marie.

She offers her hand to Julie and Julie accepts it, and is lifted to her feet. Charlotte-Marie inspects the cut in Julie's coat. 'No blood,' she says.

'What?' says Wimpffens's second.

'No blood at all. The blade has injured the cloth but not the flesh.'

Julie stands tall, kisses Charlotte-Marie. 'Again,' she says.

They face and this time, emboldened, Wimpffen comes on in fury, his sword out like a lance. She could kill him in any one of many ways now – a sweep of the wrist up to her face to deflect his blade and allow him to impale himself on hers, a circular parry to catch his blade and then a riposte to run him through, a downwards flick of the fingers to knock his blade aside and a step in to pierce him at close distance.

She opts for the last and, though she catches his blade to perfection and steps in swiftly, the point of her sword is allowed to drift wide and she finishes the move with a hefty knee to the nuts. She needs something from him before he dies.

Wimpffen goes down into the mud and she is on him, her blade at his heart, shoved just a fingernail into the flesh. He will not easily brush that point aside.

He cries out and begs mercy.

'My God, Wimpffen, what sort of dog are you?' says his second.

'One who would live! Oh sir, I beg you consider your hurt avenged, I am truly sorry.'

'Do you know me?'

'No.'

'Do you know which duke I serve?'

'No! Is it de Maurel? I never fucked his daughter, nor even dallied with her, though I beat her maid, I confess!'

'It is the Duke of Hell. Lucifer, brightest of angels!'

'Oh God. No, literally, who do you serve?'

'I am the Devil's! Now I will spare you if you renounce God.'

'You can't do that, Wimpffen,' says the priest.

'Why not? I can unrenounce him in the morning. You can see to that.'

'That will be an expensive procedure,' says the priest.

'I can pay, I can pay!'

'Then renounce him!' says Julie. 'Accept Lucifer as your master and beg to be taken to Hell.'

'Can't I just say "renounce"?' says Wimpffen.

'Accept Lucifer!' She jabs the tip in a little more.

Wimpffen swallows. 'I renounce God,' he says. 'And I accept Lucifer as my master!'

Julie pushes, feels a brief resistance and then the blade goes in easy, straight through his heart.

'For Paval!' she says.

The seconds cry out, Charlotte-Marie squeals in delight, others curse her.

'You lied!' says a second.

'What the fuck, I work for the Devil, what did you expect?'

'You must die for that! It is a matter of honour!'

'Grow up,' says Julie. 'That one wouldn't have known honour if it had bit him on the arse.'

The tinkling of bells, the smell of burned air. She is there. Lucifer, the bright one, in the silvered silks, brocade and pearls sparkling on the breeches above those fine black hooves. The seconds are still, as if stone. Charlotte-Marie stands enraptured, the other onlookers too. There are only two people moving, and they are dead. The souls of Villepin and Wimpffen stand up from their bodies.

The Devil smiles at them both. They smile back, nervously.

'I'm dead, am I?' says Villepin.

'As Adam,' says Lucifer.

'Right. Very well. Well, every difficulty brings opportunity. You are the Devil, are you not?'

'I am.'

'Well, let me say that I am an experienced courtier, used to meeting any and all needs of the reigning monarch. I am to be carried to Hell?'

'Yes.'

'I would, then, like to negotiate a privileged position for myself therein. I take it there are better facilities for the better sort? Just as in prison, you don't expect a gentleman to do without as you would a pauper. There will be a writing desk? I will be allowed servants? To organise my own food?'

'You will have everything,' says Lucifer. 'Hell will be a Heaven for you. Why, you said yourself God would be scared to face you and I am scared of you now. I dare not heap punishments on one so mighty.'

'Well,' says Villepin, pulling at the lapels of his coat, 'I should say so. Learn to do as you're told, Devil, and we shall get on famously.'

Now Wimpffen feels bolder.

'Yes, Devil, kneel to your betters.'

'I don't have a very good history when it comes to that. But I shall try, my lords, I shall try. I shall kneel to you both and, when I tire of kneeling, others shall do it for me.'

'Very good!' says Wimpffen. 'That's a fellow!'

The Devil gestures with a whip of the wrist and a circle of primroses springs up on the grass, glowing in the torchlit gloom.

'Away,' they say and both souls tumble into the circle, down into flashes of fire.

Lucifer smiles.

'Oh, Julie. How I shall kneel before those gentlemen. To bite their bollocks until I tire of their screams, and then to have a fish devil, all spines and teeth, take over. When they beg for help, I shall say the whole of Hell is too scared of them to come near. We shall have other torments too.'

Julie bows.

'Two more lessons,' she says.

'Well, stay on your feet is one of them,' says Lucifer.

'That is not a true lesson.'

'No. But let me offer you a false one. The use of the subtle foot that says it steps forward when really it steps back. The foot that shrieks "I attack!" as it prepares for defence, the foot that say, "I defend!" in the instant that it launches an attack.'

'Show me this foot,' says Julie.

So the Devil does, hooves sucking the wet ground but their steps still light and easy. Half forward, half back, long and short, fast and slow. Julie follows, sometimes slipping, sometimes standing. After hours – it must be hours – the Devil is satisfied that she has it. Still it is night. Still the torches burn, but with a steady light in the hands of the unmoving seconds. Time, it appears, is still.

Then the second lesson follows: the beat upon the opponent's blade that knocks it aside, but any fencing master knows that. Here the Devil teaches her to slide the beat in, not rap it, to flick the sword beneath the enemy's, to beat on the offside and draw a response, opening the line to the heart. Thirteen ways can such a beat be done, and they do not rest until Julie, arm aching, mind tired, has them all.

'Thank you,' says Julie.

'Thank you,' says Lucifer. 'You have brought me souls.'

'I will bring you more.'

'Perhaps. But perhaps not.'

'Why not?'

'Why look, there is one of your assailants there. Do you not recognise him, the one who came with Wimpffen? Did you not notice how he scissored his lips?'

'I will kill him,' she says.

'You will not.'

'Why not?'

'I think you both have an appointment with Mssr de la Reynie.' The Devil clicks their fingers, then Charlotte-Marie is on her, hugging and kissing her, the seconds are cursing her, the onlookers screaming murder.

A pistol shot in the dark. Torches everywhere.

'Duellists!' shouts a voice. 'Surrender to the King's Guard! You'll hang for this!'

'Run!' says Charlotte-Marie but Julie is spent. While others have lived but a breath, she has trained and fought for hours with the most exacting master in the world.

The seconds bolt, the onlookers rout. The guards rush past Charlotte-Marie and Julie – weary, exhausted, worn out – is seized, her sword still limp in her hand.

Scene Two

To Hit and Not Be Hit

Rough hands are on her, Charlotte-Marie is screaming, cursing the men that have come to carry Julie away. These men will not touch Charlotte-Marie, of course; she is too high born, too well dressed, and a woman at that. Duelling is men's business, and it is men who must pay when they transgress the king's laws.

'By order of His Majesty the most divine, splendid and radiant Louis, you are hereby arrested on the most grievous charge of duelling in defiance of the strict order of the most magnificent Louis, who stands in the place of God.'

They grab her sword, pull her arms, carry her to a waiting carriage. This is no noble's conveyance, nor even a fiacre, but an open-backed affair of the sort that might be used to carry bales of straw or faggots of wood. She is lifted up and her legs kicked from under her, made to sit down heavily by two stout fellows with cudgels. The other man, the second for Wimpffen, is plonked beside her.

'Please keep away from me,' he says. 'I am Seigneur Challont-Aymaville, you have perhaps heard of me. We are of vastly different social spheres and it is right you keep your distance.' That way of speaking, the lips scissoring out the words, trimming each to length.

She stares at him.

169

'Remember me?' she says.

'No,' he says. 'Who are you?'

'I will jog your memory before I kill you,' she says.

He snorts. 'You're not of the correct social rank to kill me. Villepin should have declined to duel you.'

'I won't duel you. I'll just cut your throat,' she says.

The man turns away from her. 'Tiresome person,' he says.

Charlotte-Marie is calling after her. 'Julie! Julie!'

'My darling,' says Julie, and she feels the words now as she says them.

'Julie?' says Challont-Aymaville. 'You are a woman?'

'I am.'

'Oh my, you're not the harpy that got loose in the garden?'

Julie snarls at him and he recoils.

'What's your name?' Charlotte-Marie shouts at the man who appears to be in charge, a captain in the Cardinal's Guard by the look of him. 'My family founded your regiment. You tell me your name because you're going to be out on your ear by tomorrow, I've never known such an outrage.'

'Orders of the king, ma'am,' says the captain. 'Nothing I can do about it.'

'We'll see, we'll see!' says Charlotte-Marie but then her maid has her hand on her arm, and she is led back to her carriage.

Julie loves her then, as she walks away. All love is fleeting, she knows, and it is dear because it is fleeting. Julie is only a toy to Charlotte-Marie, a dear and favourite toy but that is all. Julie knows that in a season, in a year, Charlotte-Marie will tire of her. Even now she is walking back to the fine carriage, to the gilded life at Versailles, as Julie is led to prison and to trial. Of course, the palace is where Charlotte-Marie is the most use – to speak to her family, to her friends and to get Julie released. But there is something more meaningful in her departure. Charlotte-Marie will not come screaming after the carriage, she will not throw herself in front of the horses. She loves Julie but she does not need her, and Julie feels warm and glad in that. It is enough in this world to look after yourself. To take on a true lover, someone who cannot live if you do not live, someone who feels every blow, every disappointment for you, is too much. Her father was like that, back in the south, bringing her up as bold and tough as any boy. He diminished when she said she was leaving to seek her fortune, she saw him fade. In the month it took her to prepare to travel, he became a smaller man. He could not have walked away. But Charlotte-Marie can. To be loved completely by someone is to hurt them. So how can you want that?

'Goodbye, Charlotte-Marie,' she says. 'I love you for not loving me. Though I will take your infatuation.'

Such sad thoughts. She guesses she will die. She is without station in life. Charlotte-Marie's father will see her as dangerous – not for the kisses she offers her daughter but for the situation of her birth. How can a girl like Charlotte-Marie give her heart to a guttersnipe?

A man walks before them with a torch, another behind and she wonders again if she has died, if this is Lucifer's procession to Hell.

But no, she is amazed that, through the night-black streets, in the golden orb of light in which she travels, she begins to recognise where she is going. They have pulled onto the wide thoroughfare of the Rue St Honoré where the houses are rich and opulent enough to obey the law and keep a light burning all night so that, in combination with the street lights, it might almost be day.

What an odd place. The world is changing, making itself anew, outgrowing nature and the sun to make its own light. It does not seem quite holy, it seems to defy God. Let light be made, said the Lord, and light was made. Now man is doing the same and it seems too easy. Where is God? Where is God? Behind her, the tinkle of bells, behind her a figure walks upright on goat's hooves, in its own inner light, invisible to all else. She feels the Devil's hunger like a breath on her neck.

One of the men with the cudgels has her sword.

'That's mine,' she says.

'Got you into enough trouble already, I'd say.'

'You cannot take a gentleman's sword. Even if he is a prisoner.'

'And yet I have.'

She looks up, sees the Palais Royal, Richelieu's old palace, pale, wide and magnificent. It dominates the street. The Opéra on the east wing is the nearest she has to home in Paris. 'Are we going to the Opéra?' she says.

The man laughs.

'No, sir, nor nowhere like it.'

They pass by the east wing and go on to the west, which blazes with the light of candles like a seam of gold in the dull black rock of the night sky.

The horses pull up and there is conversation between the men.

'You're sure it's here, sir?' says a guardsman.

'King's got ambassadors from every corner of the world up at Versailles,' says the captain.

'Has he?'

'Probably. Do you want to travel that far? Monsieur's here and as good as the king in this. Besides, Louis pardons everybody. I want a hanging. Duelling's got to stop. It's killing more officers than a division of English horse.'

'I suppose so. Let's get it over with, then.'

She is taken down from the cart. Her hands are not tied, nor anything so melodramatic, though the two guardsmen stand at her shoulder, another in front and one behind.

The Devil insinuates themselves between them, unnoticed

by the men.

'Oh, Julie, I believe I will have you soon. I do so love you.'

She shivers.

'I am not dead yet.'

'Though soon you will be, and I will await you. To kiss you with a tongue of fire on a bed of thorns. To hold you in my freezing arms on the ice-black plain of Gehenna. Or to take you through the falls of blood and encase you in the great wall of living flesh.'

'Yeah, half time,' says Julie. 'Let's see how this pans out, shall we?'

'What are you on about?' says a guardsman.

'Tell him his wife lies twice weekly with the wine seller by the Pont Neuf.'

'Cause your own mischief and woe,' says Julie. 'I've done enough for you already.'

'You have that,' says the Devil and withdraws.

She is led alongside Challont-Aymavilles who, she notices, has taken the trouble to pick up the fallen Wimpffen's silver stick. They move through splendid corridors of scarlet and gold, past paintings and sculptures, rich cabinets, plate cups. She wishes she had the chance to pocket some of this loot. Any one of the vases, she thinks, could pay Paval's mother's rent for the next forty years. And more.

Finally they come to a short, wide corridor. Here, chairs line the walls and all the guards sit, though she is still made to stand. Challont-Aymavilles is allowed to sit, as befits his rank. A footman in a bright blue coat takes a message and they are told they are lucky, Monsieur has had a cancellation and so can see them very shortly – no more than two or three hours, which the captain assures them is a blink compared to some waits for royalty.

She is thirsty, tired and her arm is heavy. The gold and red of the walls swim before her eyes.

She is back in the courtyard in Alsace, her father teaching her his tricks with the sword. The beat, the press, the graze, the use of the dagger and the back hand. He could not fence very well himself – he lacked timing, distance, patience, an eye – but he showed her well enough. She sways and in her mind, she is swaying with that soft mountain breeze that played through the days of her youth, she is swaying, swaying. A hand steadies her, a voice says 'come' and then she is marched through the open doors to meet Monsieur in his reception chamber.

'Bow before his Royal Highness, Philippe, Duke of Orléans, Duke of Valois and of Chartres, Lord of Montagris and Prince of the realm!'

Julie has seen opulence before – she has been to Versailles – but this room overshadows even that magnificent palace. Every surface shines gold and silver, rich tapestries woven through with gold thread shimmer like waterfalls on the walls, busts and statuettes, lampstands and candleholders gleam, while above, a chandelier of bright gold shines with the light of a hundred candles, sparkling like an angel's cloud chariot.

At the centre of the room, surrounded by handsome young men who posture and preen, stands a very tall and imposing woman. She wears a long wide skirt, wide as a cathedral bell. It is edged with gold and lace. Her sleeves are wide and adorned with ribbons, her bodice pulled tight to her corseted waist. Her hair is fashionably short and high, but it is her décolletage that really takes the eye. Her plunging neckline reveals what is very clearly a hairy chest.

Everyone bows low to her, including Julie, and one of the delicate young men whispers in her ear.

He then turns to the captain and says, 'What do you want?'

The captain, who still has his eyes on the floor, says:

'Begging Your Highness's pardon, we have apprehended

these men duelling in the Tuileries Gardens. This one was a combatant, the other a second.'

Now the tall lady does speak and, when she does, it is with the clear and commanding voice of a man. She speaks like a general addressing his troops.

'Duelling. I love duelling. Any dead?' He says the word 'dead' like a hungry man might say 'soup'.

'This man has killed two – the Comte Villepin and the Seigneur Wimpffen.'

'You confirm that?' says the lady. 'Two of them. Villepin and Wimpffen?'

'Two,' says Julie. 'And those were their names.'

'Indeed, Your Highness,' says Challont-Aymavilles. 'Both good friends of mine, gentlemen of taste who were marked for great things.'

'Neither of them bad with the blade, both social climbing bores,' says the lady, who Julie now realises must be Monsieur, the king's brother. He is a great soldier, a father of many children, a leader of men. She has heard the rumours that he dresses as a woman but can hardly find that scandalous, given her own disguise as a man.

Monsieur goes on. 'I wish I could duel. They won't let me. I'd pick fights all day long if they did. Can't have the king's brother getting skewered though, can we? Your coat looks a little rum, fellow. Are you the social equal of the men you killed?'

Julie realises he is addressing her.

'No, sir,' she says. 'I am not.'

'Oh God, that's awful,' says Monsieur. 'Well, you should hang. You know the law, fellow, my brother has stated it clearly. Men who duel must be hanged. Now, we can make an accommodation if a person of rank steps out of line, reputation must be defended and all that, but killing one's betters, not on, old chap, not on, even if it is on the field of honour.

You, Shallot-Potatovilles, what's your name?'

'Challont-Aymavilles, sir.'

'Oh yes. You'll have to do a little time in prison. For appearance's sake. We can't be killing our fine gentlemen, but we can't let them off without censure either. You, low fellow,' he addresses Julie, 'any reason I should let you off?'

'The law is clear,' says Julie. 'Men must hang for duelling.' Monsieur smiles. 'Er, it's normal to beg for forgiveness, to touch upon my tender heart. I know I said I would hang you, but I might let you off if you can make me laugh or cry, or something.'

'Men must hang for duelling,' says Julie.

'That's not a particularly robust defence,' says Monsieur.

'It would not be, sir,' says Julie. 'Were I a man.'

Monsieur smiles, looks at her quizzically, his head slightly to one side.

'You have a beard,' he says.

'Does the glass you have in your hand contain strong drink?'

'I should say so,' he says.

'May I take it? Not to drink but to show you what might astound you?'

'I'm all for being astounded,' says Monsieur.

He passes the glass to a handsome young man, who passes it to another, who passes it to another and so on, until it is left on a table for a servant to pick up and pass to her.

It is a strong drink, some sort of spirit like they use for removing glue in the theatre she thinks, though she has tasted very little of such things.

She dabs her sleeve into the drink, to the disgust of most of the courtiers, and rubs it against her beard. The gum that has been securing it is dissolved and the hair comes away easily. She washes her face in the drink to pull away most of the disguise.

'Well, I'll be buggered,' says a courtier.

'Inevitably and soon,' says someone else and a polite laugh goes through the room.

Monsieur approaches her, looks at her face.

'You could be a boy,' he says.

'Do I need to prove it to you?' she says, putting her hand to the front of her shirt as if to lift it.

'Won't be necessary,' says Monsieur. He laughs. 'So how did you come to be fighting men in the king's gardens?'

'They insulted me, they killed someone I love.'

'My word,' says Monsieur. And then, 'I don't believe it.'

The room is quiet. No one dare ask him what exactly he doesn't believe. Monsieur expands anyway.

'I don't believe a woman can kill a man in a duel, let alone two men. Are you passing off your own work as hers, Challont-Aymavilles?'

'Oh no, sir, she killed them,' says Challont-Aymavilles.

'She definitely did, sir,' says the captain. 'Our spies observed it.'

The silence now is profound.

'Monsieur does not believe it; therefore it is not believable and could not have happened,' says a handsome young man. 'That is as certain a fact as they come.'

'The torchlight, captain, could there not have been some question of who dealt the blows, given the lack of clear vision?' says another courtier.

Monsieur waves his hand in mild dismissal.

'We will see,' he says. 'Do you have this, person, this woman's sword?'

The captain clicks his fingers and it is brought for him.

Monsieur inspects it. 'A good blade,' he says. 'Jacques, run out and get a sword.'

A handsome young man puts his hand to his chest in shock.

He then addresses another young man, who addresses another, who addresses another, who addresses a servant. The servant goes out and returns with the sword, waiting at the door.

'Bring it in, man!' says Monsieur.

'I cannot bring a weapon into the presence of Monsieur,' says the servant.

'I say you can. Bring it in, you fool.'

The man bows and holds forward the sword in two hands, as far away from his body as he can, as if he fears it might bite him.

It ascends the social structure, passed from hand to hand until Monsieur finally takes the blade.

'Right,' he says. 'Let's set to.'

'No, Monsieur, no no no no!' Now a more serious-looking man steps from the rear of the room. He is wearing a coat so encrusted with emeralds and gold braid that she wonders if he has trouble moving any faster than his crabby, creaking progress across the floor.

'You are not my keeper, Aubespine,' says Monsieur.

'I am your protector, and the protector of the realm,' says Aubespine. 'You cannot duel, Monsieur. If you are killed, well . . .'

Monsieur lets out a short laugh.

'You think I can't beat a woman?' he says.

Aubespine reddens, shrugs.

'You think I might be in danger, from a woman!' he says.

'Accidents happen, sir.'

Monsieur sniffs. 'Not to extraordinary men,' he says. 'I managed to avoid accidents routing the Prince of Orange at Cassel, didn't I? There were a few fellows on the Dutch side fairly keen to make sure I had one, I can tell you. Keep the doors open, we will fight the length of the room and hall.'

Aubespine has the look of a man trapped in a burning

building who cannot locate the door. 'At least let me fetch some foils, sir, stops to blunt the blades.'

Monsieur rolls his eyes. 'I won't get hurt and this person was due to hang anyway, technicalities of sex aside, so stop worrying, Aubespine.'

'The problem is that she's already due to hang, sir. We can't hang her twice if she runs you through.'

Now Monsieur is angry. He reddens and he stamps. 'I told you, you damned fool, there's no chance on earth of that happening!'

'But the carpet, sir, when you kill her.'

'The cleaning arrangements of the court are no fit subject for gentlemen!' says Monsieur.

Aubespine bows and withdraws, though as he does, he brushes past Julie.

'Careful,' he whispers. 'Death comes easier at the point of a sword than it does on the torturer's rack.'

The room is cleared of furniture, statuettes, flowers and vases, though not of people. The tafettaed, silked, laced, cloaked, perfumed, primped throng presses to the walls to allow them space but so many people are there that there is no more than a strip of carpet down the centre of the room in which she can fence. Julie is reminded of Daniel in the lions' den though, unlike Daniel, she is not one for stoic endurance and these are gaudy and posturing lions. Lions nonetheless. They have teeth sharper than any beast, she is sure.

Monsieur salutes them all with his blade and comes en garde. It is hard to see his feet beneath his skirt, and when he steps forwards it is as if he glides on ice. Immediately he advances, and she can see his arm is stiff. This, maybe, is the product of the sort of fencing education where the master is afraid to tell you that you have it wrong and, when you spar, your competitors are afraid to beat you. He moves his arm like he

179

is stirring porridge, worse, no one ever stirred porridge with the elbow locked like that. She has heard he is a fierce warrior but it's one thing to cleave a man's head in two with a sabre on the battlefield and quite another to daintily pick apart the defence of a skilled opponent with a small sword – light as a needle and responsive to every twitch of the fingers.

She quickly does the calculations in her mind – she cannot win, cannot possibly cut the king's brother. But she cannot lose. Monsieur, for all his humour and his pretty dress, intends to put a blade in her guts. Or if he does not intend to, he looks as if he may achieve it through clumsiness. So she must lose but lose in a way that is really winning.

He takes two slow steps down the carpet and is within range. She thinks of stepping back – such a movement might be more allowable to a woman, who will not be accused of cowardice – but decides not. She will fight conventionally, standing her ground. She catches the end of his blade near the hilt of her sword, deflecting it aside, and offers him a slow riposte – driving the tip of her sword back towards his rear shoulder, asking for the parry.

He really has no guile, he leaps upon her riposte, blocking it out himself just as she knew he would. It would be easy to twitch her fingers, send her blade under his and rip a hole in his arm or even to go through to his heart. She restrains herself and gasps as if she cannot believe the speed of Monsieur's arm and flies back into her own parry. He tries to deceive her blade, holding back for an instant but she is wise to that, catching the sword with a second movement across her body. She makes a mistake, quite deliberately, leaving the parry a little short of where it needs to be, inviting him to renew his attack, push through and snick her tunic. He is too slow to realise the opportunity and instead pulls back his arm. If he were not the king's brother, he would now be dead; the tip of her sword would have followed his retreating arm as if pulled in by magnetic attraction and killed him where he stood.

He breathes heavily.

'This woman can fight, I give her that!'

He lumbers at her again, moving his arm far after his body, punching in the blade rather than allowing the tip to draw him towards his opponent. She simply leans aside, for now it is time to show him and the court where he stands. She catches his advancing blade, and sweeps it low to attack at his skirts. His stance is so wide that his legs can be easily missed. She stabs into the cloth, lacerates it and withdraws.

'Ah, Lord Jesus!' cries Aubespine.

'Shut your gateau hole, Aubers!' shouts Monsieur.

Monsieur tries again, this time trying a clumsy, old-fashioned rapier cut to her head. She blocks it high and answers with a flick to dislodge her opponent's tiara. 'Bravo! Bravo!' shouts the king's brother.

'Aie, aie, aie!' wails Aubespine as the crowd gasps.

Another lunge, another and another, each more predictable than the last. He makes every mistake you can make – he withdraws the arm before thrusting, sending her a signal he is about to attack; he lifts the point sending her another signal; he actually cries 'have at you!' and then, unbelievably, has at her. How is she going to lose to this lumbering oaf without allowing him to kill her? She has an idea. Now she does start backing away towards the doors at the end of the hall. If she can get to them, she may be able to run for it. She is offering nothing by way of attack now, just stepping back, parrying, stepping, parrying, stepping, allowing the clodhopping prince to come on and on. Finally she reaches the doors, but she glances behind her to see they have been bolted from the inside. She can't reach down to undo them without being run through.

Still he comes with a 'hoo!' and a 'haaa!' and a 'now then!'

How to lose, how to lose? She could beat this idiot with no weapon at all. Now there's an idea. He has her against the door now, her back foot pressed against the wood. He sweeps up her blade with his and, though it would be easy to slip off it and impale him, she allows him to take her sword from her hand, sending it spinning across the room.

'Ha!' he shouts and lunges hard for her chest, but she has learned the Devil's Esquive and pivots on her front foot, turning her body sideways to allow the blade to pass harmlessly past her chest and stick hard into the door, where it lodges as firmly as the sword in Arthur's stone.

Monsieur, who will never be king, pulls at it for an instant, finds it stuck, and then nods, wags his finger at her.

'Showed you a thing or two, didn't I, my girl? Showed you a thing or two.'

She bows deeply as he bows to the rest of the room, a showman milking his applause.

'You, Shallot-Amiables,' he says to Challont-Aymavilles. 'Three months at Le Châtelet. Middling rooms, though you can pay for more comfort. Let that be a lesson to you.'

Challont-Aymavilles bows and crosses himself, tries to make it look as though this punishment hurts. As yet he has no idea of the fees the jailers charge for the most basic of commodities, or he might be a little more genuine in his distress.

'You,' says Monsieur to Julie. 'A woman fighting, how perfectly hilarious. How very hilarious. You killed two. Even funnier!'

The room erupts into laughter.

'You are forgiven,' he says. 'Pardoned, though as you say there is no offence to answer, you being a woman. Murder, I suppose, might be seen as grave, but can it be called murder if a woman kills a man with a sword? Or can it be seen as lack of manliness on his part, his fault, his shame?'

Everyone in the room makes a sort of low braying noise.

They don't know how the king is going to answer his rhetorical question but want to make the sort of sound that shows they agree with whatever the answer is going to be.

A commotion at the door, shouting and banging.

'Not invited? I'll give you not invited, you son of a tanner's piss collector! My father is the Marshal of France! I'm my own fucking invitation!' It's Charlotte-Marie's voice.

She piles into the room, followed by her train of servants and strides up to Monsieur.

'Hello, Philippe,' she says to Monsieur. 'Favour to ask. I'm afraid one of my gentleman friends has been caught in a spot of bother in the Tuileries. I think he has been taken here and . . . Julie!'

Her face lights up and she throws her arms around Julie, kissing her madly.

Monsieur claps with delight.

'This is your gentleman?' he says, gesturing to Julie.

'Indeed yes. Oh, highness.' She offers a quick curtsey.

'This gets better and better. I had heard the rumours, you naughty thing! Tonight you will join us while we dance,' says Monsieur. 'You will be the gentleman and I the lady! Music, oh God, let there be music! What is your name, my dear, your name?'

'Julie d'Aubigny,' she says. 'Your devoted servant, sir.'

'Watch out, gentlemen,' says Monsieur. 'Mind your manners around her. She is a tigress. Two dead in duels and only a prince of the realm able to contain her. A tigress. Growl!'

Everyone claps, everyone laughs, all except one.

A gentleman steps forward, tall, spare, dressed in a coat of primrose, flapping a pristine white handkerchief. Is this a devil, a member of the Tredecim?

'I think I know this woman, sir,' he says. She feels her

mouth go dry. This is one of them, then. The sword she lost to Monsieur is still on the floor. Would it be a breach of court etiquette to run him through on the spot?

'Oh yes?'

'Yes. She has made certain threats against certain gentlemen.'

'Has she, by God?'

'Yes, sir. I have my suspicions that she might be the monster of Versailles who struck at Christmas!'

'What?' says Monsieur. 'Do you have elephant-taming skills, d'Aubigny?'

'I do not, sir.'

'No, thought not.'

The man coughs, dainty. 'If you might hand her over to us, sir, we could question her to ascertain the truth.'

The prince snorts.

'And I dare say we would never hear from her again. Listen, what is your name?'

The man blanches. This is as hard a slap as Monsieur can deliver.

'Du Bellay,' he says. 'Marquis de—'

'Never mind where,' says Monsieur. 'Look, Doubleday, or whatever your name is, this woman amuses me. If certain gentlemen have had certain threats issued, then those gentlemen should respond by duelling.'

'It would not be seemly to duel with a person of low rank!'

'Not seemly. Not seemly! No real fun is seemly. What are you, Du Bellay, a lawyer's country wife? They can duel her. It'll be funny.'

Du Bellay smiles but his eyes are narrow.

'As you say, sir.'

'Oh, by the way, Du Bellay,' says Monsieur. 'This person has my protection now. Those who move against her move against me.'

Julie imagines Du Bellay as a little plaster figure, its body crumbling away to the ground, its smile left hanging in the air.

'Very good, sir,' he says.

'Oh, I doubt she's that,' says Monsieur and the court erupts into laughter as Du Bellay backs from the room. Charlotte-Marie takes her hand and, light with the thrill of survival, with the acclaim of Monsieur, with the love of Charlotte-Marie, she skips beside her to the dance.

Scene Three

A Fugitive Spirit

It is a washed out, pale dawn that greets her as she leaves the dance. Two of her enemies are near. Du Bellay – who must be one of them if his interest in her is anything to go by – and Challont-Aymavilles, scissor mouth. She knows where the second will be very soon – in Le Châtelet, and prison. Du Bellay, she doesn't know. But she can find out.

She takes out her card from the bandage in her sleeve where she also keeps the little knife she took from Versailles and scratches off Silver Stick and Villepin.

Charlotte-Marie is at her side, her carriage waiting.

'Come with me,' she says.

'I have work at the Opéra.' Julie is dog-tired, and a nearby bed is very appealing, whatever the charms of Charlotte-Marie.

'Work . . .' says Charlotte-Marie, rolling the word around her mouth as if it were a sweetmeat she had never tasted before. 'You have no need of that now.'

'I have responsibilities.'

'Responsibilities . . .' says Charlotte-Marie, wincing as if she had just reached the unpleasantly bitter centre of the afore-mentioned sweetmeat.

'You wouldn't understand.'

Charlotte-Marie smiles.

'Can you drive a carriage?'

'Yes, can't you?'

'Of course not, you silly thing. Well then, it is fixed. You will return to my house on the Île de la Cité with me. I'll send my carriage driver to do your work.'

'Will he mind?'

Charlotte-Marie looks genuinely puzzled.

'What do you mean, mind?'

'Well, won't he object?'

'You're not making any sense,' says Charlotte-Marie. 'He's a servant. He serves. He doesn't object or mind. You don't get to object or mind until you're at least a seigneur and not even then if you know what's good for you.'

'I should go back. I'm safer as a boy at the Opéra than I am as myself at your house.'

It's cold, and when Charlotte-Marie embraces her, it feels as if she is falling into the warmest, most comfortable bed. She knows too that, should she go with Charlotte-Marie, she really will be falling into the warmest, most comfortable bed she has ever known.

Julie will not go with her, though. She must do her own work, continue her own life, remember who she is. And sleep, she must sleep.

'You will call on me,' says Charlotte-Marie.

'Of course.'

They kiss deeply.

'I want you,' says Charlotte-Marie.

'And it is my dearest wish you should have me. I will come to you as soon as I can.'

'Do.' They part, Charlotte-Marie trailing her fingers across Julie's hand. Julie waves her goodbye as her carriage slips into the dawn.

Now she knows she must hurry, though she has only a short way to go to her cot at the Opéra. Her limbs are heavy, her eyes tired. The stress of two duels has leached the fire from her blood and she is weary and spent.

She walks towards the Opéra wing of the palace and tries a little air.

'The bonds of marriage terrify me,
I fear the most tender snares.
A heart becomes so unhappy
When freedom runs away!'

She is shocked by her voice. It is stronger, not good, still not good but much stronger. The taste of her enemies' blood comes back to her. Yes, that is it, that is what is curing her – the elixir of revenge. La Moreau was right!

She makes her way around the building to the darkened rear. There is something wrong with the shadows to the side of her left eye. She turns to see a familiar figure stepping out of the darkness not three paces from her. Dreux – the cock-eyed pistolero from Versailles! Diandré's killer! Someone at the dance must have got a message to him.

This time, though, he carries no gun. In his hand is a sliver of steel – a smallsword flashing in the torchlight of the palace.

'By Jesus, you will face me alone,' he says. 'I am . . .' He seems to be working his way towards a long speech of triumph. It is interrupted only momentarily by his death. 'Weary of your games and your murders,' he says. 'Great men like me will not be bested by a mere girl. Great men . . . What's that?'

He is looking down at a heap of fine clothes that lie on the ground. Within this heap there is something that fascinates him, by the look of it. He tries to move the clothes with his foot, but his foot goes straight through the clothes as if they weren't there.

It is then that Julie sees the truth of his situation dawn on him. The heap of clothes contains his own body and the reason his foot has passed through them is that he is now a ghost.

Julie has not waited for him to finish his fine speech but slides the little knife from her sleeve and stabs him hard in the neck, cutting the ghost from him with a single blow. She licks the blood from her hand.

His ghost stands before her, incredulous.

'By Jesus! You've killed me!'

'It would appear so. A pity it was so quick. For Diandré's life!'

'Who?'

'The boy you killed!'

Vengeance feels good to her, like a warm bed on a cold day, something she can luxuriate and revel in. Where is Lucifer? She wants this piece of shit taken to Hell for his crimes.

'He had Bissy's button! He was a thief, if not a killer!'

'And the penalty for that is death? Even if what you say were true, monsieur, a boy's life is worth more than the price of a coat's button.'

'Not one of Bissy's buttons, they were exquisite!' he says, flatly. She can see he genuinely means it. Where are the bells? Where is the heavy air? Where is the Devil?

She stoops to his body, removes his purse, his rings. She will get this to Diandré's mother. It will feed her for the rest of her life. Before that, there are practical concerns. Can she leave his body here? She should cart him to the river. The streets are still empty, it is so early, so cold.

'Why are you doing this? Is it true you serve the Devil?'

'I have a bargain with Lucifer.'

'A bargain?'

'Yes, to kill each of the Black Tredecim before All Hallows' Eve. To send each of you evil men to Hell, which is where you're going, you ugly and gluttonous man.'

She pulls him by his coat towards the river, dragging him across the cobbles of the palace and then the dirt of the street. His ghost walks beside her, waving his arms and shouting:

'Ha! I was shriven not ten minutes before I came here by my priest Father Andrew of Sainte-Marie! What are the chances? I'm going to Heaven! I'm going to Heaven!'

'Lucifer! Lucifer! Come and collect your spoils!' she shouts.

The sound of little bells, the smell of primroses. She gets the body level with the river. Here the bank is built up into a quay to take the boats that come to visit the Palais and the Opéra.

Dreux rolls in with a splash. She looks around. No one. Even the guards on the west of the Palais can't see, their line of sight blocked by the bulk of the great east wing.

'So that's it? No pomp? No funeral?' says Dreux's ghost.

'They'll probably fish you out in a few days,' says Julie.

'I'd hoped for, I don't know, splendour!' says the ghost, casting wide his arms.

'I wouldn't worry about that,' says Julie.

'Which way is Heaven? Do they send someone for you? What happens?' asks Dreux.

'About that,' says Julie.

She, he, it is there: shiny hooves, brocade and bright silk, Lucifer, gaudy gentleman-woman, beast of darkness.

The Devil bows to Dreux.

'"By Jesus",' says the Devil, as if holding up the words in a pair of tongs. 'Isn't that what you said when you saw my friend here? Remind me of the third commandment again, Mssr Dreux.'

'Thou shalt not take the Lord's name in vain. Oh God, you can't get me on that!'

'And there you go again,' says the Devil. 'I'm afraid I can, and I will. What ripe punishment for an issuer of oaths? An affliction of the tongue, perhaps . . .'

'See ya!' says Dreux and the ghost hightails it down the street.

'Aren't you going to chase him?' says Lucifer.

'I can't catch a ghost!' says Julie. 'You get him!'

'I've had rather a hard day,' says Lucifer. 'Some days in Hell really take it out of you. There's the smiting, the biting, the writing. Everything's administration nowadays, I tell you. It seems you can't roast a horny priest's right nut without filling in a form. Hell's gone soft! It makes me wonder what I did to deserve it sometimes. Well, until I remember.'

'He'll get away!'

'I dare say he'll turn up eventually,' says Lucifer. 'They normally do.'

'But what will he do in the meantime?'

'He seems to be running in the direction of Le Châtelet,' says Lucifer.

'What would he be doing there?'

'Probably alerting Challont-Aymavilles to the facts of your mission,' says Lucifer. 'Telling all his former colleagues to make sure they live good, virtuous lives, fully confessed up until the last time they fumbled with themselves under the bed covers. It'll make your job harder, no doubt.'

'Will they be able to see him?'

'Yes, if he appears to them in a dream or some such other way. Most ghosts choose not to. They lose interest in the living very quickly, knowing they will soon join them. But if they wish to, they can.'

'You let him go deliberately,' says Julie.

'Not so. He ran and I didn't stop him.'

'You could have stopped him.'

'That point seems rather moot now,' says Lucifer.

'You owe me a lesson.'

'Not until the soul is in my jurisdiction,' says Lucifer. 'You must return the ghost to me.'

'How am I going to do that?'

'I have no idea,' says Lucifer. 'But I am afraid I must regard our bargain as quite void if I don't get every soul that is owed to me.' The Devil smiles, points of light twinkling like horns at their forehead.

'You are a deceitful creature,' says Julie.

'You knew when you engaged with me what my nature was. The priests warn you from the pulpits weekly. There was no deceit over my deceitful nature, only your own, your self-deceit. So you out-deceived the Devil, you proved a more deceitful creature than the queen of deceit herself. In God's eyes, how wicked does that make you? How you shall burn for that, Julie, how you shall burn.'

A tinkle of bells, a waft of perfume. The street is empty, and she feels near to collapse. The sun is rising on the damp streets. She turns towards the Opéra.

She opens the door of the theatre to find Arcand sitting by her cot smoking a pipe.

'Ah,' he says. 'I have work for you to do!'

'I need to sleep,' she says. 'And then I need a costume.'

'This is insupportable!' says Arcand. 'What do we employ you for? Where have you been? Why are you wearing a costume already? Did you ask to take that? Why are you covered in blood?'

She chooses to answer only one of his questions. 'I just did for Diandré's killer,' she says. 'And I need you to get a parcel to his mother.'

Arcand nods. 'What sort of costume do you want?'

'A priest,' she says. 'But first, I must sleep.'

She crosses 'short and stout, Villepin and silver cane' off her list. Six down, well maybe five if you remove the wandering ghost of Dreux, and February not yet gone.

Scene Four

I Curse Thy Traitor Heart!

Lucifer has given Julie an idea. If Dreux's ghost really is going to alert his co-conspirators, she can turn that to her advantage. Challont-Aymavilles is bound to want to confess his sins and be shriven. Well, she might provide at least half of that service.

Le Châtelet, where Challont-Aymavilles has been taken, is a strange mix of palace and prison: some of its rooms for ordinary prisoners, no more than spare cells; some of them designed for the upper-class prisoner who cannot be expected to suffer the degradations, overcrowding and squalor of an ordinary prison and who can enrich King Louis, the warders, vintners and whores during his stay.

She has come through the sleet of the Paris streets whose houses huddle close down towards the Pont au Change as if for protection against the raw wind coming off the river. At least most of the shit and worse than shit that mires the streets is frozen, so the city's familiar stenches are muted. The prison is near to the water and even the Seine carries no evil airs today.

She is very cold. Her priest's costume is just that – a costume. It isn't made of the heavy wool of the real thing but is constructed of much lighter cloth designed only for its appearance, not its usefulness. The wispy beard she has glued to her face does nothing to keep it warm. The wind goes through her as she scuttles through the early morning, her legs heavy from the fights and the dances of the night before.

It's Sunday and she guesses she will have until mid-morning to act. Even if Challont-Aymavilles gets a message to his church at first light, the church mass will have to come first for the priests.

Within the cassock is her little knife that she took from Versailles, sharp to pare the fruit cleanly. She intends to serve Challont-Aymavilles a dish of himself.

She rounds the corner into the Rue St-Denis. Le Châtelet is set back from the other tall houses of the street, as if they have all stood back in deference to it. To Julie it looks like a building stuck together out of bits of several others – a round tower, a square tower, a big arched roof with tall windows in the centre, a conventional house built on its side, little lean-tos built on the front. The problem with this sort of jumble is knowing where to enter.

She approaches dead centre and passes through a big arch that looks as if it might formerly have contained a portcullis. The arch is damp and the dirty snow inside it is stained yellow.

She goes on in, casts around. In the courtyard, two braziers burn while a queue of mainly women and children wait in a ragged, stamping line to gain access to a door in a long wall below a sloping roof. Just looking at them, she knows they are bourgeois – their coats drabber, patchier and probably a good deal warmer than the splendid clothes the nobles wear. Even if these people could afford the rich colours available to their betters, they would not be allowed them by law and for their general safety. A comte would not react well to the sight of a banker in a better coat than he himself wore and might take it upon himself to beat the banker for it. She looks around for where the nobles might be kept.

Stairs are cut into a tower to her left, and a guard sits swathed in coats and blankets just inside in a small office separated from the stairwell by a low swing door.

She approaches, makes the sign of the cross. Her mouth is dry, and she trembles, though she can't tell if that is with fear or with the cold.

'Challont-Aymavilles?' she says.

He gestures up.

'Top floor.'

'Any cell in particular?'

The guard laughs. 'He has the whole thing.'

He calls something after her, but his voice is muffled by his scarfs and she doesn't hear what it is as she winds up the stairs.

There are four floors and each one has a door, none of them with locks on. Of course they don't. This prison is for noble criminals and debtors. They are there at the command of the king, who is their world. They will not escape simply because there is nowhere to escape to. A poor person escaping could slip into the numberless multitudes of poor and disappear. Nobles live their whole lives in the gaze of their peers, always known, always seen. Theirs is a tiny world and, within it, invisibility is impossible.

She reaches the top of the stair and is confronted by a stout wooden door. She crosses herself, for real this time, and knocks. There is no answer, so she softly opens the door to be hit by a waft of hot air. Clearly Challont-Aymavilles is keeping a nice fire. The door opens on a well-furnished room with a good woollen rug on the floor. The chairs and table are well made but relatively plain – their curlicues and rolls in unadorned wood, not gold leaf. Another door leads out directly opposite. It's closed, so she goes to it and listens.

Nothing. She puts her hand to the handle. Then she does hear something. She puts her ear to the door.

'Forgive me, father, for I have sinned.'

He is taking confession. Shit! There's a priest in there. It's one thing to pawn your soul to the Devil, quite another to kill a priest, though she realises she needs to get rid of him. The moral considerations aside, it's just not practical. People miss priests, enquiries are ordered into their violent deaths, witnesses interviewed. When nobles are dying, the authorities tend to assume it's just a feud or has something to do with some business they don't understand. They don't look too hard into it for fear of whose toes they might tread on.

She can't let this confession go on, though. If Challont-Aymavilles goes through with it, his soul will be safe even if she manages to kill him this afternoon.

She feels inside her cassock. She has hidden most of Charlotte-Marie's money under a floorboard at the Opéra. She didn't bring a lot with her for fear of being robbed. Nevertheless, she must try to bribe the guard. She runs back down the steps to find him shivering inside his blankets.

'There's an imposter in Challont-Aymavilles's rooms!'

'Hold on,' says the guard.

'I won't hold on. Challont-Aymavilles has many enemies and I believe there's a man disguised as a priest sent to kill him with him now. I was sent to hear his confession, only me. There is someone else up there now. You have to act.'

'I don't have to, Father. My orders are to guard the gate. Personally I don't give a fuck if an aristo gets killed.'

'If he's killed on your watch, what will become of you?'

'I'm filling in, so I'll just deny I was on. If you want me to do something, then you'll need to make it worth my while. Extra duties come with an extra price.'

'Please go and arrest him. I only have one ecu.'

'Give us that, then.'

She passes it over. He takes it and pockets it.

'It's not enough.' He seems to find this very funny. 'I'll need a bit more motivation than that to get off my arse.'

'It's really hot in his rooms,' she says.

'Well, why didn't you say? I'll go and nick him now. If it turns out you're wrong at least I've had a little warm. And I can interview this imposter indoors near the fire. That could take an hour! You're a smarter fellow than you look, Father.'

He ambles up the stairs and she goes to stand in the queue for the lower jail, thinking that might be the best place to avoid notice.

After what seems like an age, the guard comes back down, a scrawny, aged priest grumbling in front of him. He looks an unlikely assassin.

'I know, Father, I know, but I have received certain information and we can't be too careful. Better safe than sorry. I'm sure we can get you a cup of hot wine while we check your credentials. I might have one myself.'

'I'm not being interviewed by the likes of you!' says the priest.

'Well, the alternative is that we have to strip search you for weapons in the middle of the yard,' says the guard.

'This is an outrage,' says the priest.

The guard takes the priest across the yard to a door beyond the queue. Julie guesses that very soon another guard will come to replace him, so she peels away from the queue and makes her way up the stairs.

At the top someone is shouting.

'You will pay for this lapse, I tell you. Pay! I am a personal friend of Monsieur, brother to the king, and when he hears how you have endangered my life, he will shake Heaven and earth. I told you I wanted my priest, not the nearest priest. I paid good money for you to get my priest and you just pick one who presents himself as a priest because you can't be bothered to shift your lazy arses over to the Île de La Cité and he turns out to be God knows what! Well, you are for it. For it!'

The diatribe continues as she ascends the stairs. Clearly Challont-Aymavilles has not quite understood that the guard has departed and that he's shouting at no one at all. Well, not quite no one. Her.

She rounds the final twist of stair to find Challont-Aymavilles isn't even facing the stairwell. He's leaning up the doorway making a straining noise like a dog complaining about being moved off a bed.

'Never been so insulted, never,' he's saying to himself. 'The doctors told me to control my temper and you, you bastards, have made me lose it. And now I'm having a turn again. Oh, my chest. Oh, my arm! They told me my heart would kill me! Oh, traitor heart!'

Julie feels like killing him just for his self-pitying purple prose. He sits down heavily on the flagstones and Julie, with her Devil-granted ghost sight, is alarmed to see the pale outline of his ghost leaning out of his body and back in again.

'Oh shit!' says Julie.

Challont-Aymavilles sways as he sits and stares at her blankly, like a drunk fixing on a single point to try to avoid crashing to the cobbles.

'Come with me, sir, with me!' She puts her shoulder under his arm and helps him to his feet, steering him back into his rooms. She sits him on the armchair, scattering its cushions to make a more even perch. Challont-Aymavilles looks very pale and shaken.

'I think you are in a grave way, sir,' she says. 'Did you take confession?'

'That man was no priest. My confession meant nothing,' he says, trembling. 'Will you take my confession now, Father?'

'Yes, yes,' she says. He could die any moment and it seems he has confessed his sins. She doesn't know whether to kill him here and hope for the best or to try to get him to sin in some way first.

At the bottom of the stairs she hears voices. 'Up here?' 'Yes. Up here.'

Guards. Shit.

Challont-Aymavilles grasps at her arm. Then he swallows.

'Oh,' he says, in his scissored way, and falls back into the chair, eyes rolling.

An elderly voice echoes up the stairs.

'If I hadn't had the captain to vouch for me, where would we be? It's not the offence to myself I count, it's the gentleman.'

Julie ducks behind the armchair as Challont-Aymavilles gargles.

'I only got halfway through his confession,' says the priest, as he enters the rooms. 'And now—'

He falls silent. 'Shit!' he says, and the guards say it too.

The priest trots over to Challont-Aymavilles; she hears his little steps.

'He's dead. Christ's balls, he's dead! Look at the colour on him.'

Julie cringes. She is expecting to hear the sound of bells and the *clop* of shiny hooves very soon.

'On my watch!' says a voice. 'Well, on your watch according to the rota.'

'We swapped out!'

'Guards!' says the priest. 'Control yourselves! This is bad for you indeed.'

'Bad for you too, Father. You only got halfway through his confession before he keeled over. Not too many aristos going to be calling for you, are there, if that's your level of service?'

'That was your fault!'

'Something I shall entirely omit to tell anyone!'

'Wait!' A voice she doesn't recognise speaks. 'Surely there is a way. We report that this gentleman was ill and called for a priest. We sent for one with all speed, the father came, heard confession, when this gentleman's situation became worse. In extremis and very quickly, the good father administered the extreme unction. If we had not acted so quickly, he would have died with his sins on his soul. Grateful family cough up large church donation and a few morsels for us. Got oil, Father?'

'Yes.'

'Splash a bit on him. Make it look good.'

'We split three ways whatever he's got in his purse!'

'Done,' says the priest.

Julie presses herself into the back of the big seat as the three rifle the rooms.

She is close enough to smell their breath as they pass but they work fast and, in a quick minute, they are gone.

She stands, goes to Challont-Aymavilles. He is very pale and his ghost hovers in and out of his body. So, still alive and only half confessed. She takes the cushion from the floor and presses it to his face. He bucks and kicks briefly, but she holds the pillow fast, pressing the ghost out of him like juice from grapes.

'What are you doing?'

She turns to see the guard from downstairs. She thought he'd gone but he's obviously come back to check the place over again to see if he can find something valuable his companions missed.

'You've stolen this man's money. You've let an assassin in. At the moment he's dead of natural causes with a priest as witness. If I were you, I'd leave well alone and fuck off now.'

The guard hovers on his toes a little. 'Off I shall fuck,' he says and turns out of the room.

Julie renews her pressure on the pillow and shortly Challont-Aymavilles's ghost steps from his body.

'The Devil's Blade?' he says.

'Is that what they call me?'

'It's what they call someone. Is it you?'

'I suppose so.' She likes the name well enough for the fear it brings.

'Devil here?'

'Will be in a second.'

'Right, I'm off.'

The ghost runs towards the door but emerging from the doorway is the exquisitely silked form of the Prince/ess of Darkness him or herself.

'Well,' says Lucifer. 'Half the tally discharged, but still so many charges to answer!'

'Are you taking me to Hell?' says Challont-Aymavilles.

'An incisive observation,' says Lucifer, with a clack of the teeth that suddenly seem very pointy indeed.

'Then get Girard,' says Challont-Aymavilles. 'He got me into the Tredecim! I hate him! He's run to the army to get away from you, he thinks an anonymous uniform and the company of soldiers will keep you away. Tell me it won't, please! Be a love and kill him too!'

Funnily, Challont-Aymaville seems a lot more amiable and pleasant as a ghost than he did as a living man.

Julie takes out her card. 'Which one is he?' she says. 'One eye, three fingers, emerald ring . . .'

'I'll stop you there,' says Challont-Aymaville. 'He's the emerald ring.'

'And where can I find him?'

'That's enough help from you,' says the Devil.

Lucifer gives a click of the fingers and Challont-Aymavilles is sucked through the ring of primroses into Hell. Julie crosses Scissor Mouth off her list.

'Now,' says the Devil, let me teach you the art of the Devil's Eye!'

Scene Five

Must I Be Mine Enemy's Saviour?

The thought of the missing ghost concerns her, but she can see no way of catching him just now. Still, she wakes nights to think she sees him watching her. A good job ghosts don't carry knives, she thinks. So she does what she must, gets on with life, concerns herself with what she can do rather than what she can't and sets out after Girard, chasing the army east.

Of course, she confirms Challont-Aymavilles's story first. She doesn't want to trek miles to find she has been led astray. She visits the Palais to ask for Monsieur. He will know the army's movements. The guards laugh at her. Of course she knows Monsieur, they say – the king's brother often associates with street sluts. She says she knows Charlotte-Marie De Mazarin and this causes more hilarity. 'They really shouldn't allow news sheets' says a guard. 'Even whores know the names of great men now.'

After a week of waiting and dodging the kicks of the guards, she sees Aubespine getting out of a sedan.

'My lord, Aubespine!'

He pauses, squints, a look of mild horror dawns on him, like that of a schoolmaster recognising a pupil who used to torment him twenty years before.

'You,' he says.

'Me,' she says.

'Shall I remove this person,' says a door guard.

'No, bring her inside. And order us coffee,' he says.

Over the steaming cups of what is basically a bitter soup, she explains that she wishes to confirm that Girard has gone east and to know the whereabouts of Du Bellay.

Aubespine raises his eyebrows.

'May I explain to you,' he says, 'that when Monsieur says you are his dearest friend and under his protection, that means it behoves people like me to protect him from you. He should not be the victim of his own generosity.'

'Tell me what I need to know, and I'll never trouble you again.'

'You'd never trouble me again if I had you hanged.'

'I think, with my friends at court, I would trouble you a great deal were you to do that.'

Aubespine tugs thoughtfully at his wig. Then he sends for a footman and instructs him to go to the barracks of the Picardie.

'These gentlemen have slighted you?' he says.

'Yes.'

'In what way?'

She says nothing, just shrugs. He sips at his coffee, replaces the cup on its little table.

'I was going to tell you to be careful,' he says, 'but I think it better if you are reckless. That way you will cease to be a problem to me.'

'Am I a problem to you?'

'A little. If you become a bigger one, I'll let you know.'

'How?'

'I'll have you murdered. At the moment I balance the fuss and inconvenience of letting you live against the fuss and inconvenience of having you killed and find the scale tips more to the former than to the latter. I warn you these scales can tip very quickly and without warning. Are there any other slights you are seeking to redress in blood?'

She nearly tells him, nearly asks for help in identifying the men on her list, but thinks again. Secrets, knowledge of intentions and plots, are a commodity in the court, she guesses. She doesn't want to give him anything more to trade.

When the footman returns, he whispers in Aubespine's ear. Aubespine nods sagely.

'Du Bellay has gone away to England or Spain or somewhere. I cannot help you with him. However, within months an opportunity will arise for you to rendezvous with Monsieur Girard in the way you would wish. When that time comes, I will furnish you with information through your friend de Mazarin.'

'I need to know now.'

'It is my needs, not yours, that concern me and I do not need Girard to die in Paris causing . . .' He searches for the word. 'A mess! Your opportunity will come soon enough. If Monsieur wishes to help you any more, he will contact you,' says Aubespine.

'I'll await his pleasure,' says Julie.

'I'd concentrate more on avoiding my displeasure, if I were you,' he says.

Girard, she discovers through Charlotte-Marie in early March, has gone east with the army, the Picardie regiment to be precise though not even Charlotte-Marie can discover what was happened to Du Bellay.

The war, it appears, has become bogged down at Philippsburg in Trier. It takes her three weeks to walk to the siege, out on the boggy road to Rheims. She is not alone – a stream of merchants, workmen and adventurers are with her, traipsing along the road to the city and then out to Verdun along the pretty River Meuse. She eats sugared almonds at Verdun – the speciality of the town – and has to stop herself from buying another handful from the market as she is sure she will be sick. It's a pretty town, surrounded by hills, but it is not untouched by war.

The army went through only a few weeks before and now, in April, there are no chickens to be bought for a pot by the fire, no mutton, no pork. The bread is scarce and expensive because the bulk of it is heading east, one way or another, sucked in to the army's long tail, of which she is a part. Beer costs a fortune, cheese is unavailable. In the end, she buys another pack of sugared almonds as there is hardly anything else to eat. Perhaps the almonds arrived in the town after the army had gone.

She sustains herself with thoughts of Charlotte-Marie. She surprised her at the Opéra one day and this time Julie went back to her grand house, spent two months with her in bed, fucking, dreaming, drinking, eating and waiting for Aubespine to send a message. She would have left earlier but she had tried a little of Mssr Pomet's tincture, which gave her many exquisite afternoons watching the sunlight through the windows as she lay in Charlotte-Marie's arms. Then she tried a lot of it, and every day. She had to force herself to leave, to get back on the road of revenge.

'Why do you torment yourself?' said Charlotte-Marie, pressing a bottle into Julie's shaking hands. 'Take the tincture with you.'

'I lose too much to it,' said Julie. 'All my will. It is spring now. I must free myself of it.'

Free herself she did, with much sweating and shaking, holed up in her bed at the Opéra, Charlotte-Marie safely back at Versailles. Three times she found she had walked to Pomet's shop without thinking but three times she came away. She took the bulk of her money to Paval's and Diandré's mothers to stop her buying any more of that lovely dreadful tincture.

She would rather be poor than a slave to a medicine. Eventually the longing faded, though the ghost of it remains with her. She is regretful now. She has wasted so much time, albeit in an ecstatic way.

She travels as a man, because it is easier that way. No one understands an unmarried woman travelling alone, or rather everyone does and everyone is wrong. They will think her a whore or an idiot, a potential victim. Better to pose as an adventure-hungry youth running to catch the army and join it on its trail through the east. Pelletier has come with her, on her request. He will work for a share of whatever spoils she gets, and he is convinced they will be big ones. He suggests that she can travel as herself if she pretends to be married to him. The thought repulses her.

She does not quite understand why the army is fighting but understands that it is to defend France. That is why King Louis has marched his men into Trier, one of the German states, and intends to march them a good deal further. Although this looks like aggression it is, in fact, only done with great regret and because France is surrounded by enemies with whom she is not currently fighting, but might one day. That is to say, they weren't fighting France until France came marching through their lands. Sérannes tried to explain it to her when he came to visit her at the Opéra, causing Arcand's eyes to nearly pop from his head. Sérannes is a dear, though she can't find him attractive. Too much angle and bone, not enough curve and comfort.

The Ottomans in the east were vexing the Holy Roman Emperor Leopold and the German princes quite badly, he says – the Mussulmans being convinced that they, not Christian men, had God on their side and making war upon the lands of the Church. King Louis took advantage of this pleasant situation to press various very rightful claims he had in the Low

Countries, reasoning that the Emperor could not fight on two fronts at once. However, God, it appears, was on Leopold's side against the heathens and the Ottomans have been quite broken, enabling Leopold to turn his attention back west. There is also a question of a grand alliance – the English, God help us, are becoming involved, appearing from their foggy little island like the vultures of legend whenever trouble flares for France, or anyone for that matter.

The important thing, however, is that the Tredecim member known as Girard has gone with the army and may, disastrously, get himself killed before Julie can kill him. This will not do. On the way along, she tries out her latest learning from Lucifer – that of the Devil's Eye. Lucifer told her that the body speaks its own language, that weakness and strength, confidence or nerves, a thousand things, may be read in the way an opponent holds their sword, even in the way someone bargains for bread. She studied long and hard in that strange no-time that surrounds the Devil until she could tell at a glance if Lucifer was about to attack, feint, defend or wait. She could tell when the Devil let themselves be scared, timid, bold or simmer with an almost invisible rage that foretold a hasty attack, all caution gone.

Now she uses that eye to make trades for food, seeing when someone is chancing their arm on a price. Sometimes she uses it to go whoring, after a fashion, as a boy, tugging off a few travellers in return for bread or for beer – so much healthier than the water in these parts. The work isn't pleasant but no more unpleasant to her than milking a cow. Actually, it is more unpleasant, a cow doesn't breathe in your face while you tug on its teat. She has to nut one idiot when he tries to kiss her. These men pay for her hand, no other part, and certainly not that piece of your soul that is given in a kiss.

Sometimes now she sings. Moreau's blood cure has worked, to an extent, and her voice has come back after a fashion.

She can manage the camp songs and the sentimental airs of the ordinary people. She would love to take on Lully now, to let her voice call the angels from the sky, but she is afraid. If she pushes things, if something breaks. Would that be it forever? She smiles to herself. She has hope at least. That has changed. There might be a life beyond this year, her dreams may not yet be dead. Yet, here by the fire, singing of a boy who waits in the rain for a girl whose love is forbidden him, she knows her dreams are different now. She no longer sees herself as the duchess, as the mother to a brood of little aristocrats, spending the duke's money and fucking his friends, their wives, their servants. She just sees herself on stage in the candlelight, setting her voice free, set free by her voice.

As they cross out of France the land flattens. In France there was little to be had, here there is nothing. All the farms have been burned, all the villages too, and all of value taken. As she travels towards the army, she sees a plain truth – war, religious persecution, all that. It's all about theft. The army has lain waste to the countryside here. Now she can get less for a tug in a bush because others are haunting the camp – thin women, hollow-eyed children, no men. They will do anything for food. A mother tries to press her infant into Julie's arms and Julie, taken by surprise, accepts the child. It is a girl of about four and she weighs nothing, nothing at all. Julie gives them the last of her bread. She is near to the siege and it will be good to be hungry. It will focus her mind, make sure she works quickly.

'You should not have done that,' says a man.

'Why?'

'They are in this condition because God wills it. To help them out of it is to oppose the will of God.'

'You sound like a Dutchman,' she says. Aren't they always talking some such shit?

His face darkens. 'Watch yourself,' he says. She thinks of the protestants Louis has forced from France, the Huguenots. They were always talking of 'predestiny' – that everything is the will of God. Well God willed them to fuck off, so off they have fucked. Is this man a Huguenot? Maybe he was one but converted to the true Church to save his skin.

That night she goes to the man while he is sleeping and opens his pack with her knife. There is a good purse of coins in there. She gives most of it to the next child she sees begging, thinking 'God willed that', though she keeps a little for herself. The life of a whore is not for her, nor for anyone if they have the money to avoid it, she thinks.

Onward, hungry, she walks to the siege. She speaks to those on the road and is happy, on the whole, in their company. Here are people that the world has put in a fixed place – poor, despised, unwanted. War lets them move, be something other than they were. There are clever folk here, a man who taught himself to read and speaks of Aristotle and the medicines of the ancients and who wanted to be a doctor but came from too poor a home to manage it.

His name is Fancheux and he is a young man of around twenty-two who speaks with an intensity and earnestness she finds endearing. He gives little cures to people on the road in return for food and he pulls a man's tooth while she watches, having first had him eat a black paste. The man makes no noise of complaint and the tooth comes out cleanly in a pair of pliers. 'From Mssr Pomet?' she says, sniffing the paste. The smell sends a shiver through her.

'Yes,' says Fancheux. 'Are you a medical man?'

'No, I have a friend who enjoys that tincture.'

'It is a cure for all ills,' he says. 'Very therapeutic. Would you like to try?'

'I am not ill,' she says.

'You don't need to be ill to find something therapeutic,' he says.

She laughs. 'It's a weird kind of doctor who says that,' she says. 'Or one who wants more business. Content yourself with ministering to the sick, there are enough of them without starting on the well.'

'There are plenty who do that,' he says. 'Does not your king take three clysters a day?'

She has heard this said, that the king holds court while someone shoots warm water up his arse to purge out the corruption within.

'If someone wants to squirt something up my behind, they can pay for it,' says Julie.

Fancheux laughs. 'You are a clever boy,' he says.

'Perhaps I should try to be a doctor and study at Montpelier.'

'They would not let you in,' says Fancheux, his expression grim. 'Why not?'

'You have not the letters of introduction,' he says.

'Ah,' she says. 'I know that problem. So why are you travelling here?'

'To be a doctor in deed, even if I can't get the education and certificate. Wars are good for people like me. A man with a musket ball in him rarely asks to see your certificate before you stop his bleeding.'

Julie likes Fancheux and stays with him, hearing all about the various humours of the body, how the blood moves always around in a circuit, as revealed by an Englishman, and how the proper condition of a person may be ascertained in the colour of their skin, their shit and their piss.

He shocks and amazes her with stories of how one man had a nail driven through his eye and lived on unharmed after it was removed. He tells how his interest in medicine grew when, as a youth, he fought a duel and was run quite through but the blade failed to pierce any of his vitals and how, in a week, he was up and running around again. He shows her the scars, one at the front, one at the back.

'Only so much of the body is useful to life,' he says. 'If a blade enters correctly it can pass without causing too much discomfort nor any harm.'

'Do the gentlemen of the medical schools know this?' she says.

'I have no idea what they know in the medical schools,' he says.

Fancheux asks her why she is travelling, and she tells her she is carrying a letter for a gentleman.

They meet others too – men of Normandy and Brittany who she can scarcely understand, a few adventurers from Ireland who speak French well but with an accent you imagine a dog might have. They are seeking 'the fortune of war', by which she thinks they mean plunder. She sings them a song that pleases them in her croaking voice. She can hold a tune, though, now and sings better than anyone else at the campfire. She knows it will not, however, be enough for the Opéra.

'The fortune of war, well I'll tell you plain,
Is a wooden leg or a golden chain.'

'Or a wooden box,' says Fancheux.

'No guarantee of avoiding that if you sit on your arse,' says one of the Irishmen and she thinks he is right. Plenty die in their beds who never see adventure in their lives. She needs to work fast. She has men to kill, and quickly. She shivers at night, lonely for Charlotte-Marie but cursing that she lost such focus by being with her. She should have sought the others while she waited for news of Girard but she was too caught up in Charlotte-Marie. Or was it in Pomet's tincture? She will say she lost the time to Charlotte-Marie because it is better to err for love than for whatever is in that medicine. Now she must concentrate on her task. Now she must outrun chance, misfortune, disease and time. These are formidable opponents. When they are beaten and her foes are nicely dead, she will return to Charlotte-Marie. She hates her enemies even more for the time they have stolen from her. She will steal a whole heap more from them. At night her fox, Furie, curls up next to her and she takes comfort in its warmth.

The whole country smells of smoke; the smell never goes away. She sees things she wishes she had never seen – burned little houses that remind her of her own in Alsace, a rag at the side of the road. When she looks closer, she realises it is attached to an arm. A barn lies burned and, when she passes it, she sees a human jawbone among the ash.

They hear the siege well before they see it. There are cries in the distance, great crashes and the sound of cannon; horses scream in protest, all the dogs they have with them and all the dogs they cannot see set to barking. Does she imagine it or does the earth shake? No, she is just nervous, and her stomach is rumbling with hunger.

As they approach the walls it is as if they have stepped out of the land of famine and into that of milk and honey. All along the hill leading to the city are market stalls, selling any sort of food, any sort of service you could require. She walks past butchers, geese staring out blankly from hooks, bakers with loaves piled in golden mountains, farmers selling everything from cabbages to pickles to lumps of iron. Everywhere is noise – the songs of the vendors, the cries of children. A smith bangs steel at an impromptu forge, a leatherworker sews boots and each trade has not one practitioner but ten or twenty or more. Around them the displaced move like ghosts – hollow-eyed women offering their bodies for bread, children running like rats between the stalls, kicked and beaten by the vendors, snapped at and bitten by their dogs. Every variety of beggar is here, limbless, diseased, young, old, some imploring, some silent and sitting as if in a shroud of despair. She buys an apple and some bread for the sort of price you'd expect to pay for a decent pair of gloves and continues up towards the sound of the gunfire, the dogs, the horses, towards the sound of war.

At the top of the hill she looks down. Philippsburg itself is a lost cause. The town sits in the elbow of a valley, all the banners of France snapping in the breeze within it. The city itself has already fallen, it seems. In front of her is the great blue ribbon of the Rhine, lazy under a cold, dipping sun. Above, on the great mound like a mountain that dominates the town, is the palace of the Elector of Trier, a formidable walled castle. She can see two protective curtain walls that an invader would have to get past even to approach the might of the stone keep – a great triangle of sturdy towers surrounding a central square tower that commands the entire river plain about it.

Big guns flash in the valley but she sees they are useless. The shots splash earth from the mound well below the walls and, when muskets flash and bang from the palace in reply, the gunners go ducking for cover. The defenders, on top of such a precipitous mountain, are at a significant advantage, it seems, though they lack any serious cannon to do damage to the besiegers in the town below.

Julie is glad. No frontal assault, no gruelling hand-to-hand battle, no slaughter so far. The chances are that Girard is still alive. She pushes down the hill to the town, trailing Fancheux behind her.

'We must find lodgings,' says Fancheux.

'I think that might be hard,' says Julie.

It is. Everywhere is full to bursting – requisitioned. The regiments of Les Vieux Corps – the oldest in the army – get the choice big houses, while everyone from the younger regiments, from the Flanders through to the Italians and the Toulouse, have set up in the meaner dwellings in the tiny, winding streets. In the end, a major from the Lyonnaise rents them a space on the floor of the goldsmith's guild. They put their packs down on the floor with a hundred farting, snoring, wanking troopers in a hall that would be a squeeze for fifty. Fancheux is called to see a man who has been wounded in the leg by a bullet. The bullet has not lodged and Fancheux says the bone is not smashed. He cleans the wound with alcohol and boiled water. 'After Hippocrates!' he says. The long name soothes the man's friends, though Julie has no idea what it means. He applies a smear of animal fat and honey on a lint bandage to seal it.

'I have never seen that,' says Julie.

'The fat keeps out bad humours from the air and keeps the wound moist,' says Fancheux. 'After Galen.'

'Galen who?'

'A learned Greek,' he says.

'I have heard of Greeks,' she says. Operas are full of them.

She sleeps well, for there is no moon and the night is flat dark. There is some hullaballoo from the town in the very early morning, screams and cries, shots. The soldiers wake but no one seems in much of a hurry to go and investigate.

An officer comes in and tells them 'at ease'. 'Just a sortie,' he says. 'Idiots in the castle trying to grab a few vittles. Good sign, they're running low. The Picardie boys have sorted it.'

She sleeps next to Fancheux, dreaming of Charlotte-Marie. Picardie is Girard's regiment – high born fellows, mainly. She knows, though, that Girard has not been killed in any action. How? Lucifer has not appeared for her.

When the sun rises, she is quick to get out. The camp is fetid. It stinks even by Parisian standards. The town is like the guildhall – meant for far fewer people than it contains.

A soldier vomits into the road. Drunk? Or the beginnings of siege fever? She must work quickly.

She finds the Picardie regiment in good time. They are billeted in what must be a nobleman's or merchants' quarters near the centre of the town – grand houses of that forbidding German style looming above well-appointed stables.

'Monsieur, monsieur!' she calls out, trying to attract the attention of one of the pale-coated soldiers, but they are all too busy with the morning's business – grooming horses, shaving, the richer ones being shaved. Men sharpen swords and knives that are already sharp, polish boots that already shine. Everyone is teetering between boredom, excitement and fear, desperate to be doing something, glad to be doing nothing, unsure if the knot in their stomach is brave anticipation or cowardly anxiety. Cooks move among them with pastries, bread, little hard eggs. She calls to a cook as he passes, and she finds a hunk of bread and two small eggs placed in her hands. This is a rich regiment, food to spare, and the cook doesn't want to risk picking a fight with some officer's relative or friend for the sake of a bit of bread. She munches, passes among the men.

She scouts around some more. How many men can a regiment contain? She doesn't know. In her coat is the letter she has for Girard – or rather a blank piece of paper sealed with wax. She could use it to find out where Girard is but carries a slight fear she might chance upon him by mistake, and then she would be in the uncomfortable position of having to hand him a blank letter.

'You!' She realises someone is addressing her. It's a fierce-looking major in a coat as red as his face.

'Sir?'

'What are you doing munching my bread? Do I know you?'

She bows.

'Monsieur, I have a letter for Seigneur Girard. A man with a fine emerald ring.'

The major grins. 'That's long gone to his gambling,' he says. 'I dare say you'll have a devil of a job delivering your little letter!'

'Sir?'

He takes a note from inside his coat, waves it and replaces it.

'Ransom,' he says. 'He got grabbed on the sortie, the fool. They want three pigs and twenty crates of ale for him.'

She crosses herself, cursing inside.

'Will you pay it?'

'Not likely. He owes the whole regiment a fortune at dice and no one here's prepared to lend him a penny more. He can wait until we take the place tomorrow.'

'Might he not be killed?'

'By this time tomorrow, according to the note. In which case his house in Paris gets sold and we all get paid. Job's a good 'un, I'd say. If I had my way, I'd delay the attack!'

With that he walks away.

Julie finds Pelletier working the pea and shell game with some young grenadiers.

'I need to get in there,' she says, nodding up to the castle.

He shrugs. 'It's very big,' he says.

'Is that a problem?'

'In some ways yes, in some no. The bigger the castle, the more chance of finding a hole in the sentry patrol. But also the greater chance of finding more sentries if you get it wrong.'

'Can you do it?'

'I will do what I can,' says Pelletier.

That night, they feel their way forward through the trees, under the moonless sky. It is so very dark, just the stars for light, and it is only the black bulk of the castle against the constellations that keeps them on course. There are four of them there. One of the men who accompanies them is so disreputable-looking and foul mouthed that, by comparison,

Pelletier seems as mild as a country priest. The other is not much better.

Over Pelletier's shoulder is the body of a pig. Where he got it from, she doesn't ask, nor what he did to secure it. An apple at the siege is the price of a pig under normal conditions. How much is the price of a pig? A couple of orchards? More?

The word she will need is in her head. She repeats it and repeats it for fear of forgetting it: '*Gefangener. Gefangener.*'

It is damnably quiet as they skirt the walls, and Pelletier taps Julie on the shoulder to indicate she should stop.

She does. She cannot speak here. The sentries on the walls will be vigilant. She leans against the cold wall in the dark silence for an age. Then, from the valley below, there is a flash of light – flame blooms in the dark, an enormous bang and a rumble goes through the ground. One of the guns has fired and men are shouting in the darkness.

She hears shouts from the ramparts and muskets flash and thump, footsteps run.

'Now,' says one of the men they are with, and they feel their way along the wall up to where the ground levels.

The going is hard; Julie slips and falls but there is enough commotion towards the front of the palace to cover the noise. She gets up, tracking the wall with her left hand. A flash, and she glimpses the three men in front of her in the frozen second of a musket flare. She keeps going, eyes swimming from the sudden brightness in the dark.

'Here?' says Pelletier.

'Here.'

The man lets out a series of chirps in imitation, she thinks, of a nightingale. Above them, another series of chirps and a rope comes down.

'We have a pig!' hisses one of the men.

"I have a good quantity of church plate,' says the voice from above. The accent is like scraping metal. German, she presumes; she has never heard a German speak before and wonders why they do not learn French better if they wish to communicate with the civilised world. Still, the word is in her mind: *Gefangener. Gefangener.*

'Send it!'

A bucket scrapes down. She can hardly see it. It lands. Another musket flash and the bucket lights up silver in the gloom. Three plates and two shiny cups.

'Good,' says the man.

'You don't want to bargain?' says Pelletier.

'No time, this is good enough,' says the man.

'No, no,' says Pelletier. He hisses up, 'Monsieur, another goblet, at least.'

The voice curses, but the bucket goes back up and returns again. Pelletier feels within.

'Do you think they have more?' he says.

'Send it up now, or you'll get us shot.'

'You can go,' says Pelletier. He hands each man a goblet, she can just make out in the gloom.

'Take the fucking lot, Danton,' says one of the men. 'These aren't going to stop you.'

Julie had expected this. She draws her sword, jabs it in the general direction of one of the black shapes. A cry.

'You cut me!'

'I'll do it properly if you don't fuck off,' she says.

The men slink away on low grumbles. Muskets pop and crack above her, the big cannon below speaks again and she feels the wall shake.

'The pig!' says a voice from above.

Pelletier tries the rope.

'You can lift it?' he says to the invisible people above.

'Yes!'

'It is a very big pig!'

'There are three of us!'

Pelletier ties the rope to the pig and the bucket and gives two good pulls above. 'Now!'

Julie sheathes her sword, uses the pig's body as a step and pulls herself up on the rope.

'I will not come back to the town,' she says to Pelletier. 'Seek me at the Opéra in a month or so if you want to continue our arrangement.'

'I will be there!'

'It's a good one, lads,' says the voice above. 'Come and give me a hand.'

The rope creaks and groans as she is lifted. It drops, she clings on, the voice above curses.

'It's a very good one, get more hands on the rope.'

She takes her knife from her sleeve. She expects to have to stab one or two at the top and a knife is better close in than a sword. She is glad she can't cross herself. Who do you pray to when you are on the Devil's business? She won't pray to Lucifer, for sure, but can she really pray to Christ? There will be time enough for that afterwards.

Straining, protesting, the rope lifts her up. She can just see now, dark shapes against the starry sky. The musket shots slow to a patter, like dying rain, their lightning flashes more sporadic. It is quiet, or the quiet of war – insults shouted, someone somewhere screaming but no gunshot any more, nor any flash.

'Heave!' says someone above and she shoots heavenward. As soon as she is clear of the parapet, she steps off. The men on the rope are all a way back, having retreated rather than pull the rope through their hands too much and risk letting it slip. As her weight leaves the rope, the pig shoots up into the air past her, landing with a wet thump on the stones.

'Pork!' shouts a voice and the men on the rope surge forwards to get at the pig. She is gone, away from the men, into the darkness, like the dark sprite she is. They haven't even seen her in their frenzy to get to the animal. She skirts around the top of the parapet. So far, she has only gained the outer curtain wall. There may be two more to go.

The whole palace outside the second wall is flat black – not a light burns despite the spring chill. These people know that they may be here through the months of a more unbearable cold. Strange voices in the darkness, that crunching, cracking tongue of German. To her it sounds like the tearing of gristle, all spiky and cold. This is a vision of Hell. No, not a vision, there is no sight, but a forewarning in stink and noise. Children howl in the darkness and a dog lets out a long cry of distress that never seems to end – hunger, she expects. That is not a good sign for the besiegers – the Germans haven't eaten the dog yet. The French army could be there for a while. She feels her heart pounding, crouches to calm herself. Fear seeps up from the ground here like a miasma from a bog. The whole town breathes it in and she is no exception.

She finds a ladder down from the parapet and walks across the inner courtyard, careful in the dark. Her knife is beneath her coat, but she thinks it more of a danger to herself than anything. She could trip and fall in this darkness, stab herself. Tents have been set across the inner courtyard and she feels her way through the ropes. Will Girard be here? She doubts it. You can't keep a captive in a tent, well, not easily. *Gefangener, Gefangener.* She bites hard down on the consonants in her head. It must sound German. It must sound German!

She suspects he will most likely be up in the keep where it will be hardest for him to escape and hardest for others to rescue him. Peering through the gloom, she can see what she thinks is the gateway to the inner courtyard, but she can't be sure. She trips over a tent rope and the men inside shout and curse, but they don't emerge. Up to the gate. Two guards, both slumped listless against the wall, bored and cold. They are thin for the army, not thin for civilians. The siege is only yet nibbling these people. She passes through without comment, she's not sure if they even see her. If they do, they don't seem overly bothered.

The inner courtyard, at last, has some light. Large tents are arrayed here, each very close by its neighbour and some low lamps burn within them, turning them into cocoons of light. If the siege outside stank, here it is worse. The air is thick with the smell of shit, animal and human, and the ground slick with God knows what. It hasn't rained in a while, so it's nothing pleasant.

She approaches the tower. A guard is at something like attention on the door. Now the word must be used, tried, like a spell.

'Gefangener,' she says. It means 'prisoner'.

He says something unintelligible back to her, a stream of crunching, clashing words. She smiles, lowers her head. He rolls his eyes and takes her around the back of the tower. Here sharp steps descend into darkness. He says something squawky again and goes back around the other side of the tower. There are no guards here and the cobbles are too hard to pitch tents but some of the poor lie against the curtain wall, ragged people but no more ragged than the poor of Paris, a city not burdened by siege.

She goes down the steps into the black. The door is cold and mossy, and she feels around. There is no lock, only a hefty bolt. She raps at the door. 'Monsieur Girard! Monsieur Girard!' No noise from within. She draws back the lock. A waft of even fouler air than exists outside, a reek like a punch in the face.

She steels herself, goes inside. It is utterly sightless here. She strains to listen, can hear breathing. She steps forward gingerly, testing the way, toe by toe. Her hand is above her head, feeling for any beam or obstruction. Then something solid, a groan.

'Monsieur, Monsieur Girard. I am here to help you!'

He groans again. Is it him?

'Monsieur. Are you Girard of the Picardie?'

'I am, God have mercy on me,' he says in his aristocratic French. 'God forgive a poor sinner!'

She kneels, puts her hand to his body. A leg. She feels upward. His face is wet with sweat, though it is cold in the dungeon.

'Monsieur, that will not do,' she says. 'It will not do. You are not dying. Be your former self. Curse God and vow to live.' She has her knife in her coat. It feels big there, too big, waiting for use. She sees Paval dead in the Bois, thinks of his mother's tears, thinks of the terrible cemetery where he now lies. She is itching to cut this man's throat.

'God receive me. Sweet Jesus, take me into your care, a penitent and sinful man.'

'Curse God and I will take you from this place!'

'Devil, fever devil, get away from me. I repent all my sins and beg the forgiveness of the Lord. I am confessed and ready to be taken into His peace.'

Ah, shit. This is a disaster.

She has no idea what state he is in, if he can even be moved. If they've left him here with only a bolt to hold him in, unsupervised, she doubts he is in any condition to go vaulting over the walls. Girard is in fear of his life and has made his peace with God. She has no option, she must rescue him and restore him to health so he can resume his sinful ways. Then she can kill him. Moving him, letting him down by rope or ladder as she had thought, will more than likely send his soul straight to Heaven. What to do?

Footsteps outside. A lamp. In the beam of its passing she sees Girard. His face is puffy, slick with sweat. His hand is swollen, pumped up like a bladder, and the arm has a raw wound in it. Then the beam of light returns. It descends and she shrinks back into the darkness, up against the wall nearest the door.

She hears a voice in German. A tone of disgust. The lamp bearer shouts at someone, a rebuke, she thinks. The door is closed, and it is bolted. She is now a prisoner too.

Scene Six

Hark, Hark, the Blast of War!

She finds the door, groping, and runs her knife along the frame until it catches on the bolt.

There is no moving it, though she works the tip of the blade against the metal, trying to persuade it free. She tries to cut at the wood of the door, to make a hole big enough for her to work a finger in and scrape the bolt open, but whoever made the door has put some thought into it. A formidable iron plate protects the wood at the level of the bolt. Furie, her fox stole, comes to life and sniffs at the door. Finding nothing, they shoot back up Julie's body to limply take their place again at her neck.

Julie thinks for a long time, but no idea presents itself. Nothing for it but to wait for the attack the next day. The night deepens, chills. Dawn seeps under the door, offering a little light. Girard's face is pale and bloodless, and she fears he will die. She has no water to offer him, nor bread.

The castle simmers with noise as the sun rises – the clangour of a smith's working, the wailing of children, the misery of dogs waking to hunger, shouts and cries in that jagged tongue. Then it is as if all the noise of the day has poured itself into one mould, a mould of a cannonball fired hard against the gates. A monstrous thump. Deep silence and then the crackle of musket fire in reply.

The thump has breached a gate – not of wood but of reason. The castle erupts in clamour, a noise like the souls of the damned receiving the judgement of God, louder, more desperate than anything she has ever heard, an orchestra of fear. Cannon fire again, so loud the guns could be in the room with her. Girard stirs. Not dead yet. Not dead yet.

Smoke drifts in, bitter, the smoke of powder, other notes too, the smoke of wood burning. Screams and the sounds of clashing metal, fusillade after fusillade of musket fire.

Fear makes her thirsty and she wishes she could drink. She grasps her knife, willing her fingers to relax on it. She wants to move, to fight if need be. But no one comes, no one comes. More smoke, more noise. Crackle and bang and scrape and scream. Footsteps running, down the steps they come. She stands, back against the wall.

The bolt is pulled aside, the door opened, a curse and a shot, so close she loses all hearing. Black powder is in her nostrils, her vision is white from the flash. A shape enters, goes towards Girard. She stabs it, hardly seeing and, as her floating vision comes back, sees a German soldier dead at her feet. Another bang, loud enough to break her deafness and a bullet strikes her, not from behind but from the front.

All the wind is knocked from her and she goes sprawling backwards against the stone, vision swimming, her hearing dead.

A moment's confusion – has someone shot her from within the chamber? There is no one there. A ricochet, she has been hit by a ricochet. Her sight blurs, fails.

Footsteps, a shout. There is a weight upon her, constricting her breath, crushing her ribs. She stabs wildly with her blade, feels it thump against something, withdraws and stabs again. When she twists, the weight falls away. Light smudges back into clear vision and another soldier is dead on the floor.

They had come to kill Girard, fearing the siege lost. She stands, a wetness at her side, her head is swimming. There is no pain but there is blood. She grabs Girard. He is a small man and she a tall woman, but his weight is immense to her. She heaves him up the steps, arms under his arms. Around her, panic reigns; men rush and shout, scream and bawl, but at what and why, she does not know and neither do they.

Now she drags Girard against the curtain wall. Getting him out is impossible, she thinks.

She lays him down. Extreme times call for extreme measures. She runs back to the dungeon. Her own smallsword will not do now. A man can be spiked by such a weapon and not die for a week. Fine for a duel but, in a battle, a man needs to know when you've killed him. She withdraws the German soldier's military sabre, feeling its weight in her hand. This will do. She hopes it will do – she doesn't know what she will face when she gets to the gate.

She limps around to the gate in the wall. Above her, muskets rattle and crack, men with sabres hack at grappling ropes, great stones are hefted and dropped over the edge of the battlements. The gate heaves and protests but it holds as twenty men of the town press to keep it shut. Facing the gate is a cannon, a good-sized gun on big wheels staffed by a crew of six. A stout man in a dark coat holds the pole of the linstock, its slow match sizzling at its end. Another man carries a bag of powder, still another a great ramrod. The powderman jabbers and crosses himself and she can see how the linstock bearer shakes with fear as he calls out prayers to Heaven. She sees the plan – if the door gives, the cannon will discharge, killing all who stand in the way. She caves in the side of the linstock bearer's head, feeling the shock of the blow, the crunch of steel on bone all the way along her arm. She picks up the pole, laying her sword on the ground. All attention is on the gate and so she has the fire at the hole before anyone can react. But it does not fire, only sizzles and smokes, and then the powderman gives a cry and the gun sergeant is on her with his own sabre. She deflects his swinging blow with the linstock but slips and staggers backwards. Time slows, she is on the ground. The powder at the hole is smoking, the sergeant raises his sabre, the powder flashes, the sabre falls, she rolls aside as the great blade drops, sparking off the cobbles. The gun roars and death is loose among them. Bone smashes, wood smashes, metal bends as the ball and a quantity of loose bolts and stones passes through the defenders, through the gate, ripping a great hole, forcing it from its hinges.

The sergeant swings again but she has found her sword and catches his blade. Even deflected, the force of the blow feels as if it will shove her through the cobbles, but he has put too much into it, committed too far and he stumbles forward. She cuts him down at the knee, sending him spiralling and wailing to the floor. Then she is up, the pain in her side suddenly sharp as the thrill of the fight is overwhelmed by her injury. Time moves strangely, each heartbeat an hour. A charnel house faces her. The defenders have been torn to pieces by the shot and raw meat extends in a bloody tongue to the mouth of the gateway. The carnage does not stop there. The cannon has turned the wood to deadly splinters, sending them flying into the party trying to lay a charge on the other side. Torn bodies in the once pale uniform of the Picardies lie sprawling before it. The gun crew briefly consider attacking her but then run for it into the castle, because it is as if a pale tide is rushing in – the French foot charging the gate.

'Come on!' shouts Julie. 'Come on! I have led the way.' A musket swivels and fires at her. She sees the flash, then the bang, hears the ball zinging off the cobbles. She is alive. She runs, around the back of the tower and towards Girard. There he is, lying where she left him, alive or dead she does not know. It takes a tremendous effort to get him upright, slumped across her shoulders. Her knees buckle, he slips from her grasp but then she has him. She staggers forwards. Now all manner of shit is being thrown from the high tower – stones, planks, pans raining down in a deadly clatter. A Picardie officer rounds the corner.

'Girard!' he says but a great shape descends above him and he is smashed down in the deep chord-like sound of a falling clavichord, white keys flying like teeth from a smashed mouth as it lands.

'Help me! Help me!' she cries.

A Picardie footman grabs Girard by the other side, then another takes over from her and they retreat under a hail of musket fire, bricks and bottles. Through the first gate, fighting everywhere. The plan – you can't call it a plan – in these sieges is slaughter, slaughter for its own sake and as a message to all others who will resist. Every man, woman and child in the palace knows it and they fight madly against their attackers with whatever they can find. The Picardies are in, others are joining them. The town is won, surely the town is won. She loses sight of Girard as he is rushed through the advancing horde. This won't do, she runs as hard as she can, the pain at her side enough to make her retch.

He has gone, he has gone. No! There he is, between the two men of Picardie. She chases hard. They are outside the palace, now, descending the slope.

'My friends,' she says. 'What are your names?'

'Roux,' says one, 'Simon,' the other.

'You will be well remembered for this kindness, but the palace falls. It falls. I cannot keep you from your plunder!'

'This man owes me money.'

'And you will be paid. I will take him to the doctor. You go and reap your reward within.'

An exchanged glance between the men, a nod. 'You take him to the billet. By the square.'

'I will.'

The men smirk at each other and then turn back to the castle, crying plunder. And then a welcome sight. Fancheux is coming the other way, clasping his big surgeon's saw.

'Fancheux, Fancheux, here!'

The doctor bounds over.

'Look to him,' she says. 'Save him!'

Fancheux bends to Girard. He spends a few minutes examining him as the camp's hangers-on – women, old men, children, dogs – charge up the hill after the soldiers, eager for plunder, eager to watch some action, if not participate in it.

'He is very ill,' says Fancheux. 'You are a better target for my attention than him.'

'Help him!'

'He is cold, Julie, ready to die!'

'Fancheux, this is a great gentleman. A great gentleman! Save him and you will have all the letters of recommendation you need!'

'He is going to die!'

'No! No, Fancheux, he is going to be your greatest achievement. This is where you will rise to the level of the great doctors of history!'

'You need me to look at your wound!'

'Later! For now save him. I do not want him to die!'

Fancheux glances almost longingly up the hill to the palace.

'Very well. I'll help.'

They drag Girard backwards down the steep hill, between them. The wound at her side hurts but she presses on until she makes the town, her arms numb.

Here the carts are assembled, waiting to carry away the booty. She finds a donkey that is towing a small handcart. It is tied but unattended and she pushes Girard onto the cart and leads the donkey away.

'Hey, where are you going?' A rough-looking fellow, a farmer of some sort, stands in her way.

'To the hospital.'

'That cart's rented to the Dauphin's regiment, find another.'

'I am taking this.'

'You are taking nothing.'

She glances left and right. A tide of men still rushing into the gate, panic, noise.

'Let me pay you,' she says.

She produces her knife.

'Pick the cart up at the Picardie billet later. You will be rewarded. Or I can pay you here, now, with this.'

The farmer looks at the knife, hard. Then he curses her and walks away.

'Get to the billet,' says Fancheux.

'You must work on him in the cart while I drive.'

'That is impossible.'

'Then your future is impossible. Believe me, Fancheux, this man has enemies and must be got away from them. Trust me!'

'We are going the wrong route. This is away from the town!'

'Exactly. And now you do as I say, or I will say you forced me to help you kidnap him.'

'Kidnap him or you will accuse me of kidnap. I see.'

'Exactly.'

Fancheux shrugs. 'Drive on,' he says.

Scene Seven

What a Thing Am I!

Fancheux treats Girard's wounds as they travel, applying poultices of strong wine. He lectures Julie on how he is following the example of clever Hugh of Lucca and someone called Chirurgia Magna, but it washes over her. Well, not all of it: she has a good swig of the wine as she steers the cart.

'Where are we going?' says Fancheux.

'To the nearest unruined place. To somewhere the army has not passed through and through which it will not pass,' she says.

'But why?'

'This gentleman must recuperate in private and in quiet. We must bring him to health. He cannot have any shocks or knocks.'

'So you are the doctor now?'

'Trust me,' she says. 'Fortune awaits you.'

'I don't trust you,' says Fancheux. 'But I have a feeling about you. You are not like ordinary men.'

'In what way?'

'Well, you are a woman, for a start.'

She laughs. 'How did you know that?'

'I am a doctor after all. Your face shape, the way your body flows in curves not angles, the absence of anything approaching a beard. But mostly, I have never once seen you piss up against the back wheel of the cart. Why do you disguise yourself?'

'The world belongs to men,' she says. 'And I would have my portion.'

They follow the road of the army's destruction at first, camping in the cold night in the cart, huddling together for warmth. Fancheux sees to Julie's wound and says it's not as bad as it appears. The bullet either grazed her or was stopped by her coat. It cut her and broke a rib but nothing more. He gives her one of his poultices.

At night Fancheux sleeps one side of Girard, Julie lies uncomfortably on the other, but sleep only really comes after dawn when the sun rises. It is cold at night but in the day spring shows it is winning the battle to change into summer. She dreams of Charlotte-Marie and of Paval and wishes life could be simpler. She could be happy as a lady's maid, sneaking to that lady's bed when her husband went away. She could have been happy as a poor man's wife, maybe. She could even be happy with Fancheux, though he is not much to look at. Wouldn't it be better to have a handsome man, she asks herself. It helps, yes, it helps but there are other considerations too. Money, renown, some sort of mastery of something counts too. Fancheux has only one out of four.

There are hills here and the donkey struggles along their tracks, head low to shield its eyes from the afternoon sun. They are heading broadly north-west, she thinks. They drink at streams and Fancheux loads grit into his little pistol to take down an unwary pigeon. They are hungry but it doesn't matter. Lots of people are hungry for lots of the time, that is the way of humanity since the very beginning.

Girard is sweating now, heavily. Fancheux says that is a good sign, the fever is leaving him, and he feeds him herbs in water, cleans his wounds with wine.

'We should drink that,' says Julie.

'It's better used preserving his wounds,' says Fancheux.

'How so?'

'What do you mean, "how so"?'

'How does it work? Does the wound become drunk?'

'You are ill educated,' says Fancheux, though he laughs as he says it.

'Then how?'

Fancheux goes to speak and then pauses. 'I was going to say that it's the wisdom of the ancients,' he says. 'But then, the wisdom of the ancients is simply that it works. No one says how. Perhaps the wound does get drunk. Or perhaps wine carries some beneficent quality, some quality of merriment, that gladdens the body at the site of the wound. Truly I don't know. It will be about balancing humours, no doubt, but I am in need of medical school to understand exactly how.'

'It seems you are ill educated too,' says Julie.

'I am,' says Fancheux. 'Perhaps this good man will provide the remedy.'

'What makes you think he is a good man?'

'Would you save a bad one?'

'Would you?'

'Yes. A doctor must treat anyone, regardless of their virtue.'

'Would you treat the Devil, knowing the harm she would cause in the world?'

'I think I shall never meet the Devil to be tested. And why she?'

'I have met her,' says Julie.

'Is she in need of a doctor?' He is not taking her seriously, she is glad. It's good, though, to talk about such things to someone, though she must cloak her true meaning behind a mask of jokes.

'Not presently,' she says. 'But one day the Devil must go to war with God. And then, she may be wounded as this fellow is wounded. Would you patch her knocks?'

'If that was God's will.'

'Ah, so you operate by God's will.'

'Whatever that is. Is it not unknowable?'

'You ask a priest,' says Julie.

Fancheux snorts. 'Then you'll get the priest's will.'

'That's blasphemy,' says Julie.

'I'm full of them.'

Julie is worried now, for Fancheux.

'Don't you go to confession?' she says.

'Not I.'

'So you are unshriven.'

'I don't believe God can be known,' says Fancheux. 'Is He really concerned if I fuck a woman or two out of wedlock?'

Julie smiles. She wondered how long it would take him to get round to that.

He goes on: 'What can God, who sets the stars on their course every day, care about the petty doings of men? Wouldn't that make Him petty Himself? Small, when we know Him to be grand?'

Julie laughs.

'God is that petty,' she says. 'I know it more than most.'

Should she tell him how she knows? There is no reason to.

The going is slow through the hills with Girard but after a week or so, the land becomes more prosperous, less depleted. They have left the army's trail and come out of its long supply route. They arrive at a farmhouse, its meadows blooming with the May sun. Inside things are not so pleasant. The farmer has just lost his son to the scarlet fever and another seems to be going the same way. Fancheux offers his services free and orders the child purged by enema before being moved to the night air. In return they receive a bed for the night.

When, the next day, the child's fever has lifted, the farmer is so grateful that he bids Fancheux stay for as long as he likes, at least until his gentleman patient is better. So Girard gets a warm room, warm wine to bathe his wounds and, when he begins to cry out in pain – a good sign, says Fancheux, a very good sign – Fancheux administers his opium. Girard falls quiet.

She waits a fortnight to see if Girard recovers. He is still delerious, though the nights are getting shorter and summer is heralding its arrival with warm blue days.

'How long will it take for him to be able to speak and reason again?' says Julie.

'I don't know. A month, maybe more.'

Julie sniffs the air. Spring is becoming summer, for sure. She does not have a month to waste. Six men left to dispatch to Hell and an errant ghost to catch and only a few months left to do it.

When Fancheux is out in the fields helping the farmer repair walls, Julie sits by Girard's bed. His arm is still heavily strapped and bandaged but the hand is no longer swollen, though it is black with bruises.

'You are recovering, my lord. Would you like a whore? A boy, a girl?'

He says nothing, does not even stir.

She thinks to take his hand, to put it to her breast. Would that count as sin enough? His hand would have offended, as it says in the Bible. She cannot be sure, though, that God would not regard that as no sin at all, Girard having no control over the actions of his hand.

She tries it, feels his clammy fingers against her. He whispers something.

'Yes?' she says, leaning close. 'Yes?'

'Jesus save me,' he whispers and falls back into his stupor.

She curses, feels like strangling him but refrains. That will not do.

Fancheux has gone sweet on her, she can tell. He smiles when she comes in, tries too hard with his jokes, compliments her all the time. She knows that the quickest way to cure most of these gentlemen of their infatuation is to give in to their demands easily. They do not want what they can easily have. She will not give in. She thinks of Charlotte-Marie. Is she in love? Or is it just that she is, like the gentlemen she mocks, wanting the unattainable or, at least, the distant. She can see no future for her and Charlotte-Marie. The gulf in rank is too great, even if she were to become a great singer.

Of that – she notices her voice is improving. She asks Fancheux 'have you any cure for this?' and tells him of the wound she suffers. He listens to her sing. 'You are good,' he says. 'Your voice is low for a woman, but it is good.'

'Good will not do,' she says. 'Unique and brilliant is what is required. It improves with the . . .' She cannot say it, must not say it and then she does. 'It improves with the death of my enemies.'

Fancheux's eyes widen.

He asks to inspect her throat and mouth, peers within.

'You have killed many enemies?' he says.

'Enough. And every time, the taste of their blood improves my singing.'

Fancheux adopts a posture of comic fear.

'And do you sing much in between these blood drinking sessions?'

'Only immediately afterwards.'

'Then it is simple,' he says. 'All you are doing is relaxing. And each time you sing, you work to relax your throat, to stretch scarred flesh, a little more. Take this and then use your seclusion here. Go to the fields to sing.'

She sips at the medicine he gives her. An opium tincture. She nearly refuses it after what happened with Charlotte-Marie. She cannot lose any more time. But her voice is worth taking the risk for. She takes a draught. She feels light-headed, warm and steps into the sun. When she goes to the fields she sings and it is wonderful to release herself, to have the sound pour forth. By the third day of trying, her voice is better – so different to what it was, so profoundly deeper but perhaps a little sweeter too. She takes the opium, sits in the sun and sings. To fight her new voice, to insist on the high notes she hit not a year before, is folly. Instead she plunges, exploring the depths she can now attain.

The Devil is there. Lucifer watches her, lies with her, kisses her, and their kisses taste of something burned and wonderful. Julie wants them to go but cannot summon the strength beneath the influence of the opium.

'You will yet be mine,' says Lucifer.

'Not easily,' says Julie. 'Why are you here?'

'To listen,' the Devil says. 'Such beauty. It comes not from your mouth, Julie, nor your throat. This is a beauty of the soul.'

'You will never have it,' she says, waking and sitting up in the middle of the meadow. Time has slipped, it seems. It is now June and the day is warm.

The birds are singing in the meadow, larks dance in the blue air. There are so many more men to kill but the tincture seems to sap her will. There is no way of getting a letter to Sérannes or Charlotte-Marie from here. Instead, she must go to Paris, discover what has become of her enemies.

On the third week of walking, dozing and dreaming, she refuses Fancheux's tincture. A sweat breaks out as she does so.

'Cured?' he says.

'A different sort of sick,' she says. 'I will stay here forever if I take any more of that.'

It's a hot summer morning when she sets off, on foot. Girard lies in his bed, not knowing the world. But the signs are good. The fever has gone, says Fancheux, and his wounds are healing nicely. He will likely live.

'Will he ever be as he was?' says Julie.

'Perhaps,' says Fancheux. 'You love him, don't you?'

'Something like that,' says Julie.

'Perhaps I should let him die.' He transfers his weight from foot to foot, hems and haws a little. 'If he were not here, would you have me?'

'No,' says Julie. 'Not until you are rich. And for that, you need Girard's letter. I will come in a month or two from Paris. I will bring fine paper and ink.'

'And if he chooses to leave?'

'Persuade him he needs to stay. His weakness is dice. Reintroduce him to the vice. To any vice. Men like this live for such things and I am sure he will recover more quickly than if recommended to virtue.'

Fancheux laughs. 'That is strange physick!' he says.

'Cure his body. Sicken his soul,' she wants to say but does not. Instead she says, 'The farmer's boy can run errands for you if you need anything. How are you for money?'

'Well enough,' he says.

'Good,' she says. 'Keep him here.'

She likes Fancheux and she would like to stay. Perhaps one more day, then, one more draught of opium, one in the company of the charming Fancheux. Yes, just one. No. Is it Fancheux or is it the opium that makes her want to stay?

She kisses him, on the lips and he leans forward to deepen the kiss. She withdraws.

'By summer's end,' she says. 'I will see you.'

Scene Eight

The Steel Caress

The road back to Paris is a long one and more than once she thinks to turn back to the farmhouse. Strange visions attend her at night – the wandering ghost of Dreux staring at her, little Diandré, searching for his head, Paval asking if he can have his blood back. She shivers through the days and thinks she may be coming down with a fever. If only she had the tincture, that would cure it. She longs for it. At one point she walks back a mile, determined to return to Fancheux and take a soothing draught of opium. Then she sees its folly. If she wants something that much, then it is better to do without it. She forces herself on to Paris.

Charlotte-Marie's note awaits her at the Opéra when she returns – 'As soon as you return, tell me, I am waiting for you. I know who your "Diablo" is!'

Pelletier is there too, in a fine coat. 'You prosper,' she says.

'Less so when you are absent,' he says.

'I'll have work for you before long.'

'I live to serve,' he says with a bow. 'Yourself,' she thinks, but that's the way she likes it. She knows where she stands with Pelletier.

Arcand is arch. 'We'll just keep the job open for you, shall we?'

She has one word for him. 'Diandré.' He lowers his eyes.

'Your revenge progresses?'

'It progresses.'

She writes to Charlotte Marie immediately, dispatching a messenger boy.

In a day the letter returns but borne not by the messenger boy but Sérannes.

'You,' she says.

'Me,' he says.

'To what do I owe the displeasure?' She is teasing him. Sérannes is interesting, for a man, and she likes him.

'Your Charlotte-Marie's father does not think your acquaintance a good one. Luckily for you, he does not know you work here.'

'I see. And you are his messenger boy?'

'A little more,' he says. 'I am here to kill you.'

'How inconvenient for you,' says Julie. 'Why does he not call the police?'

'Who knows? Perhaps he doesn't want scandal attaching to his daughter. And it won't have escaped his notice that the police have proved rather ineffective at detaining you. Almost as if they regard some of these aristocrats as best got rid of and are happy to let them keep dying for a while.'

'So I am some sort of royal rat-catcher, am I?'

'Maybe. But you are also a rat, which is why I am here to dispose of you.'

'Dispose away,' she says.

Sérannes sees her eyeing a heavy candlestick and puts up his hand to dissuade her from slugging him with it.

He smiles. 'Unfortunately, I cannot find you,' he says. 'It appears you have quit Paris.'

'I will see Charlotte-Marie,' says Julie.

'Over my dead body,' says Sérannes at the same time that Julie says, 'over your dead body,' so they both laugh at the coincidence.

'Walk with me,' says Sérannes. 'As a man, so you may not be known if we are seen.'

She takes breeches and a coat from the wardrobe, puts on a man's large hat and they walk along the Seine, arm in arm.

The river is a trickle, the summer has been dry, and it stinks worse than usual. The banks are baked bare, all trees stripped long ago for firewood, but a little way off the grand houses of the Île de la Cité rise pale in the afternoon sun.

Sérannes takes her arm.

'Your Charlotte's father is a powerful man,' he says. 'He could make a deal of trouble for you.'

'Like having me killed.'

'And those around you too. Those at the Opéra. You need to leave now, Julie.'

'I have to be here. I have men to kill.'

'Yes, well, about that. Charlotte-Marie has made a little discovery for you.'

He takes out a letter.

'That is from her?'

'Yes.'

'You read it?'

'Yes, and only me. You are lucky. Most communications in and out of Versailles are read by the king's men. This one escaped them in my pocket.'

Julie reads.

'Dearest Julie. My beastly father has confined me to Versailles and insists that, should I attempt to continue my liaison with you, or anyone like you, I shall be sent to a nunnery. Rather like exiling a wolf from the hills to the sheep's pen, I'd have thought. But nuns are dreary, Julie. Come and see me when you get the chance. I will find someone for you to kill. Diablo is very likely my father's acquaintance Du Bellay. I heard someone call him it the other day and he shushed them. The man who used the name was Godefroy and he bears extravagant roses upon his shoes! And Dreux, it appears, has a brother. You'd have thought one of them was enough. I expect you'll want to give him the chop too. A dreadful bore, he deserves worse, my darling, he really does. I must see you soon or I will go mad.'

'Can you get me to these men?'

'That will be difficult, but I think we have the solution to two of our problems here. I have been doing some asking of my own. The men who assaulted you – many things can mark them out but one thing marks someone more clearly than any ring, blemish or tone of voice. Fear. The most afraid are the most guilty, in my experience. And one man, Gourgue Viscount of Tarascon, has become very afraid recently, very pious. He claims to have been visited by a ghost – the ghost of Dreux, no less, and – on its urgings – has surrendered his life of excess at the court of Versailles to become a monk in the hills of Tours.'

'That is remarkable,' says Julie. 'First that the ghost should visit him and second that he should be so moved by the visit as to turn to God.'

'Indeed. Particularly considering his penchant for whoring and debauchery of all sorts. He takes mass at every opportunity. A sea change, as the English would say.'

Julie thinks. Gourgue is clearly afraid for his soul. She cannot get to it if he has become a model of piety. These rich men. They dance with the Devil in moonlit woods but, when real danger faces them, they cower behind their prayer books like frightened children in the dark.

'Do you think his conversion will last?'

'Until the present terror has gone. That is what he has said,' says Sérannes.

Julie thinks.

'Well, we can satisfy everyone here,' she says. 'I will leave Paris, as you ask, but to go to this monastery. You will be able to tell your master true that I am gone and that you know where I am going. You will follow to kill me. We will establish more details when we get there.'

'And what do I get for my pains?' says Sérannes.

'Me,' she says. 'You love me, do you not? Or think you do, in the way men love any pretty woman.'

'I am infatuated with you,' says Sérannes. 'It may turn to love were it reciprocated.'

'Help me in this and I might let you have me. As a wife.' The words are out before she has considered them. Sérannes is no duke, nor anything like one. But he has a roof over his head, he is near to Charlotte-Marie, so why not? She could even teach fencing with him, should she live so long.

'But I am supposed to kill you. That, I believe, would be an impediment to our future happiness.'

'The Devil's Blade will die. You will return with a sweet and homely girl you met in the country.'

'You?'

'Yes.'

'What would Charlotte-Marie say?'

'She is a sophisticated lady. She knows the necessity of husbands for women like us. Your duke might even let us nearer.'

Sérannes reddens. She didn't think such a man was capable of embarrassment. She knows what he is thinking. She is beneath him.

'You do not rush to marriage?' she says.

'No. I . . .'

'I do not blame you. You must sample before you buy. And I must sample you.'

'Sample me?' He seems appalled, amused but appalled.

'I must know you are fit for my purpose. You are the lord of the sword in these parts?'

'I have a certain skill.'

'I need to be sure of it. Come with me.'

She leads him by the hand back to the Opéra, through the winding backstage and out into a little courtyard that is catching the last of the dying sun. There is no show tonight and the building is quiet around them, save for some sparrows brawling in the eaves.

She buttons her coat and turns to him.

'Undress me,' she says.

He goes to undo the buttons, but she draws back.

'No. Not with your hands. With your blade. I need to know what I am giving myself up to. Undress me, take off my clothes. But cut me once and you shall never have me.'

He smiles and bows to her, unsheathes his sword.

He holds it daintily between his fingers like a lady with a pen, she thinks, but then the arm flashes out, the thumb presses on the grip and the point sings down. One button is cut, then another and another. A fourth, a fifth and the coat is open at the front. She stands facing him, quite still. He slices her shirt front with a single movement. He runs the point of his blade across the cloth that binds down her breasts, bids her turn around. The shirt is sliced through at the back, split from neck to tail. It falls away. He works the tip of the sword under the knot that secures the binding, pulls and it tumbles down.

She turns to face him, half naked in the dusk.

Now he runs the blade across the string that secures her culottes and cuts that too with a quick flick of the wrist. The trousers drop.

'Good enough?' he says.

'Good enough,' she says and pulls up the trousers, gathers the coat around her.

'Is that it?' he says.

'You are fit for my purposes,' she says. 'I will need more from you before you get more from me.'

244

Scene Nine

Penitence Will Be My Salvation!

Tours is light and airy compared to Paris. They reach it at the best time of year to see it, she thinks, full summer with the light dancing on the lovely Loire, its pale stone bright, its markets full of colour. They do not spend long there and head out quickly towards the abbey.

St-Denis sits just above a pretty woodland in the shadow of a great raw hill that falls just short of being a mountain. Its black flank dominates the country behind the abbey, rising above it like the hunched body of an enormous wolf. The air here is clean and sharp and, when she sings, it seems to hold a brighter note than the rotten murk of Paris.

'Your voice is strong,' says Pelletier, who walks beside her. 'A singing career isn't going to put you off devilment, is it? I made a good penny out of stealing that pig. The plate sold to a church near the Marais.'

'Have I had my share?'

'Your share was entrance to the city. The pig and the plate were my own work. Though, I admit, you are lucky for me, that's why I like you. Everywhere you go, opportunities emerge. No chance of a fuck, is there?'

'There is,' she says.

'Great! Here?' They are on the monastery road from Tours.

'There is no chance,' she says. 'You can afford a whore.'

'Yes, but they're fussy around here.'

'And you think I'm not?'

He laughs and she says, 'Take a bath at the monastery, Pelletier. Or put on some perfume if you fear catching a cold. Clean clothes too. You will find yourself more acceptable to women.'

'Oh, women,' he says. 'Why will they not take me as I am?'

'I refer you to my earlier comments,' she says. Her father used to say that when doing the Duke's legal business. It makes her laugh to remember it.

The monastery is a large affair, with many outbuildings in good pale stone. The monks here are industrious and, as she approaches, she can hear the sound of metal beating, a choir of plainsong and smell the aroma of hops in the air.

This abbey is the heart of the area, she can see, and this is a calm and peaceful country. A rough man leading a stout chestnut carthorse descends the path, a purse chinking at his side. So no fear of bandits here, then. Children run in the abbey's shadow, calling out in a game of touche-touche, a touch passing it from one to the next.

A stream runs down one side of the building and, in it, brothers are washing grey sheets while, across in the main building, a saw barks. They are constructing, or reconstructing, a doorway.

Gourgue will not be here under his own name, for sure. She is here as a letter bearer once more – or supposedly so, dressed as a boy. Monsieur Girard has something to say to the good Gourgue and has entrusted her with a most important missive.

She makes her way to the travellers' lodge and peeks within. No one is there at this time of day but there is a good area of sleeping space and even some rough blankets piled at one end of the hall. She is tired – it has been a long walk south from Paris – but she is not sleepy.

She is looking, above all else, for someone she can ask for the whereabouts of Gourgue. A boy comes in, dressed in good peasant's clothing. He looks at her like a deer staring at a strange movement in the trees.

'I am looking for a wealthy man who has recently come here,' she says. He says nothing but, like a deer, turns and runs away.

She waits for a while. In Paris you might go and search for the maître d'hôtel but here, in the country, one waits. Time moves more slowly. She thinks about that. Will her allotted year go less quickly if she sits here than if she bothers herself with chasing about trying to avoid her fate? If, in the end, any of the Tredecim survive or if one manages to get himself killed, would it have been better to have spent the time sitting in the cool shadows, smelling pine smoke on the breeze, thinking about nothing more than the next breath? But that is not her way. If time is to disappear, let us gulp at it, guzzle it. When it is gone it is gone, the same as if she had sat nibbling it by the fire.

Eventually a red-faced monk comes in. He stinks of hops, whether by production or consumption, she can't guess. Perhaps both. The boy hovers beside him.

'Yes?'

'I am searching for Gourgue. I have a letter for him.'

'No one of that name here.'

'A gentleman. Very holy, recently arrived from Paris.'

'Very fat?'

'Very fat.'

'And short?'

'No taller than my shoulder.' Sérannes has told her that.

He eyes her suspiciously.

'None here like that,' he says. 'Give me the letter and I will get it to him.' Julie smiles.

'You cannot deliver it if he is not here. I must deliver it in person. I have a quantity of money for him too. In payment of debt. You might mention Monsieur Girard.'

'I can give him any money.'

She smiles and bows.

'So he is here?'

'Don't get clever with me, son. Hand over the cash and I'll see he gets it.'

'I think I will not,' says Julie.

'Then fuck yourself,' he says.

'I would if I could,' says Julie. 'But I find my cock won't bend far enough around.'

The monk snorts and leaves but the boy laughs as soon as he is departed.

'A sou,' says Julie. 'Lead me to the short fat Parisian.'

The boy nods.

'He will be at chapel,' he says, in his thick country accent.

She passes him a coin.

'Thank you,' she says.

Julie walks out into the clear day. Somehow the woodsmoke makes the slight chill in the air that little sharper, a spice to an already delicious dish. It banishes all weariness, sharpens her sensibilities too. She is very conscious of the sword she carries at her side, the knife in her sleeve, the pistols in their case on her back. She takes a small nip of the opium tincture she has brought with her from Paris. Having cured herself of its want, she considers herself its mistress and may safely consume it again. It is a light mix, says Pomet, cut in with life-giving sugar, which is the cure for all ills. A feeling of immense pleasure sweeps over her. It is as if she is a cat rubbing the ecstasy from its body against its mistress's leg.

'Kill, kill,' she says to herself and the words seem themselves embodiments of joy.

Floating, she goes on to the chapel. It is early and the light streams through the windows. It seems to her that the sunlight is the passing of God's chariot, its golden beams lifting and caressing her. At first, her vision swimming between the chapel's contrasts of light and dark, she thinks no one is there. The smell of incense is in the air but no smoke troubles the light beams. It is past the hour of sext, before nones. The monks are at labour, not at prayer. All save one, who kneels before the altar.

He is praying:

'O Lord,

The house of my soul is narrow;

enlarge it that you may enter in.

It is ruinous, o repair it!

It displeases your sight.

I confess it, I know.

But who shall cleanse it?

To whom shall I cry but to you?'

She sits on the long prayer stool beside him. He hardly notices her, so deep in prayer is he. He has only one eye, the other covered by a patch. Her mouth goes dry with the anticipation of the ecstasy of her enemy's death.

Beads of sweat stand out on his forehead and she notices the back of his white robe is stained with red. A flagellant? Lashing himself for his sins, as if God was not more than capable of handing out stripes all on his own.

'Gourgue,' she says.

He does not acknowledge her.

'Cleanse me from my secret faults, O Lord,

And spare your servant from strange sins.'

She laughs to herself. 'Spare me from strange sins.' These men. These weaklings. As if sin descends on them from outside, unbidden. This one, this little sweaty one, has sought out sin, gone begging to find new and more outrageous offences against Heaven. None sent sin to find him. There she is, sounding like a Protestant. She crosses herself, for all the good that will do her.

'Boo!' she says, shoving him on the shoulder.

The man awakes from his rapture, opens his one eye.

'It's me,' she says.

'Who?'

'The Devil's Blade! Curse of the Tredecim! Do you know how many of your fellows I've killed?'

'Oh Jesus, save me!' he says.

She laughs.

'I am here to help you save yourself.'

'How so?'

'I offer you the chance to fight me!'

'And be skewered or trampled by one of your demons?'

'No demons. Only skewering. What do you say? You can be rid of me and go back to your whores, your drink and your dice. We'll duel.'

'No fear!' he says. 'I am a holy man until you or I are dead! I know your reputation, I'm not crossing swords with you.'

'I am offering you the chance to kill me.'

'I don't like the odds,' he says. 'Forgive me, Father, for thinking on gambling.'

'Then I'll kill you here,' she says.

He trembles.

'I'll go to Heaven, then! Dreux's ghost has told me what you're about – sending good folk to Hell.'

'Good folk won't go to Hell. And look at you, all shriven, your soul sparkly new. You'll go to Heaven in a duel.'

'Not likely! If I spike you and you die, then or later, am I not a murderer? And if I die, do I not do so in defiance of our Lord's injunction to turn the other cheek? Dreux has told me how litigious and nit-picking the Devil can be. If you want to kill me, go on, but know I'll go to Heaven and you won't have your bargain with your master.'

'Have you been communing with the dead, little man? You know what our Lord says about that!'

'They communed with me and I spent a week on my knees in here in penance since. I'll not touch dice, tit nor bottle while you live.'

'Then you might have to wait a very long time.'

'Suits me,' he says. 'I think you'll find you last shorter than you think.'

'Have you set a man to kill me?'

'That would be a sin. No. But others might. Others will.'

She smiles at him, opens her shirt to show him her breast.

'Come on,' she says. 'Would you not like to kiss me!'

'God help me, get away from me, whore!'

He stands and staggers back from her.

'God deliver me! God deliver me!' he shouts.

In an instant he will alert the other monks, she thinks. It's time to go.

She strides out of the monastery, running off down the hill. As she steals on to the back of a barrel-laden cart, concealing herself, she passes Sérannes travelling in the opposite direction.

She sits back against a barrel, presses her fingers to her side and smiles. She will have Gourgue by moonrise tomorrow.

Scene Ten

Strike, For the Love
You Bear Me, Strike!

The place of the duel is set and Sérannes has done his job. She is to meet him in the biggest clearing of the hillside wood that overlooks the monastery and there they will fight. Sérannes has explained to Gourgue that he has been tracking Julie from Paris. He has offered to stand as Gourgue's second, which means it is acceptable for him to fight for him. Her second is Pelletier, that seedy man – quite drunk but in a cleaner coat and breeches than he normally wears. He himself looks cleaner too. He's clearly taken her advice on washing at the monastery. Nevertheless, he is rolling drunk.

'Why have you come in this state?' she asks.

'I'm afraid I'll have to fight him if something happens to you.'

'You won't have to fight him,' she says. 'Nothing is going to happen to me, and he has no seconds of his own for you to get involved with.'

'Oh, all right, I got drunk because the beer's so good in these parts. And I like to be drunk. But, to matters in hand, what is the cause of this duel?' he says.

She has to come up with some reason, can't trust him with the truth. 'He has offended my honour.'

I offended your honour, you didn't challenge me to a duel.'

'I'd be afraid of catching something in getting close enough to kill you. Bad air attends you and we know how that can poison those unused to it.'

He farts, as if in illustration.

'Have you sharpened the swords?' she says.

'At the grindstone of the monastery. You would not believe the expense.'

'You're right, I wouldn't. No doubt you've doubled it for a little profit of your own.'

'I have not doubled it!'

So he has tripled it, at least.

'How much?'

'Four sou. It is not like knife sharpening, so says the grinder, more akin to needle making. Fine work.'

'Show me the blades.'

He does. Both are functional smallswords, indeed sharpened to needles. She tries her finger against one and draws a little blood. Good.

She gives him two sou and he seems well pleased.

'You have followed the rest of my instructions?'

'Yes. Are you sure you want to do this? Sérannes is a very dangerous opponent. He will kill you, very likely.'

'I do not fear death. Only damnation. You will convey my body to the monastery?'

'As you instructed. I have spoken to the monks and told them I expect one body at least in the next couple of days. They were resistant but I told them they would get good money for it.'

'And whores, you have found whores?'

'I have made whores,' says Pelletier. 'Two farmers' daughters whose virtue did not come cheap. You would not believe the price.'

'Again you are correct, I would not. How much?'

'A livre! Worth it, though. They were quite debauched, I almost blush to relate what they had me do in testing them. I could hardly come for shame.'

'Though you did.'

'And each time I did, I prayed Christ for deliverance from these bawds. After four times my prayers were answered, and I broke free of them.'

She finds it funny that he cannot bring himself to inflate the price of a whore so much, presuming it is so well known that Julie will easily spot any deception, but he is quite prepared to blow the price of sword sharpening beyond any credibility at all. Swords are for gentlemen. Therefore swords are associated with the rich, therefore anything to do with them must be incredibly expensive.

'I will pay you tomorrow.'

'You will be dead tomorrow.'

'And yet I will pay you. You have my word.'

Pelletier looks mildly puzzled. 'Oh, yes, that,' he says. 'You're virtually the only person I know to whom their word means something. I suppose I'll take it in lieu of a promissory note and your address.'

The assignation is at dusk, not full night. This is away from Paris, there is no need to hide so much here.

The abbot might object if he knew but then he might not. Gentlemen killing themselves on his doorstep is, as Pelletier has noted, a good chance to earn some funerary fees. And yet, despite the lack of need for secrecy, the hour seems apt. A time of fading light, a drawing in of attention from the wide horizons of day to the tiny buds of light from lantern and fire and so to the self. She knows she may die but she feels a thrill at the risk of it. Better to dare and stand elated or damned before creation than to hide away like a field mouse before the scythe and die anyway. Or so she tells herself. When she looks at her hands as she makes her way behind Pelletier's lantern through the pines, they are shaking. She hears the tread of the women behind her. Pelletier turns and tells them to wait. They will not be required until later.

Sérannes is already there when she arrives. He is the only one, save for a priest he has rustled up from the monastery. The man is a monk and looks slightly too excited by the prospect of plying his trade at a duel than perhaps he should. Not much opportunity for adventure in these parts, she guesses. The woods are dark now, though the clearing is light, fired by the sun that kisses the top of the pines.

She does not acknowledge Sérannes, though he offers her a short bow. Pelletier staggers across to him, offers him choice of blades. Sérannes takes one, Pelletier offers Julie the other. She takes it.

'We will commenth,' says Pelletier, who has only a little brandy left in his bottle.

'First you will know me,' says Julie.

She takes the brandy, pours it over the blade, wipes it down with a cloth. Then she applies the candle from the lantern. For an instant the blade flares blue.

'Well, as show-off tricks go, I'd account that a failure,' says Sérannes.

Julie holds up the sword.

'Know that I am Julie d'Aubigny, wronged by the men of the Black Tredecim. I have lost my love, lost my friends and lost my soul but I swear that all those who have so abused me will suffer a far worse fate. I am the Devil's, sent of the Devil to do her work!'

'Her?' says a voice from the darkness. So, as she thought, Gourgue is here.

'The Devil is a man,' says the priest. 'All the authorities agree.'

'Then the authorities are wrong,' says Julie. 'I have met her!'

The priest raises his eyebrows and crosses himself.

'Shall we stop this monstrous carnival of boasts and simply set to?' says Sérannes. 'But first, what did you do to that sword? I know tricks, madame, plenty of them. Was that for a reason beyond show?'

'It was not.'

'A poisoned blade? So the slightest nick compels me to death, and you run off into the woods to await my collapse?'

'You offend me. That was brandy, burned for the fire it brings, fire that shows the hatred in my—'

'Stop the histrionics,' he says. 'Perhaps so. But I would be of quieter mind if we were to exchange weapons. I will have your sword. You have mine.'

'As you wish,' she says.

Pelletier takes her sword to Sérannes, swaps it for his and brings his back to her.

'Would you like sacrament?' says the priest.

'God has abandoned me,' says Julie. 'I will say my prayers when He delivers me my enemies and shows He is sorry for what He has done to me.' She knows no penance or blessing can release her from her bargain.

'This is sacrilegious!' says the priest, in the appalled but fascinated way of a little boy describing a glimpse of the scullery maid's tits.

'I will take sacrament, Father,' says Sérannes.

Sérannes kneels and the priest takes wine and bread from his bag and begins the rite. As he says the Pater Noster, Julie gazes out into the woods to see if she can catch a glimpse of Gourgue, but he is invisible to her. Only as the prayer ends does she hear a voice echoing the words away in the dark.

'et ne nos inducas in tentationem;
sed libera nos a malo'

She feels a shiver knowing he is out there. It must be him. Sérannes would not commence without him present.

Sérannes takes the bread and wine, receives a blessing and then stands.

'You sure you don't want to . . .?' he says, gesturing to the priest.

'It will do me no good. And I fight better with the prospect of damnation hanging over me.'

'As you wish!'

'Ready, gents. And gentesses?' says Pelletier, who is slightly undermining the gravity of the situation by taking a substantial piss.

'Ready,' she says.

'Ready.'

'Then salute and set to!'

They salute each other and come en garde, tapping each other's blade to acknowledge the fight will begin. The fox grumbles at her shoulder. 'No, Furie,' she says. The fox can be no help to her here.

Sérannes offers his blade in a feint, or rather a cross between a feint and an invitation for her to take his blade, beat at it with her own or push it aside. It is slow but not so slow as to be obvious to any but the most perceptive fencer. She ignores it and attacks his hand. Of course, with Sérannes there are no easy wins, even were you seeking one. There is nothing she can do this early in a fight to surprise him and he easily parries, grazing down her blade to attack her arm. She yields, flicks up her sword to deflect in the guard of prime, with her hand in the position of a woman in a swoon, and stabs down at him. The blade is not so much parried as accepted, caressed, welcomed in to a deep, knee-bending embrace. It is as if his blade is made of glue, hers stuck to it immovably. But then it does move, and he extends his hand like lightning, knowing that she will mirror his parry. She does, but he has come off her sword now, avoiding it and slipping its engagement with just a movement of the fingers. She feels the blade enter under her ribs, feels it snag the flesh of her back on its exit. He has run her through, the blade sunk into her up to its hilt.

Vision blurs, her mouth goes dry. She sinks to her knees. Sérannes lets go his sword, steps back in an extravagant bow.

'I'm sorry it had to end this way,' he says.

'I'm bloody not!' Gourgue comes stomping from the trees. 'Finish her,' he says. 'Finish her!'

'She is finished,' says Sérannes. 'I do not make a habit of wasting my thrusts.'

Julie is on her side on the floor, looking at the sword's hilt in a fascinated delirium.

'She's dead?'

'She will be within a few breaths,' says Sérannes.

Gourgue kneels to her, his hand stretching out for the grip of the sword that impales her.

'No,' says Sérannes.

'No? You say "no" to me, base man?'

'That is my sword, sir, my servant in a duel with a mortal opponent,' says Sérannes. 'I allow no man to touch it and, base though I may be, you are alone here. Be thankful of the service I have given you and return to your life.'

Gourgue blows and puffs like a bulldog who has been robbed of its bone. But he relents.

'Very well,' he says. 'You, scrag-arse!' He addresses Pelletier. 'Me?'

'Yes, you. Want to earn a livre?'

'I'd prefer to earn two,' says Pelletier.

'One now, one on delivery. You will come to me in an hour at the monastery and take a letter to my friends in Paris. I'm off to get drunk and feed myself until I burst.'

'Whores, sir?' says Pelletier.

'If there are any. Of course there are some, I'm in a monastery. Can you get them to me?'

'In a trice.'

'Then do. I am free from threat, free to sin again as man was born to sin! You, priest. You can confess me in the morning?'

'Of course, sir. Though I would—'

'Need paying, of course. The whole world needs paying. It's a pity I can't confess for what I'm about to do. The Church really should try to be more convenient. If you could expiate sins in advance, you could increase your revenue and guarantee more souls for Heaven.'

'I will recommend it to the abbot the next time I see him,' says the priest.

To Julie the world is receding. She feels as if she is falling down a long tunnel, the trees, the sky just smudges of colour shrinking to nothing. She breathes in, feels the pain, so acute, then she is gone.

Scene Eleven

I Rise to Wreak Vengeance Upon You

Stone is cold beneath her back, the air is chill, and the only light comes from a chink in the doorway, a silver finger of cold moonlight stretching towards her through the dark.

She sits up, or tries to. She is in agony from the wound at her side. She steels herself and, from the most secret part within her breeches, squeezes out a bottle of Pomet's tincture, and gives it a good swig. Sérannes has removed his sword and patched her side with a bandage and lint; she feels the wad beneath her fingers.

The room warms, the silver light seems a flight of butterflies dancing before her, the pain lessens. Sérannes did his job perfectly, piercing her exactly in such a way that the needle of the blade passed through her body without causing her substantial harm – just as Fancheux had told her happened to him. Her shirt is wet beneath her fingers, though, wet with blood and she feels dizzy, despite her draught of Pomet's magic mixture.

Carefully she pushes herself upright on the morgue slab. Her head swims, not altogether unpleasantly. She breathes in. It hurts, but not too badly. The fox nudges her neck and she puts up her hand to comfort it. The little creature licks at her fingers and, for a while, she lets it, for the peace it brings.

Standing is not simple. The tincture has kept the pain at bay, but instinct tells her to keep bent over, protecting the wound. She imagines it might tear or rupture if she moves too quickly.

Of course, she has no weapon on her. Even if she had managed to keep a sword at her side, someone would have taken it by now – a monk, Pelletier maybe. Whoever put her in the morgue has almost certainly taken her knife. The only things she has in the world now are her breeches, her torn shirt, a ratty fox fur that no one would want and a bottle of poppy tincture that was hidden where none but a truly deviant man would ever look on a corpse.

She opens the door. The night is clear, all the starsplash sky stretching out above the hills, the fat moon sitting upon a cloud as if upon a table.

No one is stirring, apart from the sound of a girl's sobbing that drifts through the night air. Julie's feet are cold as she treads forward, looking for Sérannes. He is nowhere. Pelletier has gone too, no doubt to Paris, with the letter telling the gentlemen of the Tredecim that they are safe from the Devil's Blade.

Good. He will remember to mark the address to which the letter is delivered.

She notes with satisfaction that she is inside the cloister of the monastery. She had feared they might lay her out on the other side of the gates, in the servants' dwellings, cut off from the monks for the night. But no, she is at the centre of a large open courtyard flanked by covered walkways.

The woman sobs on, somehow deepening the silence Julie feels around her. She hobbles around the walkway, clinging to the shadows. There will be a dormitory somewhere and somewhere else, separate cells. She guesses Gourgue will be in one of the cells. And then, of course, she understands. The wound and the tincture had stopped her thinking. The voice of the woman. Monks were always up to their necks in whores, it was well known. But here, in the backwoods, they must find such services difficult to come by. If a woman is in there, the likelihood is that it is one of the farm girls.

She puts her ear to a door, hears nothing and opens it, but a musty smell hits her and she peers within to see rows of books upon tables. The library, then. She moves down past another door, listens there. Monks snoring. Still a third where she hears water running – the privy, very likely. At a fourth, the woman's sobs are louder and she hears a bored voice telling her to shut up. It's Gourgue, she's sure. This room smells pleasantly of pine smoke. The warming room – they must have given this over to Gourgue for his evening's sport.

She passes on until she finds what she is looking for, or rather smelling for. A deep smell of meat and a faint odour of baking bread. She pushes open the kitchen door. Long tables stretch out before her, pans and pots hung from the wall, a large fireplace furthest away from her containing no less than four spits for turning meat.

She goes down to the end of the hall, holding her side as she does. A nip of tincture at the end sends her head spinning and she sits on the table blankly for a while, pleasure coursing through her. When the rushing sensation of joy fades, she surveys her choices. There on the side she looks for what she wants. A knife? No. A steak hammer? No, too difficult to wield in her present condition. She needs something quicker and quieter. The meat spit. It's as long as a spear and sharp too.

Arming herself, she walks back, tracing the smell of the pine. She does not quite know how to go about this. If in doubt, proceed boldly, her father always told her.

She knocks.

'Who is it?'

'Me, monsieur.' She makes her voice as low as she can.

'You? The servant?'

'I am a servant.'

'Well, come in then.'

She pushes open the door.

Gourgue doesn't even look up. 'You can get me more wine and get rid of this blarting whore for me. I'll keep the other one.'

He is lying on a mattress of white linen, looking up at the ceiling, quite naked. His little cock curls beneath his belly, darker than the rest of his pale skin, sitting there like a spiralled dog turd on a pile of snow.

On the floor, one of the girls too is naked, sitting forlornly with her arms around her legs. The other one sobs in the corner, a livid bruise across her face, visible even in the candlelight.

'Good wine,' says Gourgue. 'I'll pay well.'

'Oh,' says the girl. 'Oh my, you look like a devil!' She is speaking to Julie. In her blood-soaked shirt and disordered hair, she guesses she must.

'Who asked you?' says Gourgue. 'Who asked fucking you? You keep your mouth shut until I choose to put my cock in it.'

'God forgive you!' says the girl.

'Fuck God, fuck him to fuckery. I've had enough of God to last me a lifetime in this place.'

'Hello,' says Julie.

'Hello. What do you mean, "hello"? I . . .' Finally he sits up.

'I mean "goodbye",' says Julie

'Oh Jesus fucking Christ,' says Gourgue.

He tries to get up, but his foot becomes tangled in the loose cover of the bed. She charges, the sharp end of the meat spit like a bayonet before her. She sticks him hard in the side and he goes down in a gush of blood, bellowing, screaming out 'Please!'

He tries to get up again but only makes it to his knees. She raises the spit, two handed above him.

'Please,' he says. 'Please!'

'Worship me,' she says.

'What?'

'Worship me. Call me goddess and pray for forgiveness, the forgiveness only I can grant.'

'I worship you! I beg you to forgive me. Forgive me!'

He has his arms wide, his mouth open in supplication.

'Thou shalt have no god but me,' she says as she brings the spit down. He half closes his mouth before it enters but the spike's progress is not impeded and she drives it crunching through his teeth, down into his throat and deep into his stomach.

He gargles, tries to shout, whimpers.

'Oh God! Oh God!' cries one girl, while the other still cowers.

There is a heavy bang at the door.

'Gourgue!' shouts a voice. 'I know you're enjoying yourself in there, but could you keep it down? Some of us are trying to sleep!'

Gourgue dies, slumping meatily as she releases the spit, a carcass before he even strikes the floor.

There is a silence. Even the girl in the corner has stopped sobbing, though she crosses herself repeatedly.

Footsteps leave from behind the door.

The air thickens, the sound of a bell, dissonant and deep.

'Well, well,' says a lovely, musical voice. 'What charges shall we lay at this one's door?'

Gourgue's ghost sits up from his body. He looks just like Gourgue, though he is paler, and a light green aura surrounds him. He looks at Lucifer.

'You're beautiful,' he says to Lucifer. 'How much for a fuck?'

'Absolutely no charge at all,' says Lucifer. 'I would be delighted to take you to my bed.'

'Is this Heaven?'

'I'll say this for you men of the Tredecim, you're consistent in your errors,' says Lucifer.

'Purgatory?'

'Warmer, quite literally. Third time lucky. In a manner of speaking.'

A ghost cannot really go pale, but Julie really does think she sees Gourgue blanch.

'I have given money to the poor!' says Gourgue.

'Whores don't count,' says Lucifer.

'I have . . .' Gourgue stumbles on his words, appears nonplussed.

'Run out of good works?' says Lucifer.

'I have been a good man!'

'Since your last confession you have fornicated outside marriage, you have had a god other than the Lord your God, you have beaten this girl.'

'There's nothing in the Bible that says I shouldn't hit a whore!' says Gourgue.

'All right, I'll give you that,' says Lucifer. 'But you have coveted your neighbour's wife.'

'I have not!'

Lucifer turns to the beaten girl.

'Where do you live, Madame?' says Lucifer.

'Just down the valley.'

'Neighbouring the monastery?'

'Yes.'

'And you, Gourgue, were lodged, where?'

'Here, but that doesn't make these people my neighbours.'

'I'm afraid it rather does,' says Lucifer.

'You cannot catch me on such little sins!'

'According to the Lord your God, coveting your neighbour's wife is just as bad as murder,' says Lucifer. 'Don't blame me, son, I don't make the rules. Now, to proceed, what day is today?'

'Saturday.'

'Incorrect,' says Lucifer. 'By the bells it is Sunday. The Sabbath. Yet here you are fornicating in mockery of God.'

'This is piffling!' says Gourgue.

Lucifer smiles. 'Indeed it is. Hellish, isn't it? And that, I think, will be the nature of your punishment. I will give you the chance to get out of Hell, yes. If you can find the right legal documents to present to the right demons. Of course, if you get the wrong ones, and it is mighty easy to get the wrong ones, you will incur their wrath. But, having called me piffling, you will spend your days piffling, poring over burning papers to make sure no error exists, no mistake that could confine you to Hell for another thousand years. After an eternity, maybe longer, you might be free. Or maybe not.'

'What of the salvation? The final day when God's infinite mercy extends to all.'

'I wouldn't set your hopes on that if I were you. God's infinite mercy has a way of being, shall we say, "finite".'

'I . . .'

Lucifer extends their hand and the circle of primroses sprouts on the floor of the room.

'Oh, deliver me! Deliver me!'

Gourgue is sucked into the circle and his ghost vanishes in a puff of fumes.

The girls cower, pulling the mattress over them.

'My lesson,' says Julie. Her head is swimming with Pomet's mixture, or the wound in her side, she can't tell.

'Yes,' says Lucifer. 'Today, we shall learn how to fight toe to toe. Breast to breast! Lip to lip.'

They are suddenly close to Julie, close enough that their noses touch. Julie finds a sword in her hand – it has appeared from nowhere – and lifts it. The Devil crosses blades.

'We could just forget this and go to bed,' says the Devil. 'You look like you could do with a lie down.'

Julie smells Lucifer's perfume, a rich lavender, feels the Devil's hot breath against her lips.

'The bargain is that you teach me to fight!' says Julie.

'Very well! Have at me!'

Julie pulls back her arm to stab with her sword, but the Devil puts a hand upon her wrist, stopping her from moving it. The Devil withdraws their own arm to get enough space to strike but Julie mirrors the move, holding the arm at bay with her off hand.

'Oh dear,' says the Devil.

In an instant the Devil has dropped their weapon and trapped Julie's hand by placing their hand on top of hers. Lucifer makes the shape of a question mark with the lower wrist, dropping the hand underneath Julie's but picking up a knife from their belt on the way round. Julie's wrist is locked, and the pain makes her knees give way. She is too close to use her sword properly and the Devil pushes the knife towards her throat. Her side is so painful, it feels as if the sword is still in it.

'A Japanese gentleman taught me that when I appeared to him as an ogre. He gave up its secret in return for his life! Now you try!'

Julie sticks Gourgue's meat knife into the band of her breeches. The Devil puts a hand on hers and she does the move exactly, curling under then over the wrist to make a question mark.

'Excellent,' says the Devil. 'Now you have it!'

'You are still standing!'

'Well, it's not going to work on me, is it? Practise it with your Sérannes! Now I'm going to torment Gourgue. I always love a new soul to play with!'

Lucifer steps through the ring of primroses and is gone.

The girls cross themselves and cower beneath.

'If you don't want to get blamed for this shit, I suggest you come with me,' says Julie. She bends to take a taste of Gourgue's blood, then limps from the room, grasping her side, the women trailing after.

Scene Twelve

Desire! Desire! Desire Will Lay Me Low!

The farmer will not let Julie stay in his house when he hears what his daughters have to say to him – a story of murder, the Devil striding from a great hole of fire, dragons flying in the air, a beast with the head of a wolf and the body of a horse.

Julie marvels at how fear can spark the fancy. Sérannes curls his lip and tells them they will do what he, as their better, commands. Julie thinks she should go. The word 'witch' has been mentioned and that is a dangerous enough accusation in these parts.

Still, she manages to get some sheep fat and honey from the farmer, along with a wad of linen to dress the wound. She scratches the name of 'One Eye' off the card as she lets Sérannes tend her wounds.

Sérannes pays them well enough for silence – gives them his master's visiting card, on which he scrawls his own address. 'Any problems or trouble, send for me here,' he says.

The farmer looks at the elaborate card, inlaid with silver and gold, as if it were one of the tablets of Moses passed to him by God himself. Can he read it? Probably not, but it is like nothing such a man ever sees and he is plainly in awe of it. Sérannes is sure, he tells Julie, that sight of the duke's card will be enough to bring any enquiries regarding the death of

Gourgue by the abbot to a swift end. Gourgue was a rich and powerful man, killed by an unseen hand. The idea that this may be the duke's business will mark the affair too hot a pot for him to touch. With luck he will vow the brothers to silence, bury Gourgue and insist to any who ask that he died of a fever.

Sérannes has business back in Paris, attending to the duke, but she will get back to Fancheux with Pelletier in the mule cart.

She needs a doctor, desperately, but there are none to be had outside the monastery. She feels hot, the beginnings perhaps of a fever, though she has doused her wound in alcohol, as Fancheux suggested, and smeared it with lard. She had smeared the sword with alcohol too as Fancheux had thought the alcohol confuses the bitter humours of the air as they enter the wound, making them drunk and less likely to be acceptable to the humours of the body, where they might breed corruption together. At least, that's what she remembers that he said.

Before he goes, Sérannes wants a word with her. The wound in her side is very painful and she is running low on the tincture of opium. She takes the last of it to help her doze as she sets the cart on its way east.

'You will be all right?' says Sérannes.

'I don't know. Your aim was true.'

'It tore me to do it. I have never been so nervous.'

'At least your hand did not shake.'

He smiles. 'I am Sérannes. My hands do not shake.'

'No.' She embraces him.

He takes the back of her head. 'Julie,' he says.

She leans back. 'Give my love to Charlotte-Marie,' she says.

He looks down. 'Will you never come to me?'

She holds both his hands. 'One day, when I am better, I will give you my body and my pledge if you want it. My heart, that is not mine to give.'

'Whose is it? The Mazarin girl's?'

'I think so.'

'That is unnatural.'

'Is it natural to light lamps over the streets of Paris and make it noon at midnight? Is it natural for two men to carry one other in a sedan chair? I don't see the animals doing it. Is it natural to stuff a ball into the mouth of a cannon and light war all over the world? Nature is never our best guide, particularly in this age of marvels.'

'I don't want your body, I want your love.'

'I can love men, Sérannes, but I can never love you.'

'Why?'

'Because I can love a man as you love a puppy, as a simple, silly thing, locked in its own world. You are not a simple, silly thing. I dislike complicated men for they are things of twists and knots, not depths and echoes like women.'

'You mistake me.'

'You are an actor on the stage of life. You do and you dare, you move, and you scheme. But to me you are just that – a thing in the play of life. If I were to fall in love with you it would be as one falls in love with a character in a play. The voice, the image. A woman is more.'

'How so more?'

'I could not explain in any way you would understand.'

He snorts.

'I will make you love me.'

'Love is a cloud in the sky, Sérannes. You cannot make it do anything. It is either there or it isn't.'

'For you I will summon a storm.'

She smiles. 'Summon it, then. Help me summon a storm of blood.'

'I would marry you. Now. At least do that. Innkeepers do it in these parts, don't they? No need for love to do that.'

She puts her hand to her chest.

'Me, the Devil's Blade, whose name ghosts tremble to speak? And a girl still with the Alsace shit beneath her fingernails? A fine job you'd have introducing me to your lord.'

'You should be honoured.'

'And I am.'

'Will you consider it?'

'I have said I will. When my time is up, and I am free of the Devil, I will marry you, Sérannes.'

He nods.

'Goodbye then. Try not to die.'

The journey east is a hard one – the summer sun bakes them; the hills are steep and the ways narrow.

Julie rocks on the little cart, her sword by her side, counting the deaths of her enemies. Eight so far – if she includes Dreux. Five to go. How long will it take her to properly recover? To be ready to face them? She doesn't know. Maybe a month. She must hurry. It will be autumn soon and her time will be up.

They come back to Fancheux after four days of travelling. She is weak, tired and feverish. Fancheux inspects her wound. 'This was madness,' he says. 'Insanity. If he had missed by a whisker . . .'

'Sérannes does not miss by a whisker,' she says. 'He strikes true, always.'

Fancheux cleans the wound anew and, within a week, is pleased to report that it is healing. However, he says, she must wait to see if the fever will grow and sends her to bed. It does, terribly. Visions come to her – Lucifer standing by a gate of fire, an elephant rearing at her, her father – she knows it is her father, but he wears the mask of a devil. She does not know how long she has been in that bed but when she wakes, her wound has scabbed over, stopped bleeding.

It is night, the moon a sharp sickle and Fancheux comes to her, brings her soup.

'How long?' she says.

'A while.'

'How long? What month is it?'

'September.'

'Early September?'

'Late.'

She feels her stomach tighten. 'I must go.' She tries to stand but her legs will not support her.

'Not advisable,' says Fancheux. 'Not yet.'

She drinks the warm mutton soup and tiredness takes her again.

In the morning, she has a visitor.

It's Girard. He looks well, whole, healthy. His court pallor has left him and a summer tan browns his face.

'I owe you thanks,' he says as she sits up in bed. She sees him properly for the first time now. He is of good height, dark haired and tolerably well looking, though she suspects he has been working on the farm because his muscles are displeasingly prominent, and his face is tanned. She has the almost universal prejudice that a thick arm and a sun-kissed complexion are the mark of poverty and therefore unattractive.

'Do you know who I am?' She looks around for her knife, her sword. She has no sword – the one she used to practise with Lucifer vanished with the Devil. Has this man come to kill her? Dizziness briefly overwhelms her, and she knows she is at his mercy.

'Yes,' he says. 'You are the reason I was at war. I was visited by the ghost of Dreux. He told me to look out for you. But you rescued me. Why?'

Should she lie? She can hardly say, 'to restore you to health, so you might sin again. To restore you to health so I can kill you and your soul with a single blow.'

'I wanted to make a bargain with you.'

'What sort of bargain?'

'If you name to me your co-conspirators, I will let you live.'

Girard crosses himself. 'I have sinned grievously,' he says.

'Yes, you have.'

'But I have been shriven, that is for sure. The country priest heard all my sins.'

'That must have been fun for him.'

'I think there are no abuses that would shock these priests. You have to go a long way to sin like a priest.'

'You have been a long way.'

'I have indeed. But I am sorry,' he says. 'Truly sorry.'

'Many men are truly sorry if they think it will allow them to escape Hell.'

He laughs. 'Yes, they are. But isn't that what Hell is for? It's there to keep us on the right path and to return us to it when we stray. Without Hell, why should anyone ever do anything but exactly as he pleases?'

'This is a strange sort of sorry,' she says.

'Though genuine,' he says. 'I have spent many days thinking and dreaming here. I would make amends to you.'

She sits looking at him. Would he bring Paval back to life? Little Diandré?

'For what gain?'

'For the gain of my soul. In my dreams I have been to strange and beautiful places. The tincture that Fancheux gives me sends me to them. I believe I have glimpsed Heaven and would visit there when I eventually die.'

'So how might you make amends?'

'I will contact the members of the Tredecim and have them come to where you might kill them. You will kill them, but you will spare me to continue my life of virtue and good works.'

This is an offer she might find difficult to refuse. Time is running out for her and she needs to find these men quickly. Girard's remorse is not like that of Gourgue's, she thinks. He seems in earnest, repentant, almost cleansed by his experiences.

'You can simply tell me their names. There is no need to lead me anywhere.'

'I can tell you those I know,' he says. 'But they will run as soon as you kill one. They have already run. I ran to the war. Gourgue declared for a monastery. The others could be anywhere. I can unite them and bring them in. I do that and you let me go. And I tell you this. I will never, ever recant my love of God for anything. I am a changed man. Even if you were to die in front of me, I would not go back to my former life. I am sure of the reality of Heaven and it is to Heaven I will go.'

He takes a swig on a bottle of Pomet's tincture, stands dreamily before her.

Julie feels her side. She needs to recover but she cannot waste time. Perhaps this is the best way, in the short term. She can worry about what to do with Girard later. She feels her heart softening. She needs reminding of what this man has done.

Julie smiles at him.

'You are an evil man.'

'I was, but by your kindness and the skills of the doctor I am restored and determined to set forth on the path of good.'

'You are an evil man.'

'I have expiated my sins. I have confessed and done penance. God forgives.'

'What has he forgiven? Tell me.'

'You will think very ill of me. But know I have walked away from those sins, left them in the past.'

'Tell me.'

'I have preyed on the poor, both in the houses and lands I own and in those I do not. I have forced tenants to pay their dues by whoring to me their daughters, some scarcely old enough to be called women. I have called devils, or tried to, by the sacrifice of infants, a baby in one case. I had my first wife killed – attacked by what appeared to be cutpurses but who were in reality my hired assassins. I have been a glutton, a proud man, an idle man and a lustful one. I have been quick to anger, I have envied my betters and sought to do down my equals. I have been a bad lot, but I acknowledge those sins. I have sent messages to Paris instructing that my estates be dissolved, and the money given to the poor. I will enter a monastery and spend my life in earnest devotion to the Lord.'

'Were you there when Dreux killed the boy in the woods?'

Girard crosses himself.

'It was not Dreux. He only took the head. At the instigation of great men, with regret and hesitation, it was me.'

'You cut off Diandré's head?'

He crosses himself again.

'No. I strangled him. It was Dreux who cut off the head. God forgive me for the heinous sin of murder.'

'Did he take long to die?'

'Not long. He only had a little neck.'

Julie sits with that fact a while. She doesn't think anything. Her mind feels blank. But a heat is rising in her that will cook her brain and with it all restraint if she does not speak soon.

'I have a bargain,' she says. 'You write a letter, tell the men of the Tredecim that Dreux's ghost has something to say to them and that they must summon him at his grave if they have pulled him from the river, or from the Seine itself. Include a request for payment for your good doctor here and letters of recommendation. For my part, I will never kill you while you remain a Christian man.'

'Then you will never kill me, for I am a Christian true.'

'You will swear on the Bible to do this?'

'I will swear.'

'Then so shall I, to seal our bargain,' she says. 'And then you will deliver me the remaining men of the Tredecim.'

'I only know a few of them you have not killed.'

'Who?'

'Dreux's brother. Du Bellay. Godefroy.'

The same ones as in Charlotte-Marie's letter. He is not lying, then.

'Good. Write.'

When he has done it, she calls for Fancheux.

'Go back to Paris,' she says, 'and take his letter.'

'Do I not get more reward than that?'

'You are implying I should fuck you?'

'Well, that would be good but, no, I would like to marry you, Julie.'

She laughs to herself. Not another one. She likes Fancheux, very much. He is even attractive. But, but . . .

'I cannot marry with the Devil on my back.'

Could she be a doctor's wife, grinding up herbs and potions in her kitchen? She might. And then she might find a final cure for her voice. At which point she would be off to the Opéra, breaking his heart.

'One day?'

'I am sworn to someone else. You can do better than me, Fancheux.'

'I doubt it.'

'Take the letter. Get your pay and get away from me and from these men,' she says. 'Your life will be happier and more pleasant for it.'

'Happiness and pleasantness are overrated,' he says. 'You bring a certain adventure. What are you going to do with Girard?'

Pelletier comes out carrying two packs and a letter. 'One letter,' he says.

Fancheux takes it. 'I'll be gone in the morning,' he says.

'Go now,' says Julie.

'I've packed your things,' says Pelletier.

He passes Fancheux the bags.

'I know you will not do that man harm, otherwise why get me to restore him to health?' says Fancheux.

'Go,' says Julie.

'There is a side to you that can be quite frightening,' says Fancheux.

'You don't know the half of it,' says Pelletier.

'I will go tomorrow,' says Fancheux. 'It is too late to set off today.'

Julie feels her fingers itch for murder. But she must wait.

The next day, they watch Fancheux go into the late morning sun, his mule plodding down the valley. There is a chill on the September breeze. Autumn is crossing swords with the long summer.

Julie returns to the farmhouse.

'Shall we head back to Paris soon ourselves?' says Girard. 'We have evil men to overthrow.'

'I say again, *you* are an evil man.' Julie walks to the rough shelves at the back of the room. 'And I do not forgive you,' she says. 'You killed my friend.'

'If I understand your mission, that is hardly relevant,' he says. 'I will not go to Hell, so any vengeance on me is useless. I suggest you join me in prayer and that, in the morning, we contact a priest who will work to free you from your vow.'

'I do not wish to be released.'

'From something so harmful to your soul? Only a fool would say that.'

'Pelletier!'

Julie's man has been behind Girard. Now he slips a rope around his neck and pulls him hard back into his chair. Girard's arms flail, his legs kick but he is held quite firmly. She runs around the table to take up the rest of the rope that lies in a coil on the floor, securing Girard by his legs and his arms as the breath goes out of him and he flops into unconsciousness.

'Careful, Pelletier,' says Julie. 'Do not kill him.'

'I have not,' says Pelletier. 'It's the robber's art.'

When Girard recovers, he finds himself securely tied.

'This is stupid,' he says. 'Kill me and God receives my soul.'

Julie goes back to the shelves, takes up a bottle of Monsieur Pomet's medicine.

'When you curse Him,' she says. 'You may have some of this.'

Act Three

Scene One

We Knock at the
Portals of Hell's Starless Chambers

Julie looks up at the dark bulk of the big church against clouds that sail like great ships on the ocean of stars in the Paris night. She recalls Girard's death with a shiver. It took him four days to curse God, to say that he spat on the angels and had been proud of his sins. He was delirious by the time she killed him; she strangled him in the chair where he sat, tied in his own shit and vomit. Then she took out her card and crossed 'Emerald Ring' off it. Nine down. Four to go.

Lucifer had been impressed but circumspect. 'I'm not sure this counts,' said the Devil.

'A slight on God is a slight on God,' said Julie. 'You heard what he called the angels. He is a sinner.'

'I'm not sure He would see it that way.'

'Then keep this one in Hell until the day of judgement. Then God can decide Himself.'

'Seems fair,' said Lucifer.

Girard's ghost stood forlorn by the side of his body.

'I want to go back in there,' he said. 'I want to feel the tincture coursing in my veins again.'

'I'm sure we'll find something to course in your veins, old man,' said Lucifer. A click of the fingers and a circle of primroses burst at Girard's feet and he was sucked down into Hell.

The Devil's lesson was apt – how to offer an opponent what he wants in order to trap and confound him. She has, of course, used false attacks before: she was educated by her father about the *invito* – the offering of an apparent mistake to lure an opponent in. But now the Devil teaches her how to confound an expert swordsman – how to offer the invito knowing that your opponent will only feign to take it up, how to swiftly ensnare his blade to strike at the heart. The Devil shows her the Fiend's Coupé – how to use the pressure of an opponent's sword to flick your blade over the top of theirs, feinting for the inside line, drawing the response before a mere rub of the fingers – like a man testing the quality of tobacco – sends the blade below again to pierce the heart from the other angle.

'I wonder,' says Lucifer, 'when you are planning to use these skills. You seem content to stab and strangle rather than duel.'

'There will come a time,' says Julie.

Will that time be now, this night in the churchyard of St-Denis, where Dreux was buried in the family vault after they fished him from the river? Julie hides in the shadow of a thick oak, flattening herself to the trunk. It's full autumn now, well into September, only weeks until she must fulfil her bargain. She has been watching Dreux's brother's house for weeks, following him wherever he goes, rolling his uneven gait around town while glancing hither and thither but seeing nothing. Whorehouse, church, coffee shop, inn, whorehouse, church, tavern . . . But tonight he met with two others and Julie knew where they would be going. She was there before them.

Already it is spattering with rain, the black clouds sending the half-moon racing across the sky. She is cold in her thin stage-clothes that she wears to disguise herself as a young anistocratic man.

The gentlemen arrive on foot – this business is not even for the eyes of the most trusted servant.

There are three, stooped as they walk, huddling along. Though they are only sheltering from the biting wind, they remind her of mice, terrified of the hawk. Several times he has called at a house on the Île, but it seems no one is home. She discovers this is the house of Godefroy – and when she calls, his servant informs her he is away for a month. Where, the servant will not say.

'You have the key?' one of the men says.

'Yes.'

Dreux's brother slaps his paunch as if to confirm it. My, how these aristos munch!

'Have you heard from him, the ghost?'

'Not since he warned us of her plan and told us where to find the body.' Dreux's brother sounds like him too, an impatience to his clipped and manicured vowels.

'Are you shriven?'

'Yes, for the good it will do. I manage an impure thought unbidden every second breath,' says the brother. 'You two?'

The men nod in confirmation. They are both heavily cloaked, against the rain and against sight. One is quite tall, the other less so, thinner. 'Shall we proceed?' says the thinner one. That voice, so affected. She knows it is the one from the Bois. She feels she could step from the shadows and kill him right here. That will do no good. First, they must accomplish the business they are here for.

'You are sure of the ritual?'

'I took it from the seer of the Marais. She calls ghosts nightly.'

'A pity she couldn't be here.'

'The fewer who know our business the better,' says Brother Dreux in his clipped voice.

'Descend, then.' Brother Dreux lights a lantern and the men go down the steps into the mouth of the family vault. She sees

285

Brother Dreux's rolling gait as he descends, waddle-stepping into the abyss. She creeps to the edge of the vault to watch them. Brother Dreux produces a key and pushes at the steel gate. It groans, as if it is long accustomed to disuse and resents the need to open. Open it does, though. When she thinks it is safe, Julie creeps down the steps, keeping low and pressing herself against the wall. Light flickers within. Julie thinks this really does look like a portal into Hell. She smiles to herself. It will prove so for these gentlemen.

'Set a circle of salt in which to confine the spirit,' says Brother Dreux. He is reading from a sheet. 'Who brought the salt?'

'Not I,' says a voice. 'I am no servant.'

'I wasn't asking you to be a servant, Du Bellay,' says Brother Dreux. 'I just wanted salt.'

'I have brought salt,' says someone else.

'Oh, God, just like a servant!' says Du Bellay.

'That is shameful, Godefroy, shameful,' says Brother Dreux.

'If I didn't bring it, we wouldn't have fulfilled our purpose in coming here,' says Godefroy.

'Nevertheless, rather déclassé, however useful,' says Brother Dreux. 'Candles, stolen from a church.'

'Now that was more fun,' says Du Bellay. 'I have those.'

'Almond wand?'

'Present,' says Godefroy.

'Beeswax tablet?'

'Here too.'

'I don't know why we're bothering with all this. All it took in life to summon him was the chance of meeting a whore, a duke or preferably both,' says Brother Dreux.

'The duke will not be coming,' says Du Bellay.

'And a whore?'

'Later.'

'That will do,' says Brother Dreux. 'Did anyone bring wine?'

'Why? Do ghosts drink?'

'I do,' says Brother Dreux. 'Wine for the sake of civilisation.'

'No servants, no wine,' says Du Bellay.

'We should have brought a servant.'

'We would have had to kill him for his silence,' says Brother Dreux.

'And would that have been such an inconvenience? In comparison to having no wine?'

'Suppose not,' says Du Bellay. 'Shall we begin?'

'Yes, but before we do, one thing. When my brother appeared to me in the dream, he was clear. The Devil's Blade seeks our souls, not just our bodies. However, the Devil is not a runner, or rather, not inclined to run. Therefore, if we are slain, our ghosts should run for it as quickly as possible. Life trapped as a spirit on earth is unpleasant, he says, but nowhere near as unpleasant as Hell.'

'Oh, do get on with it,' says Du Bellay.

'Sprinkle the salt in a circle,' says Brother Dreux.

'That is the work of a servant,' says Godefroy.

'Oh, for God's sake, we'll call you the chief celebrant if you like.'

'I would like that,' says Godefroy.

'Well, go on then,' says Brother Dreux.

'Call me the chief celebrant.'

'O chief celebrant, would you sprinkle the salt?'

'I graciously indulge your request and will do so.'

There is some kerfuffle and then an intonation begins.

'In the name of God, whose secret name is written on this tablet, known only to the chosen . . .' says Brother Dreux.

'What is it?' says Du Bellay. 'I can't see what she's written in this light.'

'It doesn't matter, we only have to hold the tablet up,' says Brother Dreux.

'If it's going to only be known by the chosen, then it should be known by me,' says Du Bellay. 'Pass me that lantern.'

'The person who sprinkles the salt doesn't hold up the tablet. We can't break the ritual,' says Brother Dreux.

'Not even to observe the proper respect to rank and station?' says Du Bellay.

'Read it afterwards,' says Godefroy.

'Do you know it? If you know it, I should know it. Your father ran a bank, didn't he? Hardly more than a grocer, fingers stained with ink! Trade! My line goes back beyond Charlemagne!'

'Quiet!' says Brother Dreux.

He begins again. 'By the secret name of God, by the pillars of Heaven, by the certainty of judgement on the final day, in the name of the angels Michael, Gabriel, Raphael, Uriel, Selaphiel, Raguel and Barachiel, I bid my brother's ghost attend us here. Wave the wand, Du Bellay, wave the wand!'

'I'm waving, I'm waving!'

'When the candle is extinguished, when the lamp is dimmed, appear to us and alert us to the presence of our enemy. Reveal her whereabouts. Expose her weakness!'

'Nothing,' says Du Bellay. 'Nothing at all.'

'You haven't snuffed the lantern yet,' says Dreux.

'Oh yes!' The sizzle of a wick being doused and darkness.

'It smells in here,' says Du Bellay.

'It's a grave,' says Dreux. 'They tend to. What did you . . .?' His voice trails away.

'Can you see that?' says Du Bellay.

'That patch of light?'

'Yes.'

'What do you think it is?'

'Well I was rather hoping it was a ghost,' says Godefroy. 'I don't want to stay in here all night.'

'Forever,' says a voice, very faint.

'Robert? Is that you?' says Brother Dreux.

'You will stay in here forever.'

'Feels like I've already been in here forever,' says Du Bellay.

'Constrain the spirit,' says Godefroy. 'Order it into the circle.'

'We're in the circle,' says Brother Dreux.

'You were meant to be outside it!'

'There's no room in here. It's not even a circle. It's an oval. What does it say about magic ovals in your notes, Du Bellay? You're the magic expert, aren't you, "Diablo".' Godefroy speaks with a sneer in his voice.

'Ghost. I say. Step in here, would you, old chap?' says Du Bellay.

'Outside,' says a ghostly voice.

'No, inside.'

'Outside.'

Julie quietly draws her knife. It will be tight work in the crypt and she has no sword, even if she needed one, the Devil's practice blade having disappeared at the end of the lesson.

'We know that,' says Du Bellay. 'She's not in here, she must be outside. Where exactly?'

'Outside,' says the ghostly voice.

Du Bellay sighs. 'This is exactly my experience with these spirits in the past. They cannot be tied down to specifics. More of a clue than that please, Dreux, old boy. Last time you said she was coming for us. What does she look like?'

'He,' says the ghostly voice.

'You said "she". You were quite firm it was a she. Where is she?'

'Outside.'

'Don't be so obtuse,' says Du Bellay.

Julie pushes the heavy door back.

'What's that noise?'

'Inside,' says the ghost. 'She is inside. I've been trying to appear to you, but you all have the psychic sensitivity of a harpsichord leg when you're fully awake! She's here, you mutts!'

'Did you hear that?' says Brother Dreux. 'She's here!'

'You heard at last! Thank God!' says the ghostly voice.

'I fear,' says Godefroy, 'that you presumed the ghost was being obscure when it was being literal.'

'Stay still,' says Brother Dreux. 'She can't see us. Draw, gentlemen, draw! No pistols in here, we could shoot anyone!'

She Can't see them but she can hear them.

She stabs into the darkness and Brother Dreux cries out.

Julie is shoved, thumped back into the wall of the crypt but she stabs again and there is another cry.

'Du Bellay. Help me!' She stabs down at the noise. The knife bounces off something hard – probably a skull – and she stabs again, this time the knife going in hilt deep, the hand that grasps it touching the button of a coat.

'Help yourself!' cries a voice. Du Bellay is past her, running, she sees him against the moon. Someone is groaning on the floor of the crypt.

She stabs down and the voice is silent. The bells, the smell of primroses. Two ghosts light the gloom – one is Brother Dreux's, the other the ghost of the tall thin man who accompanied him. 'Run for it!' shouts Brother Dreux, and they both try but it is as if they have hit an invisible wall. Then another light. This time it is the Devil, dressed head to foot in burning silver, stag horns of light upon their head sprinkling sparkles on the ground. One of the corpses she can see by the devil shine, bears big black roses on his shoes.

'What do you think?' the Devil says. 'Traditional horns but with a hint of glamour.'

'Beautiful,' says Julie.

'Naturally,' says Lucifer. 'Is that the best you've got?'

'Bewitchingly, brilliantly brilliant?' says Julie.

'Better. Now, what have we here?'

'Two dead and trapped, but where is the other ghost?' asks Julie. 'Where is Dreux?'

'Gone,' says Lucifer. 'These two have trapped themselves in the circle of salt but Dreux has recommenced his travels. I doubt he will come so easily again, Julie.'

'Let me out!' says Brother Dreux. 'Run, Diablo, run!'

The two ghosts leap forward, but it is no good. They are thrown back by the circle of salt.

'Summoning ghosts!' says Lucifer. 'And using the name of the Lord. Well, gentlemen, I can only endeavour to help you in your efforts. What ghosts you shall summon in Hell! What spectres shall affright you! And how the name of God will burn in your mouths!'

'We only sought to . . .'

Lucifer holds up a hand. 'I am not interested in explanations. God's law is clear, there can be no . . .' The Devil thinks for a second before finding the right word. 'Mitigation.' Lucifer says the word as if it is filthy and must be held in tongs.

'But . . .' says Brother Dreux as the floor opens in a whirlwind of primroses and the two ghosts are sucked within.

'That's what "but" gets you,' says Lucifer.

'You owe me two lessons,' says Julie.

'Well, indeed, but I must say there seems little point in me going to the trouble of offering you all this education if you are just going to go in and stab people like a street thug. Where is the finesse, Julie? Where the twiddles and the frills? This is an age of frills. You need frills. Frills!' says the Devil, up close in Julie's face.

'I will offer you frills aplenty,' she says, 'when the time comes. There are gentlemen who cannot be ambushed here, gentlemen who cannot be tricked or fooled. It is them I seek from now on.'

The Devil blows out their cheeks.

'Go on then, what do you want?'

'Your best tricks. Your greatest deceits!'

'For the souls of two scraggy nobles?'

'One soul's as good as another, isn't it?'

'Er, no, that's rather the point of Hell.'

'You know what I mean. Is the soul of a shit-shoveller worth less than the soul of the king?'

Lucifer looks offended. 'Yes, of course. The king is the pinnacle of God's order. A shit-shoveller is below. Believe me, it's hard work finding torments for some of the poor that are worse than the lives they have here. Add that to the fact you know they're going to be let off by Him upstairs on the final day, well, if the Son gets his way over the Father, and sometimes you wonder why you bother.'

'The nobles are high.'

'I suppose so. But they're always going to be damned anyway. It's harder for a rich man to enter the kingdom of Heaven than for a camel to pass through the eye of a needle.'

Wisdom rises on Julie like the morning sun lifting from a cloud.

'Of course it is. Because the temptations are so much greater. I used to think God hated the rich. He doesn't. It's just He hates sin and it's so much easier for the rich to sin.'

'Gluttony and Sloth are much easier if you actually have enough food to eat and don't have to work for a living,' says Lucifer.

'But can you be rich and virtuous?'

'You can be.'

'Has anyone been?'

'I think I've missed two from Hell over the years.'

'Out of how many?'

Lucifer counts on their fingers. 'Million, billion, trillion, er, untold multitudes.'

'So why do you need me to give you their souls?'

'Anxiety,' says Lucifer. 'I always worry I'll miss one.'

'What is anxiety?'

'Don't worry about it, just put up your sword and come en garde.'

Julie takes Brother Dreux's sword from his corpse and follows the Devil out into the graveyard.

Here Lucifer teaches her the feather step, hopping from gravestone to gravestone as light as, well, a feather borne by the air. Julie dances on the grave tops, spins and pirouettes, offers herself to Lucifer's blade, denies them and moves away. Then there is the 'statue's hand'. The Devil allows her to push their blade aside but, just as Julie thinks she has cleared the way for a thrust at the Devil's chest, Lucifer's hand goes rigid as if made of stone and, in that instant of resistance, extends the tip of the sword towards Julie, snicking the buttons from her coat.

At first Julie cannot replicate the move but then the Devil tells her 'it is as if you are with a gentleman and you'd like to know the seriousness of his intent, or see the colour of his gold before letting him explore your own treasures. You show him enough, let him feel enough and then "No, monsieur!" The probing hand is repelled, what was soft and yielding becomes hard and resistant. And for him, what was hard becomes harder, the denial increasing the wanting. He wrestles, he thrusts!'

Julie spins, letting Lucifer's sword fly by her.

'And I slip away. Gone!'

The Devil bows. 'My dear, I have little more to teach you.'

'Two souls,' says Julie. 'One more lesson and then release from our contract.'

'Three souls,' says the Devil. 'You still have a ghost to catch.'

'It will be my only endeavour,' says Julie. She licks the blood from her fingers.

The Devil smiles. 'Oh, I've watched you doing that. Quite the palliative. I wonder if I've been too hard on you. What can't be beaten down by knocks may yet be worn away by comforts.' They extends their fingers to Julie's neck, strokes gently at it.

'Try your voice,' says Lucifer.

Julie tries, engaging her belly, widening her chest. The note, when it emerges, is so pure and so strange that she falters. It is an eerie, low sound she produces, down in the contralto range, low for a woman. She tries again, lower, as low as a male baritone – a contralto basso as she has heard it called. She sings an air.

'Condemned to meet the dragon
Terrible fate, the will of the gods,
Impious rescuers attend me,
But I will bend to the will of Heaven.'

She sings it again, this time soprano.

Her range is astounding, the flexibility and purity of her voice amazing.

She sings and sings and, while she sings, she weeps with the joy of her voice restored, not for what it might bring her but for what it is bringing her – communion with the divine.

Lucifer has a tear in their eye.

'Look,' says the Devil. 'The wandering souls of this cemetery attend you.'

Faces float above the graves; the whole cemetery radiates light as an army of ghosts are before her. All around them, the dark glows with the light of the risen dead. The ghosts of the rich vaults have risen to watch, splendid in their frock coats, their medals and even their armour. The bourgeois from the graves too are there, some in lawyers' wigs or grasping pens and even the poor from the pits at the cemetery's edge are there in their rags, all leaning forward to catch a glimpse of her and to sing, to sing!

What a chorus, voices like fingers on the rims of many glasses rising in harmony with her voice.

And there, at the edge of the crowd, is Paval. He is pale, changed, a silver aura about him, his body insubstantial, translucent.

'He is called from Les Innocents to listen to you,' says the Devil.

'What of his fate and these other various spirits?' says Julie.

'What of it?'

'No Heaven, no Hell?'

'Is this not Hell? I can think of more pleasant spots.' Lucifer smiles. 'To be chained to your living existence but to be a shadow of what you were. To always think there must be an answer, a way out. To neither eat nor drink nor sleep but always wander the same patch of ground with the same distressed souls, one crying murder, another looking for the baby who killed her, another still looking for the mother who poisoned her to save her from starving. It is no Heaven, Julie.'

'These people cannot leave here?'

'They haunt the various places of their lives, their homes, their workplaces, the places they were killed and buried. They sometimes seek their loved ones, as your Paval has done here. They are looking for human contact, looking for help or just acknowledgement. But of course, when they get it, it is rarely as they imagine. Ahhhhh! A ghost!' Lucifer recoils, aping someone in terror.

'Paval!' says Julie.

She stretches out her hand to him and he comes forward to take it. She feels nothing as his ghostly fingers pass through hers.

'I am sorry, my darling,' she says.

His lips move and a sound comes forth, hardly audible. 'Don't stop singing,' he says.

She clutches her throat. The ridge of the scar is no longer there.

'I thought you did not heal,' says Julie.

'Oh,' says Lucifer. 'This isn't healing.'

Scene Two

Night Music

Julie staggers from the graves as the dead fade like fireflies behind her.

The sight of dear Paval has quite knocked her sideways and her legs are weak. She takes out her card and scratches off 'Rose Shoes' and 'Waddle Step'. She has the presence of mind to relieve Brother Dreux's corpse of a pistol and a good sword.

Two souls to go, three if you include a wandering ghost, and now only a couple of weeks in which to find them. Her restored voice mocks her. She will never sing at the Opéra now, despite her ability to call the dead from their graves by the beauty and strangeness of her voice. Hell will claim her before the Opéra ever can.

A lantern bearer calls to her and she, glad of the company, pays him his five sous to escort her out of the cemetery.

She walks for a long time, lost in ghosts. Her father, Paval, Diandré seem to follow her, she feels their presence at her shoulder, but when she turns to embrace them, they have vanished. She winds through the twisting root mass of streets, past the crammed tenements of the poor, the gaudy houses of the bourgeois and, when she nears the Palais after half an hour's walk, the big houses of the aristocrats. It is night and all good souls are in bed – the only light comes from the lamps that burn suspended in their glass cages on ropes that straddle the street and from the lantern of the man who walks in front of her. The light is good enough here for her to dispense with the lantern bearer, though she keeps him for the company and the comfort. In this part of town the streets are not so busy – though sedan chairs still plod by, laughter from within. A gentleman looks around him, up at the lamps, beyond to the stars, as if he has just been dropped from Heaven on that spot and can't quite work out where he is.

Someone is following her, she is sure of that. Not a ghost now, no. Someone sure-footed and crafty, someone who clings to the shadows like the night-calling fox and who moves just out of the lantern bearer's soft sphere of light.

She sends her own fox from her neck back to look. There is a growl, a snap, a curse and, hopping from the shadows, comes Sérannes. The fox returns to her neck, purring.

'This is a late time of night to be pressing your suit,' she says.

'I haven't come for that,' he says.

'What have you come for?'

'This,' he says. 'De la Reynie has decided it's time to clip your wings.'

'How does he know where or who I am?'

'He knows everything.'

'Shit.'

'It gets worse.'

'What?'

'The Marshal has had me followed. He knows I have been covering for you. He has sent . . .'

From the end of the Rue Marchand comes a stamping noise, like the gnashing of great teeth. From the other end too, a noise like men marching in line.

Ahead of her are the dark uniforms of a platoon of guards, behind her the lighter uniforms of regular infantry. There must be fifty men on each side, at least.

Around forty paces from Julie and Sérannes, they stop.

Two men begin to speak at the same time from opposite ends of the street.

'By order of the Marshal de La Meilleraye, I . . .' says the officer at the guards' end.

'By order of de la Reynie . . .' says the officer at the infantry's end.

'Stand down, man! A chief of police has no precedence over a marshal of France!'

'A military marshal has no precedence over the city of Paris!' comes the return.

Julie looks around her. She produces her pistol and relieves the lamp bearer of his lantern, blowing it out. He just falls in a heap on the floor, covering his head like a child who believes if he closes his eyes to the world, the world cannot hurt him.

The big lamp above them still shines as its rope in its glass box.

'Prepare to fire!' cries a guards' captain.

'Prepare to fire!' cries an infantry major.

'They can't hit what they can't see!' says Julie and fires the flintlock at the lantern.

There is a still moment after the report of the gun where it seems no one breathes, nothing stirs. The lantern is untouched. Then the lamp bearer screams and rolls across the street. 'My arse! My arse!' he says.

It seems that the errant bullet has ascended to the heavens and then descended to the lamp bearer's rump.

'Shit,' says Julie and, before she can pull out her second gun the command to fire is given. She sees three bullets arcing towards her, the rest flashing past. Her blade is out in an instant, striking them away with the Devil's Parry. A woman who can parry the blade of Lucifer has no difficulty swatting away a musket ball – to her the bullets fly as lazily as summer bluebottles.

Crack, a splintering sound; she sees a spurt of hot oil rupture from the lantern in a gush onto the behind of the lamp bearer below.

'Ahhh!' he cries.

Musket balls all around, rattling off the walls of the houses, smashing glass, pinging off railings, sending the shit on the floor up into the lamplight so it looks as if it's boiling and spitting in a pan, and then it's flat dark, everything invisible. She grasps Sérannes's hand and strokes the fox fur at her neck. 'Lead us,' she says.

Furie drops from her shoulders to the ground, her tail brushing Julie's free hand. She pinches the tip of the tail and the fox leads them to the side of the road, into the shelter of a doorway.

'Reload!' shouts a voice.

'I'm hit!' shouts another.

'Stop shooting!' shouts someone.

'We are the senior regiment. It's up to you to stop shooting first.'

'Snobs!' shouts a voice.

'Well, of course we're fucking snobs! That's how the whole world works, you shitty peasants!'

'Look down on this, fuckface!'

Another volley of musket fire. Windows smash, bullets wasp past Julie's ear. From the houses, voices shout demanding if the men below have taken leave of their senses.

'What shall we do?' says Sérannes. He seems calm, as if asking her if she would prefer to walk through a park or take a fiacre.

'Force the door.'

'I'll try.'

Sérannes puts his weight to the door but nothing budges.

More shooting, more cries. Plaster smashes above her head and people from the houses come to look out of the windows. The windows smash and they retreat.

'I thought this lot were supposed to be musketeers,' says Julie. 'They couldn't hit a cow's arse with a mandolin!' As she says so, a bullet smashes into the wood beside her. Men are screaming at both ends of the street, crying out, wounded or just scared.

'Get a lantern, get a lantern!' shouts a voice.

'Coming, coming!' says a voice from inside the house.

'Too much time fencing, too little shooting. No glamour in shooting,' says Sérannes.

'Draw weapons and advance!' comes a command from one end of the street.

'Draw weapons and advance!' says a voice from the other.

Sérannes tries the door again. Julie hears him thump against it. It won't budge.

The night is flat black, Julie can see nothing. Then the door opens, and a crack of light appears. It widens and she sees a red-coated butler who carries a candle in one hand and an ear trumpet in the other.

'Whom shall I say visits upon the master of the house?' he says, and raises the trumpet to his ear.

The light shines on Julie, on Sérannes, on the raw-arsed lantern bearer writhing on the steps and it is as if a couple of burly moths have seen it and come racing in.

'Go!' says Julie and pushes past the butler.

Before she can think properly, Julie has gone upstairs rather than down. Around a twist in the stair there is a door and she opens it to find a music room with a clavichordt, its keys bare, a stool before it. On top of the clavichord lies a small viol. She snatches a candle from a niche in the hall.

'Pick up the viol,' says Julie to Sérannes. A cat watches them, unblinking from an open window.

She plonks herself down at the clavichord and begins to tinkle out a tune.

Sérannes grabs the viol. 'I can't play!' he says.

'Just stand with it and be haughty when they come in. You can be haughty, I fucking know.'

'Your language disgusts me,' says Sérannes, arching a brow.

'That's the job, just like that,' says Julie.

The door is slammed open and a musketeer captain stands before them.

'We haven't been introduced,' says Sérannes. 'You are?' His eyebrow speaks cold contempt.

'Sorry, sir, I had no idea there was a young person present,' says the captain, removing his hat. Behind him, guards and musketeers brawl on the stairs.

'Nothing to apologise for,' says Julie, aping her best posh accent – which still isn't very good - while playing quietly away. 'Lovely to have company in the evenings.'

'Shoot at the king's musketeers, would you?' shouts a blue tunicked soldier behind the captain.

'You shot first, you posh twat!'

'That is our prerogative!'

The captain closes the door gingerly, removing his hat.

'You play delightfully,' says the captain.

There is a hard thump against the door and a shout of 'have that!'

'You should hear him sing,' says Sérannes, metaphorically adding one too many eggs to the pudding mix.

'I would be enchanted,' says the captain. 'Please, young sir. What is this tune?'

Julie smiles graciously and sings the words of the song she is playing from memory:

'Come, come, unrelenting Hate,
Come out of the dreadful abyss
Where you allow eternal horror to reign. Save me from love, nothing is so irresistible. Against too attractive an enemy,

Give me back my ire, rekindle my fury. Come, come, unrelenting Hate,

Come out of the dreadful abyss

Where you allow eternal horror to reign.'

'That's, er, lovely,' says the captain.

'I try to keep it contemporary,' says Julie.

The captain's eyes narrow. 'Do you always practise your
music armed?'

Julie flashes him her indulgent grin again. 'You can never be
too careful these days, Captain. Who knows when a platoon of
guards is going to come crashing through the door, hell-bent
on ravishing you?'

'Young man, nothing was further from my mind,' says the
captain.

'Pity,' says Julie.

The captain is clearly not going to be swayed by this approach.

'I repeat my question. You have a sword at your waist. As
does this gentleman here. And I notice a pistols in the coat
on the chair.'

'It is simply the fashion,' says Julie. 'All the young people
do it, I'm sure it comes from the king himself at Versailles.'

'You, sir,' says the captain to Sérannes. 'Will you grant us
an air?'

Sérannes paws the viol in his hands as if it is wet and he
wants to wring it out.

'I have finished my practice for the day, sir.'

'Indulge us,' says the captain.

Outside, what one must presume are junior officers are
shouting at their men, telling them not to do the work of the
English for them and to stop knocking lumps out of each other.

'Very well,' says Sérannes. 'Let me show my skill on my
favourite instrument.'

The viol hits the floor with a noise like a protesting cat and Sérannes has drawn his sword in a single movement to hold it at the captain's neck.

'Leave my house,' he says. 'I am master here.'

It is suddenly quiet outside.

There is a knock at the door, and it is opened.

'Who's in my house?' says an elderly man, carrying a candle in a holder. The top of a nightcap flops over one eye. 'What are all you doing here?'

'Who are you?' says the captain.

'Monsieur Marchand, attorney at law. This is my house and I'd thank you to leave.'

The captain turns back to Sérannes.

'Since this gentleman is in his nightgown and you are playing musical instruments in street clothes, fully armed, I would say you are perhaps the people, in street clothes, fully armed, in possession of a pistol the like of which we see here, whom we have been pursuing.'

'I have a sword at your neck.'

Into the doorway press four soldiers, one musketeer and three grey guards. All of them have muskets aimed at Sérannes.

Sérannes lowers his sword, gives a short laugh.

'I suppose even you boss-eyed poltroons wouldn't be able to miss from here,' he says. 'Gentlemen, congratulations. You have me. I am the Devil's Blade.'

'Well, then,' says the captain, 'I've got a rope for you. And one for you too, young man, I should guess.'

'I have a prior appointment,' says Julie. She runs to the window and jumps through, sending the cat hissing before her.

Scene Three

The Lights of Heaven
Cannot Gladden Us

She lands lightly, with the feather step, allowing the ground to receive her rather than falling onto it.

'Stand where you are!' comes a voice from the window but she is already running along the moonless street.

It is still dark enough for Julie to make the alley in a heartbeat and to disappear from the view of the hue and cry behind her.

There are lights flickering in windows, lit by those curious to see why a small war has developed in their street; there are lanterns that have been brought from the houses to help tend the wounded who lie groaning in the road. The brawling between the two sets of soldiers has dissipated and she sees at least one colonel of infantry in his big plume, strutting between two lamp bearers among the carnage and cursing the idiocy of his men. They stand sheepish, covered in the stinking shit of the streets where they have rolled and fought.

She curses Sérannes for getting caught and blesses him in the same thought. He has added to her list of responsibilities; she must pull him out of the hole he has dug for himself but he has saved her, freed her to complete her destiny. But she hasn't long. Already the street is filling with enterprising souls come to service the needs of the soldiers – wounded and whole. Nut and pastry sellers move among them, candles perched on their trays, alongside a clyster man with his big pump, though he has no takers. A couple of whores tug at the coats of soldiers who are trying to staunch the wounds of shivering companions.

And then it is light, light everywhere, the sky is full of it, followed by three window-rattling bangs. She looks up and golden serpents are wriggling across the sky to the south. Of course! The fireworks for the final carousel of autumn! And won't Monsieur be there in place of the Paris-dodging king? And Charlotte-Marie too! If she can find Charlotte-Marie; if she can get an audience with Monsieur!

She knows exactly what she must do – apply to Monsieur for the release of Sérannes, tell him that Sérannes is possessed by a fury and imagines that he can protect her. She must throw herself on the great man's mercy.

'Hey!'

She has snatched up a lamp from someone tending a fallen idiot and run for it down the street.

'Stop or I'll shoot!' comes a voice.

'Put that thing down, soldier! We've had enough of that sort of work for one night!' barks another.

The night is so, so black but the lamps cast a swaying corridor of light down the middle of the street and, augmented by her own light, she can just about see where she's going. She runs hard south, the mud, shit and worse of the street sucking at her boots as she squelches on.

She goes down the side of the Louvre. The palace is quite dark, all candles dimmed to better see the fireworks, no doubt. Or perhaps now Louis is in Versailles, the Sun King no longer shines his light there at night.

Down to the water. The fireworks have kept the crowds on the Pont Neuf, which shines with lamplight like a path to fairyland. The booths, the jugglers, the fire-eaters, the whores, dentists and poodle-clippers are all out in force, seemingly unmoved by the musket fire which echoed out from the streets not twenty minutes before.

There is a press of people on the bridge, squashing to the sides as a fine carriage tries to get through – its postillion carrying a flintlock and swearing to shoot anyone who comes near his lady.

She grips tightly on the hilt of her sword as she pushes through the crowd. She doesn't want to lose it to a pickpocket. She passes the big gallows at the centre of the bridge – placed there for the swiftest administration of justice to any of the murderers or robbers haunting the place.

Another flicker of light from the south and long tails of showering silver stretch across the sky.

'This is just the prelude, calling us in. Wait for the full show!' shouts a voice and the crowds press forward towards the Jardin du Luxembourg, she has no idea why. It seems to her that the view is perfectly good from the bridge.

On, on, through the crowd. She feels an unwelcome hand on her leg and pries the finger away.

'Aren't you lonely?' says a voice.

'The Devil is lonely,' says Julie. 'Care to keep company in Hell?'

She shows half a thumb of steel at the top of her blade and the man backs away.

At the bankside, the crowd burst from the narrow bridge like pus from a boil, spreading out into the streets on the way to the Jardin, each convinced their way is a little clearer, a little quicker.

She does likewise, choosing the widest road straight ahead rather than one of the winding, less trodden side streets. St-Germain is notoriously the filthiest neighbourhood in Paris and tonight it lives up to its reputation. Her boots go in to the ankle in the mud of the street; people slip and slide on the ichorous road and the stench of shit and piss, human and animal, is overpowering. Even for Paris.

She presses on as quickly as she can, heading towards the Jardin. It has been sealed for the royal visit and a press of people are up against its railings, clamouring like damned souls at the doors of Heaven. Guards seal the gates and run the length of the perimeter, using bayonet prods to stop people climbing over. It doesn't work. The railings are lit with hanging lamps but here and there they have gone out and she sees a flash of flesh, the white of an exposed back as a woman makes the top of the railing and tumbles over into the garden with a whoop of victory. A guardsman comes running towards her but loses his footing and goes arse over tit to the delight of the crowd.

Julie runs around the perimeter to the gates. Three carriages are struggling to make their way through the crowd to get in, the guards trying to push the ordinary people back, the coachmen cursing and waving their whips. Julie sees her chance. She ducks below the second carriage, grimacing at the slickness of the mud against her knees. The carriage is of the richer sort which sits the cabin on a shaft of sprung wood to absorb the bumps of the ride. It only touches the cabin fore and aft, dipping away from the underside for most of its length. She grabs on with her arms and feet, hoping the carriage isn't going to go over any bumps which will make the cabin descend towards her limbs and surely crush them. Will it do that? She really doesn't know how these things work, never having looked.

A man nips beneath the carriage. 'Shift up,' he says. 'There's room for two.'

'Fuck off out of it,' she says.

'Let me get on!'

A jolt and the man shouts as the wheel nudges his body. That gives him the hurry up to roll away through the filth.

Another jolt and they are squelching forwards through the gates – she hears a pistol shot and then 'get back in the name of the king, the next time it'll be a volley!' Then the protest of iron on iron as the gates swing shut.

The carriage stops. There is a yellowy flickering light here and, as she turns her head, she sees the skirts of two ladies and the boots and breeches of a man disembark. She tries to lower herself carefully on to the ground to avoid getting too dirty, but she is wasting her time. The carriage is on mud, thick with horse shit, and there is no way out of it but to roll. Dropping beneath the carriage made her filthy, rolling out makes things worse.

She emerges into strong lamplight – oil lamps are strung on ropes between poles. No one pays her any attention: everyone has eyes on the sky where rockets snap and flash. She pats herself down with filthy hands and then regrets the automatic gesture because it further soils her already filthy clothes. Around the perimeter of the blazing garden, twenty paces from where the guards are jabbing back fence scalers, sit rows of pavilions, each with the standard of a great house – lions and unicorns, harts and chevrons, bears, boars, diamonds and swords. Fireworks light the garden – penny fizzlers sold by hawkers sparkling red, gold and blue in the darkness. A bang, a cry, laughter. Bonfires, big and small, flare in the dark. The smell of smoke is on the cold air. Devils flip and cartwheel among the crowds – costumed acrobats cutting capers beside a boy collecting money in a hat who cries out 'for their ingenuity! For their ingenuity!'

Lantern bearers flow by in bright streams, moving with great speed and seemingly great purpose until they stop to mill and turn in whirling dances of light. Laughter is everywhere, crackling through the night with the splutter of firecrackers, with whizzes, pops and bangs.

She presses on to the centre of the garden. Here a great long stage has been erected and above it a light canopy marked with the fleur-de-lys. A throne of curves and swirls sits at the centre of the stage, two smaller and similar chairs beside it, and spreading out from the great chairs are wings of tables where aristocrats sit, or rather stand, in bored and dazzling array beneath lamps borne by servants dressed in scarlet and gold. They are waiting for Monsieur in order to be seated. You wouldn't want to sit down before Monsieur, lest the Sun King's brother get the idea that you weren't showing him the same respect you'd show the king.

She scans the ranks of nobles at the table, craning to see past the line of guards. They know they are on display and many strike affected poses, dangling handkerchiefs, standing like statues with their hands on walking sticks, pouting and posing while servants apply a dab of make-up here, a splash of perfume there. If you wanted to know who the most important people in the land were then this would tell you – the nearer to the throne, the nearer to the centre of power.

And there, next to a tall man in a shimmering silk coat, right beside the main throne, is Charlotte-Marie. She is a vision in the lamplight, a dress like blue flame, the light reflecting in the material like a sunset over a lake in Fairyland.

There is a throng of people, held back by guards, all trying to gain the attention of the aristocrats. She shoves in, calls 'Charlotte-Marie! Charlotte-Marie!' but a guard bars her way.

'Barracks is two hundred yards away,' he says. 'Go round the back door, you're strictly other ranks, love. No trade for you here.'

'I am not a whore.'

'All boys and all women are whores for the right price.'

'Have you met all boys and women?'

'No.'

'Then how the fuck would you know?'

He goes to strike her but she steps in, her leg across the back of his, and pushes him to his arse on the mud but another two guards take her arms. She cries out but Charlotte-Marie cannot hear her, and she is swept away, others pressing in to her place to try to gain the attention of the aristocrats.

They do not take her far, just a few yards, before they throw her down and rejoin the line.

She stands, calls to Charlotte-Marie, but she cannot be heard. The guard she pushed down is coming for her but then he hesitates, looks uncertain.

'Do yourself a favour and fuck off,' says Julie. He smirks at her and turns away.

'You,' says a voice, 'are coming with me,' as her sword is taken from her and she feels the prick of a knife in her side.

Scene Four

Now I Know Thee for What Thou Art!

She is flung onto the floor of a damp-smelling tent full of wooden boxes. It's dark inside and only the dancing light outside offers any vision at all.

A man stands above her, masked as a devil. In his hand he carries a pistol. Beside him, the flames dancing through him, is the ghost of Dreux.

'Well, Dreux, you have done us proud,' says the man. She guesses it is Du Bellay, Diablo, who she so lately saw at the cemetery. 'She means to murder us all.'

Du Bellay fiddles at the ties on his breeches, trying to open a too-tight knot.

'I'll fuck her first, Dreux,' he says. 'I have had a taste to fuck her ever since I saw her with Monsieur.'

Julie hears no reply.

'Do you think you can stand against the might of the Tredecim? Do you think you can slaughter us like cattle? Do you think—' Du Bellay never finishes his sentence.

'Furie, attack!'

'Aaaah!'

The fox springs from her neck and wraps itself around Du Bellay's mask, blinding him. Julie dives forward from her position on the floor to headbutt him hard in the nuts. He collapses forward over her shoulder and she puts her arm between his legs to lift him bodily upwards and cast him down with violence, dropping on top of him to drive her elbows into neck and ribs.

He is resilient, though, and gets his hands up to her neck, his arms out in front of him as if someone has described how to strangle someone and he hasn't quite got the right idea. Still, he gets his long fingers around her throat. Little lights flash up at the corners of her eyes, her head pounds. She reaches forward and squeezes the trigger of the pistol Du Bellay has tucked into the band he wears around his waist. A flash, showering sparks, a scream; laughter from outside.

Du Bellay falls aside, writhing, holding his bloodied groin. The tent is full of smoke from the flash of the flintlock.

White light flashes, within or without her head she can't tell. She is stunned, the world unreal, underwater, as if she has dived to the bottom of a great river. Something is hissing like a snake in Eden, something that is trying to impart some vital information.

Du Bellay writhes on the floor. 'Bitch, bitch,' he is saying. She feels for her knife but it has gone.

The ghost is there, Dreux's ghost. The ghost is trying to say something to Du Bellay, but Du Bellay cannot hear him. Only she, granted ghost sight by the Queen of Hell, can understand what the ghost says now, when the ghost has panicked, lost his concentration and forgotten to make himself heard by the world of ordinary men. It is trying to tell Du Bellay what the snake is saying. Nothing makes sense. And then it does. The snake is saying it is not a snake. The snake is saying, saying . . .

'Jesus!'

What occurs next was never in the present moment, it happens so quickly. It is an action that happens so fast that it can only ever be understood as part of the past, over before it is fully comprehended. She is outside the tent, rolled behind the stout beer barrels of a booth selling ale.

Du Bellay, still masked as a devil, is at the doorway of the tent, on his knees, staring at disbelief at his bloodied groin. And the snake's words are very plain to her now. The snake was saying, 'I am not a snake. I am a hissing firework, ignited by the flash of Du Bellay's gun. This is one of the tents where fireworks are stored. I'd get out of here, if I were you.'

Du Bellay says 'bitch'. It is a word of ignition. After it, everything is noise. Everything is noise and fire. The blast knocks her back flat, though the barrels shield her from the worst of it. She blacks out, comes to, looks up to see the canopy of the beer stall burning, rolls aside as it crashes. Screams of laughter and delight, feet stamping, a horse screaming. She stands in a field of flame, everything around her flickering and burning. Furie is nowhere to be seen. The little fox has gone.

The guards come running, the stallholders come running, everyone is running towards the noise and the fire and at the same time everyone is running away from it.

The Devil is there – not the masked devil but the real thing in his or her silver coat, with the shiny black hooves beneath. She, he, has on a strange hat of three corners, which they tips to Julie.

'Luck,' they say, 'is the Devil's virtue. Would you like your lessons?'

'I find myself a little out of sorts,' she says.

'Well, when you are ready,' they say. The Devil kneels to Du Bellay's charred remains, takes a little smear of fatty ash and rubs it on Julie's lips. The taste revolts her but a sensation of delight goes through her and she feels her throat relax once more.

Julie shakes herself, breathes in smoke, stands up. Her ears ring. Beside her is a cup. She fills it from the tapped barrel, drains its beer, throws it down. Her clothes are charred upon her body, blackened with soot. She is wandering through the crowd as if through violent waters that shake her this way and that, waters that do not know their own best course but that boil with indecision.

All the attention of the ordinary people has been taken by the explosion, the outer line of guards has gone. Charlotte-Marie is sitting at the table, the tall man in the shimmering silk coat beside her. Beside them on the throne is. Monsieur – broad-backed, muscular, a new Adonis of martial bearing–whose strong neck rises magnificently from his glittering dress. In front of him are four guards, bayonet muskets challenging the night. The aristocrats are showily unperturbed by the explosion and instead chat, gazing out into the night in an offhand, distracted way while around them the guards bristle like boars defending their lair.

She takes out her card from her sleeve with a shaking hand and scratches off 'Diablo' from her list.

She walks towards them. A guard levels his musket at her. 'Stand back,' he says.

The ringing stops, the smoke thins, and her head is finally her own.

'Who,' says Monsieur, 'is that low person?'

Julie thinks the dearest thought a girl can have, that of the ruin of her enemies who lie in the smoking ashes behind her. She coughs, curtseys and sings.

'Ascend, I may, the throne of Heaven,
My soul a lark seeking dawn's light.'

The sound is as pure and perfect as she has ever produced. It is as if she is outside her body singing now, seeing herself as a pure spirit singing through her soot-blackened, filthy body to transform not only herself but her listeners to angels, and the garden to Heaven.

Everything becomes silent as she sings. No firework crackles, no one cries out. Or at least, she thinks that's what happens. She feels herself descending within herself to a place where a hundred different Julies dwell, innocent – though in no way the church would recognise – guileless, someone who looked on the world with shining eyes full of hope. Her present self feels like an old gnarled tree, lightning struck, and the song sends her climbing down through the roots of herself to find a girl who never thought of devils and killing but only of the thrill of song, the thrill of being admired and wanted. It is that girl who now sings and commands the night.

'Yes, I have known the light of Heaven,
Though banished now to eternal night.'

'Julie!' It's Charlotte-Marie who brings her from her reverie. 'Is that you?'

She curtseys, she doesn't know why.

Charlotte-Marie talks excitedly to the man in the silk coat, but he offers her only a sudden movement of the hand, a flick of contempt, halfway to a slap. Julie feels her blood rise. This must be Charlotte-Marie's father, only he would love treat her like that. He Sérannes's employer. He will save him!

Charlotte-Marie stands up, pushes past the guards.

'Is it you?'

'It is.'

'My God, more scrapes?' She puts her hand to Julie's face.

'More scrapes. I need to talk to your father. Is that him?'

'Yes. He is not in the best of moods.'

'I have news that is unlikely to improve his temper. But he must hear it.'

'What can you have to say to Daddy? Oh my God, you're going to propose, aren't you! I can't marry you, Julie, you're a woman!'

Julie kisses Charlotte-Marie's hand.

'It is Sérannes.'

Charlotte-Marie returns the kiss on Julie's fingers, but her father has pushed through the guards.

'Charlotte-Marie, what have I told you about associating with guttersnipes? Get back to your seat, my girl, or I'll fetch my whip!'

'Get her to sing some more!' shouts Monsieur in his big, booming voice. 'That was enchanting, and it seems we're going to wait all night for the fireworks to restart.'

Julie kneels before the Marshal de La Meilleraye.

'Sir, I beg you, your fencing master Sérannes is taken by the Musketeers. They have wrongly arrested him, believing him to be the Devil's Blade.'

The Marshal raises a brow.

'And he isn't? It would seem to me that he's eminently qualified to cause that sort of trouble. He has been associating with . . .' he looks around him shiftily, 'one who fits that description.'

'He is a true man, sir, I beg you to save him. Send to Le Châtelet and release him.'

The Marshal smirks. 'I know all I need to know about fencing. There's nothing he can teach me. I think I'll leave him there and save myself a hundred livres a year.'

'Father!' says Charlotte-Marie. 'Please . . .'

'Mind your place,' he says. 'Sérannes has disobeyed me and written his own death warrant. Now get this thing out of my sight!'

'Sir!' says Julie. Before he can leave, she grabs his hand on instinct, her sooty fingers grasping his fine white glove. The fingers are stiff, unresponsive. She pulls off the glove in an instant.

'What in the name of the Devil do you think you're doing?'

She looks down at the glove and sees the two lower fingers have been stuffed, reinforced with wire. The man in front of her jabs at her, cursing. He has only three fingers.

'I didn't want to tell you,' says Charlotte-Marie. 'Oh darling, I thought it would all just work itself out!'

Scene Five

Heaven Without Thee is Hell to Me!

'You!' Julie says. 'Do you remember me, sir, from the Bois de Boulogne where you pushed your blade in here?' She gestures to her throat. 'You are the leader of the Black Tredecim! A Devil's man who makes it his life to ruin young girls. Know that I am the Devil's Blade, not your man Sérannes, and twelve of your companions now lie dead. You are the thirteenth, the Devil's number, and I have come on behalf of Hell to claim you.'

She takes out her card, waves it in his face.

He stares at her with incredulity.

'You?' He leans back from the card as if it stinks.

He has drawn in a breath and has his sword at her throat. She has no pistol, no sword, no knife.

'You look like you're from Hell right enough! I will kill you,' he says.

'Your name will be scratched from this card soon,' says Julie, folding the card back into her sleeve.

'I will scratch you from existence!' says the Marshal.

'Father, this is my dearest friend!' says Charlotte-Marie.

'I say, what's going on here?' says Monsieur, coming to the edge of the ring of guards.

The Marshal thrusts forward with his sword but she turns, the Devil's Esquive, twisting away like a prizefighter from a blow but

Meilleraye cuts her on the withdrawal of his arm, the edges of his sword sharp enough to send a gush of blood from her ear.

'Father,' says Charlotte-Marie. 'Father!' She pulls at her father's arm, but he lands a backhanded slap across her face, sending her reeling. He comes on again towards Julie but Julie ducks and weaves away.

'You four!' roars Meilleraye. 'Kill her!'

The guards leap forward, bayonets gleaming in the firelight. She backs away, slips, falls down and they are all around her, charging in a horseshoe of steel. The bayonets, the light, the shock of her fall. She cannot act. But she can speak.

'I'd like my lesson now,' she says.

Time stops. The bayonets shine with a frozen fire. Charlotte-Marie has her arms around her father, as if turned to stone in a moment of panic and supplication, her father's unmoving face etched in rage. Everything is still. Julie tries to move but she is rooted to the spot.

'What on?' The Devil is at her side. Julie looks up from shining hoof to silver coat.

'How to get out of this shit, for starters,' says Julie.

'Hmmm, not easy,' they say. 'Four bayonets charging in, no more than an arm's length from their targets. Not particularly clear what can be done!'

'Are you not up to it, Devil? Does your ingenuity fail you?'

'Well, there are some things that lessons can't answer. I can't tell you how to stop the sun rising tomorrow, or to stop it sinking again when the day is done.'

'And yet you have stopped time here. It seems to me that you can do whatever you set your mind to.'

The Devil puts their hand to their breast, flattered. 'You asked for a lesson. What can I teach you to defy the very ground that wants you, that pulls your weight to it in divine embrace, to which you will return one day?'

'What can you teach me?'

'Nothing.'

'Then do something. Strike one of these down.'

The Devil looks affronted. 'My dear, every one of these men has sins enough to make the foulest fiend blush. I want them for Hell. If I move against them, they become God's friend. I think we've been through this before. A shame you don't have your little fox any more, he might help. I can't stand here forever, dear, do you want a lesson or don't you? How about duelling etiquette in the palace of Pandemonium? You might be needing it very soon.'

Julie's body shakes. Is it fear? No, something deeper – a convulsive desire for life. There is too much to think about here, too little time. And then she has it. Furie!

'Give me a gift,' she says. 'Something that can help me here.'

The Devil's brow furrows. 'But I like my little trinkets,' they say. 'I like my pretty things. You've already had one and where is that now?'

'Two lessons, two lessons for a gift.'

Lucifer puts a hand to their chin in an exaggerated posture of contemplation.

'Two lessons and a forfeit,' they say.

'What forfeit?'

'It really is no fun if you know in advance.'

Time unfreezes for a breath and the bayonets inch forwards.

'What forfeit?'

A lurch and the bayonets are nearer still, not a hand's span from her breast.

'What forfeit?'

Now the bayonets are a finger from her chest.

'Very well!'

The Devil smiles and walks over to Meilleraye, whispers in his ear. Then they come back to Julie and produce a pair of ballet shoes from their silver coat. Lucifer takes off Julie's filthy shoes and ties the ballet shoes to her feet.

'What good will these do? I don't want to dance.'

The Devil smiles. 'But I want you to. The Devil takes Julie by the hand, a cold shiver travelling up her arm, and stands her up in front of the sharp bayonet tips.

The Devil clicks their fingers, Julie kicks her feet and the bayonets stab – each guard into his companion. Julie has leaped just above the heads of the ring of soldiers, allowing them each to skewer his mate.

The guards hit the wet earth. The Devil cries 'ooh, souls!' as their ghosts rise from their bodies.

The trouble is that Julie is such a long time descending. By the time she comes down, Meilleraye is nearly upon her with Charlotte-Marie hanging around his neck, spitting and shouting, trying to wrestle her father away.

'Seems a rum do!' shouts Monsieur. 'But entertaining enough. Continue, continue!'

Julie kicks again, shooting upwards to the height of a man's head.

'You owe me a duel, Meilleraye!'

'I owe you nothing.' He pushes Charlotte-Marie down and swipes at Julie with his sword, but he misses. She lands a foot on his head, kicking herself up and away from him, dislodging his wig so it falls over his eye.

Monsieur is clapping in delight, squawking and hopping like a great gaudy parrot and the rest of the nobles follow his lead, crying 'Bravo, Meilleraye, have at her!' and 'What a trick!' as Julie kicks and floats and Meilleraye slashes at her with his blade.

'You will not defy me!' shouts Meilleraye.

'I defied you when I lay with your daughter as a man and as a woman! I defied you when I killed all your devils and regained my voice. I call you for what you are, a fool and a buffoon, a man who cannot keep his daughters from vice nor satisfy a woman himself and who seeks the aid of Hell because he lacks the guile to secure the aid of Heaven in the personage of our most royal Monsieur here.'

'I will kill you!'

'You will not!'

She kicks at his head, but the ballet shoe is loosely tied and flies off as she strikes and she spins around, Meilleraye catching her wrist to pull her in with his left hand. She lands and Meilleraye tries to stab at her, but she remembers the Devil's Japanese trick and flips his wrist. A crack and he is on his knees.

'Bitch!' he shouts.

'I hear that a lot,' says Julie. 'It sort of loses its sting after a while.' Monsieur claps and whoops, the nobles clap and whoop too.

She knees Meilleraye in the face, sending him crashing backwards but he is a tough one, a strong soldier. He gets straight back up, roars and lunges at her, his left hand at an odd angle, but she spins aside with a hop. Unluckily, one foot now floats heavenwards while the other descends to the ground, leaving her in an extended kick position, one foot in the air. She tries to pull her foot down but for the moment it won't descend. She is stuck in an extravagant high kick, her slippered foot coming down with painful slowness as if held up by an invisible string.

Meilleraye snarls and comes on with his sword, lunging hard but she pirouettes, and the sword merely passes by as she turns. But her enemy is quick, spinning to come again as she finally lands. This time he makes no mistake, the point aimed straight at her heart, his lunge strong and accurate.

Charlotte-Marie comes from nowhere to throw herself in the way. Her father briefly pauses but then renews the thrust.

The sword passes through Charlotte-Marie, emerging in a rose bloom of blood at her back.

The crowd gasps and Monsieur cries, 'Now that was poorly done!' Meilleraye staggers backwards, as if physically struck, leaving the blade still in his daughter. Julie grabs Charlotte-Marie, hugs her.

'I'm very cold,' says Charlotte-Marie.

The sound of a bell, the scent of primroses.

'Renounce your sins!' says Julie. 'Is there not a priest! Is there not a priest?'

'I cannot renounce my sins,' says Charlotte-Marie.

'Why not? You will go to Hell!'

'Because that would mean renouncing you.'

A man comes running, says he is a priest.

'Give her the last rites!' says Julie.

The priest makes the sign of the cross.

'Have you anything you want to confess?' he says.

'Yes,' she says. 'I enjoyed it all. Every last second, all of it and, if I wasn't enjoying it, I was bored and angry. I hated my father for a tyrant, and I loved this woman in ways the Church hates. And, though I confess it, I regret nothing and would change nothing.'

'I can't work with that,' says the priest.

'Just bless her!' says Julie.

The priest makes the sign of the cross again and rattles on in Latin, waving his hand over Charlotte-Marie's eyes, her mouth, making a gesture to her legs and then to the part between her legs.

She catches but two words: '*Carnalis delectationis*'. Charlotte-Marie smiles.

'But why should we regret those sins? The sins of carnal delectation are delectable. That is why they are so described.'

Julie glances up. Lucifer is there, glowing in their own light.

'Say sorry for them, Charlotte-Marie, say sorry. It doesn't matter if it is right to do so, only that it is necessary. Stay out of Hell, Charlotte-Marie, stay out of Hell!'

'I hear the balls there are delightful,' she says. 'Sorry, Julie. Sorry.'

She coughs, her eyes close and the ghost stands from her body, though no one else sees.

Time stands still again as Lucifer takes Charlotte-Marie's ghost by the hand.

'You are an enchanting lady,' says the Devil. 'And so unrepentant.'

Charlotte-Marie stands above her own body, her eyes wide in surprise.

'Who are you?' she says. 'You look like fun.'

Lucifer smiles. 'Appearances can be deceptive.'

'No,' says Julie. 'You cannot take her!'

'Cannot?' says Lucifer. 'Cannot?'

'She said sorry. You heard at the end. Sorry!'

'You cannot dissemble with the arch dissembler. You cannot play the lawyer with the rules of God,' says the Devil.

'Who is this person?' says Charlotte-Marie.

'The Devil!' says Julie.

'Oh. I expect we shall get along famously,' says Charlotte-Marie. 'God never heard my prayers. Have you answered me, fiend?'

'I come for another purpose,' says Lucifer.

'Which is?'

'To carry you to Hell.'

Charlotte-Marie's ghost takes a little step back, nervous now. 'And if I decline to go?'

'There are some invitations that no one can refuse.'

'No!' says Julie. 'You aren't doing this right, you heard her apology.'

'Her fate is sealed!' says the Devil.

'Run, Charlotte!' shouts Julie. She shoves the Devil hard and Charlotte – coming to her senses – breaks free of the Devil's hand and flees across the park.

The Devil goes to follow her, but Julie blocks the way. The Devil bumps into her hard, sending Julie staggering backwards. It is a most peculiar shock, how she imagines lightning might feel, a nerve-jangling blow as the Devil strikes her but the delay has been enough. Charlotte-Marie is nowhere to be seen.

The Devil seizes Julie by the arm. It is as if she no longer commands her own limbs; they jerk and twitch with the odd, zinging energy the Devil imparts.

'So far,' says Lucifer, 'I have been your friend, or as much a friend as I ever am to anyone. You are close to making me your enemy.'

'Then I will be sure of the favour of God,' she says. She is desperate, a feeling in her like a deep hunger, an ache for the loss of Charlotte-Marie.

'Though your friend will not be, for sure. How I long to shower her with burning kisses, Julie, to embrace her in arms whose grip is as strong as the iron the Archangel Michael once used to bind me. I could catch her in a step if I so chose.'

'Leave her, at least until my task is done or failed,' says Julie. 'Then you can torment us both together!'

'I could make you hate each other,' says the Devil. 'Perhaps I could make one very happy and the other very sad to see it, spark jealousies between you. Or I could just pitch you on the fires and watch you burn eternally. Sing a song and I will think on it.'

'I thought I reminded you of the angels.'

'That was before the sword changed your voice. There is more of the pit about you now. But sing for me and I might consider your friend's fate more indulgently.'

She sings, for Charlotte-Marie, with all her heart:

'God who throws the thunder
Who made the lightning bite,
God who rages on the wind
Be soft for my love tonight.'

'Beautiful,' says Lucifer. 'You should be on the stage, you really should. You have very little time now. I will take you together, you and her. Her agony will be the greater for being delayed!'

Lucifer gives a short stab of a laugh and is gone.

Time lurches, starts again.

Monsieur is near the priest, Meilleraye pointing at Julie. She steps away, her slippered foot trying to float off so she has to force it to the ground.

'What have I done?' he shouts. 'I had no choice! She provoked my temper and I was not myself!' He clutches his left wrist

'You did this deliberately?' says Julie.

'In anger!' says Meilleraye. 'She has been nothing but a vexation to me! I tried time and again to marry her off, but no one would have her, between her temper and her wildness. I have other daughters!'

'You should hang!' says Julie, without thinking of the trouble that would cause her.

'Oh, let's not play judges,' says Monsieur. 'Meilleraye has lost a daughter and must be comforted. Whether he meant to or not is rather beside the point. He is a high man and to cry "murder" would disgrace the entire nobility. I'm sure you didn't actually intend this, did you, Meilleraye? That was said in the heat of the moment.'

Meilleraye regains his composure, bows low. 'No, sir.'

'Splendid. Now, we should settle this matter somehow.'

'Let me fight him,' says Julie. 'On even terms, sword against sword. I have fought him with no sword. Let us put ourselves in the arms of God and see who He favours.'

'The Marshal is not your social equal,' says Monsieur. 'And you are a woman.'

'A preposterous idea!' says Meilleraye. 'This is the Devil's Blade. This is she who has laid waste to the flower of our nobility like a fox in a hen house!'

Another figure emerges from the gloom. It's de la Reynie.

'Not sure it's the flower of nobility who have copped it,' he says. 'Or, if they were flowers, they contained their share of thorns. She's trimmed your party for sure, Meilleraye. Not quite the force you were at court. A certain, shall we say, equilibrium has been restored. Why, had the killer been doing the king's work and on his orders, he could not have done it better!'

Meilleraye blanches. 'Did you allow this to continue?'

'Far from it,' says de la Reynie. 'I contained it and stopped it. Eventually. The Devil's Blade is locked in Le Châtelet. What you have here is simply the woman who corrupted your daughter. And, like many of her kind, because she chooses to fuck like a man, that is to fuck women – in this case your daughter, in front of your nose – she fights enough like one too. She took you on without a weapon while you were armed and you had the worst of it. I would watch yourself, Meilleraye, I would not wager on beating this little girl in a duel if I were you.'

'She is neither little nor a girl,' says Meilleraye. 'And I am the most accomplished swordsman in France.'

'In the practice room with your fencing master, perhaps you are the best. But you have fought shy of duels, have you not?'

'I am too valuable to France on the field to waste time killing scoundrels! And beside, I have a broken wrist!'

'A broken left wrist. You wield the blade with your right. You fear she will be man enough for you, I guess. Or your man Sérannes. He normally fights for you, does he not?' says de la Reynie.

'Am I to stand here and be insulted by this . . . policeman?' says Meilleraye.

'He is my brother's man, what can I do?' says Monsieur. 'But he has a point, does he not? This sooty and soiled person has offended your family's honour. You should do something about that. And there is the matter of her singing. I would like to enjoy that for at least a short while.'

'Hang her,' says Meilleraye. 'Let her sing on the scaffold.'

De la Reynie coughs. 'If I might suggest something, sir?'

'Yes?'

'Well, if this lady dresses as a man and acts like a man, we should treat her like a man before the law. If she puts on a pair of breeches, then we'll call her a man and she can fight Meilleraye.'

'You know how my brother feels about duels.'

'Yes, but this is with a woman. Men, plural, are forbidden from duelling. Well, one man fighting a woman is not duelling because only one man is fighting, and the law says it takes two at least for a duel.'

'But she will be acting as a man, you said.'

'For honour's sake. The law recognises her, tit to twat, a woman.' He makes a gracious sweep to illustrate the area of Julie's body to which he refers.

Monsieur smiles. 'It is attractive. You know how dull I find my brother's laws. In the old days we put mettle into men through duelling.'

'That does not take care of the problem of our difference in rank,' says Meilleraye.

De la Reynie bows deeply. 'If I might suggest?'

'Yes?' says Monsieur.

'Ennoble her. Or ennoble her as a man. Then afterwards, when she reverts to being a woman, the title goes, and we don't have to have a person of low rank haunting the court pretending to be a marquis.'

'Oh, splendid!' says Monsieur. 'Splendid! That's it. Give me a blade someone!'

A nobleman reaches down to pull the sword out of Charlotte-Marie.

'Not that one!'

'Sorry, sir,' says the noble.

Another blade is fetched and also a man's coat, on Monsieur's request.

'Kneel as a man and rise as a prince!' says Monsieur.

'A prince!' says Meilleraye.

'What's the lowest rank you'll fight?'

'Knight, at the least!'

'Well, kneel then!' says Monsieur.

Julie does as she is bid, sinking down, bereft, beside the body of Charlotte-Marie.

'Rise, Seigneur . . . I'm afraid your name escapes me!'

'Then choose one, sir! I have a name as a woman, but I need one as a man.'

'Seigneur Femme!' he says. 'Arise, Sir Woman! And now sing for us.'

She rises, turns to the corpse of Charlotte-Marie and kneels to kiss her. Then she sings, as she has never sung before:

'It is love that keeps within its chains
The thousand birds we hear night and day in our woods.
If love brought naught but sorrows
Loving birds would not sing much less.
Young hearts, the world is favourable to you,
Make the best of fleeting happiness.
In the winter of our years, love is lord no more.
The beautiful days that fly away from us, fly away forever.'

Then she turns to Meilleraye and sings:

'Spirits of hate and wrath,
Demons, heed our call.
Deliver to our hatred
The enemy that we despise.
Spirits of hatred and wrath,
Demons, heed our call.'

Monsieur is rapt, clasping meaty hands to his necklace in delight.

'This is an affront!' says Meilleraye.

'Don't be a bore, Meilleraye. Don't focus on the words, focus on the music. It was enchanting,' says Monsieur. 'I will have you sing at the Opéra.' He clicks his fingers. 'Fetch Lully, would you? I want this girl at the Opéra as soon as possible. She can sing with Moreau at the end of October!'

Julie's heart skips. Moreau, the angel! Can she help with Charlotte-Marie? Surely an angel can intercede for a soul.

'Ah, sir,' says Meilleraye. 'I will need a week to make the necessary arrangements for the duel. And then I am due at the front with His Majesty the next day. Never mind the problem of getting this fixed.' He gestures to his wrist.

'You will make time!' says Monsieur.

'Well,' says Meilleraye. 'Perhaps after the show has finished. Midnight, perhaps, on the thirty-first of October, All Hallows' Eve.

'A year since your pact,' says the voice of the Devil at her shoulder. 'Don't be late killing him! Nor finding your errant ghost!'

So that was the forfeit, what the Devil whispered to Meilleraye – the date and time by which Lucifer would take her to Hell.

'I need it earlier than that. My honour must be satisfied,' Julie says.

Monsieur holds up his hand.

'No more. Set a place. The nearest to the Opéra. Where is the nearest open space?'

'The cemetery of Holy Innocents is often used for such things,' says someone, they can't tell who. Julie thinks it could have been the Devil themself, though it may have been one of the watching noblemen.

'Midnight on the thirty-first of October it is, at the cemetery,' Monsieur says.

Julie bows. 'Just before midnight,' she says. 'On All Hallows' Eve. I would not fight on All saints' Day.'

'Just before, then, says Monsieur. 'You will be there, Meilleraye?'

'My honour commands it, sir,' says Meilleraye.

'Should you last that long,' says Julie.

'I will be gone to one of my estates,' says Meilleraye. 'And I will take a platoon or two to defend me while I am there.'

'D'Aubigny!' says Monsieur. 'Play by the rules! If anything happens to the Marshal before your duel, I will have you hanged on the spot, you naughty girl, or should I say man? Good, you, now come on. You need to meet Lully and prepare for this part. He will be delighted I've found him a singer! Yes, what japes! Let there be fireworks!'

On his command the skies fill with gold, red, green and blue, rockets searing the darkness before exploding with bangs loud enough to shake Heaven.

Scene Six

Cursed Be That Tree That Holds Thy Weight!

Lully, summoned to the firework garden, throws a fit, the spare little man banging his foot like a goblin and saying 'no, no, no,' he will not have Julie, 'Lady Soot', he calls her, not in this opera, not opposite Moreau. He can find her a place in the chorus, he can find her a role as a spear carrier, a nymph, anything, but not a major role against the greatest soprano the Opéra has ever known.

He hears her sing, he has to, and he concedes he is impressed but he doesn't know her! Can he trust her to carry the full six hours of the opera, not to take fright, not to tire, not to do any one of a number of things he can't actually describe but fears might occur?

Monsieur is immovable. 'I expect to see her in a major role, Lully,' he says. 'She makes me laugh.'

'That is not a quality we seek in a work of high tragedy!' says Lully.

'You will admit her,' says Monsieur.

'I would rather die,' says Lully.

De la Reynie shrugs heavily.

'I doubt that will be necessary,' he says. 'Unless, of course we were to look again at the circumstances that led to you becoming the sole owner and director of the Paris Opéra – Mr Pierre Perrin, your partner, being so lamentably forced into bankruptcy by what many said was dishonest dealing.'

Lully looks as though someone has given his wig a biff, so affronted and knocked sideways is he.

'I hope you're not implying anything!'

'I don't imply,' says de la Reynie. 'I investigate and examine. Then I state my case quite boldly and call for justice.'

Lully reddens, pulls at his collar.

'This is insupportable,' he says.

'And yet I dare say you will find a way to support it,' says de la Reynie.

'I dare say I will,' says Lully. 'Come with me, girl, I need to put you to work.'

'I will come with you,' she says.

Before she does, though, she bows to Monsieur. 'I have a request to make.'

Monsieur surveys the field of combat, where dear Charlotte-Marie lies covered by a sheet and burly guardsmen labour to take away the bodies of their comrades. He surveys the wreck of the fireworks tent, then looks out into the smoky, bonfire bright night.

'You have had quite a lot for one night. If I didn't find you so very amusing, I'd say four dead soldiers and one dear friend so lamentably taken in an accident you caused, plus the death of some other persons unknown exploded beyond recognition, might be cause for me to get miffed.'

'The fencing master Sérannes,' she says. She pries off her ballet slipper and tucks it under her arm. Lully looks in disgust at her bare feet.

'This Devil's Blade.'

'He is not the Devil's Blade. He was falsely accused of that. He stepped in to protect me.'

Monsieur shakes his head for so long his earrings sway and sparkle.

'Such things are below the dignity of princes such as we. A fencing master is a tradesman. We can have nothing to do with him.'

Then he turns away, taking the arm of a lady scarcely less well skirted and jewelled than he, to totter off towards his coach.

Julie wants to search for her lost slipper, but Lully will allow her no time. It's all she can do to grab a napkin to put to her poor ear before he bundles her into his carriage to take her to the Opéra directly.

He opens the building with a big key he pulls on a lanyard from his tunic.

'It would be better for me to have you killed than to suffer this indignity,' he says.

Julie, who has neither knife, pistol or sword now, finds this alarming. 'I tell you straight, matey boy, I'm not an easy woman to kill.'

Lully, who is a head shorter than she and a good deal less muscular, frowns. 'I had ascertained that,' he says. 'And come to the conclusion that that course of action would be more trouble than it's worth.'

He goes down through the labyrinth of rooms to his office. 'In here,' he says. 'Don't worry, girl, I'm not going to ravish you!'

Julie towers over him. 'No,' she says. 'You're not.'

He opens the battered brown door to reveal a large chamber with a harpsichord in it.

'I have instructions,' he says, 'to give you the maximum stage time. Well, in this case that's impossible because we have an opera with precisely seven roles, one major female, two minor. I can't give you the role of Angelique, I just can't. That leaves you with one decent appearance as either Témire or Logistille. But that won't satisfy Monsieur, I am sure.'

'You are doing Roland?' says Julie.

'Yes!' says Lully, like it's obvious.

'Then let me be Médor. I can sing the man's *haute-contre* part.'

'I don't trust a woman to do that.'

'Play his part.'

He breathes out like a bulldog who has just been informed the butcher is out of bones. However, he puts the music up onto the stand and starts on the harpsichord. Even with the night she has had, getting blown up, cut, seeing her lover killed and being identified by her deadly enemy, she feels a thrill. Lully! She is singing with Lully! She puts down the bloody napkin from her ear, where she has held it since the coach. The blood has stopped, and she needs both her ears to find the note.

Lully offers her a little trill on the harpsichord to let her know she is to come in. She raises an eyebrow that he should think such a thing necessary and she opens her heart out before creation to sing.

As she sings, she thinks of Charlotte-Marie.

'Ah! This torment
To love evermore
a silence eternal!
Ah, unending torment
to love without hope!
I love a queen, alas! By what enchantment
have I forgotten her rank and my birth?
What distance does the spell of death put between us?'

Lully dips his head like a grazing swan as she sings. He must be relatively pleased.

'Very well,' he says. 'I'll give Dumensy the night off. Can you remember the words?'

'They stick in me,' she says. 'I'll remember them.'

'Good,' he says. 'Because I am going to test you.'

Julie thinks on the words. Eternal silence. A love without hope. Didn't Sérannes think like that about her? She must try to save him. But how? She has an idea.

'No time,' she says. 'I'll be back tomorrow!'

'You will stay here!' says Lully.

Julie hardly hears him. She runs down to the Opéra wardrobe, determined to find a disguise. Not a nobleman, not a lady, but a pauper. No one looks at paupers. The assassins, if such they are, can't wait all day and, even if they do, by dawn the first of the Opéra staff will be arriving. The building will be full of stagehands, painters and carpenters. She can easily slip out dressed as one.

So, as the sun rises over the Seine, she chases the river east to search for Sérannes at Le Châtelet.

'I have a message from Marshal de La Meilleraye,' says Julie as she arrives at the familiar office. 'The master Sérannes is to be released.'

'Too late,' says the jailer. It's a different one from last time, or he looks different out of his heavy blankets.

'He's hanged?'

'Gone, anyway,' says the jailer. 'He'd been taken out of his cell by the time I arrived this morning.'

'By who?'

'Whom,' said the jailer.

'Don't start that, son,' says Julie.

'Monsieur Paul Von Whom,' says the jailer. 'De la Reynie's German man.'

'On what charge?'

'Von Whom doesn't do the charging,' says the jailer.

'What does he do?'

'He's the hangman.'

'Where, where does he hang them?'

'At Buttes Chaumont!'

'The quarry?'

'There's a gallows overlooking it.'

Julie crosses herself. She feels as if she is flying as she runs towards the gibbet, through the bright Paris morning, life all around her: the bustle of the markets, the stink of the horses, the dirty kids playing in the filth, the drab beggars and the gaudy merchants, lawyers, monks, scribes, cartmen, fiacres crying out for passengers, walkers crying out for a lift. None of this for Sérannes if she does not get to him. She can't stand another death – Paval, Diandré, Charlotte-Marie, not Sérannes too, not him.

She crests a hill to get to the quarry. It opens in front of her, a great red wound in the earth where they are pulling out clay and sand.

But then, across the gulf, she sees a glimpse of blue in the sunlight, swaying from a pole. She forces herself on. At a hundred paces from the scaffold she is in no doubt – it is him. His blue coat blows in the breeze and his body sways gently. A child throws a stone at him and another joins in. He is dead. Julie can't go on.

Her legs weaken, she crouches, thinks she might retch. She feels like giving in, surrendering to desperation. But then the need for revenge tugs at her soul, as if it might fly free on the wind to strike down Meilleraye wherever he stands. He is the cause of all of this, that mighty man. He could have saved his fencing master, he could have let his daughter love as she wished, he could have dedicated himself to the good of the people, not devil worship and hate.

She will give in to revenge, yes. She will slake herself on it, murder Meilleraye and watch him writhe his last on the cold grass of Holy Innocents Cemetery. The dead will reach up and take him, crack the turf and stretch cold, hard limbs to drag him down. But she will have a greater victory than that, she will move on from him, forget him, explode into the life of the great teeming town about her. She will return, to the Opéra, to Lully, and she will practise for the performance ahead, practise song, the art of life and the blade, the art of death.

'Meilleraye,' she says, 'I am coming for you.'

Scene Seven

The Song I Sing Lasts Not Forever

Of course, there are looks, of course pencilled eyebrows are raised, rouged lips pursed, powdered noses looked down and all manner of snooks cocked at the Opéra when it is announced she will be taking on the role of the lover. No one argues, though, no one throws a fit, or even demurs. Lully is the king here and his word goes, particularly as it is well understood Julie's preferment is thanks to the intervention of Monsieur himself.

The first rehearsal surprises her. A round lady who enters munching a pastry takes the role of Moreau.

'La Moreau has prospered since I last saw her,' says Julie.

'That is not Moreau,' says Lully.

'She is ill?'

'Not ill, resting.'

'Then when will she rehearse?' says Julie.

'She will not. Never does. Or at least not with the cast, I have no doubt she is perfecting the role in the comfort of her own lodgings. This is La Laurent. She will stand in for her ably while we mortals prepare.'

The first time, with the musicians and the cast, thrills her like nothing else. She is assigned a boy to stand beside her with a candle on its stick so she might read the score. For some reason, this pleases her immensely. If only Charlotte-Marie were here to see her. She sees her everywhere now and cannot determine if it is her ghost or her memory that haunts her. Perhaps she is beside her, perhaps it's she who blows out the candle that lights her score, for mischief, for attention, to say 'I am here, do not forget me'. And perhaps it is just a draught.

The auditorium is dark, some stage candles lit – though not as many as will be lit on the night – and the house resembles one of those dark Dutch paintings she saw at Versailles. Lully himself, his score lit by a lantern, is no more than a daub of pink and yellow against the black of the auditorium.

La Laurent takes the lead, speaking of how she is forced to marry the hero Roland when it is another she loves. Her voice soars and trills – not with the power and beauty of Moreau but beautiful nevertheless. The strings swell, the trumpets turn twirls of sound through the darkened air and then comes her cue. Julie lets go, lets the sound emerge from the depths of her soul and the notes emerge pure, low, strange.

Lully taps his baton.

'All very . . . all very tutored,' he says.

'I never had a lesson in my life!' says Julie.

'Yes you did, don't lie to me. I can't think what Monsieur heard in the firework garden, his ears must have been deafened.'

'She seems adequate to me,' says the round lady.

'No one asked your opinion,' says Lully. 'And adequate is the problem. She is very adequate. This is not the home of adequate. This is the home of extraordinary! Try again.'

She does but her efforts don't please Lully or, rather, they half please him.

He sways his head from side to side like someone trying a new wine, not quite sure if they like it or not. 'The expression is novel. The voice is novel. The presentation is within the realms of decency, but, but . . .'

'What?' says Julie.

'What indeed?' says the round lady. 'She hits the notes, she projects, she has an originality to her. What is wrong? I can't see it.'

'Which is why you find yourself an understudy, not a lead,' says Lully, examining the score.

The round lady flashes out a pink tongue at him.

'There is more to come from you,' says Lully. 'Much more. I expect it on the night. Otherwise you will incur the displeasure of the divine La Moreau and it will be as if you have never existed here.'

'I need to talk to Moreau,' she says.

'Don't do that,' says Lully. 'You do not talk to Moreau. You commune with her, after making the proper offerings. She is a jewel and you are the foil, the setting. If you fail to shine, to add to her lustre, she will not entertain you long. Again!'

A kerfuffle at the door, a cry.

'What is this?' says Lully. 'This is insupportable!'

A flash. Bang! A gun discharges. Julie sees the bullet as if it crawls towards her – a woman trained to block Lucifer's blade is not to be caught by something as slow as a shot from a gun. She snatches the candle from the boy beside her and deflects it with a swift circular *sixte* parry, spinning the candlestick clockwise to knock it away.

In the same movement, she throws the candle underarm at the gunman, striking him in the face. It is not enough to hurt him but it's enough to surprise him. She can barely see his form as she leaps from the stage.

'I can't practise like this!' shouts Lully as the gunman flees.

Julie loses him in the dark. She returns smiling.

'I almost enjoyed that,' she says.

'God save us from wild women,' says Lully.

*

After that, Lully applies to Monsieur and three guards are sent to look after them – two on the door, one by Julie's side at all times. When she tries to leave to take some air, she is told that is forbidden. She will sing on the Monday for Monsieur. That is to be her focus this week. Anything she needs can be sent for.

Two hearts are beating inside Julie, it seems. One is the singer's who never has enough time to prepare, who must go on to the stage wishing she had another day, another week or month to perfect her performance. The other is that of the revenger, who waits like a hungry spider longing for a fly. For her the days are interminable, the month seems a year. October comes, with winds and rain. A heavy storm cleans the streets, at least down by the river where the drainage is adequate, and she strolls the bank in the autumn dusk. The nights darken. Winds blow. In a few days she must face Lucifer again, give two souls. One of those souls is currently residing in Meilleraye. The other, that of Dreux, is roaming free. She cannot think how she is going to solve that problem. She tries to get out, to visit one of the fortune-tellers or spirit ladies that ply their trade by the Pont Neuf. Perhaps they will know how to call and trap a ghost. But the guards are implacable. She will not leave.

If she does not succeed, she is damned. At least she will go to Hell with Charlotte-Marie, though she knows Lucifer will turn that into a torment rather than a comfort.

She practises in her breaks from singing with an old blunt foil she has found in Wardrobe. On one foot she wears her remaining dance shoe, using it like an invisible step to leap into the air, to turn and somersault to the ground, one leg always trying to descend faster than the other.

In a few days she has the technique and surprises Arcand the stage manager by leaping over his head and spinning head over heels to drop behind him, forcing her flighty shoe back to the ground point first, her other leg bent up to balance her.

'I could see your knickers,' he says. 'Though I dare say I'm not the first.'

Julie sleeps at the Opéra, in different places each night. She doesn't completely trust the guards to protect her – they fall asleep. One she spends in the attic, sleep tormented by the rattle of rats, another beneath a pile of clothes in Wardrobe, another still in a scenery box. She is right to be wary. People are moving around the Opéra by night, she can hear, people who should not be there. She hears them talking. 'In here?' 'In here?' 'I didn't see her leave.' 'You don't see anything, let's go.' 'He's offering five livres for her head, you go if you like, I'm carrying on the search.'

One night she peers out from beneath a pile of curtains to see the ghost of Dreux wandering around, rattish, worried. How to catch him? She wishes she knew.

She takes all this activity as a comfort. Meilleraye does not want to fight her. So he is scared. Good, he ought to be.

The night of the performance, she tries to put the duel out of her head. It will be at 11 o'clock. She needs to kill Meilleraye by midnight and have Dreux in the Devil's grasp by then. She will ask Moreau. Moreau is an angel, spinning light, and she will know how to snare Dreux. But Moreau does not come as the audience is filtering in, as Monsieur is taking his place with his entourage on the best seats on the stage – the best to see and to be seen. She peeks out from backstage. She has never seen so many candles; the place seems ablaze, the faces of the audience looking like souls gazing out from the burning pit of Hell.

Moreau still does not come as the appointed time for the start of the show arrives. The audience murmurs and rustles, coughs and complains. Lully paces backstage.

'Is she always late?' she asks him. He says nothing, stares past her. The audience grows more restive. Will Moreau have time for costume? For make-up?

She must come soon, or Julie will have to go to meet her assignation in the cemetery without petitioning for the soul of Charlotte-Marie, without finding out how to trap Dreux. Moreau does not come. A rumour goes around backstage. A messenger has arrived. Ms Moreau has faced robbers on her way to the theatre. One of her horses was shot. They are waiting for a replacement. Time seeps away. The show will be delayed. Her guard lounges, complacent at her side. Monsieur is brought drinks, a little food. He is not bored, he laughs with his friends, his great hand stroking his earrings as he does, his broad shoulders heaving with laughter.

Julie warms up, yes, for once she does, running scales, and warms up in her mind too for the bout ahead, running patterns of parries and ripostes, time hits and feints.

She sees how Meilleraye has trapped her. He has forced guards upon her, delayed the show by attacking Moreau's carriage. She cannot get out until it is finished and, by then, it will be too late. Lucifer will have her. What time is it? No one knows but it is late. Moreau sweeps through the backstage like a comet, a brilliant comet in gold and green. She is in full costume, full make-up and, as she takes the stage, she diminishes it in size, diminishes the hall too. It is as if she is the only person in the room, the sole source of light, and all eyes are drawn to her.

She opens her arms, opens her voice, opens creation to the audience so they might see it all in an instant, all the colours and sensations the world has to offer spilling out from that first note. She is the only one breathing, in the Opéra, in Paris, in the world. Everyone else is frozen by the beauty of her voice, their breath stopped while she sings.

At the side of the stage, the ghost of Charlotte-Marie hovers, seemingly enchanted too.

'You, dear,' says La Laurent behind her. 'Now would be good.'

Julie, in her man's coat and boots, her sword at her side, the fine wig on her head, steps out onto the stage as Moreau finishes her first part and turns her attention to Julie, who is to give the reply. It is as if Julie has come home, as if all her life this is where she needed to be. She sings her man's part, her voice low and sweet, the voice Meilleraye gave her with his stab to the throat. The audience catches its breath again, uncertain of this strange new tone. She allows the music to come through her, lets her voice blend with the violin that accompanies her, itself a voice to question and answer her. It's as if the audience is not there, as if only she and Moreau exist on the stage and, when Moreau sings in answer to her part, and when they sing together, they make the music of Heaven. Then the first part is done, and Julie is suddenly aware of Monsieur clapping, of the audience following his lead to burst into rapture.

Her head swims and she steps from the stage to allow the tall figure of Roland, or the singer playing him, to take his part opposite Moreau.

'Well done,' says La Laurent, tapping her on the shoulder.

Lully just nods at her, but it is the same as if someone else had leapt upon her and showered her with kisses. 'Good enough,' he says. 'Not brilliant, not divine, but good enough.'

Lully's 'good enough' is everyone else's 'brilliant and divine'. She is enraptured. It's here she has wanted to be since she was a young girl, here doing this.

Moreau steps from the stage, touches her arm. A tingle goes through her, like when she touched the Devil but instead of the tingle of danger, this is one of comfort, of reassurance, of bliss.

'I need you to help me,' Julie says. But Moreau looks the other way. 'Our cue,' she says. They go back onto the stage and Julie is in Heaven, all thoughts of the night banished as she exchanges melodies with the beautiful, wonderful angel that is Moreau. She is lost in the melodies of splendour, of anger, of sweetness, of love.

Only when the part comes where Moreau tells her she must go, that their love is forbidden by her father and she must marry Roland, is the rapture suspended. In three beats of silence that draw up the tension of her flight from the stage, she hears the bells strike 11 outside.

She runs from the stage to the tumult of applause. Lully is talking to her, what is he saying? 'An hour,' he is saying. 'You are off stage for an hour now. Keep warmed up but don't overdo it. Don't let your voice go cold.'

Her guard stands beside her, picking his teeth.

'I need to piss,' she says, picking up a candle.

'I have to follow you,' he says.

'Follow then.'

She runs down to Wardrobe, the stagehands clapping her as she goes, through the little door where the trough runs through the building into the street. The guard goes to follow her in, but she says, 'Are you fucking joking?' and closes the door behind her.

High above is a little window, but she sets down her candle, then takes the ballet shoe from her blouse and puts it on. She jumps, kicking the shoe like a fish kicks its tail to ascend, her arms wide and her other foot out in front of her for balance.

She floats precariously up, touching the wall to regain stability as she goes before she reaches the window. It's no more than

346

a hole with a piece of vellum stretched over it. She untacks it and pulls herself in to the wall, wriggling through. Below her is a drop of about ten feet. She pushes through the wall and falls out. Suspended by the shoe, she floats down head first, coat flapping down over her face, to land gently on her hands in the filth of the street. She wipes her hands on the wall, then runs hard for the cemetery.

Scene Eight

See the Devil, Triumphant and Bold!
(Accomp. by rhythm of cloven hooves)

The torches on the main mound of the cemetery are turning to depart as she jumps on her shoe across the cattle grid of the entrance.

She bounds up towards them in long hops. There are twenty or thirty torches flaming in the blackness before her, making it hard to discern a single face. There are guards there, for sure, soldiers with muskets and bayonets.

'Meilleraye,' she says. 'I am here, ready for our assignation!'

The torches part and Meilleraye walks forward. He is wonderfully dressed, a wide justaucorps coat of silk like a great red bell – she thinks it is red – deep as a lake beneath the torchlight. He smiles.

'You're late,' he says.

'Not too late,' she says. 'You should have had them shoot two of Moreau's horses. That way I might have missed our appointment.'

'And made your appointment with another,' says Meilleraye, coming up to whisper in her ear. 'You have scarce little time for this, girl, if my friend tells me right.'

'Your friend?'

'The one from the place below.'

'You have made a bargain with the Devil?'

'I have.'

'What did you offer?'

'Your soul, of course. The Devil seems to find it difficult to obtain on her own.'

'It is that,' says Julie. 'Could you not just have run and let my time expire?'

'I will gain many advantages if I do not. I could be king!' he whispers.

'So de la Reynie was right to trim your wings.' Has Lucifer done her a favour here, got this man in front of her with time to spare? She guesses the Devil would not like things too simple, for gambling is Lucifer's vice. Yes, the Devil wants spice and excitement, to guess at the outcome. Not having can be more delicious than possession, for possession destroys all dreams and replaces them with dull reality. The prospect of losing Julie has become as enticing as having her. Though the Devil has secured a handsome second prize in Meilleraye.

'Put up. I am in a hurry to begin, I have a final scene to get back for.'

'Do hurry, Meilleraye,' says an aristocratic voice. 'I'm deuced cold here and there's a fire at my club!'

'All in good time,' says Meilleraye. 'Though this evening, you will not be fighting me.'

'I shall!' says Julie.

'Not so. You see, I cannot handle a sword as well as I could, owing to my disability.' He holds up his hand, the one she broke in their fight, swaddled in bandages. 'Therefore, as is correct, my second shall step in for me!'

'This is unacceptable!' says Julie.

'It's the done thing!' says a posh voice.

'I'll kill you here!' she says. The guards present their bayonets.

'Very well. I say you are a coward, Meilleraye!'

'I am no coward.'

'You are no brave man. I'll kill your second and then spit on you, see how you like that.'

'If you kill my second, we will be equal. You will be tired or injured and it will be just for me to fight you. Though I doubt that eventuality will come to pass.'

'We will see! Bring him here!'

'Sérannes!'

From the torchlight Sérannes steps, his face lean and gaunt. He has his hand on the hilt of his sword.

'I saw you dead!' she says. 'I saw you hanging!'

'A rascal stole my coat,' he says. 'Meilleraye here sent for me as I was on my way to the scaffold. I owe him my life and my duty.'

'I'm so glad!' says Julie.

'It's the worse for you, my love,' says Sérannes tenderly.

A man comes from the light. He has a long box in his hands which he opens.

'The weapons,' he says.

Sérannes glances at the box.

'You intend to fight me?'

'I am a man of honour. Bound to Meilleraye by vows I took when I entered his service. I cannot break them, Julie. If this is his will, it is his will. I do not have to kill for him, but I have to defend his person and his honour. That was my solemn oath. I must keep it on pain of my soul.'

'You can't defeat me. You know who my fencing master is!'

Meilleraye laughs. 'You think you can defeat old Sérannes here? Really? I never would have taken him from the prison if I didn't think he could beat you. Old Dreux here appeared to him by night and he told him something he has been keeping from me for years.'

Dreux? Yes, she stares hard and sees beside Meilleraye the fleeting form of the ghost.

'What?'

'Tell her, Sérannes!'

Sérannes bows to her.

'I have a secret thrust,' he says. 'The Devil's Thrust. It is unanswerable.'

'There are no secret thrusts,' says Julie. 'I have learned that from the Devil. There is guile, there is practice and there is surprise, but there is nothing in fencing that does not have an answer if you can make it in time.'

Sérannes dips his head, smiles.

'I'm afraid that is incorrect,' he says.

'I will not fight you,' says Julie.

'Then I will have you torn to pieces on the spot,' says Meilleraye. 'And I will have Sérannes do it outside of the formalities of the duel. He is my man. Sworn. An oath!'

Julie shakes her head.

'Then know this,' says Julie. 'When I am done with him, I will come for you.'

'If you live then I will be delighted to fight you.'

'Despite your bad hand,' says Julie, sneering.

'Despite it.'

'Then put up,' she says.

She knows the strike, the one Sérannes administered to her. Just above the navel, below the rib, the sword angled up a little, not too much to the side. She can put Sérannes down without killing him, if he takes the cue.

The weapons are presented to her and she chooses one.

'Like in front of Gourgue,' says Julie. 'At the monastery. Only now it is I who will make the final strike.'

Sérannes's face is grim.

'Not like that, my love. This is for real.'

'Sérannes, why? You do not have to do this.'

'I am Meilleraye's sworn man. I must do what I must do.'

'There is no "must". Resign, throw away your position. Be your own man.'

'My oath would still bind me. I could break it only for one thing.'

'For what?'

'If you say you love me. For that I will go to Hell.'

Julie hugs him. 'I love you!' She squeezes him to her.

'You do not,' he says. 'I wish that you did, but you don't. You are a bad liar, Julie.'

She casts down her eyes.

'I will try,' she says.

'Love admits no "try". But what love cannot bring, death will. You will be mine.'

Julie steps back from him.

'I need to kill Meilleraye. I will not go to Hell. And if I you stand in my path, I will cut you down, Sérannes.'

'We will see!' he says.

'Gentlemen, part!' says one of Meilleraye's seconds.

'I am no gentleman!' says Julie.

'You can say that again,' says Meilleraye.

Sérannes steps towards her, kisses her hand. Then he steps back, salutes, comes en garde. With the Devil's Eye, taught to her by Lucifer herself, she can see he is more tense than she has ever seen him before. There is a tightness in his shoulder, his rear leg is slightly too straight. His hand, though, is light on the blade and hardly moves at all as it makes the shining tip cut patterns in the torchlight.

She salutes too, takes up an irregular position, blade sloping down not up. It's unusual but nothing Sérannes hasn't seen before, normally from lazy fencers of two sorts: the first simply droops his blade because he knows no better; the second imagines that such an obvious invitation to attack into the high line will be snapped at by the opponent like a fish grabbing at a hooked worm. Julie knows that Sérannes will not imagine she falls into either of those two categories, both of which can carry the same title: 'Those about to die'.

They step forwards into distance, their blades touch, the lightest pressure from Sérannes. He is asking her, teasing her, daring her to slip the point of her sword under his blade and thrust for his heart in the hope that the sudden release of pressure will move his sword aside and open the path to the target.

If she refuses, then he slides his sword down hers, pushing it out of the way, using the blade as guide for the point as it slides towards her hand.

She drops the point under his but delays the thrust, waiting for the eager block, the parry, to come too soon so it might pass by and she might have a clear hit to the chest, to the spot where the blade might slip through and do no harm. He makes the parry, but it is too controlled, just a tad too wary and she knows he has offered her this opportunity to strike, knowing that a quick reversal of his arm will trap her blade and leave her open to attack. The opportunity is declined. Sérannes smiles and dips his head in salute. 'Well done,' he seems to say. 'This might be a long night.'

She does not have a long night to play with. Very soon, the Devil will come for her.

She renews her attack, flicking out the blade to the hand but now Sérannes is talking to her.

'They say the Devil schooled you,' he says. 'But did you ask who schooled the Devil? I, Sérannes, I have devils queuing at my door to receive instruction. The Queen of Hell, if she be a queen and not a king, seeks my advice, not I hers. Death awaits you, my love.'

'You are not usually given to boasting, Sérannes!'

'I am not usually given to fighting the objects of my infatuation, but these are strange times,' he says.

'Strange indeed,' she says. 'I mean you no harm, but I must do you harm!'

She tries the False Step, half sliding backwards with her foot as her blade goes forward.

She smiles, he smiles. No buying that one, not even slightly. He doesn't even begin to block or to move.

'Oh, dear Sérannes, I hate to do this,' she says. Three raps on the blade, two on the inside, one on the out, before a thrust to the hand that dips at the last instant down to the thigh. She wants him to search for her blade there, to drop into a parry, and he does, but when she completes the move with a thrust to the torso, he has turned aside and the sword goes past, forcing her to snap back to en garde to deflect his lightning riposte.

He smiles again, acknowledging her skill.

'Death will not wait, dearest Julie,' he says. 'Death is here, can't you see him? You say can see ghosts, Julie. Are they here, the children of Death?'

They are. All around the cemetery, the ghosts are there to watch – Paval, dear Charlotte-Marie, even Dreux, still fretting, anxious, pacing.

'They are here,' she says.

'He knows, you know,' says Sérannes, his blade like a serpent's tongue licking towards her throat. 'He knows you only have minutes. Dreux knows too, and hopes to bargain your soul for his, or at least gain the Devil's favour by delivering you. Why don't you give up, Julie? You cannot catch a ghost and make another in such a short time.'

'You know why I cannot give up. For the wrongly dead, for justice and to stay out of Hell myself, of course.' She catches his blade with a wide, spiralling parry but he has slipped away with a flick of the fingers before she can launch an attack.

'I know,' he says. 'I know you cannot give up. That is why, my dearest one, you must prepare for death. Prepare for the Devil's Thrust, my love.'

'There are no secrets you can surprise me with, dear Sérannes!' She kicks on her slippered foot, floats up into the air to descend with the blade aimed at his head.

'There might be one, my darling!' he says.

He blocks her thrust, but he strays too wide, by a thumb's width, no more. It is enough. She slips off the parry and strikes for his torso, searching for the Immortal Path of Ease, the passage between liver and heart where a blade might pass harmlessly.

She thrusts and, as she thrusts, she laughs. Sérannes made a mistake, Sérannes parried too widely. No. What a fool. Sérannes does not make mistakes, Sérannes always parries exactly as he chooses to. It's a trap but a strange one. It is as if a spell has been cast to slow the clock, hold back the candle flame as it nibbles at the wick, freeze the moon in its orbit. The tip penetrates his coat, his waistcoat, his shirt. Then a judder, a thump. It has hit something solid. Her blade is momentarily snagged in something Sérannes has secreted inside his shirt.

She is shocked. That he, he of all people, would resort to cheating. She pulls back the blade, but it snags and that means she is a tiny part of a breath too slow. Sérannes envelops her blade and, with a snap of the wrist, sends it flying up into the night.

'The Devil's Thrust,' he says.

'You betrayed me,' she says.

'Never,' he says, opening his arms like a man welcoming rain. The blade falls, glimmering through the torchlight like God's lightning to strike Sérannes in the neck just above the collarbone, on the jugular notch, skewering through his chest so the point emerges from his back. Sérannes makes a gesture something like a bow, a flourish of the arm, and falls to the earth.

His ghost stays where it is.

Bells, the scent of primroses and a circle of pale flowers opens, Lucifer stepping through.

'One minute to go, Julie,' says the Devil. 'Two souls to collect.'

'Run, lord, save us both!' shouts the ghost of Dreux.

'Why did you do that? Sérannes, why did you do it?' says Julie, sobbing, furious.

'So I can do this,' says Sérannes's ghost. With a bound he is on Dreux, grabbing the other shade by the scruff of his coat.

'Leave me be! Leave me be!' shouts Dreux but Sérannes has him, dragging him kicking to the circle of primroses. At its edge, he hesitates.

'Don't!' she shouts. Sérannes turns.

'Do not forget me, Julie,' he says and jumps within. Both ghosts are sucked into a vortex of fire.

A voice cries out from the street.

'Midnight and all's well.'

'One short,' says Lucifer. 'You are mine.'

Scene Nine

You Have Taught Me Too Well, My Master!

Lucifer stretches out a dainty hand to Julie.

'A bargain is a bargain,' says the Devil.

'Take her!' cries Meilleraye. 'Rid the earth of this pestilence. Her use is at an end!'

Julie comes en garde, nothing fancy, a straight challenge, sword out front at the level of her elbow, angled up towards the Devil's face.

The Devil purses their lips and then says, 'Julie, this is hardly fair. I have kept my side of the bargain scrupulously. Have I not educated you to be a fencer nonpareil? Can you not dance lightly upon the air, skip and flip upon the breeze, offer and withdraw, promise and deny, tickle and tease, deceive and kill?'

Julie extends the sword towards the Devil.

'The bargain is unfulfilled.'

'How so?'

'There are twelve souls in Hell, released from the ties of flesh by me in this last year. Yet I have had only eleven lessons.'

'A fencing lesson won't avail you where you are going.'

'You have cheated me.'

'I cheat everyone.'

'I call you false.'

'Why, thank you.'

'I call you artless.'

'What?' Lucifer scowls. 'Surely anything but. I have used your baser instincts, your desire for revenge, your arrogance, your hate to undo you. I have led you on, led you on, led you on, until you have found yourself little by little at the edge of the cliff.'

'No,' says Julie. 'Not so. You have shoved me to the edge of that cliff. Without your interference, your oafish interjections, I would have killed these gentlemen by the spring and spent the summer idling by the river. Whenever I, by my art and guile, came nearer to my goal, you thundered in like a tavern drunk to a Versailles ball, smashing and wrecking until you got your way. If you were so interested in having my soul, you could have just breathed on Dreux's pistol shot, made Monsieur too drunk to pardon me. It would amount to the same thing. No need to play to your own gallery and convince yourself you are subtle, my lord.'

'My lord? I am a lady.'

'Not so, I think. No woman could be so dull. You are male, posturing in the fine form of a woman but lacking all our sex's finesse.'

'This is the talk that will see you roast,' says Lucifer. The Devil extends a long finger towards Julie.

'Always your intention,' says Julie. 'You never meant to cede enough power to make this interesting. You are boring, sir. I call you, sir, for I see you clearly.'

The Devil flares their nostrils and little wisps of smoke appear. Then they draw back their lips, exposing teeth like slabs.

'You will pay for your words.'

'Pay in the way a village judge makes you pay, pay like you pay a butcher presenting his tatty bill, replete with bloody thumbprints. Not pay as one pays a gentleman, much less a prince. I will forfeit my lesson, sir, to give you one. I call you out, in the manner of the nobility. Will you take me instead, like a bailiff takes a carpet, knowing only its worth, with no mind for its beauty?'

The Devil stamps a hoof and the ground splits beneath it, bones and skulls spilling from the earth. The guards cry out and scatter in terror, running into the night.

'I am no butcher!'

'You are a tradesman, handing out services, collecting bills. I should decline to cross swords with one such as you. I have been made a knight, you know!'

'I am second only to the most worthy!' bellows Lucifer.

'So where is your Heaven? Where is your grace? You are God's servant, no more, His debt collector, a workman in lace and silk, a monkey, a scapegrace. Not even the dignity of honest labour for you.'

Lucifer seizes her by the collar, lifts her bodily from the ground.

'That's right, fellow,' says Julie. 'Attack me like a footpad, not like the gentleman you will never be!'

Lucifer casts her down, sending her sprawling on the soft earth.

'Put up,' they say. 'Put up, like a duellist and a noble, though you are not a true noble.'

'Call your seconds,' says Julie.

'I will be your second!' says Meilleraye.

'There,' says Lucifer. 'Call yours.'

'I will stand for you, Julie.' The voice is faint but clear. It is Paval's ghost, close by her shoulder.

'And I.' Little Diandré is there, his head mercifully attached to his ghostly shoulders. Julie looks around her. All about the cemetery, the ghosts are massing, sitting on the colonnades, the gravestones, the pyramids of bones.

'You beware!' shouts the Devil to the ghosts. 'All of you in your wanderings. You belong yet neither to Heaven nor Hell. I may take a closer look at your cases!'

The ghosts murmur, sigh.

'I will defeat you and you will leave us all alone!' says Julie.

'I will defeat you and take you all with me to the pit!' says Lucifer.

'You asked me why I bothered to learn so much skill from you. For this, my Lord. For this! Swear to leave me alone when I beat you!'

'I will not swear,' says Lucifer. 'And it does not matter that I will not, for there is nothing you know that I did not teach you. No trick, no deceit, no nothing that can surprise or catch me!'

'We'll see,' says Julie.

The seconds call them en garde and they present their swords.

'This will be a rare fight,' says the Devil. 'A boiler and bubbler, a stew of a scrap to savour.'

'I will serve you bitter dumplings,' says Julie.

'That,' says the Devil, 'is not a phrase any gentleman should hear when facing sharp steel.'

'I thought you were a lady!'

The Devil roars and Meilleraye cries, 'Engage!'

Julie has crossed swords with Lucifer before in practice but never like this. The first rap upon her blade is so hard it shivers the steel, threatening to smash it in her hand. The second rap does not land; she flicks her blade under Lucifer's so the beat misses and she flicks out the tip of her own sword towards her enemy's throat. She is, of course, expecting the parry – Lucifer is too rare a fencer to be beaten by such an obvious trick – but she drops at the last instant out of the high line, driving the tip into a shiny hoof, showering sparks into the night.

'Ahhh!' The Devil cries but he, she, it drives its other hoof into Julie's midriff, kicking her into the air to the height of four, five men. Now Julie cries out, is sick in her mouth, as the world whirls and spins. She tenses, expects the cold smack of soil but it does not come, and she floats gently back to earth on her slipper as Lucifer hops and curses.

Steel can cut him then, yes, *steel*. The Devil, according to the tales she heard in the village, can be cut, marked and bound by iron. She can kill this fiend! She can kill it!

Lucifer's face deforms now, the snarl on the lips spreading like a wave across all the features. The teeth become more prominent, the brow heavier, the hair sparser and from the head sprout a pair of sharp black horns. The Devil is transforming in front of her, casting off the guise of a female to reveal himself: brutish, thickset, male.

'One trick I did not teach you, so a small victory to you,' he says. 'There will be no more.'

He comes on, limping but at such a pace that she has to stagger backwards to avoid his lunges. His attacks are offered and renewed with lightning speed, the lunges impossibly deep, the variety of target bewildering. Julie parries and ducks, turns and leaps to avoid the vicious blade. She is cut, first on the ear, then on the arm, then the calf. The ghosts moan and fret, the ground shakes under the sparking hooves, her own breath saws and catches like a demented violin. 'Kill her! Kill her!' shouts Meilleraye. 'Carry her to Hell!'

She kicks up into the air with her slippered foot, using it like an acrobat might use a loop of rope to turn upside down and backwards, striking up into the Devil's belly. The tip lands, releasing a hiss of steaming blood and the Devil cries again.

'Who taught you this?' he shouts. 'Who showed you such tricks?'

'None but me,' she says.

'Liar! No mortal woman could show such guile!'

'Think again!' she says, spinning in a pirouette. He has anticipated her though and, before she can complete the turn, he has grabbed her from behind.

'Too fancy,' he says. 'Too fancy by half!' He has her by the throat, his hands burning hot. He begins to squeeze.

'How's this for fancy?' she gargles.

Julie grips her blade in two hands, points her sword back towards her belly and, slipping her hips to one side, drives backwards. The sword goes straight through the Devil's body. He howls with pain and releases his grip, staggering.

They are on the main carriage road, near to the entrance of the cemetery, exactly where she needs to be.

The Devil clutches his side, then raises his hand to his face, looking in disbelief at his bloody fingers. Then he smiles.

'Shall I tell you how God made me, my dear?' he says. 'I cannot be killed. I am immortal. Everlasting, ever living!'

Julie steps back, feeling with her foot.

'You bleed well enough for one who cannot die.'

'I do that,' says Lucifer. 'I can suffer, true. I can ache and burn and scream with agony, but that agony will never be rewarded with the end of death. So stab me, puncture me a thousand times and I will still come on. Your duel is unwinnable, Julie, as long as I can stand the pain. And standing the pain is something at which I have long practice.'

'So come on!' says Julie. 'I've had enough of your talk.'

The Devil roars, and leaps at her. A blur, a howl. Furie the fox is there, leaping up to cast itself across Lucifer's eyes. The Devil growls, tears the fox away, throws it across the graveyard. But he has stumbled, taken a false step, his wounded foot landing heavily on the slippy iron of the cattle grid that covers the cemetery entrance. The hoof punches through the gap in the bars, pushing the iron aside just enough to slip through before the metal springs back to trap the Devil at the ankle.

Lucifer curses, pulls, twists and struggles but he is trapped, stuck fast. Furie runs up Julie's back to sit limp at her neck.

Meilleraye is on his hands and knees, pulling at the Devil's hoof, screaming as his flesh sizzles at the Devil's touch, then pulling at the bars of the cattle grid in crazy desperation but to no avail. He can in no way shift his master.

'Free me,' says Lucifer. 'Free me!'

'I'm trying, my lord, I am trying,' says Meilleraye.

'Try harder!'

'Can you not change shape?'

'Oh yes, I could always do that,' says the Devil.

'Then why not do it?'

The Devil boxes Meilleraye a mighty cuff around the ears.

'Of course I can't change shape while bound by iron! Don't you think I've thought of that?'

'Well, then, my lord, our situation is delicate,' says Meilleraye.

'Delicately fucked from where I'm standing,' says Julie.

Meilleraye turns around to face her.

'Release this fiend, now,' he says. 'I command you as your superior.'

'Fuck yourself,' says Julie. 'I command you as your inferior.'

'You stand against all rank and order,' says Meilleraye. 'My lord here faced you with honest blade work, with skill incomparable, with fight and fury. You laid him low with tricks.'

'As high fellows have done down all the centuries, only to claim virtue and bravery once the battle is done,' she says. 'And let me point out that the moral of this situation, its correctness, its place in the order of God's creation, is hardly what is relevant.'

'What is "relevant"?' says Meilleraye.

'That I have the upper hand and your master is trapped. Unless I release him, he might be there by dawn, all his weakness on display for the world. Imagine what might become of creation were the Devil to be caught here forever. No wars, no famine, no poverty, no Church!'

'No Church?' says Meilleraye. 'Because the priests would have no one to oppose?'

'Because they'd stop muttering into their cassocks invoking me every five minutes and doing my work whenever they stopped muttering,' says Lucifer.

'And I might find a way to open the gates of Hell,' says Julie. 'To allow all the poor souls therein to walk free upon the earth.'

'That is against God,' says the Devil.

'I thought that was your job,' says Julie.

'There are many ways to serve,' says the Devil. 'As jailer, as tester, as prover. But serve I do. Serve I must.'

His face is quite distorted now, prominent fangs in the mouth, great horns at the hairy head.

'No, my lord,' says Julie. 'There is no "must", you do not need to serve. You can stay here to the common scorn like a villain set in the stocks. I shall walk free, you will never be in a position to make good your claim on me.'

The Devil snorts.

'Are you so sure, Julie? Do you think it beyond my powers to persuade one such as this to release me? And if you were dead, you would not be here to stop them.'

Meilleraye smiles and, in an instant, he has leaped upon Julie, little knife at her neck. Furie bites him on the hand but he flings the fox away. 'You die,' he says.

'Hang on!' A voice from nowhere, from beyond the grave. She looks up to see Pelletier with Dreux's pistol levelled at the Devil. The ghost of Paval looks on. He has fetched Pelletier there.

'Now, this has an iron ball in it,' says Pelletier. 'And I am told that will kill a Devil or send him on his way at least. So unhand my mistress, sir, or I will kill your master!'

'What's that to me?' says Meilleraye. Julie is doing all she can to keep the knife from her throat. She tugs down with both hands but cannot shift Meilleraye's hand. The knife nicks her.

'As soon as you are dead, I will find someone to free me,' says Lucifer. 'And then, Julie, I will come looking for your soul!'

'Right,' says Pelletier. He takes careful aim at the Devil and pulls the trigger. The flint sparks, a mighty bang, and the Devil laughs. 'Missed!' he says. 'Such a pretty gun, so poorly made. Kill her, Meilleraye, and fetch a smith to set me free!'

A wet gargle from behind her, a cough, and Meilleraye collapses to the soggy ground. Julie turns to see his body, a neat rose of blood at the centre of his forehead.

'That is bad luck,' says Lucifer, as Meilleraye's ghost rises disbelieving from its body.

'Reload!' says Julie. 'Shoot the fiend and let him carry himself away to Hell.'

Lucifer grins.

'I am not so easily killed. You can wound me, Julie, blast out an eye, but you will never kill me. I will regrow any part of me you destroy. God hates me. He would not allow me to die.'

'Then we are at an impasse,' says Julie. 'For I will not release you, and you will not release me!'

'I can wait till morning,' says Lucifer. 'Some fool will set me free.'

'And yet you will know you have been beaten,' says Julie. 'You have weakened yourself, called for help. I offer you a better way. I will release you, but you will release me. I will fulfil the terms of our bargain, if a little late. Look, I deliver you a plump ghost, ripe for roasting!'

'I'm off!' shouts Meilleraye's ghost and runs towards the cemetery gates but Paval's ghost moans and streaks across the grass, a hundred others at his back, to catch Meilleraye's phantom and return it, wriggling, to Julie.

'Very well,' says the Devil. 'So I swear. Set me free!'

'There is one more thing!' she says. 'You must promise never to torment me again!'

'I cannot promise that,' says Lucifer. 'But I will offer you a different bargain. I will not enter your life again nor trouble you in any way, Julie, unless you call upon me yourself.'

'That I will never do.'

'Then you are safe.'

'Pelletier!' calls Julie. 'Your burglar's tools, sir!'

Pelletier unfurls his roll of tools. From within he selects a file. 'This should do,' he says.

'Release me! Release me!' wails the ghost of Meilleraye, but he is not released, will not be released.

Pelletier cuts through the bar and Lucifer steps from the cattle grid, assuming their earlier, beautiful form. They take the ghost of Meilleraye by the scruff of his neck and, though he kicks and struggles, he is held fast.

'We have our bargain,' says Lucifer. 'Kiss me, Julie, for I acknowledge you an equal.'

'You will burn me?'

'I will not.'

Lucifer bends to kiss Julie on the lips and a thrill goes through her, like stepping into a frosty morning from a stuffy, smoky room.

'We will have dealings again,' says Lucifer. 'I may have other bargains to offer.'

The primroses sprout at the Devil's feet, the vortex of fire swirls and she is gone, dragging the ghost of Meilleraye behind her. Julie crosses herself. In the confusion, the fight and the fear, she forgot Sérannes and Charlotte-Marie. There may have to be other bargains struck if she is to keep their souls from Hell.

'You owe me a drink!' says Pelletier.

'I have an opera to finish!' says Julie.

366

Paval's ghost is at her side. She reaches out to touch him, but her hand passes through.

'Go,' he says. 'I will be there, watching.'

She kisses his faint outline. Charlotte-Marie is there too. Julie turns to her, presses her lips to nothing, but gazes into the spirit's eyes.

'Do as he says,' says Charlotte-Marie.

'Yes,' says Julie. She takes the card from her sleeve, crumples it and lets it fall to the ground. Then she sweeps out of the graveyard, on towards her audience.

Recitativo Secco

So there you have it, the opening acts of the opera of the life of Julie d'Aubigny. She has beaten me, for a while, though I still hold certain cards in this game of trumps and will yet get to play them.

See her here, on the stage before Monsieur, returned from the fight. The nobles think her make-up quite convincing, the tears and mud upon her clothes only a facsimile of the marks of struggle.

We know better, do we not? Julie has struggled, Julie will continue to struggle, even as the ghost of Charlotte-Marie watches her from the wings, hand in hand with that of her dear Paval. Diandré is by her side. He will haunt the Opéra now. But others have their eyes on her.

Here is the Comte d'Armagnac, quite captivated by this magnificent performance, by the voice so beguiling, so different, so womanish man, mannish woman that it seems deliciously indecent, his wife at his side bristling to see his fascination. Is the erotic charge he feels all the sharper for the memory of her as a girl? His wife, the countess, holds a fire shield against her face. It is meant to protect her make-up from the heat of the candles, but she carries it on the wrong side, away from the light, to hide her tears from her husband. I wonder what she would give to protect her marriage from the wiles of this androgyne upon the stage.

Outside the theatre is another world, that of the poverty and stink of Paris. Here, old Sieur de Maupin of St-Germain paces by the rich carriages, or rather hobbles, for he is not as steady on his feet as he used to be. He has lost quite everything, every last sou, and his knees are sore from praying for relief from his awful condition. What just God could allow a fellow of such former repute to sink so low? He asks himself that now. What might he give to return to his former comfortable estate? You know, don't you, you know. Would he even consent to marry a country girl of no breeding just so Armagnac could have her at his side without scandal? Of course he would.

She will become La Maupin, grand diva of the Paris Opéra – once I have encouraged her husband and the Comte to take her on. Did you not hear me swear never to do Julie harm? Well, how can advancing her prospects by making her mistress to a Comte and the respectable wife of a gentleman of great family be called harming her? It cannot, I submit to you that it most certainly cannot.

I hardly yet need to do her harm, so many are waiting to do it for me. For, when the news of the unfortunate fate of Meilleraye becomes apparent, will his wife rest until his killer is dead? What if she stumbles upon his books, upon his notes on the summoning and control of devils? Again, I do Julie no harm personally, but my oath does not require me to stay the hand, stay the claws, stay the whips of the legions of Hell.

Consider too Sérannes, whose soul currently staggers through the hateful heat on the burning shores of the lake of Fire. He doesn't know it yet, but this is the least of Hell's torments. The special nature of Hell is that each new torture is so awful that it makes the sinner's soul wish for the one that preceded it. Julie is already thinking of ways to secure his release.

So, as Julie sings the final notes of the great opera and even Lully applauds from his place in the orchestra pit, as Moreau turns, flushed, to kiss Julie upon the hand, I have no doubt that one day

Julie will be mine. Julie is so easy to love, and I am not immune to her charms. One day she will return to me, ready once more to strike a bargain to become the Devil's Blade.

Author's note

This story is based loosely on the life of Julie d'Aubigny, who became known as La Maupin – diva of the Paris Opéra. Some of the biographical details have been changed but generally the mundane ones. The more extraordinary aspects of the story – the supernatural aspect aside – are true. Julie really did have an expert skill with a sword and killed many men who crossed her – on one occasion three at one go. She was often pardoned by the king's brother 'Monsieur', who found the idea of a woman killing men in duels hilarious.

Her tussles with men were not limited to swordplay. She once had to face the law for beating up her landlord and she thrashed the singer Louis Gaulard Dumesny after he repeatedly sexually harassed the women members of the opera troupe. She also had a reputation as a great wit.

Her skill with a blade was formidable but was exceeded by her skill as a singer. The Marquis De Dangeau wrote in his journal that she had the most beautiful voice in the world.

She conducted passionate affairs throughout her life with both men and women. After the death of her final lover – Marie Louise Thérèse de Senneterre – she was inconsolable and disappears from history. She is believed to have returned to her husband of convenience Maupin and then died aged 33, having joined a convent.

Note on historical accuracy

I have tried to make this novel as true to the real history as possible. However, I have allowed a little laxity in the exact date of a key event because it didn't sit exactly where it should have, if I had been in charge of things. Events are not always placed where they should be and it's up to novelists to correct history's mistakes.

Note on the Italian edition

Acknowledgments

Thanks to Richard Hornby for his sagacity and insight. And several coffees.